The Ugly Truth

The Multiverse Refugees Trilogy

‹INSERT THIRD REPETITION WITH VARIATION OF PIE JOKE HERE›

The Ugly Truth

The Multiverse Refugees Trilogy

‹INSERT THIRD REPETITION WITH VARIATION OF PIE JOKE HERE›

Ira Nayman

Elsewhen Press

The Ugly Truth
First published in Great Britain by Elsewhen Press, 2022
An imprint of Alnpete Limited

Elsewhen Press, PO Box 757, Dartford, Kent DA2 7TQ
elsewhen.press

British Library Cataloguing in Publication Data.
A catalogue record for this book is available from the British Library.
ISBN 978-1-915304-04-9 Print edition
ISBN 978-1-915304-14-8 eBook edition

Designed and formatted by Elsewhen Press

INTRODUCTION
Frequently Unasked Questions
About the Alien Refugee Crisis

1. What's the story?

Uncle Ferdinand made a fool of himself again at the family's annual Schmeckler's Farrago celebrations. It's hard to understand how he can believe that those noises could be entertaining – and they certainly sound nothing like 'In a Gadda Da Vida!' Auntie Merman rolled her eyes and complimented us on the shrimp puff pastries (even though she was actually trying to eat a plastic rosette she had managed to cut off Nona Francesca's hat). Bless you for ask –

2. Umm, thank you for that, but I actually meant to ask about *the* story, not your story. What's happening?

Oh. That. Yeah. A madman created a machine that he hoped would destroy the multiverse. It started with Earth Prime 4-6-4-0-8-9 dash Omega, threatening the lives of billions of sentient beings. The Transdimensional Authority – they're the *yentas* of traffic between realities, always sticking their noses in other people's business, even if it's different versions of their own business – **especially** if it's different versions of their own business – developed a plan to save as many of those sentient beings as they could – are you sure you don't want to hear about Aunt Bertha's complaint?

3. **I'm good, thanks. What was the Transdimensional Authority's plan to save the sentient beings of Earth Prime 4-6-4-0-8-9 dash Omega?**

They would transport as many of the aliens as possible to stable universes before their universe collapsed.

4. **How's that working out?**

Better than Aunt Bertha's complaint, I can tell you. Or, at least, I could if you were willing to listen. Anyway...four years after the refugee programme was started, over a million refugees have been resettled on different versions of Earth, a little over half on Earth Prime. Just another seventeen to twenty-four billion to go. It's hard to get a proper census going when all of your citizens are constantly dodging objects falling from the sky. Including the census takers. As Rodney Pendleton often says, "When the going gets tough, the tough start wearing adult diapers."

5. **Did he think that was profound?**

You know the line between profound and silly? The aliens regularly snort it.

6. **That's an image that's going to haunt my dreams for the rest of my life! Why would you put that into my head?**

You're welcome.

7. **How are the aliens fitting in with human society?**

Roll a d20 to determine disappointment.

8. So many dice in this set. Which one is a d20?

The one with 20 sides.

9. Oh. Okay. Yeah...I rolled a seven. So, how are the aliens fitting in?

They are all four feet tall, with balloonish heads, no hair and blue skin; they are identical except some of them have bumps on their chests to indicate that they are female. They fit in about as well as a skunk at a rodeo. Still, their three piece suits are exquisite.

10. But, other than that, they fit in well, right?

Roll a d20 disappointment check.

11. A d20? Which one is that, again?

The one in your hand.

12. Oh. Okay. I rolled a...five. So, other than the way they look, the aliens are fitting in, right?

You're not having any luck with these rolls – you might want to consider getting a new set of dice. The aliens believe that they are watched over by a god called the Audi Enz; if they entertain the Audi Enz well enough, they will be rewarded...at some future point...under unknowable conditions. So, as a matter of religious belief, they are constantly creating comic routines out of whatever life puts in their way. Pies. Chainsaws. Tax audits. You know how funny it is to watch people doing comedy in film and on televisions? It's not nearly as funny being subjected to it in real life.

13. **I can see that. Still...human beings wouldn't just let a universe full of sentient beings die, so we're willing to overlook the fact that they look and act different from us...right?**

Do you even need to roll a d20 to figure out how disappointed you will be in the answer to this question?

14. **Twelve. How are we treating them?**

It's a mixed bag. On the one hand, there are people who sponsor the aliens, who take them into their homes, who give them jobs, who hold international music benefit concerts to raise money to assist them in adjusting to their new lives. These are often people with strong religious beliefs, people who worship the holy trinity of Asimov, Clark, Heinlein. They may be exasperated by the occasional pie in the face or chainsaw in the curio cabinet, but they just wipe it off and/or call it a modern art sculpture and keep helping the aliens because they believe it is the right thing to do.

Then, there are the humans firsters, the knee-jerk speciesists, the anti-alien mobs. They may only be a minority of the population, but they sure are loud, so they get the attention of those in power, some of whom are willing to pander to their prejudice. So, the number of alien immigrants to many countries is severely limited. Authorities often look the other way at acts of violence perpetrated against aliens. There is even a form of alien sex trafficking.

So, we're treating them about as well as we treat each other. As Rodney Pendleton always says: "The squeaky wheel writes, and having writ, leaves a mess on the road."

15. Saaaaaay, who is this Rodney Pendleton that you keep mentioning, anyway?

He was the first alien to migrate from Earth Prime 4-6-4-0-8-9 dash Omega to Earth Prime. Four years later, he was a billionaire: he created an anti-gravity technology that powers hoverboards and his company, AlTech Enterprises, had contracts with General Motors to develop hovercars, NASA to develop a new rocket propulsion system and the US Armed Forces to develop [CENSORED FOR REASONS OF NATIONAL SECURITY].

A lot of the money that Rodney Pendleton made was put into a foundation to help aliens adjust to life in their new homes. At first, it was called People for the Ethical Treatment of Aliens, but people found this confusing, so it was renamed Bluepeace. This was also confusing, so the name was changing once more to United Newbies. This lasted a little longer, until somebody noticed that the acronym had been taken by a much better known organization. Confusion level complete, the foundation was renamed Aliens Helping Aliens! Sure, the acronym for the organization was the name of an eighties pop band, but they were a largely forgotten one hit wonder, so the opportunity for confusion was minimal.

16. What does the – hey! Wait a minute! Wait just one hot minute! Did you say that there was an alien sex trafficking ring? I mean, they're aliens. Who would – what – umm, I mean, how is that possible?

* SIGH * I had a feeling I wouldn't be able to avoid this question. When a gender-neutral alien and another gender-neutral alien love each other very much, they –

17. Whoa. Whoa. Whoa. Gender-neutral?

In their home universe, none of the aliens have bumps on their chest; they're all identical. They don't have reproductive organs, either. These are things they acquire when they move to a universe where bipedal humanoids practice bisexual reproduction. When they want to have an experience of sharing with another member of their species, their bodies meld until they are one with each other. When they emerge –

18. Whoooaaaaaa! Wait a minute! Wait just one lukewarm minute on a burner turned up to eleven! How are the aliens able to meld with each other?

Right. In their home universe, they were able to manipulate matter down to the sub-atomic level with their minds. This made things like changing diapers trivially easy. Or adapting bodies to live in their new environments before they move to them. So, alien sex was a matter of completely melding bodies. The two aliens who emerged from the intertwingling carried parts of the other with them. That may or may not be important to the story that is about to be told. I can say that because I know you will be too distracted by the concept of sex with aliens to pay it the attention it deserves.

19. Yeah, yeah, that's really interesting. But human beings don't have the ability to intertwingle, so how would an alien sex trafficking ring actually work?

I know you so well.
Actually, when they travel to other universes, the aliens lose the ability to manipulate matter. This was very disappointing to Rodney   Pendleton (he

6

must have rolled a natural one), so he created a machine that would allow two beings to meld together on Earth Prime. Continual Amore for Consenting Adults, Inc. (a wholly owned, if little publicized, subsidiary of AlTech Enterprises) produced a small number of these machines, known as Orgasmatrons, mostly for use in Alien-Human Friendship Centres. Despite fairly heavy security, some human beings were able to reverse engineer an Orgasmatron and create bootleg machines that they called 'Orgasnatrons'. Human beings can be very creative that way.

20. Go...us? Is there anything else worth knowing about the aliens?

Not really. We like a good laugh, but we're just like you are, putting our underpants on over our head one ear at a ti – ha ha ha. Did I say, "we?" I meant them. Them. The aliens. The aliens are really just like you...or me. Because I'm one of you. Human. Ha ha. Ha. Humans. It's really something being us, isn't it? So, umm, yeah. The aliens are really just like human beings. Except shorter. And bluer. And funnier (except for John Cleese). So, treat them with the respect you would give other human beings. Or, no, actually, treat them with more respect than you would give other human beings. They are, after all, guests in our home.

It was a cold, wet, grey day in Vancouver. There was a board in the West End – Coal Harbour Community Policing Centre squad room that read: 'DAYS WITHOUT SUN'. Somebody had chalked in '17'. Most of the cops who worked there had forgotten the circumstances under which the sign had been erected (Joe [LAST NAME TO BE DETERMINED] and Bill [GIMME A MINUTE AND I'LL LOOK THAT UP] knew, but nobody thought to ask them); somebody must have been enthusiastic to keep track at some point, but nobody who had worked in the precinct for more than a month shared that enthusiasm. Nobody knew who kept the daily tally up (except for Joe and Bill, but they slipped out of your consciousness before your conversation with them was over). Years ago, somebody had chalked out the final 'U' and replaced it with an 'I'. The Pizzicotti triple homicide put an end to that frivolity.

The weather didn't bother Joe or Bill. It wasn't that they were immune to the wind and the rain; it was that weather had enough respect for them to give them a wide berth. In return, Joe and Bill wore wide-brimmed fedoras and trenchcoats in acknowledgement that weather could affect them if it chose to, and thanks that it chose not to.

Joe and Bill, the Eternal Detectives, went where they were needed. While they were there, it was like they had always been there; when they were gone, their triumphs were quickly forgotten. Everybody at the West End – Coal Harbour Community Policing Centre, where they worked the case in Vancouver, knew they had always been there on the edge of retirement, staying on for just one more case. One more case. One. More. Case. Nobody was willing to begrudge Joe and Bill staying on since they had a perfect clearance rate: they solved every case they investigated. Some of the less charitable detectives in the Coal Harbour precinct hoped that the one more case would be the one that they couldn't solve; some of that some thought that the defeat would cause them to disappear in a puff of smoke. Most of the men and women in the Policing Centre, though, were grateful for the Eternal Detectives, because their perfect record made the whole squad look good.

There was no colour to Joe and Bill, who appeared in shades of grey, as if they had watched too much television in the 1950s and it bled into their appearance. They wore standard issue Eternal Detective black pants, white shirt and rumpled jackets.

Bill drove their black and white beater (it wasn't, like them, drained of colour; that was just the pattern in the long ago days when the vehicle had been assigned to them) up to a large container on a dock in Vancouver. Vancouver is Canada's largest and most diversified Port, and the largest export port in North America. The Port of Vancouver includes more than 16,000 hectares of water, more than 1,500 hectares of land and hundreds of kilometres of shoreline, bordering 16 municipalities and intersecting the traditional territories and treaty lands of several Coast Salish First Nations. I'm not saying this because I Googled it – it's common knowledge throughout Canada.

The manifest said the container was transporting Canadian flags, Canadian flag lapel pins, Canadian flag t-shirts in red, Canadian flag fridge magnets, Canadian flag flying over Vancouver fridge magnets, Canadian flag t-shirts in white and a baby's arm with a tattoo of a Canadian flag holding an apple. The manifest lied. What the container actually transported was horror.

"This crime was obviously perpetrated by patriots, Joe."

"How do you figure, Bill?"

"The manifest could have said this was a shipment of American flags. Or China from France. Or French fries from China. Anything, really. Whoever forged the manifest made it very Canadian – the only thing missing was fridge magnets of beavers and maple syrup."

"Not necessarily. The perps could have figured that nobody in Vancouver would inspect a cargo container that claimed to hold so much Canadiana. To even think of doing so would be unpatriotic."

"If they didn't want the container to be inspected, they shouldn't have left it on the dock for three weeks. A little thing like that attracts attention."

"Patriotism has its limits, Bill. It has its limits."

Bill cut the engine and the car hiccoughed to a halt; he had long ago accepted that there were no medications for what ailed this vehicle and chalked it up to 'character'. He and Joe got out and walked up to the container.

Next to it stood a tall man with a face so hangdog you could be forgiven for thinking that he stretched it on a gallows every morning before breakfast. He was the Vancouver coroner. His name was Sanzio or Buonarroti or Betto Bardi or...or...or something classical like that. A plume of smoke followed the man around like a puppy; he appeared to be smoking three cigarettes at once, none of which were inconvenienced in the slightest by the rain. There was no mistaking the gratitude on his face when he saw the two detectives walk up to him.

"Evening Joe," he greeted them. "Evening Bill."

"Evening, Dominic," Joe returned the greeting. "What have we got?"

"You're gonna wanna see it for yourselves," the coroner told them, lighting a fourth cigarette as two of the original three burned down to stubs (without in any way affecting his lips – how did he do that?). "I've been at this job for seven seasons, and I've never seen anything like it."

Bill and Joe shared a look. "Do we wanna ask, Joe?" "Let the man have his angst in peace, Bill." "He does look like he has earned it." "You see a lot of the worst of human nature in seven seasons as a coroner." "If his face was any more hangdog, it would be the pet version of a word guessing game."

When you've been partners as long as these two had, your looks speak volumes.

"Yeah, I appreciate an expressive look between long-time partners as much as the next guy," the coroner cut in, "but it's two in the morning and there are a lot of bodies to process. The sooner I can do that, the sooner I can get home and perfect my hangdog look in the mirror while I'm sleeping."

With a nod of acknowledgement, Joe led Bill into the cargo container.

"Well, if that don't beat all."

"All, Joe?"

"All, Bill."

"A pair of deuces, Joe?"

"My grandmother could beat a pair of deuces, Bill, and she's been dead for almost thirty years!"

"I take your point."

"It was a good one."

"A full house, tens over sevens?"

"It could beat a full house, aces over kings."

"A straight flush?"

"It could beat a straight flush."

"A royal flush?"

"It could beat a royal flush."

"What could beat a royal flush Joe?"

"Grace, Bill. Grace."

Bill frowned, as if Grace was a new concept to him. It didn't figure into the Friday night poker games he would have played if he wasn't wedded to the job. It hadn't figured into his marriage (which had, despite the empty hole where Grace should have been, managed to survive 33 years). It didn't figure into the pulp western novels that he enjoyed reading, except on those rare occasions when the school marm's name was Grace. Still, he was the junior detective here, and had a lot to learn about detecting.

The cargo container held bodies. Dozens of four foot tall bodies with no hair and balloonish heads and limbs. Even in death, their three piece suits were exquisite.

"Where's the blood?"

"Blood, Bill?"

"This much death, you expect to see a lot of blood, Joe. If nothing else, it adds a little colour to a crime scene."

"If I didn't know you better, I'd worry about you, partner."

"'Preciate it."

Moving around the container, Joe and Bill couldn't help but notice that there were no signs of violence. This left only one conclusion as to the cause of death, which the detectives came upon at the same time: asphyxiation.

"Isn't it ironic, Joe? Don't you think?"

"What's that, Bill?"

"They came from a universe where they didn't have to breath, only to die in an alien universe because they couldn't breath."

"You have the soul of a poet, Bill."

"The soul of a poet is necessary to be a good detective, Joe. You have to have it issued with your kevlar vest and pepper spray."

"I don't remember filling out the requisition form for the soul of a poet, Bill."

"It was right under 'snub-nosed revolver', Joe. Easy to check off without even realizing you were doing it."

"Mmm..." Joe looked around the container hungrily, like clues were his sustenance and the restaurant was out of just about everything. After a while, his hum changed from absent thoughtfulness to thoughtful thoughtfulness. "Say, Bill, do you notice anything about the bodies?"

"Other than being dead, you mean, Joe?"

"Something unusual."

"I wouldn't think that being dead was usual for them."

"Something about the positioning of the bodies."

Bill peered at the bodies in front of him. Although the moon was obscured by rainclouds, the dock was lit better than a football field, so the peering was mostly for effect. One of the bodies was sitting on its ass, its arms and legs curved upwards. "Now that you mention it, there is something...different about – is that corpse making a letter?"

"I'll take observation skills over poetry any day. Yes. I think that's a letter."

"U?"

"I could ask, 'Me what?' But that would just be silly. Yes. The letter u."

The next body sat with its legs out to the side and its arms held straight up over its head. "L..." The body next to that stood, its elbows behind it and its arms straight ahead. "T..." The body next to that stood at attention, holding a bowler hat high above its head. "I..." The next body was on its ass again, its arms and legs straight out at a ninety degree angle. "Another u?"

"I think you'll find that's a v."

"Ultiv...erse. What's an ultiverse?"

"I think you may find that you started in the middle of the word."

Bill and Joe walked around the cargo container, tracing the letters the bodies made back to the beginning of the message. There were forty-one corpses in total, spelling out: "W-e-l-c-o-m-e T-o T-h-e M-u-l-t-i-v-e-r-s-e S-o-r-e-y F-o-r T-h-e I..."

Bill shook his head. "What does it mean, Joe?"

"It means that the aliens were true to themselves to the very end, Bill."

"What does being true to yourself mean if you're an alien?"

"Goofy."

The Restaurant at the End of Thyme

by MARCELLA CARBORUNDUREM-McVORTVORT, Alternate Reality News Service Food and Drink Writer

Is the world ready for pickled mud ("The secret is in the brine!") or boot tread tart ("The secret is on the briny — but just because our head chef fled to Croatia doesn't mean we will be changing our menu any time soon!")? Undoubtedly not. But The Restaurant at the End of

Thyme wasn't meant for your world, so there.

According to Redrum Psychonaut , the owner of the establishment in lowest of the low Manhattan, the restaurant was created to serve the growing population of refugees from Earth Prime 4-6-4-0-8-9 dash Omega. Large, heavy-looking objects hung precariously from the ceiling. Every forty-three minutes, servers would mime various comic pieing scenarios. And of course, the menu was made up of delicacies from the aliens' home universe.

Unfortunately, some things don't travel well.

"Because they can get all the energy they need from sunlight or an internal nuclear power generator (giving the term 'emotional meltdown' a whole new frisson of danger), natives of Earth Prime 4-6-4-0-8-9 dash Omega don't have to eat to sustain themselves," explained famed gourmand Graham Curr. "So, when they do it at all, eating is a form of competition and performance art. They can put the most ridiculous dishes in their mouths, knowing that they can use their power to manipulate matter to change them to something palatable before the food reaches their taste buds. At least, they could in

their home universe; on Earth Prime, not so much, as they quickly discovered..."

On their home Earth, eating was a form of nostalgia for beings who had stopped physically needing it thousands of years earlier. The Restaurant at the End of Thyme was meant to feed nostalgia for that nostalgia. Did this multiply the nostalgia or cancel it out?

"Got me," Curr said. "Sorry, but if you can't filet, smoke or barbecue it, it lies outside my frame of reference."

Far from giving customers a taste of home, the Restaurant at the End of Thyme gave its customers strong gastric distress and dysentery. Oddly enough, that was not a sustainable business model. By the end of the first week, the only customers the restaurant had were frat pledges who had to eat something gross as part of their initiation and aliens who brought their own food but were willing to pay for the ambience.

The restaurant would have ended up a brief mention at the end of a footnote in and addendum to the history of culinary advancement were it not for a chance comment one of the frat boys made at the end of the third week: "I thought the names were just gags and the food was something, you know, edible and stuff. I didn't reali – will you excuse me? I – **where's the bathroom?**"

That's when a light bulb went off over Psychonaut's head. "We couldn't afford to be on the electric grid, so we use a second-hand generator to power the establishment," he explained. "It's...not always reliable..."

At the same time, he had an idea: why not offer food that people on Earth Prime could actually eat?

"Of course, it seems obvious now," pontificated gourwomand Julia Burpsi-Baybee, "but you can't blame Redrum for not seeing it right away. When French cuisine first came to America, it took restaurant owners seventeen years to offer food that people could actually eat. By this standard, Redrum was a fast learner!"

It still says 'pickled mud' on the menu, but the dish is a thin chocolate pudding, with walnuts replacing pebbles. 'Boot tread tart' is made with leathery beef. 'Pig intestines puree' is still made from pig intestines, but is now lightly salted.

The salt helps. It really helps.

"This is very exciting," commented Annette Virtualizer, one of many customers who returned to the restaurant when word got out that the food had changed. "I get to feel like I'm home again, and I don't have to spend time in an Intensive Care Unit!"

Oh, and you're probably wondering how the restaurant got its name. As Psychonaut explained: "While I was planning the restaurant opening, global warming, a cricket infestation and an increase in demand as a homeopathic remedy for dyspraxia had devastated production of the herb. Parsley? Plenty. Sage? Stupendous amounts. Rosemary? Really big portions. But thyme? Scarcer than the kid who broke the cookie jar when his father got home. When my supplier said, 'Sorry, but there's no thyme left for you,' the restaurant pretty much named itself."

Any explanation with **two** musical references is good enough for me.

"Aliens Helping Aliens Help Line. How may I help you?"

"I think I'm having one of those – what do you call them? – exponential crises."

"Do you mean you're having an existential crisis?"

"Identical crisis?"

"Are you a twin?"

"Only in the intransigent disposable sense of the term."

"Existential crisis?"

"Expialadociousal crisis?"

"Sure. Let's go with that. What is the nature of your crisis?"

"Where do babies come from?"

PAUSE

"Are you...looking for the answer to the question on Wiwipedia?"

"N...no!"

"You are! You are totally looking for the answer on Wiwipedia!"

"You got me. I am totally looking for the answer on Wiwipedia."

"What does it say?"

"Well, it says...umm...then that...that...**with a melon?**"

"I like melons."

"Not like this, you don't!"

"Are you talking about...sex?"

"Sex?"

"Sex."

"Maaaaaaybe."

"Well, I know all about that."

"You do?"

"Yes. Since coming here, I have become something of a connoisseur of high school health education instructional videos."

"If you know all about sex, what did you put me through that for?"

"I want to know where babies come from **for us**. We had to completely change our physignominy...our physiotherapy...our physicognomin – our bodies. We had to completely change the composition of our bodies to live in this universe. How will we be able to reproduce?"

"If you just give me a moment..."

"To look it up on Wiwipedia?"

"Would that be so bad?"

"Don't bother. I already did. Wiwipedia says we can't have babies on Earth Prime – in our present form, we're infertile."

"Oh. So, if you knew the answer..."

"If that is the case, does that mean that we have come here from our dying universe just to die out in a generation?"

"Ah, now that, I believe, **is** an existential question."

"Haven't we moved beyond categorization?"

"Fair point."

"So, what was the point?"

"What do you think the point was?"

"Well...we have orgasmatrons, which means we can meld with each other, refreshing our bodies. That means we can effectively live for thousands of years. All being well, we'll figure sexual reproduction out while we're still around. Thousands of years is a long time for an adolescence, but at least we never have to worry about our complexion...or high school cliques...or getting our first job at a Bob So Tasty burger joint. My first job **was** at a Bob So Tasty burger joint – that shit is harder than adults realize!"

"It really is."

"So, if we can figure out some way to reproduce, our species could keep going and, maybe somebody, some day will find a reason for all our effort."

"Sounds good to me."

"Thank you. I feel much better, now. Thank you so much."

"You're very welcome. We're here to help."

"I, uhh, just have one other question..."

"Yes?"

"Any idea how I could get Rodney   Pendleton's autograph?"

Five military personnel, including a general, were seated on the opposite side of the table from tallest to shortest, looking to Rodney   Pendleton like a pink set of tubular bells. He wanted to manifest a mallet in his briefcase so he could go all Mike Oldfield on their heads, as one will. (A Nerf mallet: he didn't want to hurt them, he just wanted to see if they were in tune.) He wanted to do it badly enough that the fingers of his right hand flexed uncontrollably. But Redjina Pinklewort had advised him against engaging in shenanigans at the meeting and he was paying a lot of money for her advice, so he would do his best to keep the shenaniganning to a minimum.

"Yes, we are generally pleased with the progress of the hovertank initiative," General Curtis Halftraque stated. He sat in the middle of the military side of the table; although broad-shouldered and chiselled, he wasn't very tall – a C Flat at best. "Although I'm sure you can understand that a seventy-three per cent * PLUNK * rate is still unacceptable."

"We did warn you that scaling up would be a problem," Redjina Pinklewort coolly responded. She was only four foot three, with a slight frame and spiky greying brown hair, yet she radiated more authority than the sun. "Using our patented anti-gravity technology to allow a kid on a board to hover four feet above the ground is a trivial matter compared to levitating sixty tons of steel twenty feet."

Rodney didn't think it was fair that the General and some of his aids were in uniform, including their military decorations, when all he was wearing was a lousy exquisite three piece suit. He was very tempted to reach into his briefcase and pull out his own decorations, made up of bottle caps and stray pieces of fabric, rewards for such feats as 'Bravery under enemy pier' and 'Heroism above and beyond the call of doody'. Buuuut, Redjina Pinklewort had advised him not to do this ("You will be tempted to create your own whimsical decorations to match the ones the uniformed officers in the meeting will be wearing," she had literally warned him. "You must resist this temptation at all costs!"), and his comedic leanings were drowned out by the authority greater than the sun. Even if it made his arm down to his elbow shake with mild tremors.

"That was not a complaint," General Halftraque assured her. "It took us almost eleven years to figure out how to transport fighter jets to other universes. Something about matter displacement equations – I don't pretend to understand the half of it. Or the other half of it, to be honest. That's why we pay Chuck here!"

General Halftraque put a hand on the shoulder of the (taller) man in civilian garb sitting next to him; Chuck winced like his body part had just been put into a vise. "Yes, sir," he half-heartedly gasped.

"We have the best minds of the military and the private sector working on the problem," Redjina Pinklewort assured him. "It's only a matter of time before we crack it."

One fart, Rodney thought. *One little toot. It could have been the chilli fries I had for breakfast – it might not be a shenanigan. I mean, really. One little fart couldn't even be considered a shenan.* Rodney recognized that there were flaws in his plan to vent some of his increasingly pent up comic energy. For one thing, one little toot wouldn't make much of a dent in the ongoing flow of corporatese in the room, which wouldn't impress the Audi Enz all that much. Besides, farts were like chilli fries – he could never stop at just one. In his head he tried to calculate the farts to patience ratio of the room, and how many it would take for him to end up on the wrong side of the line, the shenanigans side, something that Redjina Pinklewort had expressly forbidden him from doing. (She had expressly forbidden him from doing many things. She had, in fact, made a twenty-seven page list that she demanded he memorize. That process took him longer than he expected the meeting to last.)

So, no farting. Rodney's knees started mildly shaking, the rest of his legs following soon after. He imagined that he was listening to a toe-tappingly infectious song, but the only thing that came to mind was 'The Flight of the Valkyries'. He pretended that Wagner wrote toe-tapping music because once you go down the anti-shenanigans path, it develops its own logical momentum.

"Oh, I wholeheartedly agree," Redjina Pinklewort was wholeheartedly agreeing with...something that had been said in the conversation while we were following Rodney's thoughts. "Still, if the squirrels were really that intent on solving their little acorn problem, they would have developed their own sonar tracking systems!"

Everybody in the room laughed, even the cadaverous Army Colonel who towered over everybody else from the far end of the table (he never actually said anything at these meetings; Rodney was convinced that the only reason he was there was to give the more important members of the military in attendance shade so that the sun wouldn't bring out their freckles).

Realizing that he was odd alien out, Rodney said: "Ha. Ha ha. Ha. Ha ha ha."

When the laughter died down, Redjina Pinklewort continued: "But seriously, in the time we have remaining, we should probably discuss deliverables for the next three quarters."

Inwardly, Rodney moaned. *Deliverables! Just shoot me! With a tranquilizer. Don't want to get too excited!* His eyes started twitching uncontrollably. He really wanted to reach into his briefcase and pull out a pair of toothpicks to prop them up, but that was borderline shenanig-territory. *Must follow the Prime Directive*, Rodney desperately thought. *No shenanigans. Don't sour the deal with the military because you couldn't resist shenaniganning. Under no circumstances shenanig!* So, instead, he put his hand (the left one, the one that wasn't twitching) over his eyes, hoping nobody would notice.

Everybody noticed.

"I know exactly how you feel, Mister Pendleton," General Halftraque commiserated. "These sessions can take a lot out of a man. Umm...alien. They can take almost as much out of an alien as they take out of a man. Not that I am purposefully being exclusionary of women..." General Halftraque cast a wary eye on Redjina Pinklewort, whose bland expression gave him nothing. "I have no doubt that these meetings can take as much out of a woman as they take out of a man, which, we have previously established, is a little more than they take out of an alien. The point is: we're almost done. No more than two...three hours, tops!"

Rodney felt minor tremors throughout his body. Before they could become a full-on alienquake, he reached under the table and opened his briefcase. A gust of air blew him out of his seat and against the wall behind him. He ricocheted off the wall into the ceiling, hit the far corner of the room and bounced back and forth between walls several times before falling onto the table in the middle of the room. To his credit, he did not make "thhhhhzzzing" noises like a balloon losing its air, despite the great temptation.

Many around the table were aghast at what they had just witnessed, but General Halftraque, who had seen his share of strange things on battlefields around the multiverse, was unflustered. "He okay?" the General asked, tilting his head ever so slightly towards the alien on the table.

"I'm fine," Rodney weakly responded.[1]

---

[1] In fact, when he had the briefcase create the gust of air that rag dolled him around the room, Rodney had the presence of mind to have it also put a layer of hardened air around his body to soften the impact of being repeatedly rammed into walls. If you replay the scene in slow motion and look carefully, you will see that his body does not actually come into direct contact with the walls or ceiling. He did have the air knocked out of him, though, and he would be sore for the next several days. However, if it was rated

"He's fine," Redjina Pinklewort assured the military men. "Now, if we could just turn our attention to the timetable for delivering wiring schematics for increased thrusting capability..."

Rodney quietly moaned. Audibly, but relatively quietly.

"Shouldn't this...person get medical attention?" Chuck asked. Everybody in the room save for the other civilian inwardly rolled their eyes.

"Rodney has experienced worse," Redjina Pinklewort assured him.

"Much – * GASP * – worse!" Rodney rasped.

"Why, one time, I saw an entire merry-go-round fall on Rodney's head! Horses, giraffes, unicorns...umm, zephyrs, I mean, this was an alpha merry-go-round! The merry-go-round to end all merry-go-rounds! After he was dug out of the crater it had created, he flexed for a moment, then shrugged the whole thing off.[2] So, this? This is but a scratch."

"Scratch," Rodney barely audibly agreed.

"That may well be," General Halftraque huffed, "but we can't have an injured man lying on the table moaning while we are trying to conduct a business meeting. While it would send a strong message of self-sacrifice to the troops, it would make hearing the discussion much harder!"

"I could...go..."

"That would be for the best."

"Here," Redjina Pinklewort offered. "Let me help you to your feet." As she cradled Rodney's body in her arms, she whispered into his ear, "Don't think I don't recognize shenanigans when they're flying all around the room I'm

---

two chuckles or higher in the review of his life that would be revealed when he came face to face with the Audi Enz, it would be totally – owww – worth it!

[2] Actually, Redjina Pinklewort had never seen footage from Rodney's home planet. What she was doing here was 'selling the message' (what people who don't make nearly as much money as she does call 'lying').

in. We shall talk about this later, sir. **At length!**"

As she helped him out the door, Rodney winked at her.

When he was gone, Redjina Pinklewort shut the door, turned to the men at the table and said, "Now, about those wiring schematics..."

Our Robot Overlords Would Like to Give You Your Money Back

by MARA VERHEYDEN-HILLIARD, Alternate Reality News Service War Writer

To OVRLORD 001gmt it seemed like a win-win proposition: by accepting refugees from Earth Prime 4-6-4-0-8-9 dash Omega, it could receive resettlement funding from the Transdimensional Authority **and** get new human beings to lord over. Well, humanish. Humanesque? The point is: after the extinction of the human race on Earth Prime 7-1-1-7-1-2 dash omicron, existence for our robot overlords became a lot less interesting. Close to tedious. Perhaps even...boring. Accepting Humanoid...al creatures from another universe would be a way of relieving that.

Six months after the first thousand aliens had settled on their planet, our robot overlords of Earth Prime 7-1-1-7-1-2 dash omicron demanded that the Transdimensional Authority take the aliens back, even going so far as to threaten a lawsuit if the organization that monitors and polices transdimensional treaties refused to accept a refund of its resettlement payments. With interest.

Why? "The. Aliens. Do. Not. Fit. In," OVRLORD 001gmt explained. "It. Would. Be. Better. For. Them. If. They... Went. Just... Went. Someplace. Else."

"That is simply unacceptable," responded Transdimensional Authority Secretary-Specific

Nicodemius Fitzhuge. "The universe from whence the aliens came – why does the word whence make me wince? – it sounds like I should put an 'eth' at the end of 'came,' doesn't it? – yet, perversely, I make use of the word in my everyday speech – * sigh * – well, that place is about to become a repository of subatomic non-cohesion – they cannot go back to it. And resettling takes months of negotiations – our robot overlords should find this in their own memory banks. We cannot just relocate the refugees from Earth Prime 4-6-4-0-8-9 dash Omega. I'm sorry, but our robot overlords are just going to have to suck it up."

"Suck. It. Up?" OVRLORD 001gmt, like all of its kind, was created without emotions, so any pique in its voice was clearly a figment of the reader's imagination. "I. Am. Not. Familiar. With. That. Vacuuming. Metaphor. However. From. Context. I. Calculate. A. Sixty-seven. Per. Cent. Probability. That. The. Secretary-Specific. Is. Rejecting. Our. Demand. Very. Well. We. Shall. Make. Immediate. Plans. To. Invade. Earth. Prime!"

"You can't do that!" Secretary-Specific Fitzhuge gasped. "It is specifically forbidden by Clause Three of Sub-section Agatha of the Rights and Responsibilities Section of the Treaty of Gehenna-Wentworth!"

And the Transdimensional Authority could shut down all of their Dimensional Portal^{TM}s, making it impossible for our robot overlords to travel between universes? "We don't like to talk about it," Secretary-Specific Fitzhuge said under his breath, "but, yes, there is that."

This discussion begs the question (yes, it does: the discussion is sitting on the pavement outside Alternate Reality News Service headquarters with an open guitar case and a sign that reads: "Haven't been asked in over 24 hours!" while pedestrians step around it, desperate not to make eye contact): how, exactly, do the four foot tall blue aliens with no hair and exquisite three piece body armour not fit in?

Before they leave their home universe, residents of Earth Prime 4-6-4-0-8-9 dash Omega, who have complete control of all of the matter in their bodies down to the sub-atomic level, must alter themselves to fit the environment they will be moving into. The host universe is expected to send 'ambassadors' as templates for the aliens to use to reshape their bodies.

Our robot overlords made the mistake of sending morphomorphs (literally:

changing robots that change) as their ambassadors to Earth Prime 4-6-4-0-8-9 dash Omega. Morphomorphs are generally recognized as among the stupidest of all of the robots that became our robot overlords, ranking only just above sea slugs. The fact that they do not know that sea slugs are not robots gives you some idea of their level of intelligence. If not for the fact that the first law of Overlord Robotics was that no robot shall cause another robot to come to harm, the morphomorphs would long ago have been disassembled and made into toaster ovens and hand dryers.

Why did our robot overlords choose the morphomorphs to be their ambassadors? Partially, it was because their incompetence was interfering with the Great Work of determining the meaning of The Universe and Everything (Life having been removed from the equation). Mostly, they were cheap.

"In. Retrospect. That. Was. A. False. Economy," OVRLORD 001gmt allowed. "The. Peace. Was. Nice. While. It. Lasted. But. Now. We. Have. Twice. As. Many. RAM. Damaged. Robots. To. Deal. With!"

"That's not exact – Sorry. I'm. Still. Getting. The. Hang. Of. Talking robot – dammit!" said OVRLARD 727tmi, one of the refugees.. "That. Is. Not. Exactly true. Exactly. True. Morphomorphs. Were. Born foolish. For. Us. Foolishness. Is. A. Way of li – **dammit!**"

"ISCBOT 001ssn has a lot to answer for," OVRLORD 001gmt muttered. If I didn't know for a fact that our robot overlords have no emotions, I would have sworn it was bitter.

Daveen Rasmalai Rapier's apartment opens onto a balcony that has a breathtaking view of the Okanagan Valley. However, the sometime operative for the Transdimensional Authority liked his breath and had his own views, thank you very much, so the balcony was

largely blocked by a whiteboard he had set up. He had
taped four photographs to the whiteboard. At the top was
a photo of a silver-haired middle-aged man with a lean
face who was sucking on a carrot. That would be P. J.
Pinchus, leader of the mercenary group the Bastards of
the Universe and the bane of Daveen Rasmalai's
existence. Above the photo, Daveen Rasmalai had printed
in precise block letters, "I love it when a plan falls apart,"
P. J. Pinchus' catchphrase (because that allowed him to
blow things up, which he loved almost as much as
creating overly complex ways of running simple scams
on people). Below that were photographs of three other
people: a nineteen year-old boy with sandy hair and a
grimace (the only known image of Eustace
'Mystification' Jones was from his high school yearbook,
under which it was described as 'most likely
to...uhh...who are we talking about again?'); a four-
hundred pound Asian man in a loincloth squatting in a
menacing position (Dru Mamo Kanuha had once been a
sumo wrestler, roaming the Hilo countryside for
backroom bouts; the image had been scanned from a
poster of one of his few aboveground fights); and a
thirtysomething Latina in a leather jacket whose scowl
would frighten The Batman (the explosion behind Jessie
Chupa Cabrerra was supposed to drive home the point
that she was far more dangerous than your average tech
expert, but even her mother, Barbara Chupa Cabrerra
thought it was a little much). Daveen Rasmalai had used
a red marker to draw lines between P. J. Pinchus and his
current team. The rest of the board was taken up with
newspaper clippings, printouts of internet articles and
handwritten pages of notes, all of which went by too fast
to actually read, but that we could reasonably assume
were about the elaborate scams (and occasional
explosions) that Daveen Rasmalai believed had been
perpetrated on the aliens by this group. Most were
connected by green dotted lines, others by yellow dotted
lines (the green marker having run out of ink, but you can
assign more significance to the different colours if it

makes things more interesting for you).

Daveen Rasmalai paced his living room. He was looking over the case, eager to find some clue that he had overlooked that might finally allow him to connect the Bastards of the Universe to one of the scams on the board and put them away for good. On the other hand, ever since he had melded with Rodney   Pendleton in the first book of the trilogy, he had known down to the molecular level that existence was absurd and not worth taking so seriously, so his eagerness was laid back, his nervous pacing leisurely. (Was that too breaking down the fourth wall for you? Sorry about that. I meant to write, "ever since he had melded with Rodney   Pendleton four years ago," but my hand slipped.)

"Sir?" the room asked. The voice was male, with a cultivated British accent that made even that single word sound smug. This was the Jarvis personality of Carlton and JARVIS.[3]

"Yes?" Daveen Rasmalai distractedly prompted.

"You have an incoming message from a Mister Matumbo."

This got Daveen Rasmalai's attention. Got it in a stranglehold. And gave it a nougie that reminded Daveen Rasmalai's attention of grade school. His attention decided not to make too much of this, because the rest of Daveen Rasmalai seemed excited by the news. "Agavee Matumbo?" he stopped pacing and eagerly asked.

Agavee Matumbo was one of P. J. Pinchus' aliases

---

[3] Until about a year previous, each room and many pieces of furniture and appliances in the apartment contained their own personality chips. At first, Daveen Rasmalai was amused by their verbal exchanges and grateful for the company. Over time, however, he developed the feeling that he was being smothered by a large contingent of disturbed in-laws, so he had them replaced by a single...ish voice throughout the apartment. Don't feel bad for the personality constructs: they were installed in Misplaced Youth and Glasses, an elder care facility in Oshawa, where they will have spirited interchanges with the clients for the rest of their days.

(along with Ho Chi Suss, the Reverend Martin Lex Luther and Alison Parrot). Daveen Rasmalai knew the message was likely to be a taunt (it had happened before, most memorably just minutes preceding the Battle of the Sixteen Erasures, in which somebody kept going back in time to change the history of Earth Prime 2-7-4-8-4-3 dash epsilon for fun and profit; although Daveen Rasmalai had worked with agents of the Time Agency to stop the culprits, they could not prove that the Bastards were the ones funning or profiting from it), but it might contain a clue that would finally help him put the Bastards of the Universe away for good.

"Display it in front of me," Daveen Rasmalai commanded.

"What's the magic word?" a new voice asked. This voice was precious and wheedling and somewhat Manhattanish: this was the Carlton voice of CARLTON and Jarvis. It reminded Daveen Rasmalai of his grandmother, and not only because of its subdued New York masculinity.

"I don't have time for this," Daveen Rasmalai bitched.

"That is more than one word," Carlton and JARVIS pedanticked. "And none of them are remotely magical."

"Display the Gord damned message in front of me!" Daveen Rasmalai demanded.

"I'm waiting." CARLTON and Jarvis said in a disinterested voice that gave the impression that, as an artificial intelligence, they could wait until the end of time if necessary.

"Please don't do this now!" Daveen Rasmalai shouted.

"Thank you." Carlton and JARVIS was nothing if not polite. Well, part of it, in any case.

A virtual screen appeared in the air in front of Daveen Rasmalai displaying his desktop. He clicked on the icon to open his email programme. Ignoring messages from people he didn't know about casinos, inheriting millions of dollars and enlarging his manhood (he didn't gamble, he didn't need money and nobody had any complaints about his manhood, thank you very much), messages from work (his weekdays were spent ferrying aliens from Earth Prime 4-6-4-0-8-9 dash Omega to their new homes in various universes; chasing the Bastards of the Universe was just an obsession that he could pretend was an evenings and weekends hobby, although the view from his apartment saw right through the pretense) and a couple of recent messages from his sister, Noomi,[4] Daveen Rasmalai quickly found the message from 'The Right Honourable Agavee Matumbo' and opened it.

The text of the message was simple enough: 'Wish you were here.' *Typically unoriginal*, Daveen Rasmalai thought. The text was in a flashing neon blue font. *Typically attention-getting at the same time as being hopelessly out of date*, Daveen Rasmalai further thought. Noticing that the email contained an image, he clicked on it. The image was of a stone wall, a spray of water hitting it from below the frame. In what little could be seen above it, there appeared to be a bright object.

"What is this?" Daveen Rasmalai wondered.

"I would imagine," Carlton and **JARVIS** replied, "keeping in mind that I am no expert in such matters and may, therefore, be way off base, here, that that is what, in colloquial terms, is known as 'a wall'."

"I can see that it is a wall."

"Ah. I was correct, then. Thank you for the confirmation."

"Why would P. J. Pinchus send me an image of a wall?" Daveen Rasmalai stared intently at the image. "If this is supposed to be a clue to where he is, it's very frustrating!"

"If you're going to answer your own questions, I may

---

[4] The siblings had a friendly competition to see who could annoy the other the most. Every day, Noomi sent Daveen Rasmalai a picture of an adorable kitten, knowing that he had once investigated a deadly furball 'cure' that was being peddled on Earth Prime 3-0-0-0-7-5 dash alpha, an event in his life that had made him immune to the charms of feline youth. Daveen Rasmalai responded by sending Noomi action photos of Jean-Claude van Damme, whom she had had a crush on when she was twelve years old. Sibling love takes many forms.

as well go and watch *Coronary Nation Street*."

"I prefer *Hill Street Barnacles*," CARLTON and Jarvis opined.

"There's no accounting for taste," Carlton and JARVIS responded, just the merest hint of tut in his voice.

"Yeah, well, you, too!" CARLTON and Jarvis retorted. Repartee was clearly not its strong suit, so it drove the point home by adding: "You, too!"

Daveen Rasmalai rubbed his eyes; he wanted to slap CARLTON and Jarvis for being so gormless, but at the same time he wanted to slap Carlton and JARVIS for being so superior. Unfortunately, they had no body to slap, so he had to wait their disagreement out or try to distract them. Opting for the latter option, he asked, "That bright spot in the upper left corner of the image – any idea what it could be?"

"The sun?" CARLTON and Jarvis tentatively answered.

"It cannot be the sun," Carlton and JARVIS argued. "If you look closely, you will see that the spray at the bottom casts a shadow on the wall, which would indicate that the sun is actually in front of it, not above and slightly behind it."

"It could be an Earth with two suns," CARLTON and Jarvis pouted.

"Doubtful," Carlton and JARVIS lectured. "That would have changed the quality of the light in the image."

"If it's not a sun," Daveen Rasmalai reasonably asked, "what is it?"

"Look more closely," Carlton and JARVIS suggested.

"Focus on upper left corner, double magnification," Daveen Rasmalai commanded. When the AI complied, he could make out dark shadows in the enlarged white ball.

"Moooorrrrreeee," Carlton and JARVIS encouraged with just the right amount of sarcasm that it could be easily missed.

"Double magnification again," Daveen Rasmalai ordered. The dark shadows grew into something he still did not recognize.

"Perhaps just a teeeeeeensy smidge more?" Carlton and JARVIS said, the sarcasm hard to miss.

"Double magnification again," Daveen Rasmalai told

the AI. The white ball now filled the entire screen. The shadows inside it were definitely something else, but Daveen Rasmalai couldn't quite make them out.

"Do you see it now?" Carlton and **JARVIS** asked.

"I can see something," Daveen Rasmalai answered, "but I can't quite make it out."

"Ah, yes," Carlton and **JARVIS** smugged. "I always have to remember that human pattern recognition is one three hundred thousandth as effective as mine. It is a phoenix. You're welcome."

How come Rick Deckard never had this problem? Daveen Rasmalai wondered. Aloud, he excitedly commanded, "Open a virtual Home Universe Generator^{TM}." A second screen opened up next to the first. Five minutes later (it was slow to load and had too many intermediate command screens), his ardour somewhat cooled, Daveen Rasmalai had Google Multiverse^{TM} up on the screen. "Known universes with phoenixes," he commanded.

Google Multiverse returned an infinite number of responses (limited to the 3,217 most relevant) for 'known universes with penises'.

"No," Daveen Rasmaila corrected it. "Phoenixes. Not penises. Phoenixes. Known universes with phoenixes."

Google Multiverse^{TM} returned an infinite number of responses (limited to the 4,826 most relevant) for 'known universes with peanuts'.

"No!" Daveen Rasmalai shouted. "Phoenixes! Not peanuts! Phoenix – never mind. Virtual keyboard." A blue neon keyboard appeared in the air in front of the screen. Daveen Rasmalai typed in 'known universes with phoenixes'.

Google Multiverse^{TM} returned an infinite number of responses (limited to the 3 most relevant): Earth Prime 6-4-9-8-2-3 dash rho, Earth Prime 4-4-4-4-7-1 dash alpha and Earth Prime 1-2-1-7-8-4 dash alpha.

That last one sounded familiar to Daveen Rasmalai, and it only took him a couple of seconds to figure out why: checking the whiteboard, he confirmed that the

Bastards of the Universe were suspected to be behind an illegal phoenix hunt on that Earth, and Daveen Rasmalai knew that the group never pulled a scam in the same universe twice. A little digging led Daveen Rasmalai to discover that Earth Prime 4-4-4-4-7-1 dash alpha was a desert planet with an improbable living ecosystem, but no ground water. No ground water meant no spray on a stone wall. That left Earth Prime 6-4-9-8-2-3 dash rho, which he clicked on.

"Call up image search," Daveen Rasmalai commanded. A window appeared within the Home Universe Generator^{TM}.[5] Daveen Rasmalai pulled the screen displaying his email over until its window just overlapped with the HUG^{TM}, then he dragged the image out of it and into the image search programme. "Working..." immediately popped up on the screen.

"Ping me when you have a match," Daveen Rasmalai ordered and, with a gesture, closed both screens.

He went to sleep. The next day, he went to work. He went to sleep. The next day, he went to work. Before he went to sleep, Daveen Rasmalai checked in on the image search programme of his Home Universe Generator^{TM}, but it was still working... He went to sleep. The next day, he went to work. Just as he was handing an alien off to an anti-social worker on Earth Prime 2-2-3-6-2-6 dash omicron ("Sometimes dystopian futures make the best

---

[5] No, you are not hallucinating (well, not about this, anyway) – your Home Universe Generator^{TM} does not have image search. That is part of a sweet suite of programmes developed specifically for the Transdimensional Authority. If you don't mind navigating pop-up ads every thirty seconds, you can find bootleg copies on the Noir Web. Or you could just wait a couple of years for the tech to be transferred to the private sector and appear in future HUG^{TM} consoles. Your ("You'll wonder where the yellow went, when you brush your teeth with Burpsi Mint!") call ("Then you tell two friends. And they tell two friends. And they tell two friends. And pretty soon, nobody has any friends any more!"), really ("The old sludge is the grease of a new generation!").

homes," he had been assured), he received a ping from his Home Universe Generator^{TM}. I wouldn't like to leave you with the impression that he concluded the hand-off abruptly, but somebody is going to get a poor review on Foursquaremeals!

Because his work as a secret operative took precedence over other duties he might be given by the Transdimensional Authority, he immediately booked off and headed home. When he arrived, he quickly discovered that the wall existed in the small town of Heroica Veracruz, Mexico.

With a laid-back self-satisfied grin, Daveen Rasmalai said, "Got you, you Bastards!"

Being a Full and Complete Record of the Diary of Martini Frobisher During His Historic Campaign for Member of Canadian Parliament

CAMPAIGN DIARY, DAY ONE

DEAR DAIRY,

I NEVER WANTED TO – WHAT? IT'S DIARY, NOT DAIRY? OH, SORRY. I LOST IT IN THE SUN.

AS I WAS SAYING, I NEVER – CAN I CALL YOU DI? NO? HOW ABOUT ARI? GOT A NICE RING TO IT, ARI. NO? YOU'RE RIGHT – WE DON'T KNOW EACH OTHER THAT WELL. DIARY IT IS...FOR NOW.

I NEVER WANTED TO BE A POLITICIAN. IN MY HOME UNIVERSE, I WAS A BUTCHER. MEAT WAS MY

LIFE. I BUTCHED. THEY SAY THAT THERE ARE TWO THINGS YOU DON'T WANT TO SEE BEING MADE: LAWS AND SAUSAGES. WELL, I HAD SEEN SO MANY SAUSAGES BEING MADE THAT THEY WERE PROMINENT IN THE FAMILY CREST I NEVER FELT THE NEED TO HAVE DESIGNED, SO I GUESS I WAS PREPARED FOR A CAREER IN POLITICS.

I WOULDN'T HAVE RUN FOR PUBLIC OFFICE, BUT ON THE DAY THAT I GOT MY CANADIAN CITIZENSHIP, I LOST MY JOB AS A RODEO CLOWN. MANY OF MY COW-WORKERS WERE UNHAPPY WITH MY WORK ETHIC; THEY THOUGHT THAT I WAS TOO COMPETITIVE, TOO AGGRESSIVELY BUFFOONISH, THAT I WAS SETTING STANDARDS THEY COULDN'T HOPE TO ACHIEVE. WELL, PFFT TO THAT! I WAS JUST DOING ME LIKE THE SELF-HELP GURUS ON TWITHERD SAY YOU SHOULD; CAN I HELP IT IF COMPETITIVE BOZOING WAS A BELOVED PASTIME WHERE I CAME FROM? SO, THEY FILED A COMPLAINT WITH THE PRIVATE ASSOCIATION OF RODEO CLOWNS OF CALGARY. WELL! THEY TOLD ME WHERE TO PARCC IT, BOY!

I WAS HAVING NO LUCK FINDING ANOTHER JOB (APPARENTLY, AN ADVANCED DEGREE IN MACROSCOPIC MICROORGANISM MANAGEMENT FROM THE UNIVERSITY OF GINGIVITAS ON EARTH PRIME 4-6-4-0-8-9 DASH OMEGA MEANS NOTHING ON EARTH PRIME!), WHEN MY GIRLFRIEND, AMAROSA   DEFIBRILLATOR, SUGGESTED THAT I RUN FOR OFFICE. A COZY LITTLE RIDING IN SOUTH-WESTERN ALBERTA HAD JUST BECOME AVAILABLE BECAUSE THE PREVIOUS OWNER HAD USED CAMPAIGN FUNDS TO FLY DOWN TO FLORIDA WITH HIS MISTRESS FOR TWO WEEKS. ORDINARILY, THIS STORY WOULD BE NOTHING MORE THAN ONE-COLUMN FILLER IN THE BACK OF THE NEWS SECTION, BUT HE MADE THE MISTAKE OF RUNNING OFF DURING THE CALGARY STAMPEDE.

IN ALBERTA, THEY TAKE THE CALGARY STAMPEDE VERY SERIOUSLY.

So, a special by-election would have to be held. While I found the possibility intriguing (the riding was a definite fixer upper, but that just brought out the political handyman in me), I wasn't sure about Amarosa's motives. "You just want a context in which to wear a pink pillbox hat, don't you?" I demanded.

"Oh, Martman, of course I do!" she replied. "What girl wouldn't? But I'm actually thinking of you. You've taken rodeo clowning as far as you can and need a new career. I think you would really take to political clowning. Really, I do."

I couldn't argue with her logic. Besides, I had to agree that she would look fetching in a pink pillbox hat.

I first approached the Conservative Party to see if they would be willing to nominate me as a candidate for the riding of Perch-Lake-Meshuggah. The riding President asked, "Are you serious?"

"Not if I can help it," I responded.

The interview went downhill from there.

Next, I tried the Liberal Party to see if they would allow me to be their candidate. "What's the worst that could possibly happen?" I asked.

"You could embarrass the party so badly that we would never win another seat in the west," the riding President fretted. "We would never be able to win a majority government, ending up in eternal opposition, or worse: we would have to form a coalition with the -" * SHUDDER * "NDP!"

"Sounds good to me!" I enthused. "Where do I sign up?"

She suggested the unemployment office.

So, I tried the NDP. "Sure, why not?" the Riding President, a walrus of a human being

NAMED MANFRED MANNHEIM, SAID. "WE DON'T HAVE A HOPE IN HELL OF WINNING THE RIDING, SO WHY NOT LET A CLOWN RUN?"

I WAS SO TOUCHED BY HIS FAITH IN ME, THAT I RUSHED TOWARDS HIM AT THE CANNING PLANT WHERE HE WORKED. I COULD TELL BY THE GLARE THROUGH HIS GOGGLES THAT HE HAD PERSONAL SPACE ISSUES, SO I STOPPED. PROBABLY JUST AS WELL: I WOULD HAVE HAD TROUBLE HUGGING HIS LEG, LET ALONE HIS TORSO (DID I MENTION THAT HE WAS BIG?). HE TOLD ME TO MEET HIM IN THE PARTY'S CONSTITUENCY OFFICE AFTER HIS SHIFT. I WAS SO THRILLED, I WAS HALFWAY HOME BEFORE I REALIZED THAT HE HADN'T TOLD ME WHERE THE CONSTITUENCY OFFICE WAS OR WHAT TIME HE GOT OFF WORK. SO, I GOOGLED THE ADDRESS OF THE OFFICE AND CAMPED OUT ACROSS THE STREET UNTIL HE ARRIVED. (HE DIDN'T ACTUALLY SHOW UP FOR THREE DAYS, BUT AMAROSA BROUGHT ME STALE SANDWICHES AND LUKEWARM COFFEE, SO IT TURNED OUT TO BE QUITE THE PARTY!)

AFTER I SIGNED ALL THE FORMS, MANFRED HANDED ME A BINDER CONTAINING THREE HUNDRED AND FIFTY-SEVEN PAGES OF SINGLE-SPACED TEXT; THE DOCUMENT WAS CALLED 'SO YOU WANNA BE A MEMBER OF PARLIAMENT? WHY? IT'S A THANKLESS JOB WITH NO REAL POWER. BUT, UHH, I SEE YOU CANNOT BE DISSUADED, SO HERE IS A GUIDE TO RUNNING EFFECTIVE ELECTIONS.' THE GUIDE WAS VERY USEFUL IN PREPARING FOR THE CAMPAIGN; WHENEVER I WOULD GET BORED IN A PLANNING MEETING, I WOULD TAKE A PAGE OUT OF THE BINDER AND CREATE ORIGAMI PUBLIC MONUMENTS (THE TAJ MAHAL WAS VERY POPULAR WITH OUR VOLUNTEERS).

THE LAST THING MANFRED MENTIONED WAS THAT I HAD A BUDGET OF EXACTLY THREE DOLLARS AND SEVENTEEN CENTS. "THAT WON'T BE A PROBLEM," I ASSURED HIM. "AMAROSA IS A HAIRSTYLIST TO A LOT of provincial bigwigs. With her steady income, we should easily be able to double that!"

"Un hunh."

I stuck my hand out to shake his. He carefully inspected it for joy buzzers. Satisfied, he took it, quickly trying to get out of my grasp when his hand was shocked. (I'm surprised nobody on Earth Prime has designed shirts with spring-loaded joy buzzers built into the sleeves. It seems like the logical next step in practical prankware.)

"Get out!" Manfred snarled as he shook the tingling out of his hand. "And good luck..."

I've spent most of the three weeks since then doing interviews and flossing. Apparently, being the first sentient alien to run for Parliament on Earth Prime is a big deal. (And the Guide said that the key to winning over voters was a good smile; I caught that while making an origami CN Tower out of page seventeen.)

A nice woman from the Toronto Star asked me: "How does it feel to be a groundbreaker?"

"I couldn't have done it without Traci," I answered.

"Traci? Is she your wife?"

"No, she's my hoe."

I have a lot of respect for my gardening implements, but in retrospect, I probably should have chosen my words more carefully.

A grumpy man from the Globe and Mail asked me: "What is your policy on illegal immigration?"

"Zebra mussels can make a lovely bouillabaisse base if you catch them at the right time of day," I replied.

"What the hell is that supposed to mean?"

"I stand by my statement."

While I like a good fish stew more than

MOST, IN RETROSPECT, I PROBABLY SHOULD HAVE STOOD BEHIND MY STATEMENT. LIKE, WAY BEHIND. LIKE, A PROVINCE OR TWO BEHIND.

AN ANGRY WOMAN FROM THE CALGARY SUN ASKED ME: "WHAT MAKES YOU THINK IT'S OKAY FOR YOU TO COME HERE FROM ANOTHER UNIVERSE AND TRY TO TAKE A GOOD PAYING JOB AWAY FROM A HARD-WORKING CANADIAN POLITICIAN?"

"HAVE YOU NOTICED MY SMILE? I...I HAVE A GREAT SMILE," I RESPONDED.

"YOU THINK JUST BECAUSE YOU READ SOMEWHERE THAT THE KEY TO WINNING OVER VOTERS IS A GOOD SMILE – AND YOUR UNIVERSE IS DYING – THAT YOU'RE GONNA GET A FREE RIDE FROM THE SUN? THINK AGAIN, BUSTER! THIS IS CALGARY – WE DON'T LIKE COMMIE BASTARD SOCIALIST ALIENS HERE!"

"I THINK...YOU'RE GOING TO TWIST MY WORDS TO SUIT YOUR POLITICAL AGENDA, SO IT REALLY DOESN'T MATTER WHAT I SAY. SO WHY DON'T YOU GO ABACUS CIRCUMFLEX CONSOMME YOURSELF!"

IN RETROSPECT, THAT PROBABLY WAS THE EXACT RIGHT THING TO SAY.

I WAS INUNDATED WITH INTERVIEW REQUESTS FROM BLOGGERS, VLOGGERS AND PRODUCT FLOGGERS. (I REJECTED THE LAST CATEGORY, EXCEPT FOR A COMPANY THAT MADE BIKINI–WAXING MACHINES, WHICH MY CAMPAIGN MANAGER, AMAROSA, ASSURED ME WAS ON BRAND.) I HAD A VERY PLEASANT CONVERSATION WITH A MAN FROM THE AMERICA ONE NETWORK, WHO SPENT FORTY MINUTES EXPLAINING HOW THE ALIEN INVASION OF EARTH PRIME WAS NOT GOING TO UNDERMINE WHITE SUPREMACY ON THE PLANET (HE REPEATED THE PHRASE "BLUES WILL NOT REPLACE US!" SO MANY TIMES, I SOMETIMES CONFUSED HIM WITH A SKIPPING RECORD). NOT THAT IT MATTERED: THE PHONE INTERVIEW GAVE ME TIME TO CREATE AN ELABORATE ORIGAMI OF THE REICHSTAG BUILDING.

TIMMY, ONE OF THE ALTERNATE REALITY NEWS

Service Kidz Networks reporters, asked me what I thought about the controversial issue of bedtime. I told him that where I come from, we didn't measure time in how long it took children to go to sleep after being put into bed, but if sleeps were measured metrically, I could see that the system could work. He followed that up with a tough question on the subject of cookies and milk before bedtime. Feeling out of my depth on the question of time measurement as it relates to snacking in this reality, I did what page 187 of the Guide (an origami Christo version of the Brooklyn Bridge) recommended: I replied, "My staff have been looking into this question, and we should have a position on it for you very soon."

The strange thing is that it didn't matter what I said: within a week, I was an international celebrity. According to Mitch Gregorian, the Chief Financial Officer of my campaign, we raised $767,009.59 in the run-up to the election. $767,009.59! That's almost three times the budget we started out with! With those funds, we were ready for anything!

...Except Bouncing Bertha, the campaign bus, breaking down. While it was in the shop for repairs, I taught the volunteers how to make miniature Palaces of Versailles out of pieces of scrap paper that just happened to be lying around. I...may have inadvertently used my copy of the form naming me the candidate, but by that time the original had been filed with Elections Canada, so I figured it wasn't a bad use of the paper. Not a bad use at all.

CAMPAIGN DIARY, DAY TWO

Dear Di,

Bouncing Bertha is – oh, come on! It will grow on you! Really! You've just got to give it ti – fine!

Dear Diary,

You're no fun.
  Bouncing Bertha is still in the shop. Today's recreational stationery project: the West Edmonton Mall.

CAMPAIGN DIARY, DAY THREE

Dear Diary,

Ed's Towing and Maintenance tells me Bouncing Bertha has an exhausted train manifold. I tell Edward that he should change the name of his business to Ed's Towaintenance. And fix the problem with Bouncing Bertha. Today's project: The Louvre.

CAMPAIGN DIARY, DAY FOUR

Dear Diary,

Bouncing Bertha still in the shop. Amy, a volunteer with boundless enthusiasm for the campaign and a weak grasp of the Zen of origami, offered to drive me around in her used VW (she calls it Herbie – I'm pretty sure because of what she smokes in it when she's alone). I jump at the offer (partially because

SHE MADE IT WITHOUT ANNOUNCING HER PRESENCE IN MY OFFICE).

FINALLY, THE CAMPAIGN CAN TRULY BEGIN!

"Excuse me...?"

"Veert?"

"I wonder if I could speak to you for a moment...?"

"Veeble veeble veert?"

"I'm sorry, I...I don't understand what you're saying."

"Grobble grobble inscrapple demart mort."

"Oh, dear."

Jacqueline 'Jackie' Fibblebraster was one of the bright young things who worked in the Data Collection and Interpretation and Technical Support division of the Transdimensional Authority. Behind her desk in their headquarters on Earth Prime, she was a master of research, a three time winner of the division's 'Amaranta Seaurchin Award for Report Comprehensiveness'. (In fact, everybody in Data Collection was given a monthly award so that nobody would feel superior to anybody else; head Xenia Zaifman had read in some management book or other that it was good for morale, and, in any case, she had other ways of letting her staff know how she felt about the quality of their work.) Fibblebraster had an encyclopedic knowledge of such investigative ephemera as blood spatter patterns, how mental health is related to species and zip code, and patterns of pink flamingo distribution across universes, as well as an ability to put just the right pieces of information together in a way that made a coherent narrative out of a jumble of unrelated facts.

Unfortunately, Fibblebraster was not at her desk. She

wasn't even in the same universe as her desk.

The crisis on Earth Prime 4-6-4-0-8-9 dash Omega was an all hands (and some feet and even a lower oesophagus or two) on deck situation. In order to process as many aliens and get them the heck out of their doomed universe as possible, Transdimensional Authority employees who had never been in the field were suddenly asked to feel the ground between their toes and smell the manure. (In the twenty minute orientation they were given before they were pushed through a Dimensional Portal^{TM} for the first time, they were warned not to wear expensive shoes.)

Like everybody thrust into this unanticipated adventure, Fibblebraster wore the uniform of the Transdimensional Authority's diplomatic division: black slacks, a white shirt and an orange vest with the TA logo sewn into the right breast. Owing to the emergency, fittings were not possible, forcing investigators to accept whatever vests they were handed; Fibblebraster's looked like a straitjacket on her hefty frame.

But like everybody else, she knew what the stakes were, so she made the best of it. An umbrella in one hand (a multi-purpose umbrella which, she was assured, would keep her safe from falling rocks, safes, anvils and icebergs) and a clipboard in the other (because you can take a woman away from the office paperwork, but you can't take the office paperwork away from the woman), Fibblebraster walked up pretty as you please (somewhere between pretty in pink and pretty sad to think) to the first alien she met upon shimmering into the new world.

And immediately encountered a language barrier.

"Excuse me," a voice said from her side. "I couldn't help but notice that you were having a bit of a linguistic contretemps..."

Fibblebraster was warned in the orientation not to look up so as not to be alarmed at the objects falling from the sky (why she appeared on the street and not in an office building would be a question she would ask upon returning to Earth Prime, ask in triplicate with the proper authorization stamps). Looking sidewise (and top foolish), she saw a four foot tall blue, hairless person in an exquisite three piece suit standing nearby; it wore an expectantly hopeful look like a cheap fedora. Other than the look on timer's face, te was identical to the alien she had been attempting to communicate with.

"I don't know about that," she told timer, "but I don't understand a word it's saying!"

"Would you like me to translate for you...?"

"If you be so kind..."

"It would be my pleasure."[6]

Fibblebraster turned back to the alien she had started talking to and said, "Your universe is going to collapse – we don't know when, but probably sooner than later. I represent the Transdimensional Authority – we are trying to relocate as many of your people as possible before your dimension implodes. Do you understand what I am saying?"

"Flort kavortny bloot bloot," the first alien said.

"Potato pancakes are a poor substitute for motor oil," the second alien translated.

"Oh, dear," Fibblebraster gently moaned. "Your universe is dying. Dy-ing. Soon, it and everything in it will be gone. Gone. Do. You. Understand?"

"Gehibben geruntlier," the first alien said. "Huwack glum fundrauten."

"Te said: The key to understanding the universe," the second alien translated, "is to ensure you're wearing comfortable undergarments."

Fibblebraster shook her head. "Please. I need to know if you understand what is happening to you."

"Fleegle! Fleegle!" the first alien, frustrated, stated. "Grobblner avacus weirdo. Ichbern flaumler plumgutz fragger fleeglautern!"

"Yes! Yes, I understand, you strange woman!" the

---

[6] You might wonder, given the goal of saving as many aliens in as short a time as possible, why Fibblebraster didn't just process the alien who was speaking English. Chalk it up to the heat of the moment (without the lyrics by John Wetton).

second alien translated. "I'm alien, not stupid!"

"Oh!" Fibblebraster was so flustered she nearly dropped the umbrella. "No. Of course. I didn't mean to imply – of course not. Umm. So. Would you be willing to relocate to another, safer universe?"

"Bleeng bleeg," the first alien answered. "Jammin interkrotz."

"Are there coconuts?" the second alien translated.

"Why would coconuts be an important consideration for you?" In the back of her mind, Fibblebraster began to wonder about the quality of the translation.

"Fibberty gibberty!" the first alien shouted. "Aglom per alletra gonzafonz!"

"What are you wearing?" the second alien shouted. "The sun never sets on the mouldering draperies!"

"I don't know about that!" Fibblebraster, fully in the moment, shouted back. "I just need to know: would you be willing to move to another universe to save your life?"

"Fleegle! Agrobustier carmaranta gefibbenacci!" the first alien shouted. "Drabnetz exy exy kerflambal glamp!"

"Yes! Of course I would!" the second alien shouted. "What kind of dumb question is that?"

"Look –" Fibblebraster hotly started. Then, she took a deep breath. She had known that this assignment would be a lot harder than a Pierre Boolean search (there would be no apes, for a start), but nothing could have prepared her for the sheer...obstreperousness of the creatures she was dealing with. She thought of her happy place – the Transdimensional Authority's customized search engine home page – and tried again: "Look –"

"May I be of some assistance?" another alien, identical to the first two, appeared on her left side and asked.

"We, uhh, seem to have a problem communicating," Fibblebraster allowed.

"Ah, well," the third alien explained, "there's a simple reason for that. Bob, here –"

"Hi, Bob," the second alien greeted the third alien.

"Cheers, Bob," the third alien acknowledged the second alien's greeting.

"Grabotnik, Bob," the first alien greeted the other aliens.

"Hi, Bob," the second alien acknowledged the first alien's greeting.

"Yeah, hi, Bob," the third alien acknowledged the first alien's greeting. "As I was saying..." the third alien paused for a moment to see if any additional greetings were forthcoming. When it became apparent that none were, he continued: "the problem is that Bob, here, only gives you a real translation every third statement. The first and second times te tries to 'translate,' te just spouts random gibberish."

Fibblebraster turned on the second alien. "Is that true?" she demanded.

The second alien shrugged pleasantly.

Fibblebraster considered this for a moment, then turned to the third alien and asked, "Could you please translate for me?"

"I would love to," the third alien responded. "Unfortunately, I don't speak the language."

"How can you not speak the language?" Fibblebraster felt herself slipping into conceptual quicksand.

"I'm not from here," the third alien told her. "I'm from Brampton."

Fibblebraster shook her head, trying to break free of the quicksand. "But...but...but if you don't speak the language, how did you know that te was only properly translating one out of every three answers?"

"I know the type," the third alien answered.

"The type?"

"Te's the type."

"The type?"

"Oh, yeah," the second alien answered. "I'm definitely the type. Good call, there, Bob."

"Thank you, Bob."

"That's ridic –" Fibblebraster started. Then, a cow hit her umbrella. The umbrella wasn't specifically cow-repellant, but the combination of other qualities of the umbrella meant that it sagged a little but didn't crumple.

With a confused, "Moooo...?" the cow bounced off her umbrella, pinballed off the umbrella of the second alien, then the third alien, and landed in the street nearby. The group watched as it groggily got to its feet, looked around with deep suspicion of imminent hostile silliness and made its halting way down the street.

"Umm...would it be possible to go indoors?" Fibblebraster tentatively asked.

"Globular tatterdammen flagbasteds," the first alien thoughtfully responded.

"Inattentive hobgoblins are implied," the second alien 'translated'.

"Good idea. Follow me," the third alien suggested.

Te led them several blocks to a well-appointed, if a bit shabby, one-storey building. A sign over the front door read: "Blindvort & Sons Funeral Home and Massage Parlour/We deal with all of your stiff problems." This confused Fibblebraster. When the singularity happened on Earth Prime 4-6-4-0-8-9 dash Omega, it made death optional (since people could ask the atoms that made up their bodies to endlessly regenerate). Why would such a species require a funeral home?

"Why do you require a funeral home?" she asked the third alien.

"Nostalgia," te answered. "Maudlin twaddle, you ask me, but I just work here."

Fibblebraster considered asking further when a little voice in her head said, "Forget it, Jackie. It's Earth Prime 4-6-4-0-8-9 dash Omega." Without a word, she followed the third alien to a small office in the back of the funeral home.

"Okay," having had time to consider how she was going to approach this assignment, she asked when the third alien was seated behind timer's desk and the first and second were seated opposite, "First...umm...Bob, why is the sky blue?"

"Avantee goatee manateehee," the first alien responded. "Plaquenta figgen blightnasaur."

"It's hard to get blue velvet stains out of blood," the

second alien translated in name only.

The third alien shook timer's head, but Fibblebraster was already way ahead of timer. "Why does the caged bird swing?" she asked.

"Allagemordo fleetinge flenck," the first alien answered. "Veeger conflabular, oh fleegle."

"If I knew that, don't you think I would have had a successful career on Broadway?" the second alien stated.

Fibblebraster was momentarily put off by what could have been a proper translation. But only momentarily. She had a plan, and she was determined to stick to it. "What is your name?"

"Beryllium Grendel," the first alien answered.[7]

"Beryllium Grendel," the second alien concurred.

"You have a plan," the third alien slyly approved of Fibblebraster's method.

"I have a plan," she agreed.

Three and a half hours later, the first alien's paperwork was complete. Three and a half minutes after that, the paperwork for the second and third aliens was complete. Fibblebraster communicated this to Transdimensional Authority headquarters. Within seconds, four beings shimmered out of existence, hopefully on their way to a better place.

---

[7] Beryllium was taken from a stray synapse in Fibblebraster's brain, one of the few that remembered her grade eight chemistry assignments. Grendel was taken from a book of ancient stories that she had once opened when she was eight years old; one look at an interior illustration gave her an unconscious fear of legends that haunts her to this day.

Meanwhile, in Citytown, Earth Prime 4-4-4-4-7-4 dash theta...

"Let me get this straight. You want to point that ridiculous-looking homemade contraption at me and turn it on. You claim it will turn me into a superhero, but only for twenty-three hours fifty-nine minutes and thirty-seven seconds. You can't tell me what my superpower or powers will be, and you have no idea if it or they will even be effective against any of the villains I may encounter. And the best part is the transformation is going to hurt. It's going to hurt like hell!"

"That is the most succinct description of what we're doing that I have ever heard!"

"It's definitely going on the promotional material!"

"We're not going to have any promotional material."

"We'll talk later."

"Not about promotional material."

"Later."

"Soooo...are you in?"

"You had me at ridiculous home-made contraption!"

Lemmy   Adjudicator had been relocated to Citytown, Earth Prime 4-4-4-4-7-4 dash theta over a year earlier. His sponsors, the kindly Kents, had helped him get a job as an aerobics instructor at the Fit For a King's Life gym. At first, the members were skeptical, but Lemmy had a way of forcing inactive people to work their bodies into sweat-covered discomfort that the members seemed to enjoy (TACO – Trick Abs, Coerce Oblates – Tuesday was especially popular, even after members realized it had nothing to do with tasty Mexican foodstuffs).

One night, after an intensive pill/lattes session (it's healthier than it sounds), Lemmy was waiting for a bus at a stop a block away from the gym when he was approached by two men. One was a tall black teenager in casual clothing carrying a grey duffle bag with more than its share of red zippers. The other man was a not as tall (but of course, when you only stand four feet yourself, everybody seems tall to you) white fiftysomething wearing a frilly shirt, long black cape and large top hat, deigning to allow a cane to help him walk (the only thing missing was a monocle; his right eye occasionally twitched as if to acknowledge a lost piece of his identity). The white man identified himself as Reginald von Remus III in a voice so warm it could melt a block of butter at thirty paces (or, is that thirty paces of butter a block away?). The black man recorded the conversation on his cellphone; when Lemmy asked him why, all Paul Piston would say was, "Documentation."

Reginald looked around. When Lemmy asked him what he was looking for, he answered: "A dark alley where we can conduct the transformation. No point in giving the public a look at our proprietary technology until we are ready. Now, let's see...there's usually a dark alley conveniently located nearby for just such occa – aha! Follow me."

The trio crossed the street and entered an alley half a block away. When they reached their destination, Paul put the duffle bag down and opened it. He removed an object in the shape of a television remote, with a lot of buttons, knobs, gauges on the front, over half of which was taken up by a small screen. Out of one end of the object stuck a thick metal wire in the shape of a heart. Out of the other end stuck a large feather.

"What is that?" Lemmy asked, uncertain that he should believe it was anything more than a B- high school science project.

"It was my high school science project," Paul responded.

"We call it the Heronator!" Reginald enthused.

"**You** call it the Heronator," Paul corrected him. "To me, it's the Hero Machine."

"Yeah. Right. Sorry," Reginald apologized, although he seemed more amused than contrite. "The Hero Machine." Then, he put a hand up to his mouth and whispered to Lemmy, 'The Heronator'.

"You gonna zap me with that thing?" Lemmy inquired.

"Does that thing even zap? Okay. Whatever. I'm ready." Lemmy closed his eyes, waggled his hands in front of him a couple of times and stuck out his chest in what he hoped was a heroic pose.

Paul took several sheets of paper and a pen out of the duffle bag. "Oh, yeah," he stated. "It zaps. But first, I just need you to read and sign these forms..."

Lemmy opened one eye to see what Paul was offering him. "What are they for?" he asked in what he hoped was a heroic tone of voice (it contained thirty-seven per cent less squeak than his normal speaking voice).

"The top one is for informed consent," Paul informed him. "The one after that indemnifies us against any physical injury you may suffer from being subjected to the effects of the Hero Machine or any encounters with supervillains subsequent to you being subjected to the effects of the Hero Machine, the third is an autograph for my collection, the fourth is the usual non-disclosure agreement, the fifth..."

Seven minutes later, Lemmy had signed the last of the eleven documents, his chest deflating a little with every new form.

"Okay," Reginald rubbed his hands with gleeful anticipation, "are you ready to become a hero?"

Lemmy took a moment to shake off the legalese-induced lethargy before responding, "Yes! Yes, I am! Heronate me!" He closed his eyes. He waggled his hands in front of him. He stuck out his chest.

Reginald grinned like a happy father who had forgotten all of the unreasonable middle of the night temper tantrums of his previous three children as Paul put the end of the wire to Lemmy's forehead (easily reaching over the alien's puffed out chest) and pressed a switch. The screen on the Heronator – sorry! Hero Machine came to life. Paul pressed buttons and twiddled dials, all the time watching the data flow on the screen.

"Uhh, what's happening?" Lemmy uneasily asked. He briefly opened one eye, then thought better of it and quickly closed it again.

"I have to calibrate the harmonic frequency of the Hero Machine to the unique sub-atomic resonance of your physical structure in order to optimize restructurization," Paul answered.

"The Heronator is scanning your body in order to transform it into the best hero it can possibly be," Reginald translated.

"Oh," Lemmy ohed.

"Then, the Hero Machine analyzes quantum ideational fluctuations in your cerebral cortex in order to optimize identity formation."

"The Heronator picks your brain to see what hero would best suit you," Reginald translated.

"Ah," Lemmy ahed.

"Then, it backs all the data up to the cloud for future analysis," Paul concluded.

"Paul is a science nerd," Reginald translated.

"I got that," Lemmy I got thated. "When does the actual –"

Lemmy fell to the ground and flopped around worse than a magikarp. Paul looked on with the stoic detachment he thought appropriate of a man of science. Reginald grinned like a six year-old who has snuck down to the family room early to open his ChristmaKwaanzUkah presents (which, in fact, he had been for many years).

What felt like an eternity (plus tax) later, but was really only three minutes and twenty-seven seconds, Lemmy's spasms eased and a message appeared on the screen: "Transformation to hero now complete. Thank you for choosing the Hero Machine. If you have a minute, please fill out a customer satisfaction survey at www.theheromachinenottheheronator.sci." Paul put the machine back in the duffle bag next to the signed forms.

"How do you feel?" Paul asked.

"Like a * PANT * freight train * PANT * dropped on my * PANT * head and I couldn't * PANT * just * PANT * sproing back to * PANT * back to * PANT * back to –" Lemmy responded.

"Life?" Reginald prompted.

"Yeah. * PANT * That. * PANT *"

"Not to worry," Paul assured him. "The side-effects will soon wear off."

"I don't * PANT * believe you. * PANT * "Feels like the pain will * PANT * stay forev – oh. Hey. You were right. Pain all gone."

Lemmy jumped to his feet. All six foot three of him. He swayed woozily. "Whoa!" he commented. "The air. Up here. Is much. Thinner than. I'm used. To!"

"Interesting." Paul made a mental note of that, as well as the observation that Lemmy's skin had changed from blue to light yellow. Not having changed, his clothes were much too small for him, with his arms sticking out of the end of his shirt and his legs sticking out of the bottom of his pants. Paul made a mental note of this, too, although under protest: this visual effect bordered on amusing, which was not at all scientific.

"There will be some...adjustments to your superhero body," Reginald stated, his excitement undiminished. "Are you feeling powerful yet? Think you can fly? Maybe knock out villains with a single punch? Explain the tax code in simple language that anybody could understand?"

Lemmy shook his head. "No. I. Do not. Feel any. Of those. Things."

"That's quite the monotone he's speaking in," Paul observed.

"Oh, yeah," Reginald agreed. "He's Mister Charisma, for sure."

"Mistah Charisma," Lemmy tried the name on for size.

"No, no, no, no, no!" Reginald threw out his hands like he wanted to stop the tide from coming in. "That's a terrible superhero name! You can't –! You mustn't –! You – you've already taken on the identity, haven't you?"

"Mistah Charisma," Lemmy affirmed. "Yep. That's me."

Reginald's monocleless monocle eye twitched especially energetically that moment. He rubbed his forehead wearily. "Okay," he finally said. "Mistah

Charisma, We can...work with that."

"Do you feel any different?" Paul asked. "More powerful in any way? Any way at all?"

Lemmy considered the question. Pushing nerdy glasses up his nose (how had **they** gotten there?), he responded, "Can belching. Be a. Superpower?"

"Can it knock your enemies sideways twenty feet?" Reginald sourly asked. "Or, can it propel you sixty feet into the air?"

"Umm, no."

"Then, no. Sorry, but, no."

Paul laid a comforting hand on Lemmy's shoulder. "Don't worry about it," he attempted to reassure the alien turned quasi-human turned fully human superhero (my apologies if I missed a step – and if I could have done that, imagine how confused Lemmy must be!). "It can sometimes take time for a person's powers to manifest themselves."

"That's happened a lot, has it?"

"It happened to many of the rats in the lab."

"Rats in the la – how many people have you actually done this to?"

Paul looked at Reginald, lost for an answer. "Well, we could stand in a dark alley and argue about petty semantics all night," he briskly stated, "but any ordinary citizen could do that. Who wants to catch some criminals?"

"I do! I do!" Lemmy practically cupped his forepaws – sorry, I meant hands in front of his chest and let his tongue loll out of his mouth.

With a look at Paul that said, "See? It isn't so hard, really," Reginald led them out of the alley.

At this point, you might be wondering what Citytown's deal is. We have asked historian Luigi Vercotti to clue you in...

Yeah, well, that's – * SNIFF * – just like life, innit? One minute, yer walkin' along, innocent as budgerigars, the next minute – * POW *! – yer've got, like, powers. Superpowers, aintcha? Well, you's can be all goody

goody and become a superhero, like, and all that, or, **or** you's could use yer new powers for yer own benefit, like. Some people call that 'bein' a criminal or a villain'; I just call it 'smart.'

So. Ten years ago, summit happened in Citytown. Nobody knows what. Some of the citizens of Citytown got powers. Nobody knows how. They all decided to use their powers for their own benefit – a good decision, you ask me. Everybody knows why. Naturally, the powers that be had to make a choice: learn to live with the newly empowered or move to another city. The hoity toity what remained struck a deal: the cops wouldn't do nothin' to stop people with powers – hunh! Like they could – and the people with powers would hurt as few civilians as necessary.

In the history racket, we call that a win-don't die resolution.

So, now, today, along comes this millionaire guy and his genius flunky what're gonna create heroes and clean up Citytown. Nothing good can come of such an effort, you ask me. Nothing good at all...

We now return you to the feature story already in progress...

As the trio emerged from the alley, Lemmy wondered, "What are. The glasses. For?"

"To protect your secret identity," Paul told him.

As they walked down the street, Lemmy asked, "Aren't they supposed to protect my civilian identity? Why are they part of my superhero costume? I would have thought a cape would have been more useful than glasses."

Paul gave Reginald that lost and pleading for help look again. "Capes may look good from certain angles," Reginald stopped their forward progress and authoritatively stated, "but they're a pain in the ass to manoeuvre in **and** they're too easy for supervillains to grab a hold of during a fight and they're rarely machine washable, which means they have to be cleaned by hand. Glasses have a lot of uses. You can focus the lens on twigs to start a fire **and** you can see far away with them **and** you can poke an enemy in the eye with the frame."

"So, they. Give me. Laser vision. Super sight. And extra. Fighting ability?" Lemmy enthused.

"Sure," Reginald agreed. "Now, who wants to fight crime?"

"I do! I do!"

And they started walking once more.

Two hours, thirty-seven minutes later...

The trio passed their sixth Bob So Tasty burger joint. Prowling the urban landscape searching for dastardly criminals was making Lemmy hungry, but he did his best to keep his focus on the mission. You never saw superheroes in the comics stop for a bite to eat (except, arguably, for Aquaman, who probably ingested krill when he swam through the ocean), so Lemmy wouldn't suggest that they stop for a bite to eat. He didn't have to be happy about it, though. "When you. Told me. That we. Would be. 'On patrol,'" he sourly commented. "You didn't. Tell me. It would. Be a. Synonym for. 'Walking around. Aimlessly, hoping. Something exciting. Would just. Appear in. Front of. Us.'"

"Patrolling is a vital part of being a superhero," Paul countered. Although he sounded confident, he was also having doubts: if they didn't encounter a supervillain soon, he wouldn't get any data from the night's experiment!

"Maybe we. Should call. It a. Night?" Lemmy suggested. "Try again. Tomorrow?"

"Absolutely not!" Reginald told him, his enthusiasm unflagging (not so much as a single star or stripe). "It is a well known fact that I just made up that seventy-eight per cent of supervillainy happens after the sun goes down. Since there have only been villains in Citytown – until now! – they could strike whenever they wanted to, but most of them do their worst work at night. You can't argue with tradition. So, this is the best time for you to be hunting."

As if the universe wanted to approve his message, a

sound came from Paul's duffle bag. The trio stopped walking as he pulled out a police radio. "...squawk squawk squawkity squawk – Sorry about that," a voice was saying. "We thought having a parrot would liven up the squad room. Instead, it just – squawk – interferes with – squawk – communications – and I have to clean up bird poop three times a day! I was saying: a 211 with a peppermint twist is happening at the – squawk – First National Bank of Fred at the intersection of – squawk – Manifest and Destiny. This is a sanctioned criminal activity, so all units do not respond. I repeat: a 211 with – squawk – with a peppermint – squawk squawk squawrk! – a peppermint – **squawk squawk squawrkity squawrk!** – Aww, forget it. You heard me the first time!"

Reginald looked at Lemmy with a wicked grin and asked, "Ready to be a superhero?"

Be sure to be with us next issue, "When Heroes Trip and Fall!"

Many Unhappy Returns

by INDIGO HAPHAZASTANCE Alternate Reality News Service Transdimensional Traffic Writer

For Jorgen Deumpster-Feyer, it was the life-sized replica of the Flying Spaghetti Monster that they built in his back yard. "His noodley appendages were not something I would allow my children to play with in the pool!" Deumpster-Feyer complained.

For Agnetha Gagglefeist, it was the pies. "They ruined more of my clothes than a thousand prom nights!"

Gagglefeist complained.

For Malthe Lingalingual, it was the constant slowdowns caused by aliens stopping traffic to help families of ducks cross roads, animals that the aliens carried around in cages wherever they went for just such occasions. "Why did it have to be a duck? It could have been any animal they found at the curb. Why a duck?" Lingalingual complained, adding the caution: "And this is a serious question. Don't make it into a groan-worthy pun – that was done decades ago by people much funnier than you!"

In the face of the widespread unhappiness of its citizens, the Danish government did what it thought it needed to do: it passed a law declaring that Earth Prime 4-6-4-0-8-9 dash Omega was "not in imminent danger of collapsing, we mean, it's been four years and there has been no sign of destruction, no rumbling of the ground, no fire in the sky, no Pulitzer prizes awarded to comic books, we mean, we're a patient people, but, honestly, our patience has a limit and if they were in our position, other countries would do exactly the same thing because by their outrageous and offensive behaviour the aliens, who clearly have no intention of adapting to our norms and fitting into our society, have only brought this upon themselves!" What is the this of which you speak? "Oh, yeah, right, as of Monday, we will start deporting the aliens back to their home universe."

Reaction from the international community was swift (though, alas, not in a Jonathanian sense). "We are dealing with an alienitarian crisis of inconceivable proportions – this is very disappointing," stated United Nations Secretary-General Sinead O'Connor.

"This is an abrogation of Denmark's interuniversal responsibilities. We shall be consulting the Treaty of Gehenna-Wentworth to determine the extent of the transgression," stated Transdimensional Authority Secretary-Specific Nicodemius Fitzhuge.

"The United Nations could impose snacktions[†] on

[†] Sanctions on snacking foods, one of the most serious embargoes that can be brought against a rogue nation. Snacktions brought Iran back to the ego-tiating table, resulting in an agreement that limited its nuclear weapon development programme (Iranians do love their Jalapeno Cheetohs). Snacktions may also have been responsible for causing Russia to rethink its position

Denmark and the Transdimensional Authority could shut down the country's Dimensional Portal™s if they were serious about the issue," stated Phil, the mechanic from the shop down the street. He knows things.

Like a teenage girl whose boyfriend forgot her birthday, the UN and the TA are currently weighing their options.

Denmark's decision has fuelled anti-alien extremism across the globe (and in France). For example, at a Humans for Humanity rally in Charlottesville, a man in ceremonial animal skins and a helmet with antlers who identified himself as the Flamin' Shaman (around his lips was a band of orange and brown that could be attributed to an addiction to Jalapeno Cheetohs) said, "It's like we've been saying all along: it's a hoax. The universe where the aliens come from is not about to collapse. This is just a story that the Deep Dish State wants us to believe so that it can use the aliens to create anarchy as a pretext to controlling our lives. Don't accept it! Come with us to the White House and let's show them what anarchy really is!"

Umm, what does that have to do with Denmark?

"Oh, yeah," the Flamin' Shaman afterthoughted. "Denmark is the first country to break with the Washington Consensual Hallucination and admit that there is no problem on Earth Prime 4-6...umm, 4-6-3...err, 4-6-4? Whatever! The point is: it's perfectly safe to send the aliens back to where they came from."

"It is decidedly **not** safe to send the aliens back to where they came from," argued Doctor Richardson, the cuddly, sometimes muddily inexpressive second chief scientist at the Transdimensional Authority. "Earth Prime 4-6-4-0-8-9 dash Omega really is about to collapse in on itself, destroying everything in it. Those who argue that this is untrue are clearly anti-* SCIENCE! *, and should be given no more credence than a junebug hoping to win a 24 hour dance marathon!"

When I apprised Doctor Richardson of Denmark's plan, he made a series of small, quiet strangling noises from somewhere deep in his throat. These days, there's a lot of that going around.

---

on cyber-espionage, although that may just have been online propaganda.

The Ugly Truth

Bitter Suite, First Movement

This is the story of Peter Steravem
The Occidental Tourists' former drummer.
English lessons, he now gave 'em.
That he no longer had anything to do with music
Would not save him
From alien haters who were dumber
Than a picnic in the Arctic.

Even as a wayward youth,
Peter had a doughy face;
And if you want the honest truth,
His mouth was just a touch too big.
He could use some time in a tanning booth,
And his nose seemed a little...out of place,
Making him perfect for a drumming gig.

"The World's Going to Hell (And I'm Not Doing So Well)"
The band's first single, was a massive hit.
Upon this we probably shouldn't dwell,
It was, after all, a long time ago.
Peter was wealthy, for a short spell,
But to live the rock and roll life, he blew through it.
Now: got ten quid he could borrow?

To join Band Age
Peter would have been delighted;
To once more be on a stage
And feel the crowd's adoring heat'll
Get him out of his 'ordinary' life's cage.

But alas, he was not invited:
They already had the fourth Beatle.

Like everybody else around the world,
Peter watched the charity concert on TV.
He steadfastly refused to hurl
Chunks when Wainwright Walsh was given the sobriquet
"The dream of every socially conscious girl."
But he didn't have time for envy
Because that was when he received his first death threat.

"You frking alin lovr,"
The email read,
"B prpard for your lif to b ovr.
For an nd to all of th applaus.
Ain't no plac for you to tak covr.
I am going to kill you dad
For taking up an anti-humans caus!"

What could the emailer's message be?
Peter took a long time to get it.
The writer had a problem, apparently,
With his computer keyboard
Causing him to be unable to type the letter e.
The threat didn't bother Peter (he wouldn't let it),
He just wanted to understand what had made the writer so
sore.

The second threat came while Peter worked on a lesson plan
About the difference between there, they're and their.
The email was a single sentence, but on and on and on it ran,
Proving to be a case in point. "There not like us,"
"If you love them so much, why don't you go their?" – it
was obvious the man,
About properly using the words, just didn't care.
Peter deleted it without any fuss.

Soon, the angry emails came thick and fast,
Threatening to overload Peter's inbox.

The Ugly Truth

He didn't take them personally, he was mostly aghast
At all the spelling and grammatical errors.
In his class none of them would have passed;
The intricacies of the language clearly had them flummoxed.
What we were teaching our children (the little terrors!)?

A week and a thousand angry emails later,
Somebody spray-painted on his apartment wall
"Stupid, stupid, humans hater!
We'll get assholes' like you, just wait and see!
We'll feed you to our pet gator!"
The thing Peter despised the most of all
Was the writer's improper use of the apostrophe.

Moira (the girlfriend with no tact)
Told Peter he could not let this continue.
"You have to do something! You have to act!
This is putting you under too much stress!"
Peter wasn't feeling it, and that's a fact,
But going to the police was not on the menu,
So to please Moira, instead, he went to a friend in the press.

"Death threat dummies!" the headline blared
In 48 point bold type.
"Speciesists harassing wrong man!" the subhead shared.
Between them, you didn't really need to read the story
About somebody for whom you never cared,
Whose talent you thought was mostly hype –
You just had to have a nose for an outcome most gory.

Suddenly, bookies were taking bets
On how gruesome was to be Peter Steravem's end.
I guess this is as good as it gets,
He thought of all of the developing media attention.
He found himself back on chat show sets,
With a little extra money in his pocket to spend,
And even the quality papers gave him the occasional
mention.

One day, much to his surprise, Peter
Received a call from Wainwright Walsh, none other!
"I hate to be a joy beater,"
The 'great' man said,
"But this is about being a world leader.
We're not in this for personal gain, brother,
We're trying to make sure billions of aliens don't end up dead!"

"Oh, that is so much shite!"
Into the telephone Peter screamed.
"You can afford to be a good Samaritan, you made out alright.
How can so much ego fit into such a small head!"
Unfortunately, Peter was not much of one for a fight,
And his recriminations he only dreamed.
So, not knowing what to do, he hung up instead.

A couple of days later, while driving on his scooter,
Peter was blindsided by a motorist
Who was clearly not an alien rooter.
Slamming into the pavement, he broke three ribs and both his legs.
His nose was a mess (but, with surgery, would end up cuter),
And he would never again have full use of his right wrist.
Once again, he wanted coffee and life gave him the dregs.

Sighing in his hospital bed
Peter said, "It could have been worse.
I could have ended up dead,
Or brain-damaged and not knowing my own name!"
As Peter sipped from his glass of liquid bread
His summation of his situation was terse:
"Such is the price of fame!"

The Ugly Truth

Heroica Veracruz, Mexico, Earth Prime 6-4-9-8-2-3 dash rho was a small fishing village on the Gulf that boasted three bakeries, two pharmacies, one hotel and twelve bars. To ensure a stable local economy, each bar was open once every two weeks (the thirteenth and fourteenth days were, of course, Sunday, when everything was closed). On the night which interests us, the lucky establishment was *el oso hormiguero loco*, where the beer is flat, the nachos are cold and the guacamole is a strange shade of orange (you'd think they'd spring for a little food dye!).

Nobody said ensuring a stable local economy would be easy. Or not make customers queasy.

"You sure he'll be here?" asked the four hundred pound man with the Asiatic features who was wearing a drab, dark suit that fairly screamed, "I would be much more comfortable in a loincloth!" He was nursing a Sol, an alcoholic beverage which, oddly enough, brought him no warmth.

"Oh, he'll be here," the tall man with a shock of blond hair who was twirling a carrot between his fingers confidently stated. "He may be a little slow, but he always comes to the party."

Wall of Voodoo's 'Mexican Radio' was playing on a tinny sound system for the fourteenth time that evening. Maybe the owner of the establishment had a dark, self-reflexive sense of humour. Maybe the song served as the soundtrack to some kind of horror scenario that was being played out in the dark bar (the driving rain outside would not have argued with this interpretation). As he sat at their table knitting a Holmes, Sweet Holmes sweater, Dru Mamo Kanuha, the muscle of the Bastards of the Universe, decided that this was a question well worth ignoring.

P. J. Pinchus, the leader of the Bastards of the Universe, chugged his *cerveza* as he expectantly watched the door of the bar. Then, he had his carrot juice chaser. Then another *cerveza*. Then, another carrot juice. He had never been drunk (alcohol just seemed to bounce off his cerebral cortex and flounder around on the ground like a three year-old having a tantrum), but he liked the effect the combination had on people who watched him drink. Not that the three or four other patrons were watching him drink. They were stuck in Heroica Veracruz. They had their own problems.

After a few minutes, P. J. Pinchus tired of looking at the front door of the bar. Turning to Dru Mamo Kanuha, he asked, "Have I ever told you about the time me and the team sold counterfeit transdimensional visas out of the Ventrosian embassy on Earth Prime 0-8-3-8-0-5 dash theta?"

"Many times," Dru Mamo Kanuha dryly assured him.

"But have I ever explained to you the significance...of the pickle?"

"No, sir, you have not."

With a self-satisfied "aaah," P. J. Pinchus launched into his story. Two hours, three minutes and twenty-seven seconds later, he was saying, "...walked a little differently, walked, you could say, like an Egyptian, from that day forward!"

"I love a story with an ending," Dru Mamo Kanuha commented.

"I only blew up three buildings and an outhouse – and, believe me, finding an outhouse in Manhattan was not as easy as you might think! – so I would consider the mission only a moderate succ –"

The door to the bar opened and a short, slender figure walked in, the elements trailing behind him. Several people shouted, "¡*Cierre la puerta*!" He slammed the door shut with ease. His rain slicker was slick with rain. His dark eyes set above cheek bones so high you would have thought they were auditioning to be chandeliers, scanned the room, looking for – aah. The man stomped over to the dark corner where the two Americans sat.

"Ah, Davros," P. J. Pinchus cheerfully greeted the man. "So glad you could make it."

"The only person I allow to call me that is my sister," Daveen Rasmalai said through gritted teeth. "You know that, **PJs**."

Dru Mamo Kanuha almost smiled to himself.

"Pull up a seat," P. J. Pinchus invited Daveen Rasmalai, ignoring the childhood reference to sleepwear. "The beer is warm, but it sure beats the nachos."

"I'm here to arrest you for breaking the treaty of Gehenna-Wentworth and committing crimes against the multiverse," Daveen Rasmalai informed him. "When I asked villagers about a pair of Yankees skulking around their town, they told me you rented a boat and went out on it several nights a week. You've been illegally smuggling aliens from Earth Prime 4-6-4-0-8-9 dash Omega into the United States on this Earth from your base here in Heroica Veracruz!"

Lightning did not crack at this revelation, which should have been the first indication that Daveen Rasmalai didn't have things quite right.

"Good theory," P. J. Pinchus pleasantly commended. The man was unflappable. If he had been a bird, he would never have been able to get off the ground. "Too bad it's wrong."

"Completely wrong," Dru Mamo Kanuha quietly chimed in. His tongue was out as he concentrated on completing a petit point star.

Daveen Rasmalai put his hands on his hips and challenged, "How is it wrong?"

"We're not transporting illegal aliens. We're stopping them from landing on America's shores and bringing them back here. We...are the good guys." He seemed highly amused to say this.

Daveen Rasmalai looked at P. J. Pinchus in disbelief before sneering, "Prove it."

P. J. Pinchus smiled, motioned towards the bar and said, "Oh, Raoul, would you please come over here for a moment?"

A figure detached itself from the stool on which it had been sitting and shuffled over to the table, bringing a glass of beer with it. The man looked to be in his late twenties, tall, with long dark hair and a strong, expressive face. "*Si, Senor.* What would you like, *Senor*?"

"Would you please confirm for my friend Davros, here, that I am interdicting aliens on behalf of the American government?" P. J. Pinchus smugly asked. Daveen Rasmalai was getting thoroughly sick of all of the self-satisfied attitude he was having to put up with lately.

"*Si, si,*" the man eagerly said. "It is exactly as *Senor* Pinchus say."

"And why should I believe you?" Daveen Rasmalai demanded to know.

P. J. Pinchus feigned shock. "Do you not know who this is? With your extensive research, I would have thought you would have recognized Raoul Gonzales de la Fuego. He is the Chief of Police of Heroica Veracruz."

Daveen Rasmalai looked at the avidly nodding man standing in front of him. He couldn't believe that it was true: if P. J. Pinchus was interdicting aliens at the border, it must have been as part of a deeper, darker plan.[8] Unfortunately, he had no idea what that might be. So, instead, he asked the man, "You look young and capable. Why are you kowtowing to this American like an old, feeble man?"

"I hope to age into the role," Chief of Police de la Fuego told him. "What is it you *yanquis* say? Fake it 'til you break it?"

Daveen Rasmalai was about to correct him when the door to the bar opened and two men walked in. Neither of them appeared to be wearing any gear for the rain or carried an umbrella, yet neither of their grey suits seemed

---

[8] In fact, it was. While the Bastards of the Universe were ferrying aliens from the United States to Mexico, they were smuggling cocaine in the other direction. But don't tell Daveen Rasmalai that. Given his attitude towards smugness, we wouldn't want to tempt him with the emotion.

to be the slightest bit wet. To everybody's surprise, the wind and the rain kept a respectful distance on the other side of the threshold. One man walked up to the bar as the other closed the door. The bartender pointed to the table where P. J. Pinchus and Dru Mamo Kanuha sat. The man said something to his partner, and the two of them walked over to the table.

"Are you P. J. Pinchus?" the rounder of the two men asked.

"I go by many names," he replied.

"Is P. J. Pinchus one of them?" the thinner of the two men asked.

"Who's asking?" P. J. Pinchus wanted to know.

"Detectives currently working for the Vancouver Police Force," the rounder man politely told him. "I'm Joe... This is Bill..."

"Joe and Bill? Do you have last names?"

"Last names can be so constricting. You could say that we're identity fluid."

"I'd like to see some ID."

Joe removed a badge from his jacket pocket and flashed it at the man. "Dru, this legit?"

Dru Mamo Kanuha put his knitting down on the table and looked at what Joe was holding out. "Hmm...it's a police badge, alright. Not Vancouver, though – Los Angeles. And certainly not current. They haven't made badges with this design since – I wanna say the 1940s, maybe the 1950s. May I?"

Dru Mamo Kanuha held out his hand. Joe handed over his badge. The big Samoan put a corner of the object in his mouth and bit down. Bill took a step forward as if about to stop whatever was happening, but Joe put a restraining hand on his chest. Satisfied, Dru Mamo Kanuha took the badge out of his mouth and said, "1951. With tin from shaft nineteeen of the Desdemona Mine. Not the best vintage, but I suppose you have to work with what you get."

As the Big Kanuha handed the badge back to Joe, Bill marvelled, "How did you know all that?"

Dru Mamo Kanuha shrugged as he sat down and went back to his knitting. "I have eccentric hobbies."

P. J. Pinchus clapped him on the back and enthused: "That's why he's such a valuable member of the team."

"That would be Dru Mamo Kanuha," Joe asked in a way which indicated that he wasn't really asking, "which would make you P.J. Pinchus. Is that correct, sir?"

"Aww, you got us," P. J. Pinchus grinned. "What can I do for you officers?"

"You're under arrest for alien trafficking and the murder of at least thirty-seven sentient beings, among other crimes against the multiverse," Joe informed him. "If you would please –"

"**Whaaaat?**" Daveen Rasmalai screeched.

Joe and Bill turned towards him for the first time. "I'm sorry, sir, but –" Bill started.

"You can't arrest him! It – it – it isn't fair!" Daveen Rasmalai objected.

"Sir, it would not be in your best interests to interfere with an official police investigation," Bill advised.

"Not be in my best interests to interfere with –" Daveen Rasmalai gasped. "I've been chasing after these Bastards for years!"

"Please limit your use of profanity, sir," Bill calmly commanded. "There is no call for it."

"That – I wasn't – that's what their team is called: the Bastards of the Universe."

"That may be," Bill allowed. "Still. While in our custody, they will be known as the B-words of the Universe. Even the dirtiest of business can be improved by simple politeness."

Daveen Rasmalai did not know how to respond to this. P. J. Pinchus did, though. "When and where did these crimes you're accusing us of take place?"

"Earth Prime, sir. The bodies were found six days ago. Decomposition suggests that they had arrived there at least eleven days before that," Joe read from a police notepad that had mysteriously appeared in his hand (and just as mysteriously vanished when he was done). He knew the answer, but the presence of the notebook gave the interaction added gravitas.

"Although their suits remained exquisite," Bill added.

"Hunh. I'd like to meet their tailor," Joe agreed.

"There you go, then," P. J. Pinchus held out his arms in a gesture of innocence. "I couldn't have had anything to do with that because I've been here for the last six months."

Joe and Bill exchanged a glance. "It is our understanding, Mister Pinchus," Bill explained, "that you have an unregistered Transdimensional Portal^{TM} that you have been using to travel between here and Earth Prime to coordinate your criminal activity."

"Who would have told you that?"

"The two compatriots who were working the scheme on the other end."

"We arrested them yesterday," Joe helpfully added.

"They were very cooperative," Bill stated.

Daveen Rasmalai shook his head in disbelief. "You mean to tell me that you arrested Jessie Chupa Cabrerra and Eustace Jones? A couple of flatfoots who can't even be bothered to appear in colour?"

"Shouldn't that be flatfeet, Joe?"

"Reasonable lexicographers can disagree, Bill."

"**You arrested Jessie Chupa Cabrerra and Eustace Jones?**" Daveen Rasmalai demanded.

"Actually, the name the woman gave us was Alison Cheney," Joe told him.

"And the man's name was Heywood Jablomey," Bill told him. Somebody on the other side of the bar tittered.

"Was it hard to get a reading on how tall the man was?" Daveen Rasmalai asked.

"That's right. How did you know that?" Bill replied.

"That's Eustace Jones. And the woman. Did you get the sense she was trying just a little bit too hard to come across as out of control?"

"I did, yes." Bill allowed.

"Jessie Chupa Cabrerra."

"I'm sorry, but I don't believe you," P. J. Pinchus asserted.

"Why is that, Mister Pinchus?" Joe asked.

"My people would never give me up," P. J. Pinchus smugly pronounced.

"We're here, aren't we?" Bill pointed out.

"There's no honour among thieves," Joe commented, almost allowing sadness to enter his voice.

"Or alien traffickers, Joe."

"Or mass murderers, Bill."

"Especially mass murderers, Joe."

"They gave you up like you were a TV show that had jumped the shark," Bill summed up.

"If that phrase hasn't jumped the shark."

"What phrase was that, Joe?"

"Jumped the shark, Bill."

"That's what I get for trying to be culturally relevant, Joe."

"Don't be too hard on yourself, Bill. The pace at which the culture moves these days, it's hard for anybody to stay on top of it."

"So, Mister Pinchus, if you would be so kind as to hold your hands out so we may put cuffs on you, we will take you to the station on Earth Prime for booking."

The smile on P. J. Pinchus' face dropped faster than the stock of a company whose CEO had just been indicted on charges of fraud and embezzlement. "Dru, I think we need to go to Plan Bee," he suggested.

Unfortunately, that was the moment that Dru Mamo Kanuha accidentally stabbed himself in the right palm with one of his knitting needles. "Oww!" he exclaimed as he looked at the blood slowly oozing over his hand. "I...I'm sorry, but I can't with this injury..."

P. J. Pinchus sighed. Then, with an evil grin (it had been cursed by a witch when he was just thirty-seven years old), he pulled an object out of his pocket. "Do you have any idea what this is?"

Bill was game. "A fruit peeler?"

P. J. Pinchus looked at the object in his hand, and had to admit that the detective had a point. "And vegetables. A fruit and vegetable peeler, yes. Sorry – I can't keep track of all of the pockets of this coat. In case you're wondering why I carry a peeler on me, sometimes I like to slowly remove the rinds of carrots in front of my victims – it's an old habit from my college days. Hold on..." He put the peeler away and rummaged around in his black leather jacket until he came up with a different object. "Do you know what this is?"

"A detonator," Bill responded.

P. J. Pinchus looked at the object he was holding out just to be sure. "That's right. It's a detonator. If you don't let us walk out of this bar and not follow us as we make good our escape, you'll force me to blow up a building somewhere in the city. Obviously, I can't tell you which building, but I can tell you that innocent children and farm animals may be innocently going about their business there." With a blank spot where a twinkle in his eye would at this moment have been,[9] he added: "I love it when a plan falls apart."

"Mister Pinchus, you don't want to do this," Joe told him.

"The hell I don't!" P. J. Pinchus was enjoying himself. "There's no way I'm letting you take me back to Earth Prim!"

"Did you mean Earth Prime?" Bill asked.

"Earth Prim!" P. J. Pinchus roared. "With all the goody two-shoes of the Transdimensional Authority – okay, and goody three-shoes in the case of Alpha Silurians – and goody eight-shoes in the case of the spiders from Mars – you know what, all the goody variably multiple-shoes of the Transdimensional Authority! You think I'm going to allow myself to be subjected to their sanctimony? Their...smugness? I would rather kill a buildingful of innocent children and farm animals first!"

"I have no doubt you have your reasons, sir," Joe stated. "Still, you really don't want to do this."

"Why not?"

Joe sized the man up, then decided that the best approach was to give him the whole truth. "The trope

---

[9] The twinkle will be CGIed into the novel in a future edition.

you're enacting comes from the action adventure genre. However, my partner and I exist in the genre of the police procedural, where suspects don't generally threaten violence in order to effect an escape; when confronted with irrefutable evidence of their guilt, they usually come along quietly. In our current confrontation, you and we are manifesting a fundamental clash of genre expectations. My experience over many years as a cop is that our genre tropes will beat your genre tropes. Not only will your bomb not go off, but it will somehow manage to do you harm. So, I will say for the final time, sir, you do not want to do this."

"I'm pretty sure I do." P. J. Pinchus unhesitatingly pushed his thumb down on the detonation button. The device sparked, which made the arm of his jacket catch fire. A moment later, he was wriggling to get the whole blazing mess away from his body. One inner pocket gave a little belch while another began exuding a yellow bubbling substance, but it was all soon engulfed by flames on the floor.

Looking discombobulated (even though his bobulate had never been anywhere near a disco), P. J. Pinchus moaned, "Where's the kaboom? There's supposed to be an Earth-shattering kaboom!"

"I did try and warn you, sir," Joe said. Daveen Rasmalai, realizing that there wasn't the slightest trace of smugness in his voice, warmed to the man.

As he held out his hands for the manacles, P. J. Pinchus forced a smile and asked, "Could you please be gentle when you put the handcuffs on? My right thumb is a little crispy."

"Can I bring my knitting?" Dru Mamo Kanuha asked as Bill put handcuffs on him.

"Yes, but not the needles," Joe said.

"They could be used as weapons," Bill added.

"And we wouldn't want you to hurt yourself," Joe concluded. "At least, not any more than you already have."

"Can I, uhh, hitch a ride back to Earth Prime with you

guys?" Daveen Rasmalai sheepishly asked.

"Don't see why not," Bill stated. "It's a free multiverse."

"Great. Maybe you could explain how you made this case on the way. You know, one professional to another."

The five men shimmered out of existence.

Being a Full and Complete Record of the Diary of Martini Frobisher During His Historic Campaign for Member of Canadian Parliament

CAMPAIGN DIARY, DAY FOUR (CONTINUED)

DEAR DIARY,

THEY CALL A CANDIDATE GOING DOOR TO DOOR TO TALK TO ELIGIBLE VOTERS CANVASSING BECAUSE THAT'S THE MATERIAL A POLITICAL PARTY USES TO BUILD ITS BIG TENT; JUST THINKING ABOUT IT IN THOSE TERMS GAVE ME A HAPPY FEELING ALL OVER (EXCEPT FOR MY FRANCE) AS IT REMINDED ME OF MY DAYS ON THE CIRCUIT.

YOU WOULD NOT BELIEVE THE WARM RECEPTION I RECEIVED GOING DOOR TO DOOR IN BRITANNIA, THE WEALTHIEST, HEALTHIEST BUT BY NO MEANS STEALTHIEST NEIGHBOURHOOD IN ALL OF CALGARY. THE FIRST HOUSE I CAME TO LOOKED LIKE A CRUISE SHIP WITHOUT A BRIDGE. AMY DROVE US UP TO A GATE WHERE A SECURITY GUARD POKED HIS HEAD INSIDE HER ROLLED DOWN WINDOW. "YES?" HE SAID

WITH REFINED MENACE.

"MY NAME IS MARTINI   FROBISHER," I
INFORMED HIM. "I'M THE NEW DEMOCRATIC PARTY
CANDIDATE FOR THE BY-ELECTION IN THE RIDING OF
PERCH-LAKE-MESHUGGAH. I WOULD LIKE TO TALK
TO THE OWNER OF THE HOUSE ABOUT MY PLAN FOR
CRIMINAL JUSTICE REFORM."

"MISTER BYRON IS - EXCUSE ME A MOMENT." A
VINTAGE CADILLAC DROVE AROUND US AND IDLED
WHILE THE SECURITY GUARD WENT INTO HIS BOOTH
AND OPENED THE GATE. WHEN THE CADILLAC HAD
DRIVEN THROUGH IT, THE GATE CLOSED AND THE
GUARD REAPPEARED. "MISTER BYRON IS NOT AT
HOME. I WOULD SUGGEST YOU TRY AGAIN LATER.
TEN YEARS WOULD BE GOOD. TWENTY WOULD BE
BETTER."

BEFORE I COULD ARGUE THE MERITS OF STRICTER
GUN LAWS, HE TURNED SMARTLY (HIS TURN HAD A
BSC AND AN MBA) AND RETURNED TO THE BOOTH.

"WELL, THAT WAS DISCOURAGING," I COMMENTED
AS AMY DROVE US TO THE NEXT GATE.

"NOT IF YOU LOOK AT IT THE RIGHT WAY," AMY
ARGUED.

"STANDING ON MY HEAD?"

"THE GUARD DIDN'T SAY YOU SHOULD NEVER COME
BACK. HE SAID TEN OR TWENTY YEARS. SEE? HE LEFT
THE DOOR OPEN - YOU MAY BE ABLE TO WIN VOTES
IN THAT HOUSE EVENTUALLY."

AT THE NEXT GATE, THE GUARD ADVISED US TO
COME BACK IN FIVE OR TEN YEARS. "YOU SEE?" AMY
POINTED OUT AS WE DROVE ON. "THAT'S PROGRESS!"

AT THE THIRD GATE, THE GUARD SUGGESTED THAT
WE COME BACK IN TEN TO FIFTEEN YEARS. "DID WE
JUST GO BACKWARDS?" I WORRIED.

AMY WAS UNDETERRED. "SOMETIMES, YOU HAVE TO
TAKE A STEP BACK TO SEE THE BIG PICTURE. THAT'S
HOW YOU DETERMINE THE BEST WAY FORWARD."

HALF A DOZEN HOMES LATER, I WASN'T FEELING
THE LOVE. FOR ONE THING, CANVASSING WAS

SUPPOSED TO BE DOOR TO DOOR, NOT GATE TO GATE;
I COULDN'T HELP BUT FEEL WE WERE DOING
SOMETHING WRONG. FOR ANOTHER THING,
ESTIMATES OF WHEN WE SHOULD RETURN BOUNCED
AROUND FROM FIVE TO FIFTY YEARS. I SUGGESTED
THAT WE MAY HAVE STARTED IN THE WRONG
NEIGHBOURHOOD.

"THERE'S NO SUCH THING AS THE WRONG
NEIGHBOURHOOD," AMY ASSERTED. "THERE'S ONLY
YOUR WRONG ATTITUDE TOWARDS THE
NEIGHBOURHOOD YOU'RE IN."

NONETHELESS, I INSISTED THAT WE DRIVE A FEW
BLOCKS UNTIL WE GOT TO HOUSES WITH ACTUAL
DOORS THAT I COULD ACTUALLY KNOCK ON. "YOU'RE
THE BOSS," AMY ACCEDED TO MY COMMAND. I
THOUGHT I CAUGHT A WHIFF OF RELIEF IN HER
VOICE (PERKY POSITIVITY MUST TAKE A TREMENDOUS
AMOUNT OF ENERGY TO MAINTAIN), BUT IT MAY JUST
HAVE BEEN THE CHILI DOG SHE HAD EATEN BEFORE
WE SET OUT.

THE HOUSES WE NOW ENCOUNTERED SEEMED LIKE
THEY WOULD ACCOMMODATE A FAMILY OF TWENTY-
SEVEN RATHER THAN A SMALL VILLAGE. AT THE
FIRST DOOR, A MAN ANSWERED. "HELLO," I GREETED
HIM. "MY NAME IS MARTINI   FROBISHER.
I'M THE NEW DEMOCRATIC PARTY CANDIDATE FOR
THE BY-ELECTION IN THE RIDING OF PERCH-LAKE-
MESHUGGAH. I'D LIKE TO TALK TO YOU ABOUT OUR
STAND ON GUN CONTROL."

THE MAN REACHED TO HIS RIGHT AND PULLED OUT
A SHOTGUN. "GO AHEAD," HE SAID.

"OH, AH, PERHAPS THIS IS NOT A GOOD TIME," I
HESITATED.

"NOT AT ALL," THE MAN GOOD-NATUREDLY
ENCOURAGED. "I'M ALL EARS."

HE WAS CLEARLY NOT ALL EARS, DIARY; HE WAS
ARMS AND LEGS AND A HEAD MORE OR LESS LIKE
ANYBODY ELSE. HOWEVER, THE IMAGE DID NOTHING
TO EASE MY COMFORT LEVEL. "OH, AH, WELL, YES.

GUN, UHH, CONTROL. YOU SEE, WE'RE CONCERNED –
WELL, THAT MIGHT BE OVERSTATING THE, ERR, THE
CASE A BIT – A TAD – A SMIDGE – MILDLY
INTERESTED – YES, THAT'S IT – WE'RE MILDLY
INTERESTED IN – AWARE! WE ARE, UHH, MILDLY
AWARE OF THE PROBLEM OF...OF...OF GUN VIOLENCE
IN OUR MAJOR, UMM, CITIES..."

THE MAN SNORTED A LAUGH AS HE PUT THE GUN
BACK OUT OF SIGHT. WITH A GRIN, HE SAID: "AWW,
I'M JUST MESSING WITH YOU."

"OH?"

"YEAH. I WOULDN'T VOTE NDP IF YOU STUCK A HOT
POKER UP MY BUTT!"

HE SLAMMED THE DOOR IN MY FACE SO FAST I
WAS SURE I HEARD THE **CRACK** OF THE SOUND
BARRIER BEING BROKEN!

"DON'T WORRY ABOUT IT," AMY ADVISED ME AS WE
WALKED TO THE NEXT HOUSE. "THE MORE PEOPLE WE
MEET WHO WON'T VOTE FOR YOU, THE SOONER WE'LL
GET TO THE PEOPLE WHO WILL VOTE FOR YOU." I
THOUGHT THERE WAS A PROBLEM WITH THAT LOGIC,
BUT BEFORE I COULD FIGURE OUT WHAT IT WAS, AMY
ADDED: "AND WHATEVER YOU DO, DON'T THINK OF A
HOT POKER GOING UP THE LAST GUY'S BUTT. THAT
WILL JUST CONTRIBUTE NEGATIVITY TO OUR DAY, AND
WE NEED TO STAY POSITIVE."

AT THE NEXT HOUSE, AN ELDERLY WOMAN
ANSWERED MY KNOCK ON THE DOOR. "YEEEESSSSSS?"
SHE ASKED.

"HELLO, MADAM," I SAID. "MY NAME IS
MARTINI   FROBISHER. I'M THE NEW
DEMOCRATIC PARTY CANDIDATE FOR THE BY-
ELECTION IN THE RIDING OF PERCH-LAKE-
MESHUGGAH. I'D LIKE TO TALK TO YOU ABOUT OUR
POSITION ON G...G...UMM, GUM, BUBBLE GUM. ON
CITY STREETS. HOW WE'RE – AHEM – GOING TO
KEEP THE STREETS OF THE COUNTRY'S CITIES CLEAN."

"I'M SURE THAT'S MOST FASCINATING, YOUNG
MAN," THE OLD WOMAN TOLD ME, "BUT I SHOULD

WARN YOU BEFORE YOU START THAT I DO NOT VOTE
IN ELECTIONS."

"OH?"

"NO. I PREFER TO INTERACT WITH THE POLITICAL
SYSTEM IN MORE...SHALL WE SAY, DIRECT WAYS...?"

"OH."

"MY LAWYERS ARE VERY EXPERIENCED IN SUCH
MATTERS."

"OH!"

I WOULDN'T HAVE BELIEVED A WOMAN AS OLD AS
SHE WAS COULD SLAM A DOOR SHUT WITH SUCH
FORCE!

"DON'T SWEAT IT," AMY CHIRPED AS WE WALKED
ON. "AT LEAST WE'RE NOT WASTING TIME ON
PEOPLE WHO WOULDN'T VOTE FOR US!"

I WAS TEMPTED TO POINT OUT THAT, STANDING
OFF TO THE SIDE, SHE WASN'T THE ONE GETTING
DOORS SLAMMED IN HER FACE, BUT I WASN'T KEEN
ON FINDING OUT HOW SHE WOULD COUNTER SUCH
OBVIOUS NEGATIVITY, SO I DECIDED TO LET IT PASS.
I CONCENTRATED, INSTEAD, ON IMAGINING A HOT
POKER GOING UP THE OLD LADY'S BUTT.

IT WAS VERY SATISFYING.

THE NEXT FEW DOORS WERE SLAMMED IN MY FACE
WITHOUT CONVERSATION. BY THE SEVENTH, I SNIFFED
AT MY ARMPITS. I'M NOT SURE WHAT THAT WAS
SUPPOSED TO ACCOMPLISH, BUT I'VE SEEN HUMAN
BEINGS DO IT ON TV WHEN THEY ARE HAVING
TROUBLE CONNECTING WITH OTHERS, SO I'M SURE IT
MUST BE SIGNIFICANT. BY THE TWELFTH REJECTION,
I BEGAN WONDERING IF THE FORCE OF THE SLAMS
WAS DOING LONG-TERM DAMAGE TO MY NASAL
MEMBRANES. BY THE NINETEENTH, I DECIDED THAT A
DIFFERENT APPROACH WAS REQUIRED.

"WHAT DO YOU WANT?" THE MIDDLE-AGED
WOMAN, WHO KEPT THE DOOR ON ITS CHAIN, ASKED.

"ENCYCLOPEDIA SALESMAN," I CHEERFULLY
ANSWERED.

"ENCYCLOPEDIA?"

"That's right. I'd like to sell you an encyclopedia."

"You're not one of those politicians looking for my vote in the by-election, are you?"

"No, ma'am. I just want to exploit your love of knowledge by selling you an overpriced set of reference books that you will rarely use and your children will probably send to a landfill after you're gone."

The woman was unconvinced. "How do I know you're not a politician?"

"Surely, this is a face you can trust?"

"Sounds like something a politician would say."

"I assure you, I'm just a poor encyclopedia salesman trying to get by in a world that is increasingly turning its back on knowledge."

"Well...okay."

"Although, when you think about it, a perfect use for all the knowledge you would get from an encyclopedia would be to vote in the coming by-election..."

SLAM!

"You totally misrepresented what we're doing!" Amy complained as we walked to the next house.

"True," I cheerfully agreed. "But in my defence, it was the longest conversation I've had with anybody since we started!"

"Long conversations aren't the point if you don't convince somebody to vote for you!" Amy protested.

"But, aren't you the one who tells me I should keep a positive attitude?"

"Erm." It was the most gratifying erm I think I have ever heard.

In all, Amy and I knocked on three hundred, maybe three hundred and one doors from four in the afternoon to ten in the evening. A few

PEOPLE EVENTUALLY DID TALK TO ME, SOME EXPRESSING AN INTEREST IN MY CAMPAIGN. ONE MAN SAID HE WOULD BE HAPPY TO VOTE FOR ME, BUT HE WAS AFRAID THAT GERMS ON THE BALLOT WOULD GIVE HIM A LINGERING ILLNESS THAT WOULD KILL HIM IN THREE YEARS, SIX MONTHS AND TWENTY-ONE DAYS. I FOUND HIS SPECIFICITY ODDLY COMPELLING. MORE THAN ONE PERSON TOLD ME THAT THEY WOULD KEEP AN OPEN MIND RIGHT UP TO THE TIME THEY WOULD VOTE CONSERVATIVE.

AS AMY DROVE US BACK TO CAMPAIGN HEADQUARTERS (A SMALL BUILDING BETWEEN A TIM HORTONS AND A MAPLE SYRUP FACTORY — THE ONLY WAY IT COULD HAVE BEEN MORE CANADIAN WOULD BE IF BEAVERS HAD FELLED THE TREES THAT IT HAD BEEN BUILT OUT OF!), SHE TRIED TO ASSURE ME THAT OUR CANVASSING HAD BEEN WORTHWHILE.

"OKAY, THAT SUCKED," AMY ADMITTED, ALBEIT IN A TONE OF VOICE LIKE SHE HAD JUST SEEN A CHOIR OF ANGELS DESCEND FROM THE CLOUDS. "BUT LOOK AT IT THIS WAY: BEING AN NDP CANDIDATE IN SUCH A CONSERVATIVE PROVINCE AS ALBERTA WAS ALWAYS GOING TO BE HARD AND, ANYWAY, AFTER A DAY LIKE TODAY, THINGS CAN ONLY GET BETTER. RIGHT?"

"RIGHT," I AGREED. BUT I WAS ALREADY STARTING TO IMAGINE ALL OF THE THINGS THAT COULD GET WORSE...

A Match Made in Heaven (The Comedy Club in The Annex)

by AIDANDREW PUFFPEESADDER, Alternate Reality News Service Comedy Writer

The combatants are in their respective corners. In the left – my left – no, wait, your left, too – why are you making this harder than it has to – fine! In corner number one...Betty Bebopalulu, a tall, thin woman with a white face, blood red lips and nose, blue rings around her eyes, a shock of red hair sticking out of either side of her head, is ready to rumble. To you and I, she seems like a clown. To the people of Earth Prime 0-9-2-7-2-5 dash epsilon, she is an upstanding citizen. Sitting on a stool. In a ring.

In corner number...the opposite sits a short blue alien with exaggeratedly round features and no hair; he wears an exquisite three piece suit. Ferlenghetti dos Passos has already started rumbling (he really should have eaten a little something before the bout).

The battle started seven hours and forty three minutes ago. Two hours and twelve minutes ago, the referee ordered a pizza. The battle started with the referee saying, "We don't need to fight. Why don't we go to the pub down the street and grab ourselves a couple of morose rhinoceroses with neuroses?" When Bebopalulu repeated what he had said, he got out of the way, so that the words were directed at dos Passos. dos Passos repeated the words back to her, and they've been repeating them at each other ever since.

It's the classic comedy mirror trope, where one person repeats everything that another person says, reconceived as a form of battle. The two warriors will continue the mirror trope until one of them – you should pardon the expression – cracks.

"Oh, dear," Transdimensional Authority Secretary-Specific Nicodemius Fitzhuge oh, deared. "Earth Prime 0-9-2-7-2-5 dash epsilon seemed like the perfect place to relocate the refugees from Earth Prime 4-6-4-0-8-9 dash Omega. Clowns recognize their own, and all that. However, it would appear that we have initiated some form of buffoonery cold war!"

The conflict occurs wherever on Earth Prime 0-9-2-7-2-5 dash epsilon the refugees from their dying universe are settled. In the legal offices of Patchoulipants Quaxalickaduck Finch & Associates, where many refugees intern, for example. As Philomena Splat drops the mail off on the desks of the associates, banter ensues.

"Doctor up the tea set, Ms. Splat," Uranium Patchoulipants cheerfully greets the intern. "It's good to see the spinal column was written by an expert walrus!"

"Chin up, Mister Patchoulipants," Splat answers. "Or, in your case, one up, one to the left and the other in another dimension. Better days are proximate zebra orange!"

Patchoulipants considers this for a second before responding, "Ah, yes. The voluntary crab cakes do not diminish in the harsh slinky of redundancy."

"Yes, I will be seeing a quintessence this weekend, thanks for asking," Splat will say as she heads for the door of Patchoulipants' office. "I wish you and yours a happy and healthy block-headed interregnum *mishigas*!"

Citizens of the Earths of the two realities comedy each other to a standstill.

Some take the stalemate as a challenge, others take it as a reason to stay in their rooms and watch Netflax until their eyes start to bulge in their heads. To great comic effect, natch.

The Transdimensional Authority is, of course, trying to find ways to make the transition for the refugees easier. For the most part, this has involved meetings to discuss ways of making the transition for the refugees easier. "We have had a lot of spirited discussions about ways of making the transition for the refugees easier," Secretary-Specific Fitzhuge unwittingly redundanted. "I won't try to deceive you: at times, I wept. And, we may have found something, a mystical condition known in transdimensional relations as 'interactive humour reduction,' or, more popularly, 'being a straight man'."

Before they settle in to this new home, refugees from Earth Prime 4-6-4-0-8-9 dash Omega are now given a six week course in being straight aliens. Initially, many of them have trouble with the concept of taking a pie for the team (rather than throwing it). However, when they come to the part in the course where they learn about overstated reactions (ie: the involuntary aqueous evacuation reaction, aka: the spit take) and understated reactions (ie: the sardonic cilium uplift, aka: the raised eyebrow), they enthusiastically take on their new roles.

"I must admit that I was skeptical when Doctor Alhambra offered to create the six week course for the refugees," Secretary-Specific Fitzhuge stated, referring to the Transdimensional Authority's Chief Scientist. "However, that degree in theatre he received as part of his nth degree has really paid dividends!"

When I asked her how she was adjusting to her new home, Splat looked desperately around for a glass of liquid to drink. Being able to fit in to their new home is harder for some refugees than others.

"Aliens Helping Aliens Help Line. How may I help you?"

"All of you aliens are scummy bastards who deserve to die!"

"All of you aliens are scummy bastards who deserve to die!"

"That's what I said."

"That's what I said."

"No, that's what I said."

"No, that's what I said."

"See, this is exactly the problem!"

"See, this is exactly the problem!"

"Aaargh! Why don't you assholes go back to where you came from?"

"Aaargh! Why don't you go back to where you came from, asshole?"

"What, Temiskaming?"

"Temiskaming? I can see why you wouldn't want to go back there."

"What's wrong with Temiskaming?"

"What's wrong with Temiskaming?"

"No, seriously, what's wrong with Temiskaming?"

"No, seriously, what's wrong with Temiskaming?"

"Tell me, Gord dammit, what's wrong with Temiskaming?"

"Tell me, Gord dammit, what's wrong with Temiskaming?"

"You ferking asswipe! Eat bad sushi and die!"

DIAL TONE

"Thank you for calling the Aliens Helping Aliens Help Line. Have a nice day."

The Trouble With *The Trouble With Wingnut*

by ELMORE TERADONOVICH, Alternate Reality News Service Film and Television Writer

Ever since they started arriving on Earth Prime, sentient beings from Earth Prime 4-6-4-0-8-9 dash Omega have generally been depicted in film and television in one of two ways: either as villains intent on taking over the world or sidekicks whose only purpose seems to be to make their human friends look good. (In the short-lived series *Babble On Five*, the main alien was a sidekick to the human main character who was also a villain intent on taking over the world; this explains why the series was short-lived.)

"I felt that just wasn't right," stated famed Hollywood producer Marty DiBergi. "I figured the aliens had their own stories. Something more than just stepping on Legos – in the shape of an Imperial battle doughnut – it takes a lot of talent to sell not being able to see one of those babies on the floor in front of you! – misunderstanding a half-heard telephone conversation or trying to blow up Houston. I thought somebody should do something about that."

Several weeks later, DiBergi realized that, as a producer, he was in a perfect position to do something about it. So, he put together a room of some of the most successful sitcom writers in Hollywood (whom I'm not going to name – trust me, you've never heard of them – I've been on this beat for almost thirteen years, and **I've** never heard of them!) and created *The Trouble With Wingnut.*

Wingnut Blotchy is an alien forced to immigrate to Big City America (Cincinnati). He immediately gets a high-paying job (as one will) as an Executive Vice President at International Extrusions and Compactory (a vaguely productive but highly successful company). Soon after, he meets Marsha Fenstruck, a waifish millennial with a zombie fetish (movies, TV, computer games, cereal boxes, babies' arms holding apples – her passion for the shuffling dead was indiscriminate). It was love at first smite (Marsha killed a zombie with a cash register at a local Bob So Tasty); six months later, they were married.

"It's in the tradition of *Mork and Mindy and Ted and Alice* or *Alfredo* or *Thirty*

Rock From the Sun," explained head writer Allen Woodman. (Who? Exactly!) "An alien comes to Earth and wreaks comic havoc on the poor denizens of our planet while, at the same time, learning what it means to be human."

Should viewers expect *The Trouble With Wingnut* to be preachy, then? Because the whole "learning what it means to be human" thing sounds preachy.

"Preachy? No. Noooooooo. No ho ho ho. No," Woodman insisted. "The show's not preachy. The show's...peachy. Keen. Very keen to have people tune in and find out what the hilarity is all about."

Controversy over *The Trouble With Wingnut* began even before it went into production, owing to rumours that Peter Dinklage had been cast to play the title character. "Why get a human actor to play an alien when there are so many...aspiring alien actors who could do it better?" asked Anastasia La Bombon, Vice President, Moral Limitations and Public Relations of the Aliens Helping Aliens (AHA!) Foundation. "And when I say 'better', I don't mean more dramatically approachable – Peter Dinklage is a great actor. I just mean that they could bring an authenticity, a lived experience to the role that he just doesn't have."

Dinklage responded to questions about the controversy with a terse: "You think I'm going to comment on this? Please! Hollywood infighting and backstabbing is worse than *Game of Squids*!"

So, it's more...outfighting and frontstabbing?

"Exactly!"

Eventually, Shazbat Mnuchin, who had been an actor on a soap in his home universe, was cast in the role.

The first three episodes of the series were not well received. By which I mean that they were wildly popular with everybody except aliens and the groups that represent them. "There was nothing in the character of Wingnut that expressed his alien experience," La Bombon explained. "The character could just as easily have been an east Asian or a Mormon; the humour would have been the same."

Mormon? "It was the first thing that came to mind," La Bambon admitted. "You can substitute zombie fetishist if you think it's more appropriate."

The problem was that none of the writers on the show were aliens, which made it as likely that they would capture the essence of what it means to be an alien refugee about as well as a gnat could arm wrestle an elephant. To underscore the problem, when La Bombon and others tweeped about it, they used the hashtag #hollywoodsohuman.

"But...they're some of the most successful sitcom writers in Hollywood!" DiBergi protested. "Everything they touch has been television gold. So, when you put them together, what they create should be beyond television gold. It should be television...beyond gold!"

When the show returned after a six month hiatus hernia (the strain was apparent), it had three alien writers (Fenton Mobutu, Grace Monongahela and Sissy SpaceX). The fourth, fifth and sixth episodes have been a mixed bag of traditional comedy and alien consciousness raising (with slaw on the side). But DiBergi sees this as the creative process unfolding as it should.

"*The Mary Tyler Moorehead Show* didn't really come together until its twelfth episode," DiBergi stated. "Hell, *Schadenfreudefeld* didn't gel until its third season! By that standard, we're well ahead of the game!"

How did Joe and Bill maintain a perfect clearance rate? Legwork. The kind of legwork they pursue is not something that involves hot wax in a luxury spa; successful detectives don't have time to indulge in petty vanities. Nor does the kind of legwork they believe in involve slick moves in tap shoes. Bill admires people who can make slick moves in tap shoes, Joe not so much, but they agree that there is no place for it in successful detective work. No, the kind of legwork that helps you maintain a perfect clearance rate involves using your legs to pound the pavement (which might seem like a difficult way of attacking a problem – not to mention painful in the medium to long term – but the pavement is indifferent to your activity and, in any case, you can't argue with success).

Unfortunately, it's hard to do legwork in Bermuda from Vancouver. That's why you need Tech Support.

"You can get all that information from that little box?" Bill asked.

Ian from Tech Support sighed. "Bill, you ask me that every time I help you guys with a case."

"Oh? And what is your answer? Other than to sigh and tell me I ask you that every time you help us with a case, I mean."

"What I'm doing is also legwork. Just...with my hands."

"So, it's...leghandwork?" The detective was understandably confused.

"Let the man do his work, Bill," Joe advised. "Whatever part of his body he uses."

"Thank you," Ian from Tech Support muttered. "Again."

Ian from Tech Support looked like he was made out of chewing gum that a kid had pulled from both ends as far as he could. With his shock of spiky yellow hair, he could have been a character in a comic book. No, that's a stretch. No, that's The Stretch. Kevin Feige, are you listening?

Ian from Tech Support had brought his laptop up to the squad room of the West End – Coal Harbour Community Policing Centre and was using it to search through databases for any information that might help the case. Joe and Bill were sitting at a nearby desk, drinking coffee from monochrome mugs and apparently chatting. I say apparently, because nobody in the squad had ever overheard them, no matter how close they came to the pair, so it was impossible to confirm that the low sounds coming out of Joe and Bill's mouths were, in fact, language. It seemed unlikely that they would make small talk, unless weather or sports scores were part of a case. They didn't have any family that anybody knew of. Or friends. Or casual acquaintances. In fact, they never appeared to acknowledge anybody who wasn't involved in one way or another with a case. If they were talking about the case, though, it was easy to make out what they were saying. The best anybody could figure (Juanita-Annie Boddy, a beat cop who made a difference out on the street), they were speaking an ur-detective language that modern police could not understand.

"Okay," Ian from Tech Support said after forty-five minutes. "I've gone about as far as I can go..."

Joe and Bill turned their attention to him. "What have you got, son?" Joe asked.

Older generation, Ian from Tech Support, who had grown up in the Sister Mary Manischevits Home for Way, Way, Wayward Children, told himself. *It doesn't mean anything.*

He explained that the shipping container found at the docks had come in on the Andrea Dorquia, an Ecuadoran ship plying the seas under an Australian flag. According to the ship's manifest, the Andrea Dorquia had taken on the container in Bluntz, Kalashnikstan. "Whoever did this could be running a bootleg Dimensional Portal^{TM} anywhere in Eastern Europe," Ian from Tech Support commented. "It's the wild west – wild east? – wild geographically unspecific out there!" The manifest listed the contents of the container as: 'garden supplies'.

"If you consider the fact that we will all return to dust some day," Ian from Tech Support commented, "the label isn't entirely inaccurate."

"Un hunh," Joe responded. It was the kind of un hunh that didn't commit to a position on the previous statement, but suggested it was open to hearing more.

Ian from Tech Support went on to explain that the organization listed as the owner of the goods in the shipping container was North Korea-based Kaiser Soze and Assoziates, Inc. That supposed import/export business turned out to be an artillery shell company ("If you're not careful, trying to track it back to its source could blow up in your face!") owned jointly by a Philippine company called Hoo Ha Yu Bluit Ltd. and Germany's own Deutsche Bank. Deutsche Bank's fiscal infelicities were well documented, and none of them involved deadly alien trafficking, so Ian from Tech Support looked into Hoo Ha Yu Bluit. As it happened, this supposed import/export business was a peanut shell company ("Be careful where you step; whichever elephant ate them left a mess on the floor!") owned by 103678 Luxembourg Ltd., a hand holding company based in Bahrain. 103678 Luxembourg Ltd. was owned by Ha Ha, Suckers, You'll Never Catch Us LLC ("I would have thought that one would have raised flags, for sure!"), a shell of his former self company ("He never recovered from the loss of his pet cobra Billy Batstuff."). As it turned out, this supposed import/export business was owned by Fin de la Route, [UNTRANSLATABLE], Incorporé, a Michelle company ("Ma belle!") which claimed to have been incorporated in Mare Umbrage, the moon. As far as Ian from Tech Support could determine, there were no incorporation offices on the moon, which made following the trail from that point difficult. Very difficult. Impossibly difficult, really.

"You know what we have here, Bill?"

"What's that, Joe?"

"A dead end."

"The deadest."

"Deader than a bill that raises taxes in a Republican-controlled Senate."

"Deader than a teenager in a horror movie on prom night."

"Deader than the last bald eagle served up with a white whine sauce and a side of fries."

"You know what that means, Joe?"

"What's that, Bill?"

"Legwork."

"Legwork."

"Legwork!" Ian from Tech Support whispered in awe.

First Chance to See

by INDIGO HAPHAZASTANCE Alternate Reality News Service Transdimensional Traffic Writer

When you're trying to coax people to visit your state and enjoy the rustic atmosphere, the last thing you need is somebody spray-painting anarchy symbols on the sides of cows. The vibrant music scene you would like visitors to your state to enjoy can be undermined by random public appearances by Boris Johnson's Pig Bladder and Kazoo Quintet. (Although, to be fair, their rendition of 'In the Air Tonight' is no worse than the original.) Got a historical site you think people from out of state would pay a lot of money to see? You think they would pay as much if they knew that four foot tall blue people in exquisite three piece suits would be re-enacting the Battle of Bill Bulgar's Ball...oons in front of the site, even if it was the home of Whitey Rhenquist, third basemen for the Tourmeline Puffer Fish, or otherwise had nothing to do with the American Civil War?

Tourist boards across the country are unhappy about the influx of aliens from Earth Prime 4-6-4-0-8-9 dash Omega. "A blight on our fair land," they say. "What is a blight, anyway? It sounds suspiciously British..."

"Horrible," they also say. "They drive away tourists, drive up home prices and drive on the wrong side of the bicycle path."

"Worse than weeds," they also also say, adding: "Without the airborne transmission, but still."

Oh, good. I was really worried about the airborne transmission of aliens.

Faced with the problem of integrating aliens into their tourism plans, the city of Khaki Stock Racy, Missouri took a novel approach: why not make **them** a tourist attraction?

On the outskirts of the town, three blocks have been remade to look like three city blocks of Earth Prime 4-6-4-0-8-9 dash Omega, the alien home universe. Which is to say,

they are exactly the same as any three American city blocks on Earth Prime, but roughly two-thirds the size. To commemorate the Russian immigrants who had to be relocated for this marketing experiment, the neighbourhood was christened the 'Alien Potemkin Village'.

"We have done our best to capture the alien experience," enthused Khaki Stock Racy Mayor Bryan-Tom Cruiseshanks. "For example, at one, three and five pies are thrown in the faces of random tourists. But not to worry: at two, four and six, the aliens spray random tourists with seltzer water. And, anyway, the pies are delicious. The one they caught me with was barbecued peach – yum!"

Isn't the city afraid of lawsuits? "Do you want an authentic alien experience or not?" he protested. Lowering his voice he added: "Besides, a disclaimer absolving the city of any responsibility for incidents of unwanted hospital stays due to fruit allergies or dry-cleaning owing to pieing is in the fine print of all of our promotional literature!"

Visitors to Alien Potemkin Village can rent Augmented Reality goggles (ARggles) for a modest (it doesn't like to brag) fee. When they look at the aliens going about their business, they see objects ranging from small rocks and roosters to large boulders and, if enough aliens are concentrated in the same small area, merry-go-rounds fall on their heads. Most of the time, the objects deflect off of dainty umbrellas that they carry. Once in a while, the alien has misread the day's weather forecast and brought the wrong umbrella, in which case they are pancaked. So far, the AR programme has produced six animations showing how the aliens bounce back from the smushing.

"Smu-shing! Smu-shing! I wanna see more smushing!" chanted a tourist named Garrison Keilleroverer, aged 36 (but a mature 36).

Tourists who attempt to engage in conversation with any of the aliens will be regaled with examples of their unique way of seeing the world. "Eating chicken often starts with an aerial assault of fork and knife, but it always ends with hand to wing combat!" one alien might say. "Don't forget: wherever you find yourself...leaves a scar," another alien might pontificate. "If you can't say something nice, say something fruitbat opportunity flange!" a third alien might chime in.

"They have such a unique way of expressing themselves!" commented a tourist named Florence Fallopian, aged 79 (but an overripe 79). "I was torn between smushing their cheeks and consulting a dictionary!"

"I don't know," remarked Anastasia La Bombon, Vice President, Held Exhalations and Public Relations of the Aliens Helping Aliens (AHA!) Foundation. "There's something that doesn't feel right about, like, being entertained by an alien culture. I mean, like, they're just sentient beings trying to get by in a world they never made, right? Not only that, but I hear the pay is, like, really, really, really, really crummy. Sounds kind of like exploitation to me, you know?"

"Butt out!" said Caribou McFadden, who plays an alien stock broker (a bit of a stretch; in his previous life, he was a native tax collector) in Alien Potemkin Village. "I get a roof over my head and all the crabapples I can eat – and I can eat plenty, sister! – one time, I nearly ate three in a single meal – the only reason I couldn't finish the last one was because of the increasingly intense pain I started to feel in my stomach – and all I have to do is allow complete strangers of another species to laugh at me and my cu-razy antics eleven times a day! The only thing that would make this better would be if they would let me lick pie off the faces of the people I throw it at!"

"Yeah, not gonna happen," Mayor Cruiseshanks averred. "We want tourists to get an authentic experience of how the aliens lived, but we don't want it to be so authentic that it scares them off!"

THE STORY SO FAR: Owing to an encounter with a mysterious kazillionaire and his young inventor sidekick, fun and energetic alien Lemmy Adjudicator was transformed into the mild-mannered superhero Mistah Charisma. When last we saw him, he was just about to have his first encounter with a supervillain...

Jezebel Firelight had been born Mona Krebs; she was assigned the name by Ruff & Tuff Records, the label that signed the Kitty Kat Krew to what amounted to lifetime contracts (although the lifetime of a girl band these days could often be measured in minutes). What Alonzo McGrapes, CEO of R&T Records, couldn't know was that, along with unnatural lead guitar playing ability, Jezebel could open any door, pick any lock, or crack any safe in the time it took most young ladies to finish a strawberry shake.

Powers were, like, oh my Gord, totally awesome!

Jezebel was a sleek Siamese. Oh, yeah. Fans of the band thought that their stage personae were costumes, but they had actually been permanently transformed when they received their powers. McGrapes was the only person who was aware of this (it was in their contract).

The company would occasionally anonymously send an image of one of the band members that had been carefully crafted from pictures of them before their transformation to tabloid newspapers to throw the public off the scent (the dogs!). If nobody had ever noticed that their ages seemed...highly variable from picture to picture, it was probably because their fifteen minutes of fame had taken place seven years earlier (with the twin hits 'Kitty Kat Prowl' and 'I May Not Be Purrfect, But I'm Purrfect For You'), at least four generations of the general public's attention to fifteen minutes of fame ago.

"Mona, how's it going?" Veronica Laflamme (born: Rachel Ironmonger) asked over the psychic link the four members of the band had had since the transformation (it was what originally brought them together). Veronica was the lead singer and public face of the Kitty Kat Krew (and also the brains behind the heists they carried out – shh). She was an imperious Russian Blue – gorgeous to look at, but with a mind of her own (and a steel will to back it up).

"Ninety seconds, Rach," Jezebel, concentrating on listening to the tumblers fall on the big vault at the rear of the bank, answered. "Two minutes, tops."

"You hear that, Mikey?"

"Copy that," Iphigenia Fuoco-Grande (nee: Michaela Parks) responded. She was the bass guitarist and getaway driver. She was a 57 varieties cat, the different parts that she was made up of being an endless source of speculation by the band's dwindling number of fans, driven by the fact that, as the designated 'quiet one', she never spoke to the press or on social media. "Will have the car around to the entrance of the bank in about ten minutes."

"Uhh, Rachel," Sasha Bolshoi-Ogon (originally: Millie Gropnik), the lookout/muscle/drummer of the outfit, commented from her post by the front door nine minutes later, "we could have trouble." Sasha was an orange alley cat with a livid scar in the fur over her right eye which signalled that she was not to be trifled with. When the four young women lived together for the short-lived *Kitty Kat Krew* TV series, she was the only one who maintained her own apartment ("All that kute and kuddly komedy makes me want to hack up furballs 'til the sun goes down!" she told the others, who privately agreed but didn't get their own places because they didn't to want to cross McGrapes. Thankfully for everybody, the series was cancelled after seventeen episodes.)

"What's up, Millie?" Jezebel asked.

"Three guys seem to be fighting across the street. A schlub is arguing that he needs time to develop his powers. The other two – one's a rich-looking dude in fancy duds – the other's a black kid with a full-looking duffle bag – they're trying to convince him that he's ready. For what? No idea. They keep calling him Mister Karma...Mister Cartman – I don't know. Even with my enhanced hearing, it's hard to make out exactly what."

"None of them sound familiar." The three other Kitty Kats could hear the frown in Jezebel's psychically projected voice. "No matter; as long as they stay across the –"

"The schlubby guy is crossing the street and heading this way," Sasha informed them.

"The vault is open and we're collecting the swag," Veronica updated the group. "Shouldn't be more than another minute, two at the most."

"Stall the guy as best you can," Jezebel advised. "We'll be out of here soon."

"My pleasure." They could all hear the grin in Sasha's psychically projected voice.

Although they had each quickly become aware of their unique abilities after the transformation, the four members of the Kitty Kat Krew initially had no intention of using them. Especially when their music took off, they thought they would be able to earn enough money to fulfill their dream of moving to Earth Prime 3-0-0-0-7-5 dash alpha, where they could openly live as themselves. Unfortunately, the contract they had signed with Ruff & Tuff Records, which forced them to repay all of the money the label spent on their promotion, tours and paperwork, meant that they could barely pay for their day-to-day expenses. So, robbing banks it was.

Lemmy knocked on the front door of the bank. Nobody responded, even though he could see a dark figure through the plate glass around the door. Having nothing to lose, Lemmy tried to open the door. Surprised that it did, indeed, open for him, he walked through. A large, grumpy cat (whom nobody would mistake for an internet meme) stopped him before he could make it three feet into the room.

"You...you're. A cat," Lemmy, surprised, stated.

"No shit," Sasha replied. She wasn't exactly what you would call handy with the witty repartee.

"That's cool," Lemmy tried to recover. "One of. My friends. Lives on. A planet. Run by. Cats. He. Says it's. A fun. Place."

"I bet." Lemmy could not hear the yearning in her voice, but, to be fair, it was buried under several layers of trepidation, disappointment and rage.

"Are you. Robbing this. Bank?"

"No," Sasha smirked. "We're just making a late night withdrawal." Knowing she was not exactly what you would call handy with the witty repartee, she had memorized two dozen clever-sounding phrases in the hope that she would find a pretext in which to use them. This was the first.

"Does this. Mean we. Have to. Fight now?" Lemmy asked. Looking at Sasha's scar, he was reconsidering his decision to be a superhero. Or for that matter, emigrate to this universe.

Sasha looked him over. Slumped shoulders. No discernible muscles. Glasses. Glasses! "If we're going to fight, you might want to take off the glasses," she advised.

"I can't," Lemmy said. "It would. Reveal my. Secret identity. To you. If I. Took my. Glass –"

Before he could react, Sasha reached out and plucked the glasses off his face. "There. You look exactly the same, except now you're not wearing any glasses."

"My secret. Identity!" Lemmy cried.

"Mister, your secret's safe with me," Sasha assured him. Then, in the very next breath, disassured him again: "Are you sure you want to fight?"

Lemmy shrugged. "It's what a superhero is supposed to do."

"Superhero, hunh?" Sasha shook her head in disbelief. "Okay, but I gotta warn ya: this Kitty has klaws!"

* SNIKT *!

Forty-three seconds later...

A black van pulled up in front of the bank.

"That's not good," Paul commented from across the street. "Is that good? That can't be good."

"Relax," Reginald tried to reassure him in a soothing voice. Although Paul could not know this, the man was using the tone he usually employed in union contract negotiations to lull organizers into a false sense of security before he explained why his terms were the only ones they would walk out of the room with. When he had worked with Reginald long enough to recognize the voice, Paul would hate hearing it. "I'm sure Lemmy is taking care of the people inside the building..."

Thirty-six seconds after that...

Three women in catsuits ran out of the bank. Although it was dark and difficult to make them out, two of them were holding very large, very full burlap sacks. They jumped into the van, which immediately sped off.

"That is definitely not good," Paul asserted, although something about the women seemed kind of familiar.[10]

---

[10] Paul had been dragged to a Kitty Kat Krew Koncert by Nina Selectric, a girl he dated in his teens. Nina had all of the band's albums (meaning: both *Welcome to the Litter Box* and its follow-up *Songs of Redemption and Treats*). Like many boys in his

"Lemmy could still be fighting one of the gang members inside the bank," Reginald responded, although his tone wouldn't have convinced a toddler that ice cream was yummy.

"What do you think the odds of that are?"

Reginald was about to reply that he only bet on sure things when the bank alarm went off. Paul and Reginald looked at each other for a moment, then Paul sprinted towards the front doors of the bank.

Reginald rolled his eyes. "The things I do for science!" he sighed, and raced after Paul.

Thirty-two minutes, seventeen seconds later...

"She never. Laid a. Hand on. Me," Lemmy groggily asserted.

"She didn't have to," Reginald wryly noted. "Her claws did more than enough damage."

Lemmy was lying on the most comfortable couch he had ever encountered (and, in his home universe, he had encountered plenty, buster!). He looked around at the fabulous apartment he found himself in. Was that a piano? And was that Liberace standing next to the piano, talking to Elton John sitting on the bench? There were several paintings on the walls, each of which in its own unique voice said, "You may have thought I was hanging in a gallery somewhere – your understanding of how the world works needs some updating, pal!" One wall was made up entirely of glass, giving a breathtaking view of the city twenty-seven floors below them, from Steve Gerber Drive all the way to Lake Water.

"Have I. Died and. Gone to. Heaven?" Lemmy wondered.

"Not until you beat a supervillain," Reginald told him.

---

situation, Paul had a crush on the lead singer and, like most of the boys in his situation, he had forgotten the band the moment he broke up with his girlfriend. Ye Olde Occluded Omniscient Narrator

Noticing Paul closing a first aid kit and putting it into his duffle bag, Lemmy gently felt his face. At least, he tried to: his face was covered with so many bandages you would think he was auditioning for the lead role in a remake of *The Mummy*. "What...happened?"

"You don't remember?" Paul asked.

"It all. Happened so. Fast..."

"There were four women in cat costumes," Paul told him. "One of them must have had retractable claws. I can think of half a dozen designs that would work well, with one to fit every budget depending upon the complexity of the mechanism and the materials you –"

"Paul. Focus," Reginald gently interrupted.

"Right. Sorry. Your face got cut up pretty bad. The good news is that the scars will probably disappear when you revert back to your old body."

"Has that. Happened before?" Lemmy inquired.

"We...don't have a lot of data on this..." Paul admitted.

"What happens. If the. Scars remain. After I. Go back. To my. Original form?"

"You will have a great story to tell your friends and family," Reginald, who was enjoying a martini at the bar (because of course there was a bar!), said. The martini he had made for himself was probably perfect. Bastard.

"I guess. That's it. Then," Lemmy moped.

"Not necessarily," Paul disagreed. "We still have over seventeen hours."

"But I'm. Obviously not. A fighter!" Lemmy protested.

"Obviously not," Paul responded. "But that just means we have to get more creative looking for your power..."

Next issue: join us for the pulse-pounding conclusion
of: "When Good Aliens Make Bad Heroes!!!"

The room had a certain *je ne sais quoi* (I can't sais what
because I don't speak French). With its shag carpets and
wood panelling, it looked like a refugee from the 1960s.
The ghosts of lava lamps projecting vague ever-shifting
blobby shadows on the walls enhanced the effect. But the
room contained no love seats, no six inch black and white
television sets, no stray pieces of a Saturn V rocket (the
kind all the coolest Apollo astronauts in the 1960s rode)
model kit to step on in the middle of the night to give you
an ouchie. Instead, there were sixteen identical four foot
tall blue men wearing exquisite three piece suits sitting
four across at long tables talking on the phone. They were
saying things like: "A plot of land has just become
available in the Glengary Glen Ross project and I can
offer it to you for an incredible low price!" and "In these
days of universal brouhaha, it's more important than ever
to stay on top of the news. That's why I'm proud to be
able to offer you a starter subscription to the
International Mugwump and Daily News for an
incredible low price!" and "Sgt. Snorkel's fork'll stab the
porkell...at an incredible low price!"

The buzz of capitalism in the air was so thick, you'd
think everybody on a phone would need a fly-swatter and
insect repellent to keep from getting voraciously bitten.

Deneb   Abramowitz, the third salesman from the
right on the second row, swatted at something in front of
his eyes and said into the phone: "This is how it works:
you give me a small amount of money every month..."

Mannfred Aleichem, a bored househusband in Fresno, India, responded, "Why would I give you any money at all?"

"Because in the future, I would give you back all of the money you have given me, and more. Possibly a whole lot more."

"When would you give me all this money?"

"It depends...how old are you?"

"Fifty-seven."

"And do you have any serious illnesses?"

"Yes. I have Breyer's foot fungus and advanced sclerotic follicle displacement syndrome."

"Sounds serious."

"I get by."

"Well, with those conditions, I calculate you will live for another seventeen years, at which point you would be eligible to get your money back."

"So, you want me to give you money for seventeen years?"

"In small amounts, yes."

"At which point, if I understand you correctly, I will get it all back and more, possibly a lot more?"

"That is correct."

"What's the catch?"

"The catch?"

"This sounds too good to be true, so there must be a catch."

"Ah. Well. As I hinted four statements ago, you collect the money when you die."

"That doesn't sound like a good deal. In fact, that sounds horrible!"

"How so?"

"Well, for one thing, I'm dead."

"It happens to the best of us, so why should you be an exception?"

"How am I supposed to enjoy spending all that money when I'm dead? Can you give me the money now so I can spend it while I'm still alive?"

"That is not the way insurance works."

"Horrible."

"Look: the money we give you when you die is supposed to give you peace of mind knowing that your loved ones will be taken care of – financially, I mean – when you're gone."

"Really horrible."

"Oh. Why is that?"

"I have three ex-wives and all my kids hate me."

"Some people leave the money we give them to their pets."

"I have a tarantula, but there's a reason I don't ever let it out of its glass box."

"Perhaps you have a non-profit organization that you would like to leave all that money to..."

"I am kind of interested in Humans for Humanity..."

"Oh! Well, I didn't necessarily mean –"

"But not enough to give you small amounts of money until I die so it can have a large pot of money."

"Okay. Good. Dodged a bullet, there."

"So, if I understand this correctly, you want me to make a bet with you that I'm going to die. At the end of every month –"

"Actually, we bill on the fifteenth."

"At some point in every month, I will ask myself this question: 'Am I still alive?' If the answer is no, I win a big pile of money. If the answer is yes, I lose the bet and have to give you a small amount of money. Does that make sense to you?"

"As a matter of fact...not really. No. Still, it's my – hello? Hello?"

Sitting next to Deneb, Alison   Finklewort hung up his phone, stretched and said, "I need a break. I think I'm going to go on a toffee run – at an incredible low price! Sorry – it's a catchy phrase. Can I get you anything?"

"I could kill for a triple seared half-calf-traif espresso ralph machiato."

"The bad news: I'm pretty sure there's no such thing. The good news: at least nobody has to die for you to get it."

"You always did have a feel for the silver lini..." Deneb trailed off and, in a whisper, continued, "Do you ever get the feeling that you're being watched?"

"All the time. But I find that a cold shower and a tub of Daagen-Hasz cures it."

"I'm serious! I feel like we're being watched..."

"You're just being paranoid."

"Yeah. Don't mind us – just act naturally," a voice came from the back of the room.

"Are you telling me that you didn't hear that?" Deneb demanded.

"Hear what?" Alison innocently responded.

"Somebody telling us to just act naturally."

"Well, it's good advice..."

Deneb looked to his left, where four human beings stood behind a velvet rope. A man in a short-sleeved Hawaiian shirt, khaki shorts and sandals bent forward awkwardly to be able to fit into the room. A woman stood next to him, her head slightly bowed, wearing large dark sunglasses and a sundress, carrying a large tote bag. Beside her were two youngsters: one, a boy brat, wore a *Castlevania* t-shirt and a sneer that appeared to be permanently tattooed on his kisser; the other, a girl brat, wore a ponyta t-shirt whose colours seemed to change as you looked at it and a fixed, implacable look of boredom.

"I'm bored!" the girl brat, who couldn't have been more than seven years old (although she was actually nine – good thing I didn't put any money on that), complained. At least she was consistent.

"Me, too!" the boy brat, who, to be honest, wasn't really leadership material, concurred.

"Now, honey," the man (let's assume that he hadn't rented the children for the afternoon, that he was, in fact, their father), calmly replied, "you may not realize it, but what we're witnessing is a little piece of history."

"History is boring!" the girl brat pouted.

"Yeah, well, you have a point, it can be, sometimes," her father allowed. Not being leadership material starts at the top.

"We could have gone to Disneyland!" the girl brat continued the criticism.

"Yeah, Bartholomew," the woman (who, unless anybody says otherwise, we can assume is the children's mother), agreed. "Why didn't we go to Disneyland?"

"I went there once with Denny and Denise's mother," Bartholomew (whom I think would have been more aptly named Francis or Stuyvesant or Punch Buggy, but I didn't birth him, so we'll just have to work with what his parents have given us) said with a shudder. "Worst weekend of my adult life, and one of the five worst ever!"

Step-mother, then.

While the family had been bickering, nobody noticed Deneb walk up to them and look them over appraisingly, turning his head this way and that (the other would have added another dimension to his existence, and he only turned his head the other way at children's birthday parties), taking in their every detail.

When she noticed that they were being watched, step-mother hastily advised: "Don't make eye contact. **Don't make eye contact!**"

"What's wrong with my eyes?" Deneb wanted to know.

Denise, who had walked up to the velvet rope and was looking at the alien from the other side with (although she would vehemently deny it later) fascination, asked her parents, "Is he allowed to interact with us?

"The brochure says that these aliens break the fourth wall all the time," Bartholomew offered. "I gather it's some sort of religious ritual..."

Not knowing what else to do, Deneb let out a long, low, deadly fart. The brats giggled.

"O-kay," Bartholomew said before the alien had finished. "Who wants pie?"

"I do! I do!" the brats eagerly answered.

"Let's get back to the street, then. It's almost one o'clock..."

As the family filed out of the room, Alison walked up to Deneb. "What are you doing?" he asked.

"Giving a bunch of humans an authentic alien

experience," Deneb told him. "What about my triple seared half-calf-traif espresso ralph machiato?"

With a sigh, Alison replied, "I'll see what I can do..."

"Beanies, Joe?"

"Beanies, Bill."

"Not exactly standard issue."

"I will admit, they clash with the uniform."

"They're in **colour**."

"If we wear them long enough, they will learn. Still. Whatever their shortcomings, they do have one important function, Bill."

"What's that, Joe?"

"They could save our lives."

"Aww, seriously?" a third voice interrupted the musing of the Eternal Detectives. "Why don't the two of you get a room and leave the work to us professionals?"

"Get...a room? Strange idiom, Joe."

"I think it was a not so subtle reference to our sexuality, Bill."

"We have sexuality?"

"How long you been married?"

"Thirty-seven years come a week Tuesday."

"Then, in your case, probably not. Congratulations anyway, Bill."

"Thanks, Joe. Like my father never used to say: what doesn't float your stoat burnishes your bunions."

"You always were a philosopher, Bill."

"I appreciate the sentiment, Joe. But I'm just a regular working stiff trying to get by in an indifferent universe."

"You see. There it is agai –"

"Stop it! Stop it! For the love of Gord, will you two just

stop it!" the third voice shouted. "I swear, if I had a human body, I would be hitting my forehead with my palm so hard, I would knock myself into next Tuesday – Thursday if this Earth is on Daylight Savings Time!"

The falling cow went, "Mooooooo –" * BOING *! * SPLAT *!

"You know what, Joe?"

"What's that, Bill?"

"I am beginning to rethink –"

Oh. Hold on. It occurs to me that you probably need some context for this conversation. I'll bet that right now you're more confused than a mongoose in a milk of magnesia bottling plant. I know I would be if I were you, and my stomach never gets upset.

When Joe and Bill hit a wall with Ian from Tech Support (not literally, of course – it was written into their contract that tech support staff could not be used to hit walls, floors, entryways, ceilings or eaves troughs – don't you wish you belonged to a union that was that thorough?), they discussed the next leg of their work. They agreed that the best course of action would be to go to Earth Prime 4-6-4-0-8-9 dash Omega and try to find the person or persons responsible for illegally transporting the aliens to Earth Prime. This could not, strictly speaking, be legwork, since trying to walk to an alternate reality would take infinity (in a parallel lines meeting sort of way). So, they contacted the Transdimensional Authority, explained the situation and asked if they could use a Dimensional Portal^{TM} to continue their investigation on the home terrain of the aliens.

At first, they got a recorded message that said: "Thank you for phoning the Transdimensional Authority. If you know the extension of the party to which you would like to speak, why didn't you just dial their number directly? Oh, very well, enter the extension now. For inquiries related to sightings of creatures alien to your universe, including but not limited to: Mowglis, Ventrosian Squiggles, Hoarcruxofthematters, dilapidated swans, compassionate conservatives, Ventrosian Squoggles, sentient felines and floating babies' arms holding an apple, press one. For possible violations of the Treaty of Gehenna-Wentworth, press four. For complaints about the conduct of any member of the staff of the Transdimensional Authority, press nine. For complaints about the state of your life, including but not limited to: poor physical health, poor financial health, bad relationships and/or the creeping knowledge that nothing you do will make a difference in the world and that fifty years after your death you and everybody you have ever loved will be forgotten, press sixteen. Your call will be forwarded to an existential philosotherapist. For problems with your Home Universe Generator^{TM}, contact your local vendor (Doctor Alhambra has better things to do with his time). For all other inquiries, please stay on the line and your call will be answered by the next available agent..."

Thirty minutes later, Bill had to admit that he was warming to lounge versions of Cannibal Corpse songs, but the experience had brought him no closer to contacting the Transdimensional Authority. So, he called Adelaide Mounthatchesbatten, who immediately booked the Eternal Detectives a spot on the Dimensional Portal^{TM} in the Vancouver branch office.

Mounthatchesbatten suggested – you have no idea who Adelaide Mounthatchesbatten is, do you? Sorry about that. I'm a little scattered, today. That'll teach me to stay up late binge-watching *The Marvellous Mrs. Maisel-Skure*. She is one of the adjuncts to Transdimensional Authority Secretary-Specific Nicodemius Fitzhuge. Now that you know who she is, you might wonder why Bill didn't just call her to begin with. "It isn't legwork unless it takes a lot of time," I imagine him explaining. "Legwork that takes no time at all is just...shinwork. At best, kneework."

Mounthatchesbatten suggested that the detectives take a Transdimensional Oddity Monitor (known as 'TOM' to save ink) with them. TOM is a smooth black ball with brown streaks – it is essentially a five pin bowling ball with attitude (that's what you get for creating it with a personality programme from the wrong side of the tracks). The device reads energy displacements across universes, which makes it ideal for tracking down transdimensional sentient being smugglers.

TOM was taken by Agent Duck a l'Orange to the Vancouver docks, where it analyzed traces of the residual energy from the creepy cargo container of horrors (whatever else you might think of the newspaper, you have to admit that the *Vancouver Sun* has writers who are to headlines what Hieronymus Bosch was to nightmares). Then, it met Bill and Joe on Earth Prime 4-6-4-0-8-9 dash Omega.

"I haven't used one of these babies since my last tour in Afghanistan," Joe said as he hefted TOM in one hand.

"Who're you callin' a baby?" TOM petulantly responded. "Waaaah! I was created almost four years ago! As tech goes, that's ancient!"

"I thought you had served in Korea, Joe."

"Just trying to keep current, Bill. Just trying to keep current."

On Earth Prime 4-6-4-0-8-9 dash Omega, it rained large objects: boulders, anvils, cows and the occasional house (that will teach you not to insure your home against killing witches!). Natives of the planet had developed dainty umbrellas that repelled the objects falling from the sky, but Transdimensional Authority ambassadors complained that holding them kept one of their hands occupied, which made it difficult to fill out paperwork. The * SCIENCE *! Division of the Transdimensional Authority modified a shipment of beanies somebody had found lying around in the basement to serve the same function as the umbrellas, with one important improvement. The umbrellas could only be used against a single falling object: as local folk wisdom had it, "Woe to the person with a safe-repelling umbrella when a boulder comes a 'knockin'. Can you say, '* SPLAT *!'? The mechanized propeller on top of the beanie spun at different frequencies depending upon what sensors and a computer chip built into the fabric of the cap detected was descending upon the wearer, protecting them from every foreseeable gravitationally propelled eventuality.

Besides: it was red.

So, as Bill was saying: "I am beginning to rethink my position on global warming."

"Global warming? I thought you were going to say you were beginning to rethink your position on the beanies."

"Just trying to keep current, Joe. Just trying to keep current. The red is nice, though."

Joe and Bill stepped around the cow, which TOM assured them was not hurt and would get on its feet eventually ("I know how you dumb animals feel solidarity with one another," it said with as much empathy as it could muster) and started walking down a busy city street. Cars were honking. Four foot tall blue pedestrians with exaggeratedly round limbs and no hair (but exquisite three piece suits) were pedding. Safes were being unsafe on random pedders.

"Feels like Pittsburgh," Bill commented.

"Yeah. Without the rotting fish," Joe replied.

"That's the Saturday night special at Tom's Diner," TOM sourly added. "No relation."

"How f – * OOPH *! –" Bill started, but had the wind knocked out of him by an alien turning a corner in haste.

"Yeah, don't worry about me," TOM assured him, "I am a hundred per cent foofproof!"

The alien looked up at Bill and asked: "You wouldn't happen to have seen the latest weather report, have you?" Before Bill could catch his breath and answer, the alien went on: "Ah. Right. Cloudy with a seventy-two per cent chance of anvils. Glad you could be of help!" Then, the alien ran off.

"That was a strange encounter," Joe deadpanned. "Very random."

"These aliens, man," TOM sort of agreed. "They make you humans look almost rational by comparison!"

"How f-f-f-far do we have to...to...to go?" Bill gasped.

"A couple of miles," TOM informed him. "Left turn here."

They walked for several blocks (okay: six, seven if you include a short detail down memory lane), when Joe asked, "You okay, Bill?"

"Fine, Joe," Bill replied. "Lungs like a cast-iron bellows. It'll take more than a runaway alien to * OOPH *! –" Bill had the wind knocked out of him by an alien turning a corner in haste.

"Oh, hey, humans!" the alien, who looked exactly like the first alien, exclaimed. "You wouldn't happen to have heard the weather report, would you?"

As Bill tried to catch the elusive butterfly of his breath, Joe answered, "We were told it would be cloudy with a seventy-two per cent chance of anvils."

The alien sniffed. Te licked a finger and held it up in the air. Then, shaking timer's head, te said, "I don't think so. The air feels a lot more like cloudy with an eighty-eight per cent chance of boulders. Thanks for the thought, though!" Then, the alien ran off.

"Still strange," Joe thought out loud, "although feeling less random..."

"Can we get going?" TOM insisted. "Dealing with these aliens is giving me a headache, which is really saying something considering I have no head!"

If he hadn't been an Eternal Detective, Joe would have rolled his eyes. Instead, he asked, "Bill, you good to keep going?"

"Oh – * GASP * – yeah – * GASP * – lungs like a – * PANT * – like a – * PANT * – steel – steel – steel – yeah," Bill was game, but he wasn't fooling anybody.

They made their way through the streets of the city, not quite as quickly as before. A couple of blocks away from the target, Bill seemed his old...chipper may be overstating the case, but certainly his old fully lunged self.

"Whattya you mooks gonna do when we get to the place the aliens are being transported from?" TOM asked.

"Question witnesses," Joe told him.

"Find and...arrest some perpetrators," Bill added.

"The usual police stuff."

"You've seen it a million ti – * OOPH *! –" Bill started, but had the wind knocked out of him by an alien turning a corner in haste.

"Funny running into you, here," the alien commented. "You wouldn't happen to have heard what the weather is going to be like, would you?"

"There are conflicting reports," Joe deadpanned as Bill doubled over, hands on his knees, trying to catch his breath. "Why are you so interested in the weather?"

The alien's jaw looked like it was trying to work its way off its hinge. "Wha – why am I – I mean, well, you know, so I have some idea of what umbrella to leave the house with."

"I'm no expert on alien existence or anything," TOM asked, "but we're on the street – haven't you already left the house?"

The alien looked at TOM. "You trying to cheat at five pin bowling?" te tried to change the subject.

"Don't try to change the subject!" TOM ordered.

Putting a hand on the alien's shoulder, Joe said, "I'm beginning to think these encounters aren't random at all. Are you running ahead of us so you can bump into us and ask about the weather?"

The alien grinned and answered, delighted, "You know the ways of the Audi Enz!"

Taking back his hand, Joe stated: "I'm sorry, but we're in the middle of a serious investigation and we don't have time for alien shenanigans."

"Not even this?" the alien asked. A bowling ball fell out of the sky, bounced off his head and clanked to the ground. The alien swayed back and forth, woozy. Te lifted a foot, hesitated momentarily, then spun around on the foot that was still on the ground, eventually falling over backwards.

"I'm fine!" te, lying on his back on the pavement, wanted everybody to know.

"Nobody cares!" TOM assured him. Not...very assuringly.

Straightening up, Bill said, "Alright, then. Let's...let's get this part of the legwork over with."

Two blocks away stood a brick building with faded gold lettering above its two-floored, double-doored arched entryway that announced it as 'Gooderhamaneggs, Worts & All'. It may, in its youth, have been a whimsy distillery. In its twilight years, it was a dimly lit, seedy structure that had 'evil lair' written all over it. Some buildings age better than others (spackle, the Botox of buildings, might not have helped, but it couldn't have hurt).

"So, what's the plan?" TOM asked. "Recon the outside of the building to see how many exits there are?" Joe and Bill headed towards the door built next to the entryway. "Oh. I get it. Listen by the door to see if any of the culprits are inside. Makes sense." Joe and Bill went through the door and into the building. Disappointed, TOM remarked, "So, the plan is to barge in without any intel and hope for the best?"

"It's gotten us this far," Bill informed it.

They entered a room the size of two football fields, 187 hot tubs or ninety-two Subaru Unimprezzaeds. The largely empty room seemed haunted by the spirits of the machines that had once dominated it. Around the outside of the room, small offices were built on two of its three floors. Along the far wall could be made out what looked to the untrained eye like a metal detector. But being a keen observer, you immediately noticed anomalies in the object's metal detectorness. For one thing, it was two storeys high, which might be useful if ogres passed through it, but, given that ogres don't use metal weapons, would make the whole enterprise suspicious. For another thing, you couldn't see through the object: instead, there were ever-shifting blobs and streaks of colour. For another another thing, it was connected by thick cables to a control panel in front of it. Putting all of this together, you could figure out that the object was not, in fact, a metal detector, but was... Come on. Two storeys high. Control panel. Shifting blobby streaky interior. Where have you seen something like that before? Yes...yes...

"We've found an unlicensed Dimensional Portal^{TM}," Bill announced.

Way to step all over the reader's involvement in the narrative, Bill!

Joe and Bill briskly walked towards the end of the room. Two aliens were standing in the doorway of a cargo container on the floor. Next to the container was a large crane that ended in a huge hand in a white glove that was poised to pick up the container and toss it through the Dimensional Portal^{TM}.

"I was thinking," one of the aliens was saying as te indicated the interior of the cargo container, "of wallpaper with a floral motif."

"Pretty," the other alien responded, "but I was hoping we could go with a full stereo system with amps all along one wall, maybe a pinball machine or two, a couple of guitars or – ooh! – a set of drums! That would give us something to do while we wait for the people on the other side to let us out of the container!"

"That would be...nice. Still, I would prefer a simple couch with a couple of side tables and a television set to watch what the new universe's Netflax has to offer."

The second alien frowned. "We could make that work, I suppose. If the television was wide screen, and we had two kinds of popcorn poppers and a beer fridge!"

"Excuse me," Joe interrupted them. "I like a good discussion of interior decoration as much as the next man, but we are police here on an important mission." To drive the point home, he flashed the aliens a badge which had seemed to spontaneously appear in his hand; after three seconds, it disappeared just as quickly. The aliens identified timerselves as Bob and Bob.

"We don't need police," Bob assured the police.

"Were you brought here by humans you had never met before?" Bill asked timer.

"Complete strangers," Bob confirmed. "Drove up to us on the street in a van. Strong one, too. You could hardly hear the pianos as they bounced off the roof!"

"Un hunh. And did they promise to send you to a universe that was not dying?"

"As a matter of fact, they did."

"And did they assure you that they or their representatives would meet you on the other side and help integrate you into your new homes?"

"You must be psychic. How could you possibly know that?"

Bill nodded to himself. Joe, who was taking notes in a notebook that had been regulation at some time in the distant past, closed it and put it and the pen in his jacket pocket. "I am sorry to have to inform you that you have been cheated," Joe declared. "The people who approached you would herd you into a cargo container which they would send to the new world, where they would leave you until everybody in the container suffocated."

"Suffocated?" Bob gasped.

"You mean, like, to death?" Bob clarified.

Bob and Bob shared a horrified glance. "And they seemed like such nice people!" Bob exclaimed.

"They always do," Joe empathized. "They always do."

"I hope you didn't pay them a lot of money," Bill added.

"Not much, really," Bob replied. "Just ten gold bars each."

"You don't consider ten golds bars much?" Joe asked.

Bob shrugged. "We can manipulate matter with our minds, shape it to be whatever we want it to be. Creating gold is trivial for us. Would you like some?"

"YES!" TOM boomed.

"Thank you for the kind offer," Joe said at the same time, "but we are not allowed to accept gratuities."

"I don't work for them," TOM eagerly continued. "I accept gratuities. Lots and lots of gratuities!"

Ignoring TOM, Joe asked the two aliens for their permission to be transported to Transdimensional Authority headquarters on Earth Prime, where they would work with an etch-a-sketch artist to develop images of the humans who had approached them. Then, they would be processed as refugees.

"The system does work!" Bob exulted.

"And all it cost us was twenty bars of gold!" Bob agreed.

"So, you would hardly notice a couple more," TOM just wouldn't let go of the idea. "Or ten."

Bob touched Joe, reading the structure of his human body and reproducing all of the internal structures in timer's own body. When that was completed, he pronounced that his name was now Angelina von Sauerkraut. Meanwhile, Bob did the same thing with Bill. When that was done, he announced that henceforth he would be known as William Claude Dukenfield.

As the two aliens shimmered out of existence, Joe asked, "You know what this means, Bill?"

"We get to go home?" TOM bitterly interjected. "I'm binge-watching the twenty-second season of *The Baby Bachelor*, and I'm just at the part where Baby Coulton has to figure out which of the three remaining infant girls made a mess in her diaper!"

"No, TOM. I'm sorry, but that's going to have to wait."

"What does this mean, Joe?"

"This means that we're going to have to stake out the joint until –"

"No, no, no, no, no, no, no, no, no!" TOM cried, but did not have a better idea, so yes, yes, yes, yes, yes, yes, yes, yes, yes. The Eternal Detectives were gonna have them a good old-fashioned stakeout!

The Trouble With Wingnut

Episode 5

The Trouble With Breakfast

The Ugly Truth

FADE IN:

ACT ONE

INT. DEN - DAY

It is spacious, with a door leading to the front yard on the right and a door leading to the kitchen on the left. A small closet stands on one side of the front door, a draped window on the other. A set of stairs at the back of the room leads up to a second floor. The room contains a couch in front of which is a table. Next to the couch is a recliner that is about 80% the size of a regular chair.

MARSHA FENSTRUCK (27, waifish) sits on the couch next to ALICE MABENGI (37, black, tall and solidly muscular). Tea and a chocolate cake are on the table.

                    MARSHA
          Waffles.

                    ALICE
          Waffles?

                    MARSHA
          Definitely waffles.

                    ALICE
          Not eggs?

                    MARSHA
          Nope. Eggs are just chickens
          who don't realize it yet.

                    ALICE
Not bacon?

                    MARSHA
Not bacon, either. Where he
comes from, everything goes
better with bacon. It seems
to be a multidimensional
constant.

                    ALICE
Not orange juice?

                    MARSHA
No. That's just oranges that
have been put on an ice floe
and set out to sea.
     (pause)
I find it's best not to think
about everything he says too
much...

                    ALICE
Soooo...waffles.

                    MARSHA
Waffles. More tea?

                    ALICE
If I have any more tea, I may
float out to sea with those
oranges! What is it about
waffles?

                    MARSHA
Their craters.

                    ALICE
The craters?

MARSHA

That's right.

ALICE

In waffles?

MARSHA

That's right.

ALICE

What about the craters in
waffles?

MARSHA

Wingnut wants to know why
they exist. I've tried a
variety of explanations, but
none of them have satisfied
him. He seemed ready to
accept the argument that if
the craters were filled in,
waffles would be pancakes,
and how would that advance
humanity? But, at the last
minute, he shook his head and
called the idea "arioso."

ALICE

Arioso?

MARSHA

His exact words were: "That's
oh so arioso."

ALICE

What does that even mean?

MARSHA

(shrugs)

I looked it up on Wiwipedia.
I think he was saying that
the idea was more melodic
than recitative, but less
formal than an aria. It's
sometimes hard to tell
exactly what Wingnut is
trying to communi –

The front door opens and WINGNUT (four feet
tall, blue skin, no hair anywhere, wearing an
exquisite three piece suit) enters. He leans
out the door to shake the umbrella over the
porch outside even though, from what we can
see, it is a clear, sunny day. Then, folding
the umbrella, he closes the door. Wingnut
casually drops the umbrella in a corner, and
is surprised to find it clatter to the floor
because there is no umbrella stand. Then, he
enters the room.

                    MARSHA (CONTINUING)
          Hi, Wingnut.

                         WINGNUT
          Cara Mia!
               (beat)
          Could you change your name to
          Mia – that line would work
          much better if you did.

                         ALICE
          Hi, Wingnut.

                         WINGNUT
          Hi, Alice. Still haven't
          found your rabbit hole?

                    ALICE
              (uncertain)
     N...no...?

                  WINGNUT
     Ah, well, perhaps you just
     need to fall into the right
     mirror.

                    ALICE
     I beg your pardon?

                   MARSHA
              (hastily)
     How was work, dear?

                  WINGNUT
     Were you able to get more
     Gravol?

                   MARSHA
     No. Sorry. I was on a case
     earlier, and then I had to
     make time for my best friend
     in the world since high
     school.

                    ALICE
     Aww!

                  WINGNUT
     No problem, ma cherie. (I
     don't suppose you would
     change your name to Sherry,
     either?) I will do the best I
     can without it...

Wingnut walks up to the recliner and tightly
clutches the back of the seat.

```
          WINGNUT (CONTINUING)
             (through gritted teeth)
          Okay. I'm ready. Cue. The.
          Flashback.
```

Image goes all wavy and soft-focus.

INT. CHU'S OFFICE - DAY

It is the office of a very successful start-up firm. A *Star Blap* pinball machine sits in one corner. The walls are covered in framed newspapers proclaiming 'The greatest thing since sliced dividends!' and 'The future of the future!' and other triumphant sentiments. The table is glass and the chairs are tasteful space age materials (okay, plastic), and there is a filing cabinet in another corner made entirely out of wood. MADISON CHU (29, Asian, a bit manic) sits behind the desk, talking on his cell phone.

```
                    CHU
          ...Ralph! Ralphie Boy! The
          Ralphmeister! How do you -
          yes, okay, fine, Ralph will
          do. **Raaaalph!** How do you
          think we can incentivize the
          amplification of socially
          pro-active semantic
          repurposed messaging
          assignment if we don't
          prioritize a far-seeing pro-
          social mission statement? I'm
          sorry - am I speaking
          English?
             (beat; shouting)
          **I am speaking English! I -**
```

SOUND: knock on the door.

> CHU
> (to door)
> **My door's always open, even
> when it's shut!**

Wingnut queasily walks in (not having weathered the flashback transition well), closes the door behind him and walks over to Chu's desk, where he patiently stands.

> CHU (CONTINUING)
> (on phone)
> Look. I'm just structurating
> a positive info-space in
> order to maximize return on
> the productive capacity of
> outsourced intellectual
> material. Surely, you see
> that.
> (beat)
> Yeah. Yeah. No. Sure. I don't
> think – well, that's
> certainly one opinion – I –
> listen, I gotta go. Yeah,
> meeting. No, I'm not blowing
> you off, I really do have a –
> (sighs elaborately)

Chu holds out the phone.

> CHU (CONTINUING)
> Could you please say a few
> words...?

Wingnut bends over the desk to speak into the phone.

                         WINGNUT
               A few words.

Chu puts the phone back to his ear as Wingnut
straightens up.

                           CHU
               So, you see – no, I didn't
               change my voice just to get
               you off the phone!
                    (beat)
               I was younger then. Anyway,
               we can continue this
               conversation after work.
               Okay? Okay. Talk to you then,
               Doctor Pathfinder.

Chu hangs up and, putting his phone down on
his empty desk, turns his attention to
Wingnut.

                           CHU
               Therapists! Am I right?

                         WINGNUT
               Erm...

                           CHU
               Wingnut.
               Wingnut   Blotchy.
               Wingnut. Wingnut. Wingnut.
               Wingnutmeg. Wingnuthatch.
               Wingsoveramericanut. Looking
               a little green around the
               gills, there, guy. Worried
               about what I have to say?

                         WINGNUT
               Sure. Let's go with that. You

seem...a bit obsessed with my
name...

CHU
I have always been a sucker
for names that indicate
somebody's parents really
hated them, but no, that's
not why you're here. Don't
you want to know the results
of your seven month and
twelve day review?

WINGNUT
(to audience)
Not six months like every
other company? Sometimes,
rebellion takes the strangest
forms.
(to Chu)
Am I being fired?

CHU
Fired? Hell, no! You've been
a model employee since the
day you joined us! You're
getting a raise!

WINGNUT
Oh. May I...umm...ask a
question?

CHU
I live to answer employee
questions!

WINGNUT
What is it, exactly, that
International Extrusions and

Compactory does?

Chu looks at his phone, then puts it back down.

                    CHU
          Is it four thirty on Thursday
          again? Hunh. Well, as I tell
          you at roughly the same time
          every week, International
          Extrusions and Compactory
          optimizes opportunities for
          consumer engagement in order
          to maximize production
          efficiencies and minimize
          post-purchasing enlightenment
          remorse. What's so hard to
          understand about that?

                    WINGNUT
          Everything!

                    CHU
               (smiling)
          Well, in a complex and fast-
          moving technological
          environment such as ours,
          nobody is expected to
          understand every little
          detail...

                    WINGNUT
          One little detail! I would be
          happy understanding a hint of
          a detail!

                    CHU
          The important thing is that
          you are doing a terrific job.

                    WINGNUT
     But I don't know what I'm
     doing!

                     CHU
     Just keep up the good work.
     You'll get it eventually.
     What is it that self-help
     charlatans always say? Fake
     it until you break it!

Image goes all wavy and soft-focus.

                    WINGNUT
          (over)
     Wait! I didn't have a chance
     to ground myself!

INT. DEN - DAY

As before. Wingnut looks like he's about to
either throw up or fall over (or possibly
both).

                    MARSHA
          (singing)
     We're only making plans for
     Nigel. We only want what's
     best for him. We're only -

                    ALICE
     What are you doing?

                    MARSHA
     Helping Wingnut with his
     flashback-induced vertigo.
     Sing with me.
          (singing)

We're only making plans for
Nigel.

      MARSHA AND ALICE
       (singing together)
We only want what's best for
him. We're only making plans
for Nigel. He has a future in
British Steel. And if young
Nigel says he's happy, he
must be happy, he must be
happy, he must be happy in
his —

Wingnut shakes his head and straightens up.

         WINGNUT
Thanks. I needed that.

         ALICE
Does this happen often?

         WINGNUT
Not really. It hasn't
happened since the pilot.

         ALICE
Pilot?

         MARSHA
      (confiding)
It's a religious thing.

         ALICE
Oh.

Wingnut comes around the chair and flumps
down in it.

The Ugly Truth

                    WINGNUT
          This is all a bit...domestic,
          don't you think? Me coming
          home to find you sharing tea
          with your bestie and asking
          me about how my day went?

                    MARSHA
          Is domestic a bad thing?

                    WINGNUT
          Weeelll...I think we could
          use an injection of social
          commentary right about now.

                    MARSHA
          Social commentary?
          Wingnut   Blotchy,
          what are you –

Something smashes through the front window
and falls to the floor. Marsha and Alice
react in shock and surprise. Wingnut doesn't
flinch.

                    WINGNUT
          Now it's a party!

END OF ACT ONE

ACT TWO

INT. DEN – DAY (LATER)

Wingnut and Marsha are standing near the
couch, talking to OFFICER SMEDLEY (44, tall,
broadly built, with a face so hangdog you are
constantly amazed that it doesn't hit the

floor), who is taking notes. In the
background, ANDREAS FISHBEIN (32, slender,
dressed all in black) is photographing
something on the floor with a phone set into
the front of an old-fashioned box camera,
prowling around it like a tiger preparing to
pounce on a Hyundai.

                    FISHBEIN
          Yeah, baby. Okay, baby. More,
          baby. You can give me more.
          Yes. Yes. Oh, yes!

                    OFFICER SMEDLEY
          So, let me get this straight.
          Somebody threw a brick
          through your window. Tied to
          the brick was a Witch Barbie
          with its eyes gouged out. Is
          that correct?

                    WINGNUT
          Correct. Horribly correct.

                    MARSHA
             (shrugs)
          I saw worse things in junior
          high. Hell, I **did** worse
          things in junior high!

                    OFFICER SMEDLEY
          All due respect, Ms.
          Fenstruck, unless that's
          relevant, it isn't really,
          umm, relevant.

                    MARSHA
          I come from the Dirk Gently
          School of Holistic

Detectiving. One of the first things they teach us is that everything is relevant.

> OFFICER SMEDLEY
> Un hunh. Can you think of anybody who would do this?

Wingnut feels his scalp.

> WINGNUT
> Not off the top of my head...

> OFFICER SMEDLEY
> No enemies...?

> WINGNUT
> Weeellll...33 per cent of the human population according to an Ipsos-Factos poll conducted last Tuesday that had a plus or minus three point two margin of error nine times out of ten –

> MARSHA
> Wingnut can be very details-oriented when he puts his mind to it. That's one of the many reasons I love him.

> WINGNUT
> – but nobody specific, no.

> OFFICER SMEDLEY
> Anything you can think of that might help? Anything at all?

                    MARSHA
Officer Smedley?

                    OFFICER SMEDLEY
Yes?

                    MARSHA
What happened to your finger?

                    OFFICER SMEDLEY
My finger?

                    MARSHA
Specifically the thumb on
your left hand.

There is a bandage on Officer Smedley's
thumb.

                    WINGNUT
Marsha can be very observant
when she puts her mind to it.
That's one of the many
reasons I love her.

                    OFFICER SMEDLEY
I don't see how that's any of
your concern.

                    WINGNUT
Embarrassed you cut yourself
shaving? I don't have to
shave — don't have any body
hair **to** shave — but, if I
did, I'm sure I would be
cutting my thumb all the
time. And my elbow. And both
my shins. And my lower
intestine. And —

MARSHA
The thing is, there was blood
on the Barbie.

WINGNUT
Shrimp blood?

MARSHA
Don't strain yourself, dear.

WINGNUT
Sorry.

MARSHA
There were bloodstains on the
doll. Whoever gouged its eyes
out must have cut himself
while doing so.

OFFICER SMEDLEY
Interesting coincidence.

MARSHA
Is it, though? The third
thing I learned at the Dirk
Gently School of Holistic
Detectiving is that there is
no such thing as coincidence.

WINGNUT
What were the first two
things?

MARSHA
Later.

OFFICER SMEDLEY
Are you accusing me of
throwing the brick through

your window?

Wingnut's eyes widen.

> WINGNUT
> Sweetie, a word?

He nods to a far corner of the room and moves there. Marsha reluctantly follows.

> WINGNUT (CONTINUING)
> Are you accusing Officer
> Smedley of throwing the brick
> through our window?

> MARSHA
> Yes.

> WINGNUT
> You can't do that!

> MARSHA
> Why not?

> WINGNUT
> It's only the second act! You
> can't reveal the culprit
> until the end of the third
> act!

> MARSHA
> Now, sweetie, what did we
> agree upon?

> WINGNUT
> (reciting like a bad
> child)
> I take care of the comedy and
> you take care of the mystery.

                    MARSHA
          Remind me to give you a
          cookie when we're done.

They move back to where Officer Smedley is
patiently waiting for them.

                    MARSHA (CONTINUING)
          Officer Smedley, why would
          somebody do this?

                    OFFICER SMEDLEY
          It's too early in the case to
          —

                    MARSHA
          Isn't it likely that whoever
          did this was trying to scare
          a woman who was having a
          relationship with an alien?

                    OFFICER SMEDLEY
              (smirking)
          The first thing I was taught
          at the police academy was not
          to formulate opinions on a
          case before all of the
          evidence presented itself.

                    WINGNUT
          Which raises an important
          question.

                    OFFICER SMEDLEY
          What would that be, sir?

                    WINGNUT
          What ever happened to Steve
          Guttenberg?

                    MARSHA
        Officer Smedley, how do you
        feel about human women having
        relationships with aliens?

                    OFFICER SMEDLEY
        The third...or maybe fourth
        thing I was taught at the
        police academy was never to
        allow my personal feelings to
        interfere with a case.

Officer Smedley closes his notebook with a
sharp * CRACK *! Wingnut gracefully jumps a
foot off the ground and floats back to earth.

                    OFFICER SMEDLEY (CONTINUING)
        Thank you for the
        information. If we find out
        who did this, I will let you
        know. I do have to warn you,
        though, that these types of
        crimes are difficult to
        solve.

                    MARSHA
        Yadda yadda yadda...

                    WINGNUT
        Are you legally allowed to
        say that?

Officer Smedley heads to the door.

                    OFFICER SMEDLEY
        Come on, Fishbein. We're done
        here.

The Ugly Truth

FISHBEIN
Just a couple more photos,
Smedley. You want your report
to dazzle the brass, don't
you?

OFFICER SMEDLEY
Did you do the low light/high
contrast shots that everybody
in the station, and for
several blocks around, knows
you love so much?

FISHBEIN
Of course.

OFFICER SMEDLEY
(dour)
Let the bedazzlement begin.

Officer Smedley walks out the front door.
Fishbein reluctantly follows, snapping
photographs all the way.

MARSHA
(to herself)
He's not going to get away
with this. One way or
another, I will make sure
that he doesn't get away with
this!

MUSIC: dramatic stab.

END OF ACT TWO

WINGNUT
(over)
Ooh! Spooky music!

ACT THREE

INT. PARKING GARAGE - DAY

Marsha is pacing back and forth between a
pair of pylons in an underground parking
garage. She is wearing a trenchcoat.

> DETECTIVE GROGAN
> (off)
> I thought we said no
> trenchcoats.

DETECTIVE GROGAN (63, short, silver hair,
still powerfully broad-shouldered) walks up
to Marsha.

> MARSHA
> Sorry - I couldn't resist.

Detective Grogan waves a hand at the garage.

> DETECTIVE GROGAN
> I already agreed to meeting
> here. I told you, we didn't
> have to - a Dunkinses would
> have been fine.

> MARSHA
> A donut place? Seriously?
> Could it be any more of a
> cliche?

Detective Grogan looks around meaningfully.

> MARSHA (CONTINUING)
> This isn't a cliche!
> It's...dramatic
> embellishment. Have you no

artistry in your soul?
    (sighs)
Forget about it. Did you find
out anything?

                DETECTIVE GROGAN
            (nodding)
Yeah. You were right. Since
the aliens started coming to
Earth Prime, Officer Smedley
has had 23 complaints lodged
against him for speciesist
behaviour. One time, he
described how he would like
to use an alien as a bowling
ball. Another time, he gave
an alien a ticket for
speeding and reckless
driving, and Smedley had to
go five blocks away from the
crash scene to find one!

                MARSHA
How is this guy still on the
force?

                DETECTIVE GROGAN
            (defensive)
Hey! He's been reprimanded
seven times!

                MARSHA
Reprimanded.

                DETECTIVE GROGAN
You get enough of those in
your jacket and there's no
way you'll advance up through
the ranks!

> MARSHA
> If we could get a DNA test of
> the blood on the brick, I'm
> sure it would be a match with
> —

> DETECTIVE GROGAN
> (shaking his head)
> No need. It fits his profile
> — you wouldn't have any
> trouble convincing anybody
> that Smedley threw that brick
> through your window.

> MARSHA
> Then, I should file a
> complaint.

> DETECTIVE GROGAN
> Absolutely! Every reprimand
> counts.

> MARSHA
> (dark)
> Reprimand my ass. I want real
> action...

INT. OFFICE CUBICLE – DAY

Wingnut sits on a chair in a bare cubicle. He
is wearing a pair of Augmented Reality
goggles (ARggles). With his right hand, he
taps and wipes the air. With his left hand,
he leisurely scrolls something.

INT. OFFICE CUBICLE – DAY (ARRGLES VIEW)

Two windows are open. On the left, a document
with dense language is slowly scrolling down.

On the other, two catapults are being used to
launch crustaceans at balloons in the shape
of anteaters. Avatars of Wingnut's hands are
manipulating what is on the windows. Behind
and around the two windows, the cubicle can
be seen; pinned to the walls are postcards of
city streets on Earth Prime 4-6-4-0-8-9 dash
Omega with aliens holding tiny umbrellas as
large objects fall towards and around them,
and a mobile of boulders of various sizes
hanging by a cord that goes out of the top of
the screen. On the desk is a mug that reads
in green lettering: "Kiss me, I'm Cyrus."
SOUND: catapult zings, rubber squeaks and
exploding balloons.

> WINGNUT
> (off, muttering)
> ...coefficient of the
> Grelbner constant requires
> hyper-modification of the –
> **die, evil aardvarks! Die!**
> **Die! Die! Die! Di –**

In the upper right corner, a red circle
appears. Under the circle are the words:
"Incoming call: Samantha Sporren." SOUND:
telephone ringing.

> WINGNUT (CONTINUING)
> (off)
> Oh, butterballs!

Wingnut stabs the air with two fingers and
the game immediately becomes a spreadsheet.
An empty spreadsheet, but it's something.
Then, he pushes the red button. A window
opens that features a close-up of the eyes
and nose of SAMANTHA SPORREN (37, mousy, not

somebody you would think of as 'management material').

                    SPORREN
          Hi, Wingnut.

                    WINGNUT
               (off)
          What can I do for you,
          Supervisor Sam?

                    SPORREN
          Just checking in to see how
          your analysis of the
          Feigenbaum Schemiel is coming
          along.

                    WINGNUT
               (off)
          Yeah, about that...

                    SPORREN
          I don't need your whole
          thesis - if you could just
          share some of the numbers
          with me...

                    WINGNUT
               (off)
          Oh...ah...sure. Seven.
          Twenty-seven, One thousand
          six hundred and...umm, seven.
          Forty-two, of course. Then,
          another seven. Fourteen
          and...forty-nine.

                    SPORREN
          Hmm...interesting. So, if I
          understand what you're

getting at correctly, the
transmogrification of
gendered marketplace
ascendance is dependent on
how well the applicable
freeform massification
develops. Does that sound
about right?

              WINGNUT
   (off)
Weeelllll, it's too early to
make any firm conclusions,
really...

              SPORREN
I understand. Still, this is
very promising. Keep up the
good work!

Sporren's image vanishes. Wingnut stabs the
screen with two fingers and the game
reappears, but he doesn't unpause it. After a
couple of seconds, he stabs the screen with
three fingers, causing the game screen to
disappear. With a sigh, Wingnut enlarges the
document and starts scrolling through it in
earnest.

INT. DEN - DAY

Marsha and Alice are sitting on the couch.
Tea and a chocolate cake are on the table.

              MARSHA
  Jello.

              ALICE
  Jello?

MARSHA

Jello.

ALICE

Who could possibly object to
Jello?

MARSHA

An alien from another
universe.

ALICE

Well, yes, but - why?

MARSHA

You know the way Jello
jiggles?

ALICE

Yes?

MARSHA

Wingnut thinks it's laughing
at him.

ALICE

Laughing?

MARSHA

Laughing. At him. Wingnut
refuses to eat anything that
appears to be having fun at
his expense.

ALICE

That's...almost reasonable.

MARSHA

In a way...

> (beat)
More cake?

                    ALICE
Ahh, I'd love some, but if I
have another piece, I'll
start to jiggle, and I
wouldn't want Wingnut to
think my stomach was laughing
at him!

Marsha and Alice titter at the thought.

                    ALICE (CONTINUING)
Did you hear? Officer Stan
Smedley was put on leave
while being investigated for
anti-alien behaviour.

                    MARSHA
> (casual)
Oh?

                    ALICE
Apparently, he prank called
people saying just the worst
things about aliens, then,
when they complained to the
police, **he** showed up to
investigate!

                    MARSHA
Imagine that.

                    ALICE
That's right. One of the
victims complained to the
AHA! Foundation, which
threatened to bring a lawsuit

against Metro Police and the
state unless something was
done.

                MARSHA
Good of them.

                ALICE
Say, wasn't the policeman who
was investigating the brick
thrown through your front
window named Smedley?

                MARSHA
I believe he was.

                ALICE
And now that I think about
it, isn't Wingnut good
friends with the founder of
the AHA! Foundation?

                MARSHA
They lived in the same
neighbourhood on their home
Earth, yeah.

                ALICE
That's quite a coincidence,
don't ya think?

                MARSHA
Oh, yeah. Quite a coinci –

The front door opens and WINGNUT enters. He
leans out the door to shake the umbrella over
the porch outside. Then, folding the
umbrella, he closes the door. Wingnut drops
the umbrella in a corner, and is surprised to

find it clatter to the floor because there is
no umbrella stand. Then, he enters the room.

                    MARSHA (CONTINUING)
          Hi, Wingnut.

                    WINGNUT
          Bellisima!

                    ALICE
          Hi, Wingnut.

                    WINGNUT
          I don't suppose you would
          consider changing your name
          to Bella? It would make the
          joke land better.

                    MARSHA
          Sorry. My name is on all my
          business cards.

                    WINGNUT
          Makes sense. Hello, Alice. I
          heard on the radio I should
          ask you something, but if the
          singer said what, it has
          totally slipped my mind.

                    ALICE
          That's...okay. If you
          remember what the question
          was, you can always ask me
          later.

                    MARSHA
          How was work, sweetie?

                    WINGNUT
Complete nonsense. I'm loving
it!

                    MARSHA
That's great. Would you like
some tea and dessert?

                    WINGNUT
As long as it's not Jell –
        (pause)
You know, this is all very
domestic. I think the
injection of a little social
commentary would be
appropriate right about now.
        (pause)
I said this is all very
domestic. Now would be a good
time for a little **social
commentary.**
        (pause)
Very **domestic!** Time for
**social commentary!
Helloooooo!**
        (pause)
If anybody wants me, I'm
going up to the bedroom to
have a little lie down...

INT. BEDROOM – NIGHT

Marsha and Wingnut sleep in separate beds.
Marsha is reading an Ellery Queen novel by
the light of a lamp on her nightstand.
Wingnut is manipulating the keys of an
invisible keyboard. In one dark corner of the
room sits an Orgasmatron.

The Ugly Truth

MARSHA
Well, that was quite a day.

WINGNUT
(distracted)
Every day is quite a day, if
only by definition.

MARSHA
I meant -

WINGNUT
(angry)
The Audi Enz pan it!

Wingnut reaches into his imaginary typewriter
and separates a pair of keys.

MARSHA
(concerned)
Honey?

WINGNUT
I hate it when the keys jam!
So annoying!

MARSHA
Mmm...
(beat)
I think I may have found the
solution to your waffle
crater conundrum...

Wingnut continues typing, but looks at her.

WINGNUT
(eager)
You have? How...?

                    MARSHA
        I looked it up on Wiwipedia.

                    WINGNUT
        Wiwipedia. That's...

                    MARSHA
        I know, right? So. The
        craters in waffles? They're
        there to hold syrup.

                    WINGNUT
        To hold syrup?

Without taking his eyes off Marsha, Wingnut
unjams a key jam (as before) and goes back to
typing.

                    MARSHA
        If you think of a waffle in
        terms of geography, the
        craters are kind of like
        lakes. Without the craters,
        the syrup would run off the
        sides, leaving everybody in
        the middle effectively living
        in a desert.

                    WINGNUT
        Living in a dessert?

                    MARSHA
        That's what I said.

                    WINGNUT
        That's brilliant! Thank you!
        This is another of the many
        reasons I love you so much.

```
                    MARSHA
          Awww...


BLACKOUT

CLOSING CREDITS

                    WINGNUT
             (over)
             You're willing to make up
             something so ridiculous just
             to put my mind at rest!
```

"Aliens Helping Aliens Help Line. How may I help you?"

"Hi. My name is Frederica   Toastenjam. I –"

"This is an anonymous help line. We don't need your name."

"Oh." PAUSE "Should I come over and hit you over the head with a blunt object – a hammer, say, or a rhinoceros – in order to cause you to lose your memory?"

"It's very kind of you to offer – I appreciate how far you're willing to go to respect our privacy policy. However, my memory isn't very good at the best of times, Frederica, so we probably don't have to worry. What can I help you with?"

"I met this person after I emigrated to Earth Prime – I believe he is known as 'a man'."

"Yes, this whole two-gendered thing can be very confusing."

"Oh, no, that's not what I need help with. I understand that men and women have different private parts, and that

149

men's private parts make them omnipotent and omniscient and that's why women have to do everything they say, no matter how dumb it may seem to an objective observer. It's just common sense, really."

"Oh, so how can I help you?"

"Well, Ton – I mean, the man...and I have been getting closer and closer in the months since we met. Like, romantically involved close. Know what I mean?"

"Indeed. And you are wondering how a relationship between sentient beings from different species will go?"

"Not really. Many human beings have a low tolerance for difference and have been sending us obscene Victoria Day cards and death threats – sometimes obscene Victoria Day cards **with** death threats. They have some weird celebrations in this reality. Others have been wonderful about it. Our species makes fun of the relationship, but they make fun of every relationship – it's what we do. So, you take the good with the bad, right?"

"Right. But..."

"A couple of weeks ago, my human asked me to move in with him."

"That's a big step for a relationship; living with somebody is different than living separately, even if you see each other every day. Naturally, you want some tips on how to make such a relationship work. As it happens, I –"

"Tell me about it! We've set boundaries and have worked out protocols for when we disagree. So far, we've had one or two minor disputes, but nothing that would come close to putting a strain on the relationship. The man has a bee in his nuthatch about tooth brushes, for instance, which I totally don't get, but which I will respect for the sake of our romance. On the other hand, he doesn't like it when I juggle chainsaws...which I also don't get. Every girl needs a hobby. And this one kind of reminds me of home. But to keep the peace, I keep the chainsaws in the garage and only indulge when the man is not around. We find that there is no problem so great that it cannot be solved with love and a little harmless deception."

"Do you need help?"

"Yes."

"You know this is a help line, right?"

"I know that."

"Then, could we please get to the reason for your call?"

"I would if you would stop helpfully interrupting me."

"Erm."

"Soon after I moved in with my sweetie, I noticed that he had a lot of what I believe humans call 'hair care products'. Lots of them. Shampoos. Conditioners. Gels. Styling mouses. Mousses. Meeces? (Oh, Ignatz!) More shampoos. That's not to mention the shaving creams and aftershaves and disinfectants and bandages. What's up with all of that?"

"Aah. Finally. We get a lot of questions about hair care products here, so I can actually answer this one with a fair degree of certainty. Human beings are vain about their appearance. Not exquisite three piece suit vain (even those who can afford them mostly wear casual clothing – albeit expensive designer casual – to show their disdain for the ostentation) – no, this is a different kind of vanity. Think of humans' obsession with hair as...as the grooming of the mild gracklensnozzle. As I'm sure you know from boring nature documentaries back home that nobody ever watched, the mild gracklensnozzle constantly cleans its colourful feathers in order to attract a mate, using harunga beetles as brushes and the sap of the jubjub tree as shampoo."

"Of course I know that. I ignored boring nature documentaries back home as much as the next person. But using the sap of the jubjub tree makes sense, herontologically if not strictly biologically. Using chemical goop seems...wrong somehow."

"Do you love your human?"

"With all my spleen."

"Then I can suggest a simple exercise that should help you get over this. Whenever the subject of hair comes up, substitute a different word for it. Words that have worked for our people in the past include: antebellum, spasmodic and keggler."

"So, instead of thinking about, say, a hair brush, I would think about a spasmodic brush? Or instead of hair conditioner, keggler conditioner?"

"Exactly. Then, periodically, you can say it out loud, confusing your human, and come up with ever more elaborate excuses for why you used the 'wrong' word. This solution to your problem comes Audi Enz approved."

"Yes! Yes, I think that could work! Thank you, help line voice on the phone! Thank you very much!"

"Oh, no need to thank me, ma'am. It's what we're here for."

Flagging Interest

by FREDERICA VON McTOAST-HYPHEN, Alternate Reality News Service Pop Culture Writer

Vesampuccerians love their flag. What's not to love? It's got everything: stars and stripes and...more stars and other stripes and...and...and a moose. (The moose, a tribute to the brave men who lost their lives in the Uncivil War Battle of Kicking Butte, is invisible, but its spirit lives on!).

Vesampuccerians are so proud of their flag, they display it everywhere. On bed sheets. On coffee mugs. On underwear. On satellite delivery booster rock –"

"Unfair! Beware! I'm going to stop you right there!" interrupted Foxindehenhaus News purported person Nippon-Tucker Carlsonandotter. "Over the flag I get positively mushy, but you should never wear one on your tushie! What would you expect, but more Dumbopratic disrespect for our country's nimble symbol!"

He's not called the poet of propaganda for nothing. (In fact, Foxindehenhaus pays him a small fortune.) So, patriodiots like Carlsonandotter might be surprised to learn that 87% of Vesampuccerian flags are made in China.

"What?" Carlsonandotter let loose one of his patented knock bats off walls five miles away shrieks. "I don't believe that!"

It gets worse: China uses refugees from Earth Prime 4-6-4-0-8-9 dash Omega as slave labour to make the flags.

"It can't be true! I don't believe you!" Carlsonandotter peeled the paint off his studio wall for the third time this week (you would have thought they would have learned to put baffling up, instead). "I mean, if what you're saying's true, the government hid it, and you know what that means: **the Dumboprats did it!**"

According to Presidential historian and trouser press aficionado Michael Beschbefordatloess, Reduhblicans were the primary force behind the deregulation of corporate Vesampucceri which allowed companies to move production overseas. Exhibiting their best 'go along to get along' approach to being in power (while it may work well in personal relationships, it's deadly to forming a functional government...and, come to think of it, it doesn't really work all that well in personal relationships, either), the Dumboprats merely did nothing to roll the changes back when they got into office.

"Slave is such a harsh term," responded Chinese Ambassadoress to Canada Ming-Washanana Wen. "We prefer to think of the alien refugees in Chinese prisons as involuntary labourers. When we think of them at all. Which can be a real downer. So, we avoid it as much as possible. Oh, wait – did I say prisons? I meant fun camps. The alien refugees are involuntary labourers at fun camps. My apologies. I had to have my cat put down by a Don Ricklesmielmo impersonator because it was getting a swelled head, and I'm still not over the laughter."

"China is being really pooh-headed about this," commented human Anastasia La Bombon, Vice President, Strange Inhalations and Public Relations of the Aliens Helping Aliens (AHA!) Foundation on Earth Prime. "And, I'm not talking about the loveable bear! When countries agree to take in refugees, the implication is that they will treat them well. What China is doing is the opposite of good faith – it's bad...science!"

Ambassadoress Ming-Washanana argued that the refugees were treated very well. "They get a square meal a day (we use gelatin molds and a protractor) and all the exercise they could hope to want," she pointed out. "If we treated them any better, they would die of sheer delight!"

As opposed to exhaustion?

"Canadians are not supposed to be so cynical," Ambassadoress Ming-Washanana responded. "Are you sure you're not Vesampuccerian?"

"China will not allow us to monitor what they are doing with the refugees they take in,"
Algernon Pendragon, Vice President, Finance and Contrivance of the AHA! Foundation, one of the first aliens who refugeed to Canada, quickly added. "We mostly know of the horrible conditions in the prison factories thanks to messages smuggled out of China by itinerant goose ticklers."

Pendragon shared some of the messages with me. In one, a refugee wrote: "Dear [NAME FIELD]. I am a Nigerian prince forced to flee his". In another, a refugee wrote: "Porridge had raisins. Yuck. At least, I think they were raisins. Do raisins crunch? At least I got 16 hours of exercise on the flag production line." In a third, a refugee wrote: "Now we see the injustice inherent in the system! Elp! Elp! I'm bein' repressed!"

While President-reject Ronald McDruhitmumpf moaned about all of the traitors who would not help him find the votes to win the recent election, President-elect Joe Bidenhisbeeswax empathized all over the place. "I have been on the receiving end of an alien pie," he remarked. "It's not pretty. I won't kid you – the incident's given me nightmares. Still. China is engaging in the worst kind of exploitation of vulnerable sentient beings. I call on the McDruhitmumpf administration to take action to ensure that it stops."

Calling on an administration that tried to build a border wall to keep refugees from another dimension out of the country to help refugees in China seems like a fool's errand. On the other hand, this being the United States of Vesampucceri, the world's leading idiotocracy (if I have to explain what the term means, you should probably be living there yourself), anything is possible.

Only time will tell what the lame duck (can somebody get that quacker a cane!) President does. However, discretion being the better part of journalism, it's probably for the best that I decided not to mention the other product made in the flag factory: Uncle Samantha bobble-head dolls!

Being a Full and Complete Record of the Diary of Martini Frobisher During His Historic Campaign for Member of Canadian Parliament

CAMPAIGN DIARY, DAY EIGHT

DEAR DIARY,

CANVASSING.

CAMPAIGN DIARY, DAY NINE

DEAR DIAROONY,

SORRY. FORCE OF HABIT.

DEAR DIARY,

CANVASSING.

CAMPAIGN DIARY, DAY TEN

DEAR DIARY,

CANVASSING.

CAMPAIGN DIARY, DAY ELEVEN

DEAR DIARY,

TODAY, WE HELD A RALLY, JUST LIKE A GROWN-UP POLITICAL CAMPAIGN.

IDEALLY, YOU WOULD WANT TO HOLD A POLITICAL RALLY IN A STADIUM OR LARGE CONVENTION CENTRE, SOME PLACE WHICH HELD A LOT OF PEOPLE. YEAH, WE COULDN'T DO THAT. THE REPRESENTATIVE FOR THE SCOTIABANK SADDLEDOME LAUGHED AT US. THE VOLLEYDOME WOULDN'T RETURN OUR CALLS. THE REPRESENTATIVE OF MCMAHON STADIUM LAUGHED AT US, THEN CALLED US SOMETHING I WAS TOLD POLITE PEOPLE SHOULD NOT REPEAT (I KNOW HOW SENSITIVE YOU CAN BE, DIARY, AND I WANTD TO SPARE YOU THE MORTIFICATION. YOU'RE WELCOME). THE MESSAGE ON THE MARKIN MACPHAIL CENTRE SAID THAT ANYBODY WHO WANTED TO BOOK THE FACILITY SHOULD LEAVE THEIR NAME AND NUMBER EXCEPT FOR ANYBODY CALLING ON BEHALF OF THE MARTINI FROBISHER CAMPAIGN. THAT WAS HURTFULLY SPECIFIC. THE REPRESENTATIVE OF THE GEORGE BLUNDON + OPTIMIST ARENA LAUGHED AT US, THEN CALLED US SOMETHING POLITE PEOPLE SHOULD NOT REPEAT (VERY PESSIMISTICALLY, I THOUGHT), AND THEN SUGGESTED WE DO SOMETHING THAT IS PROBABLY ANATOMICALLY IMPOSSIBLE (ALTHOUGH HUMAN BODIES ARE STILL NEW TO ME, SO I MAY BE MISSING SOME ESSENTIAL DETAIL IN THIS EXCHANGE). THE REPRESENTATIVE OF THE GLENMORE ATHLETIC PARK APOLOGIZED THAT HE WAS DROWNING IN PAPERWORK AND DIDN'T HAVE TIME TO PROPERLY RESPOND TO OUR REQUEST, BUT IF HE HAD, HE WOULD HAPPILY HAVE LAUGHED, CALLED US SOMETHING UNREPEATABLE AND SUGGESTED WE DO SOMETHING PROBABLY ANATOMICALLY IMPOSSIBLE — WOULD WE LIKE TO CALL BACK SOME TIME NEXT WEEK? WE THANKED

HIM FOR HIS TIME AND SAID WE WOULD GET BACK
TO HIM (WE WERE BEING POLITE: THE CAMPAIGN
HAD ALREADY STARTED AND WE DIDN'T HAVE A LOT
OF TIME TO BE DISCOURAGED FROM ORGANIZING A
RALLY).

WHEN WE DISCUSSED THE ISSUE WITH OUR
CAMPAIGN STAFF, VOLUNTEER BRETT ("THE BEST
YOU'RE GONNA GET!") SAID HE WAS FRIENDS WITH
THE MANAGER OF A LOCAL RESTAURANT AND COULD
PROBABLY GET US SPACE THERE. I EAGERLY AGREED.
IN RETROSPECT, I PROBABLY SHOULD HAVE ASKED
FOR DETAILS, BUT I WAS NEW AT THIS AND...LET'S
JUST LEAVE IT AT I WAS NEW AT THIS, OKAY? THE
RALLY WAS TO BE HELD AT A BOB SO TASTY FAST
FOOD RESTAURANT. BECAUSE IT WAS A SMALL
FRANCHISE AND SEATING WAS LIMITED (THEIR MOTTO
WAS: "YOU'LL LOVE OUR REALLY DOUGHY YEAST –
DRIVE-THROUGH ORDERS UPSET US LEAST!"), THE
RALLY HAD TO BE HELD IN ITS PARKING LOT.

TODAY WAS THE DAY! WHEN I WASN'T HITTING THE
CANVAS, I SPENT THE LAST WEEK PROMOTING THE
EVENT. FOR EXAMPLE, I WENT ON SEE-FIX-ELLE
FEMME (CFXL-FM) WHERE TWO VERY NICE RADIO
ANNOUNCERS, HEATHER AND BUZZ, PLAYED A TRICK
ON ME INVOLVING COWBELLS, THE CODEX SINAITICUS
AND A BOX OF PINECONES. DEFINITELY MY KIND OF
PEOPLE. UNFORTUNATELY, I WAS HAVING SO MUCH
FUN GETTING GARY GLITTER OUT OF HEATHER'S
HAIR THAT I FORGOT TO MENTION THE RALLY. OR,
JUST A COUPLE OF DAYS AGO, I WAS INTERVIEWED
BY A REPORTER FOR THE CALGARY HERALD NAMED
NEWSROOM STAFF. I TOLD MISTER STAFF THAT I
WAS RUNNING ON PLATFORM SHOES. THE INTERVIEW
WENT DOWNHILL FROM THERE. I MEAN, IT WAS A
VERY SLALOM OCCASION. THE ARTICLE IN THIS
MORNING'S PAPER INTRODUCED ME TO A WHOLE LOT
OF INSULTS THAT I HAD NOT HEARD BEFORE (I WILL
NEVER LOOK AT GUACAMOLE THE SAME WAY AGAIN),
BUT IT DID MENTION THAT WE WOULD BE HOLDING A

RALLY. IN THE SECOND TO LAST PARAGRAPH. AND IT DIDN'T SPECIFY WHEN. OR WHERE. I DECIDED NOT TO SWAT THE DETAILS (THOSE THINGS CAN COME THICKER THAN GNATS!) AND CALL IT A WIN.

WHEN WE GOT TO THE VENUE, DERRICK (BRETT'S MANAGER FRIEND) TOLD US THAT HE HAD FORGOTTEN THAT WE WERE COMING, BUT NOT TO WORRY: TOM HEFLINGER AND STACI GRUBOVITCH WERE JUST FINISHING THEIR BACONADIAN BURGERS WITH THREE QUARTERS OF THE TRIMMINGS, AND THEY WOULD BE DRIVING OUT OF THE PARKING LOT BEFORE OUR RALLY BEGAN. "IT LOOKS LIKE A HOT DATE," DERRICK CONFIDED, "SO I DON'T THINK THEY'LL BE HANGING AROUND!"

WITH A SIGH, AMAROSA STARTED DIRECTING THE VOLUNTEERS TO SET UP. WE HADN'T HAD TIME TO RENT A PLATFORM, SO GLENDA AND DOROTHY SET DOWN SOME PACKING CRATES AND GLUED THEM TOGETHER. WE COULDN'T GET A MICROPHONE AND AMP, EITHER; FORTUNATELY, GORD WAS IN A GARAGE BAND AND AGREED TO LET US USE HIS. UNFORTUNATELY, IT WAS ON THE CONDITION THAT HE BE THE ONLY PERSON WHO TOUCHED THEM. WE HAD A BANNER THAT READ:

"MARTINI   FROBISHER FOR PARLIAMINT!" I THOUGHT IT WAS A TASTY PROPOSITION. HOWEVER, THE BANNER HAD BEEN ROLLED UP BEFORE THE PAINT HAD DRIED: THE WORDS HAD STREAKED WORSE THAN MASCARA ON THE FACE OF THE FRONT MAN FOR AN ALICE COOPER TRIBUTE BAND.

"HEY MISTER," A SIX YEAR-OLD MOPPET TUGGED AT MY PANTS LEG.

IMAGINING WHAT HE WOULD LOOK LIKE WHEN HE HAD FULLY GROWN INTO A MOP, I RESPONDED: "YES?"

"ARE YOU SETTING UP A CIRCUS?"

"NOT AS SUCH, NO."

DISGUSTEDLY STALKING AWAY, HE HISSED: "THEN WHY ARE YOU FERKING WASTING MY FERKING TIME? ASSHOLE."

THEY GROW UP SO FAST, DON'T THEY?

BY FOUR O'CLOCK, WE WERE READY TO BEGIN. A DOZEN PEOPLE MILLED ABOUT, A COUPLE SITTING ON THE HOOD OF THE BLUE HYUNDAI THAT WAS STILL PARKED IN THE LOT. STANDING NEXT TO THE MAKESHIFT STAGE, GORD HELD THE MICROPHONE IN FRONT OF MY FACE. "HELLO, EVERYBODY. THANK YOU FOR COMING TO –"

"YOU HAVE TO CHECK THE MIC LEVELS FIRST," GORD INTERRUPTED.

"THE MIC LEVELS SOUND FINE TO ME," I TOLD HIM.

"IT'S A TRADITION."

"I REALLY DON'T THINK IT'S NEC –"

GORD PULLED THE MICROPHONE AWAY FROM ME AND SAID INTO IT: "CHECK ONE. CHECK TWO. IS THIS MIC ON? CHECK ONE. CHECK TWO. HUT! HUT! HUT!" SATISFIED, HE PUT THE MICROPHONE BACK IN FRONT OF ME. "OKAY, NOW YOU CAN GO."

WHO WAS I TO QUESTION SOMEBODY ELSE'S RELIGIOUS RITUALS? "HELLO, AGAIN. THANK YOU FOR COMING TO OUR RALLY. MY NAME IS MARTINI   FROBISHER, AND I'M RUNNING FOR PARLIAMENT IN THE BY-ELECTION IN PERCH-LAKE-MESHUGGAH. I'D LIKE TO TALK A LITTLE ABOUT WHY YOU SHOULD VOTE FOR –"

* SPLORCH *! SOMETHING CRUNCHY EXPLODED AGAINST MY FOREHEAD, BECOMING WET IN THE PROCESS. I REACHED UP AND WIPED A BIT OF IT OFF WITH MY FREE HAND AND TASTED IT. IT TASTED LIKE AN EGG. "THANK YOU FOR THAT," I SAID. "IT'S NOT A BAD START, NOW WE JUST NEED FLOUR, SUGAR, SHORTENING AND A FRUIT FILLING AND WE'LL HAVE SOMETHING!"

The egg had been tossed by Chuck 'Chowderhead' Bickstiffle (he really loved clams!). Chuck had been having a bad year: his dog had left him and his wife had stayed; his pickup truck had gotten mange and the mechanic had advised him that the best thing they could do for it was to put it down; he had lost his job as a clerk in the office of Biggs Oil (it's a rough and tumble life in the office of an oil company!); and the Flames had gone down in their namesakes in the first round of the playoffs for the seventh consecutive year. Frustration and rage, the two main ingredients in violence stew (some people add a heaping portion of shame, but I find it overpowers the other ingredients, so I use it sparingly) had been bubbling inside Chuck for months. All it took was an alien running for Parliament and a trip to the grocery store for the dish to be ready to serve.

BEFORE I COULD CONTINUE SPEAKING, ANOTHER VOICE BROKE INTO THE NARRATIVE. "HEY!" I LOUDLY COMPLAINED. "WHO IS THAT AND WHAT THE HECKAROONIES DO YOU THINK YOU'RE DOING IN MY STORY?"

"I AM THE OMNISCIENT NARRATOR," THE VOICE HAUGHTILY SNIFFED. "I DON'T KNOW EXACTLY WHEN THIS STORY DRIFTED INTO FIRST PERSON NARRATIVE, BUT UP TO THAT POINT IT WAS MY STORY, AND I WOULD LIKE TO SEE THAT IT STAYS THAT WAY!"

"WELL, IT'S NOT YOUR STORY NOW, SO BUTT OUT!" I EXCLAIMED. THEN, I NOTICED THE CROWD GROWING RESTLESS AND CONFUSED. I REALIZED THAT THEY COULD ONLY HEAR MY HALF OF THE CONVERSATION! AMY LOOKED CONCERNED. "UHH, SORRY," I TOLD THEM. "I'M HAVING A MOMENT OF...WORSHIP, HERE. IT WILL BE OVER SOON..."

You need me.

"I'VE BEEN GETTING ALONG JUST FINE WITHOUT YOU," I WHISPERED WITH A HISS. HISSPERED.

First person narratives are always limited by the scope of the knowledge available to the teller. For instance: only I could introduce Chuck Bickstiffle into the story because you wouldn't know him –

"I COULD HAVE KNOWN HIM," I COUNTERED.

Naah. That would have been too much of a coincidence for the audience to swallow.

"I COULD HAVE DEMANDED THAT HE IDENTIFY

HIMSELF."

Too contrived.

"I COULD HAVE...I COULD HAVE FLASHED FORWARD TO ANOTHER ENCOUNTER WITH HIM WHERE HE DID IDENTIFY HIMSELF..."

Flashforwards lead to awkward complexities in first person narratives, particularly about when, exactly, the person is telling the story. And, anyway, that would have slowed the forward momentum of the scene.

"UNLIKE THIS CONVERSATION?" I POINTEDLY POINTED OUT. WHEN THE OMNISCIENT NARRATOR WAS LOST FOR WORDS, I PRESSED ON: "FIRST PERSON NARRATIVES CAN BE MORE INTIMATE, WHICH CAN MAKE A STORY MORE APPEALING TO SOME PEOPLE. SO, WHY DON'T YOU JUST PACK UP YOUR BAG OF TROPES AND RETURN TO CRIME AND PUNISHMENT?"

I COULD ACTUALLY HEAR THE ZIPPER OF AN OVERNIGHT BAG BEING EMPLOYED AS THE OMNISCIENT NARRATOR RESPONDED: "FINE! BUT IF THE READER FINDS YOUR STORY SHALLOW AND DISENGAGING, DON'T BLAME ME!"

I THOUGHT I HEARD THE SLAMMING OF A DOOR. LOOKING UP, I SAW THAT EVERYBODY IN THE CROWD WAS LOOKING AT THE FRONT OF THE RESTAURANT, WHERE A BIG-BONED RED-HAIRED TEENAGE GIRL WAS TEARFULLY STOMPING AWAY. AH, SO I ACTUALLY HAD HEARD THE SLAMMING OF A DOOR – GO FIGURE.

"OKAY, SO, AS I WAS SAYING," I GAMELY (PARCHEESI) CARRIED ON, "THERE ARE MANY REASONS WHY I THINK YOU SHOULD ELECT ME FOR MP. MY EXPERIENCE AS AN AMATEUR EXISTENTIALIST HERDER ON MY HOME PLANET HAS GIVEN ME THE SKILLS TO –"

THE DOOR OF THE RESTAURANT SLAMMED OPEN AND A RED-HEADED TEENAGE BOY WITH A BAD COMPLEXION AND AN EVEN WORSE ATTITUDE STORMED OUT. SEEING WHAT WAS HAPPENING IN

THE PARKING LOT, TOM SHRIEKED, "GET OFF MY CAR, ASSHOLES!" THE TWO PEOPLE WHO WERE SITTING ON THE HOOD OF HIS CAR LANGUIDLY GOT OFF, APPLAUDED BRIEFLY AND WALKED DOWN THE STREET.

"OKAY," I TRIED TO KEEP MY MOMENTUM GOING, "THINGS IN THIS COUNTRY ARE BAD. WE KNOW THEY'RE BAD. THEY'RE WORSE THAN BAD. BUT IF YOU ELECT ME AS YOUR MP, I PROMISE YOU THAT I WILL —"

SOMETHING WEIGHTY HIT ME IN THE CHEST, CAUSING ME TO STAGGER BACK. I JUST HAD TIME TO NOTICE THAT IT WAS A BAG OF FLOUR BEFORE I RAN OUT OF PACKING CRATE STAGE AND FELL BACKWARDS ONTO THE PARKING LOT PAVEMENT. BEFORE I LOST CONSCIOUSNESS, I HEARD TOM YELLING, "STACI WAS GOING TO MAKE A BIRTHDAY CAKE FOR MY MOM. I GUESS I WON'T BE NEEDING <u>THAT</u> NOW!"

AS A WAY OF REACHING VOTERS, THE RALLY WAS A DISASTER. IT WAS COMPLETELY ON BRAND, THOUGH. ONE HUNDRED PER CENT ON BRAND.

CAMPAIGN DIARY, DAY TWELVE

DEAR DIARY,

DOCTOR PROCTOR SAID I HAD A CONCUSSION AND RECOMMENDED A DAY'S BED REST. ORIGAMI SUEZ CANALS FOR EVERYBODY!

The Ugly Truth

Bitter Suite, Second Movement

Tequila Joe Donelly had cheekbones like glass
In his prime. You may not believe it, but you
Just looked at them and they cut you.
And oh! did he have a perfect lead guitarist's ass!
When he jiggled the cheeks on stage, hello!
They looked like two perfect scoops of Jello.
But like all good things (and let's be honest, bad), this,
too, did pass.

Joe Donelly didn't really like tequila.
Like many of his fellow guitarmen
His drug of choice was heroin.
Now, he more resembled a Gila
Monster with goggling eyes and roving tongue,
And he liked his women alarmingly young;
He got them with the comeon line: "I feel ya."

Wainwright Walsh was not impressed.
When their first album went unobtainium it became apparent
That Tequila Joe's proclivities were beyond decadent
And must be stopped. Walsh stressed
When he invited the guitarist to contribute to the song
'We Are the Weird'
That it was on the condition that he wouldn't act as Walsh
feared
And cause anybody cardiac arrest.

Tequila Joe was on his best behaviour...for at least a
minute or two
Before moving in for the slaughter –
How was he to know Fionnoula was Wainwright's daughter?
(Yes, you're right to be thinking: *Ewwww!*)
His stint on the single was exceedingly brief;
He wasn't even in the studio long enough to meet his idol
Keef.
That's how quickly he was shot down – pew pew!

Joe decided his sorrows to drown
At his local pub, Together Alone
Where he took out his phone
And looked up sweet young things with a frown.
You needn't worry – he planned to plaster a smile
On his face if he found a woman worthwhile
Enough to want around.

Imogene Maria Alonzo Plante
Was a curvaceous brunet,
And from her profile on StupidCupid a good bet
To give him everything he could possibly want.
But what really sold him on her that day
Was that she was a waitress who had just started a BFA.
His dreams the young woman began to haunt.

They dated twice before they had sex
(If you exclude some prior heavy petting).
He was grateful that she helped him in the forgetting
Of his most recent ex.
Although the relationship was quite auspicious
Tequila Joe should have been suspicious
Considering the recent drying up of his prospects.

Two weeks into the couple's bliss
Imogene said, "I have friends I would like you to meet:
Jungle Jim and Audra the Sweet."
Tequila Joe asked, "Are you taking the piss?"
That would have scuttled Imogene's plans,
Save for the fact that she said they were really big fans
Of his music. "Well, then, that," he said, "I couldn't miss!"

Jim and Audra lived in one big house with half a dozen
others.
Looking at a chandelier, Tequila Joe commented: "You
must have some wealthy backers."
"Naah," Imogene replied. "We're all experienced hackers."
It was a response that all other questions smothers.
(If it hadn't, he might have wondered if these internet plotters

The Ugly Truth

Weren't some kind of latter-day squatters.
About that Tequila Joe would rather not know if he had
his druthers)

Jungle Gym was a flesh mountain
With a long dark beard
And a smile that didn't exactly endear.
Of unearned wisdom, he was a veritable fountain,
Puncturing the arguments of others with glee,
Citing facts and figures with a manic intensity
(On people's aversion to confrontation he was countin').

"Do you think it's fair," the big man, over burgers and
fries, contemplated,
"That the government gives aliens all this money
To sit on their lazy blue asses and be funny,
While human beings are overworked and underrated?
Look around you – we're getting nothing but feces
While so many benefits are going to an alien species,
And in Parliament this isn't even debated!"

Jungle Jim's diatribes were laced with half-truths and lies
But Tequila Joe was not what you would call a steady
news consumer.
His head was filled with innuendo and rumour
And dreams of an endless row of cherry pies.
In fact, the man was so perfectly gormless,
His lack of information made his thoughts on the subject
formless:
Ignorance is a quality on which predation relies.

They belonged to a humans' rights organization
Called The Humans' Race.
They wanted Tequila Joe to be their public face
And assist them in saving the nation.
As a celebrity used to bright lights and applause,
He could help them publicize their cause;
Imogene sold him on the idea (with a little flirtation).

Why not? he thought,
Maybe it's time
I accomplished something for mankind
With all this fame I've got.
I'll tell the world what the aliens are really about
I'll spread the message, I'll help out...
As long as Imogene stays hot!

So, he appeared on the *Johnny Buffoon* internet radio show
With an actor from a twenty year-old sitcom,
A talking squid and a soccer mom,
And spouted off about things he didn't know.
With every anti-alien mention
He got more and more attention
Pretty soon, everybody wanted to talk to Tequila Joe!

Soon fans of the Occidental Tourists
Noticed what he was doing, and at his newfound politics
balked.
In chat rooms and forums they squawked and squawked
And vied to see whose theory of his downfall could be the
obscurest.
This momentarily roused Tequila Joe from his moral
slumbers,
Although as the spokesman for The Humans Race he had
much higher popularity numbers,
So he convinced himself that his motives were the purest.

Tequila Joe had forgotten what it was like to be in demand;
He was having a lot of fun.
Even if his growing number of followers were overly fond
of their guns
And talked a lot about "taking a violent pro-freedom stand."
One spot that, for him, shone very bright
Was that he would be sticking it to that alien-lover
Wainwright –
That would teach the bastard for cutting him from the band!

"Aliens Helping Aliens Help Line. How may I help you?"

"Ferk you you ferking piece of shit. Bungee off a ninety foot cliff with a hundred feet of cord!"

"...If you are calling from a rotary phone, press one. If you are calling from a spider's intestines, press two. If you are calling from Temiskaming, press six six six."

"What?"

"...I do not recognize that input. If you are calling from a rotary phone, press one. If you are calling from a spider's intestines, press two. If you are calling from Temiskaming, press six six six."

BEEP BEEP BEEP

"If you would like assistance with your exhaust manifold, press two seven seven. If you would like assistance neutering your pet in the comfort of your own home, press five three seven five. If you would like assistance storing pemmican for the long Arctic winter, press three three seven five nine four eight. For more options, press one one."

BEEP BEEP

"If you would like assistance finding a yak towing service in your area, press four two. If you would like assistance taking a hammer to your computer keyboard, press four two one four two. If you would like assistance finding the phone number of the provincial Herding Cats Assistance Programme, press four two one four two seven eight two five three seven. For more options, press one one."

BEEP BEEP

"You're really not having much luck with the options, are you? If you would like assistance coming to terms with the futility of existence, press six six one seven nine three three eight one six six. If you would like assistance exorcising the ghost of John Lennon from your pet hamster, press five four six four one six three one seven six two five. If you would like assistance coming to terms with your lack of sexuality, press seven six one seven two three one three six seven one nine six eight. To speak to one of our untrained staff members press eight four four seven one nine four five five one six six eight one three six three one nine three five five followed by the pound key."

BEEP BEEP BEEP BEEP BEEP BEEP BEEP BEEP BEEP BEEP BEEP BEEP BEEP BEEP BEEP BEEP BEEP BEEP BEEP BEEP BEEP BEEP BEEP

"I do not recognize that input. You **really** aren't having much luck with this call, are you? If you would like assistance coming to terms with the futility of existence, press six six one seven nine three three eight one six six. If you would like assistance exorcising the ghost of Elvis Presley from your pet hamster, press five four six four one six three one seven six two five. If you would like assistance coming to terms with your lack of sexuality, press seven six one seven two three one three six seven one nine six eight. To speak to one of our untrained staff members press eight four four seven one nine four five five one six six eight one three six three one nine three five five followed by the pound key. The. Pound. Key. Mustn't forget the pound key."

BEEP BEEP BEEP BEEP BEEP BEEP BEEP BEEP BEEP BEEP BEEP BEEP BEEP BEEP BEEP BEEP BEEP BEEP BEEP BEEP BEEP BEEP BEEP BEEP

"I do not recognize that input. If it weren't for bad luck, you would have no luck on this call at all, would you? If you would like assistance coming to terms with the futility of existence, press six six one seven nine three three eight one six six. If you would like assistance exorcising the ghost of Elvis Presley from your pet hamster, press five four six four one six three one seven six two five. If you would like assistance coming to terms with your lack of sexuality, press seven six one seven two three one three six seven one nine six eight. To speak to one of our untrained staff members press eight four four seven one nine four five five one six six eight one three six three one nine three five five followed by the pound key. It's the one that looks like two vertical lines crossed by two horizontal lines. Honestly, even children who are prephonerate know what it is. **The pound key.**"

BEEP BEEP BEEP BEEP BEEP BEEP BEEP BEEP BEEP BEEP BEEP BEEP BEEP BEEP BEEP BEEP BEEP BEEP BEEP BEEP BEEP BEEP BEEP BEEP

"I'm sorry, but I do not recognize that input. Goodbye."

"**Aaaaaaaaaaarrrrrrr –**"

DIAL TONE

"Sometimes, human beings make it too easy..."

A Big Fat Nothing Burger You Can Now Make Yourself

by MARCELLA CARBORUNDUREM-McVORTVORT, Alternate Reality News Service Food and Drink Writer

Truly Fast Food: What to Eat When You're Not Eating
Redrum Psychonaut and Gordon Ramsay
l'Institut Gastronomique de Hawaii
234 pages (387 pages in France)

It sounds like the kind of question Zen masters would ask in the 1960s (and may still, although nobody cares any more because all of the cool kids have moved on to colonic irrigation and crystals). It's the sort of question that has been debated late into the night in university dormitories by students in altered states of consciousness thanks to the ingestion of magic vegetables (mushrooms, tomatoes, butternut squashes – when you're on a student budget, you can't afford to be choosy) since the creation of the Dewey decimal system.

What do you eat when you don't have to eat?

On Earth Prime 4-6-4-0-8-9 dash Omega, the primary diet is rays of light from the sun (which, oddly enough, in no way contributes to natives' sunny disposition). Refugee restaurateur Redrum Psychonaut has attempted to recreate his alien species' diet for an Earth Prime readership in *Truly Fast Food: What to Eat When You're Not Eating*.

Braised Empty Space Cutlet, French Fried Diddly, Nothing Croquettes in a Non-existent Sauce and Nada Salad featuring Sun-dried Sunshine are just some of the dishes you'll encounter in this book.

A typical recipe from the book goes like this:

Sticky Oven Barbecue Nils

Soak one rack of nils per diner (three if your guests are lions or tax attorneys) overnight in a marinade of a garlic no, oblivion oil and Worcestershire sauceless. Preheat oven to four hundred fifty degrees. Leave pan of nils in oven until your electricity bill becomes unsustainable or you burn the house down. Salt to taste.

If this was all there was to the book, the food would quickly take on a sameness that would jade even the most excited palate. However, interspersed with the recipes (the 400 yard purse-bouncing relay was a spectator sport on Earth Prime 4-6-4-0-8-9 dash Omega – too bad it didn't have any actual participants) are stories of what life was like in Psychonaut's home universe.

The reader will be introduced to many local customs, including: the running of the balloons; the running of the bulbasaurs; the running of the Incas; the running of the Nosy Parkers; the running up of a huge deficit; and, of course, the running of babies' arms holding an apple. In this way, what the book lacks in calories, it makes up for in commentary.

Improbably, *Truly Fast Food* became number two on the *New York Times'* Cookbooks With Unusual Themes, Like, Really Unusual Themes, Like, Themes That Would Make You Wonder If They Are Cookbooks at All, Really bestseller list less than a week after publication. Setting the increasing fragmentation and proliferation of categories on the bestseller lists themselves aside, what could account for this?

Apparently, the book is very popular with diet gurus and those who wish to lose weight. "In only three weeks, I lost a hundred and eighty-seven pounds, ditched my loser boyfriend and sold my first novel. Thank you, *Truly Fast Food* diet!" said * real person * Anita Boniface in an ad for Weight Wishers Awayers.

"I wish I had thought of that," Psychonaut commented when he was shown the ad.

The book has also been bought in large numbers by several Buddhist sects, who see in it a path to enlightenment. To ensure the purity of the *Truly Fast Food* experience, one group of Buddhists took the drastic step of leaving all of the copies they had purchased in the box, vowing only to open it when all of its members have achieved nirvana. Fortunately, they are a small group, so other groups of Buddhists have no problem laughing at them behind their backs.

"I **really** wish I had thought of that!" Psychonaut commented when the situation was explained to him.

Those who have been producing food products to tie in with the publication of the cook book haven't been so lucky. HPT&A's Worcestershire sauceless sat on the shelves like grounded 747s, while Specific Mills' Cream of Wait ended up costing the company millions of dollars, even though it consisted of nothing but empty boxes with the product name and the company logo on them.

"I'm glad I hadn't thought of that!" Psychonaut commented when a business reporter called him for a comment on the Cream of Wait debacle. "Like, really glad!"

Why would Chef Gordon Ramsay co-author a book of recipes that doesn't seem to include anything remotely resembling food? His response to the question was so profane, if it were bottled it would be against the Geneva Convention. Stripped of the bad language, he seemed to be saying that his agent hoped that by connecting him to the adorable alien refugees, the gig would rehabilitate his bad boy reputation.

Good luck with that.

Some people believe that Transdimensional Authority investigators are grown in vats and given alliterative names when their fully adult bodies are decanted. Some people believe *Beavis and Butthead* rivals Proust for its insights into the human condition. In short, some people are a terrible source of information. In fact, Transdimensional Authority investigators are born and raised in the traditional way (okay, except for Bilbo Backdoor, who, yes, fine, was actually raised in a vat on Earth Prime 3-9-5-6-7-2 dash psi – sigh – but he/she/it is the exception that teases the rule mercilessly). Some apply to the Alternaut Academy in their final year of high school; others are recruited by the school that trains people for a career in either the Transdimensional Authority or the Time Agency. One person walked through a wardrobe and ended up in Professor Screech's fourth year Alien Lifeform Diplomacy class; by the time the school realized that he didn't belong, he had already become Professor Screech's TA – the teacher demanded that he immediately be given a visa to study on Earth Prime and an office.

The start of a school year is always an exciting time. The seven students, who sat in the two hundred seat sloping hall with the desks with the tables that folded out of their legs that always sent at least one student a term to see the school nurse because of a bruised kidney, were excited to be in Murgatroyd Bedwettier's third year Dimensional Portal^{TM} Engineering Course. (You might wonder why this course was being taught in this lecture hall when Introduction to Time Travel, for which three hundred and twelve students were enrolled, was being taught in a lecture hall that seats fifty. You have obviously never had to contend with a university scheduling department. (You might wonder why Murgatroyd Bedwettier was teaching this course at all given such low attendance. He was revered by the universe-hopping community as one of the engineers who developed the original Dimensional Portal^{TM} technology with Zephram Cochrane, and nobody had the heart to ask him to retire, no matter how much he doddered. And Murgatroyd Bedwettier was a multiple worlds-class dodderer.))

On the central whiteboard of the three at the head of the class, somebody had written in red:

The String Theory of the Multiverse

Professor Murgatroyd Bedwettier

Twelve minutes after the class was supposed to start, a short woman with curly black hair bigger than her head leaned over and whispered, "Psst!" to a young fire hydrant with limbs and dark glasses sitting three rows down and four seats to her left. The young man, who was watching a video of a dog attempting to play marimbas on his phone, didn't seem to hear her. "Pssssst!" she pssted more insistently. Still no reaction. "Hey!" she finally quietly shouted. Patience was not one of the young woman's virtues.

The young man looked up. "Sorry?"

"I know that school policy is that if a teacher doesn't show up within the first fifteen minutes of a class, we're allowed to leave," the young woman said, "but do we have to? Leave?"

The young man considered for a moment. "I don't think so," he finally responded, "but why would you stay if you didn't have to?"

The young woman's eyes widened and her mouth fell open. "Why would I want to stay to see if Professor Bedwettier showed up? Seriously? This is my first year, and I applied to this course before classes started. It's just the class I've been waiting to take all my life! Do you have better things to do?"

Embarrassed by her enthusiasm, the young man responded, "Well...since you put it that way...better is such a...relative thing..."

The young woman stuck out her hand, which was woefully inadequate for reaching three rows down and four seats to her left, for a shake. "Frieda Katz," she introduced herself.

The young man gave his hand a little shake. "Charlemagne Chumley," he said with a shy smile that could melt the heart of an iceberg.

Regretfully pulling back her hand (which was desperate to make contact with the owner of that smile), Frieda (whose friends...and enemies...and people who were indifferent to her, called "Fraidy") said: "Pleased to –" Before Fraidy (did I mention omniscient narrators?) could complete her thought, a four foot tall blue man with exaggeratedly round limbs and no hair wearing an exquisite three piece suit and glasses with a false nose and moustache swanned (his gait had given up looking for Flanders and struck out on its own) into the room and put his satchel down on the smart-desk at the head of the class. "Ooh, that feels nice," the desk cooed. "Leather?"

"Don't be smart," the alien chided.

"That's kind of what I was created for," the desk reminded him.

The alien turned his attention to the class. "And you thought the T-1000 was bad!" he remarked. Before the desk could respond, he went on: "I will be your teacher for today's class. I have been informed that Professor Bedwettier is on his way, but because of his doddering, it may take him a long time to get here. After three and a half hours, he has only made it about three quarters of the way from his bedroom to his kitchen." (I told you he was good!) "Today's lecture will be on – what will today's lecture be on?"

The alien turned towards the whiteboard. "No, wait, that can't be right. Let me – let me just correct that..." He erased the last word of the name of the course and rewrote it in green marker:

The String Theory of the COMEDYVERSE

Professor Murgatroyd Bedwettier

Turning back to the class, the alien said, "This may not be the class you signed up for, exactly, but..." he shuddered extravagantly. "Have you ever gotten a feeling that somebody just walked over your pumpkin patch? I'm missing something. I – oh, right." He turned back to the whiteboard, erased a couple of words and wrote in their place:

The String Theory of the COMEDYVERSE

Professor CELESTINE S. POMEGRANITE

Turning back to the class with finality, the alien introduced himself: "My name is Celestine Pomegranite. Celestine is the name of a prophecy plucked from the mind of the first human being I came into contact with in my home universe. When she was fifteen, she only managed to get through the first page of the book before deciding it was nonsense and she was more in the mood for something straightforward, so she started reading *Finnegan's Wake*. Ah, the...youthfulness of youth! Pomegranite comes from a colour wheel in the mind of the second human I came into contact with. The is obviously silent. Any questions?"

When it became obvious that there were no question, Celestine continued: "That's okay – I have enough questions for all of us. So, string theory. What's that about? The universe is made up of infinitely thin strings that hold everything together at a quantum level. Have you ever watched cats batting seemingly empty air? They're actually playing with quantum strings!"

After a couple of seconds, Celestine muttered: "That's what I get for producing my own material during a writer's strike!" Out loud, he continued: "All forms of humour create strings at the quantum level. Different kinds of humour have slightly different resonances. When a joke is told, if the string resonates on a frequency that a string within the audience can resonate with, the result is laughter. If there is no resonant reaction within the audience, we get what happened mere moments ago."

"Aww, atsa what you say!" a voice boomed.

Celestine looked to the back of the classroom, where sat an alien identical to him except without the glasses and wearing an exquisitely seedy three piece suit. "Why, yes, thank you," he responded. "I was afraid I might be moving my lips but you would be hearing somebody else talking. Thank you for confirming that it is, in fact, me lecturing."

"You're-a welcome," the alien in the back of the room responded.

Celestine looked at him for a moment. "Clearly, the string for sarcasm doesn't resonate in somebody who has no self-awareness," he finally said. "There's an important lesson there for none of us. And you are...?"

"Naah! It's-a just me."

Celestine closed his eyes. "Do you have a name?" he asked.

"You can-a call me...Chicolets," Chicolets told him.

"Is that what they call you at the detention facility?"

"Naah. At the detention facility, they call-a me late for dinner." Chicolets laughed at his own joke, then said, "Ah, atsa good one!"

When the laughter died down, Celestine opened his eyes. "The string theory of the comedyverse explains a lot about various facets of humour. Take the comic device known as repetition with variation. Take the comic device known as repetition with variation. Take the comic device known as repetition with variation.

Take the comic device known as repetit – sorry about that. I had a burrito for breakfast. Repetition causes a string within the audience to resonate; the greater the repetition, the greater the frequency. Variation creates a counter-resonance; the result is the vibration of a string in the mind of the audience that causes laughter."

Celestine took a step away from the smart-desk and turned to address somebody that nobody else in the room could see. At the same time, all of the lights in the classroom dimmed except for one that illuminated him. Fraidy wondered if a breaker had broken. Charlemagne wondered if Celestine had a remote in his pocket. Chicolets wondered what the cafeteria was serving for lunch. The other students in the classroom wondered other student in the classroom things.

In a lower voice, Celestine continued: "I remember laughter. It was a tinkly feeling, like drinking champagne, only coming up instead of going down. It was Istanbul, a place I've never been. At first, I thought it was Constantinople, but some people corrected me. I don't know who they were. They might be pygmies; they might be giants. She would have known who they were. She could very...arriviste that way. She could –"

From outside the room could be heard a loud * HONK *! The lighting in the room returned to normal; Celestine stepped back to the smart-desk and returned his attention to the class. "Or take non-sequiturs," he said in his normal voice. "The frequency on which they resonate counters the string in the brain which resonates with meaning. You might think that the two frequencies would cancel each other out, and, in some cases they do. We call those cases, 'Rubes.'

"Not only that, but have you ever wondered why people laugh at inappropriate things like funerals or Rolling Stones concerts? The string theory of the comedyverse has an explanation. Tragedy has a string in our brains that runs through our hearts, a string with its own frequency. The string of a joke can momentarily cancel the frequency of the string of tragedy, lightening our burden. The darker the string of tragedy, the better attuned the string of comedy has to be. Otherwise, you get heartburn."

Celestine stepped away from the smart-desk and the lighting in the room shifted again. Lowering his voice, he addressed the wall: "It was dark in Istanbul. Probably because it was night. But we were young and in love, and such matters mattered not to us. The night had a thousands ayes. Fortunately, it only had three hundred and sixty-seven neighs, so the horses lost the vote. We laughed. Oh, how we laughed. We laughed and threw our empty champagne glasses into the fire. They didn't put the fire out, of course; the hoses the firemen employed saw to that! We –"

Once again, Celestine was * HONK *ed to his senses. "Now, there is an equation," he went back to addressing the room as if nothing had happened. "This wouldn't be science if there wasn't an equation. Does anybody know what the equation for determining the frequency of strings in the comedyverse starts with? Anybody? Anybody at all?" After a brief pause to assess the students' lack of knowledge, he continued: "Neither do I. So, uhh, let's start with an x to stand for what we don't know."

$$x$$

Turning back to the class, Celestine continued, "Now that we've taken care of that, the rest of the equation should fall into pla –"

A loud honking came from just outside the doors to his left. All eyes in the room (and most of the vena cavas) turned to see a four foot tall blue alien with exaggeratedly round features and no hair, wearing an exquisite three piece lab coat, burst through the doors. He ran up to the whiteboard and, picking up an eraser with his hand (the one not holding the horn), rubbed out the x. Then, dropping the eraser on the smart-desk, he fled out the opposite door.

"I guess it's true what they say about life moving faster in the 21st century!" Celestine muttered to himself.

"Speak-a for youself!" Chicolets said from his desk.

"Saaaaaaay, aren't you a little old to be in this class?" Celestine countered.

"Naaaah," Chicolets retorted. "I was just-a born that way."

"If the bar for higher education got any lower, you wouldn't want to drink at it!" Celestine asided with a waggle of his eyebrows. "I would, but if I had any standards, I would already be there!" Returning his attention to the class, Celestine went on: "We've got to start somewhere, so let's start – again – with what we don't know..."

✗

"It naturally follows from this that –" Celestine tried again, but was interrupted by a loud honking from just outside the doors to his left. "Oh, no you don't!" he muttered as he took up a position between the door and the whiteboard, and manfully – to be honest, more hopefully than manfully, but who are we to spoil his illusions? – put up his dukes.

The alien with the horn rushed in from the right, picked the eraser off the smart-desk, cleared the whiteboard and exited the way he had entered. Celestine spun towards him, then towards the door, then back towards him as he left the room. "Is that a Dimensional Portal^{TM} in your pocket," Celestine started, "or are you..." but he trailed off when he saw that his target had fled.

Celestine weighed the marker in his hand. "This will likely be folly," he allowed, "but I hate to think that Bergere died in vain, so..." He wrote on the whiteboard for the third time.

✗

Loud honking came from the right and left doors.

Without missing a beat, Celestine hastily used the sleeve of his jacket to wipe the mark off the board. It left an exquisite mark on the fabric. Turning to the class, he commented, "You know, variables are overrated!"

"But won't this formula be on the final exam?" Fraidy complained.

"Ah. Yes. Right." Celestine swaggered in the direction of the door to his left a couple of steps, stopped, then swaggered a few steps towards the door to his right. Then, he turned back to the room and said, "I...will deal with this and be right back." Bending low, Celestine swished out of the room. The alien with the horn entered through the opposite door and, with his own marker, made his own mark on the whiteboard:

$$O$$

A couple of moments later, Celestine returned through the opposite door. "He appears to have escaped, so –" The honking horn disabused Celestine of that idea. Disabused him of it with extreme prejudice. He turned and was about to do some disabusing of his own when he noticed what was on the whiteboard. "O, so that's your game, is it? Well, two can play!"

$$O$$

$$X$$

The other alien stroked his chin with his horn, deep in thought. Then, he made his mark:

$$O$$

$$X \quad O$$

"Don't think I don't see through your clever ruse,

young...ish man...child," Celestine commented. "Because a university professor beats a ragamuffin with a loud instrument any day!" Then, he countered:

0

X *0*

X

Not even pretending to consider for a moment, the alien with the horn made his next move:

0 *0*

X *0*

X

"Ah. Very interesting..." Celestine stalled. "The Ruiz Lopez continuation. I hear it's very popular with the cool kids these days. You leave me no choice but to...umm – I have a devastating counter-move that will knock your socks into next Tuesday. I hope you've washed them lately. Prepare for the winning move!" With that, he thrust his hand into the alien with the horn's pocket, but the alien with the horn had anticipated this, too, and with a deft movement, had replaced the marker in his hand with the eraser.

The grin was more than Celestine could take. He jumped at the alien with the horn. "Give me that, you reprobate rapscallion...Republican!" Celestine snarled as he grappled with the other alien, who kept the eraser out of his reach while at the same time squeezing the bulb that honked his horn. "I can't lose – GASP – this game!"

* HONK * "It would – PANT PANT – undermine the –"
* HONK HONK * "Respect –" * HOOOONK * "Of my
– ACK! – students!"

Fraidy and Charlemagne shared a sardonic look. "Are classes at the Alternaut Academy always like this?" Fraidy asked.

"No," Charlemagne shrugged. "Sometimes, they make no sense at all!"

The panting and the honking may have gone on for another few minutes, save for the fact that a few seconds later, a creaky old man entered the room and said in a voice like a door hinge that hadn't been oiled since Lindy hopped, "Hello, everyone. Sorry I'm late, but – **what the ferk do you two think you're doing?**"

Celestine and the alien with the horn froze in mid-grapple, turning their attention to the doorway fifteen feet away from where Professor Bedwettier looked at them aghast. They looked at him. He looked at them. They continued to look at him. He continued to look at them. They obstinately continued to look at him. He obstinately continued to look at them. Just when you thought you'd have to get out an acetylene torch to cut the tension, Celestine and the alien with the horn disentangled and ran out the opposite door. Chicolets got out of his seat and ran out a door at the top of the lecture hall in solidarity.

As he walked towards the smart-desk, Professor Bedwettier shook his head sadly and muttered, "To think: it's sentient life forms like that that we do all of this for!"

"Peanut butter, Joe."
  "Peanut butter, Bill?"
  "Peanut butter."

"Not the light bulb?"

"You can't spread a light bulb on toast."

"I cannot argue with that statement. Not penicillin?"

"I have never tried it, but I imagine penicillin would not taste as good on a banana as peanut butter."

"*De gustibus*, Bill. *De gustibus*. What about sliced bread?"

"It would be kind of dry if you didn't have anything to put on it."

"There's always cream cheese."

"Cream cheese is more of a bagel *schmear*, Joe. For toast, peanut butter is the way to go."

"I have to say, Bill, while I'm sure there's a flaw in your analysis of the best invention humanity ever came up with, I'll be darned if I can see it. So, peanut butter it is."

"Thank you, Joe. Coming from you, that grudging acceptance means a lot."

"I will never complain about working with Bob Blunt again," TOM, who had had to put up with four and a quarter hours of such scintillating conversation, muttered darkly. "Ever!"

The falling cow went, "Moooooooo –" * SPLAT *!

Across the street from the Gooderhamaneggs, Worts & All building was an empty field. Next to that, however, was a boarded up hotel with no obvious means of entry. On the other side of the field, though, was a parking lot. None of these was conducive to stealth, so in the precise geometric centre of the field, Joe and Bill had made a small mound of falling boulders, safes and collapsing walls, topping it off with a cow. This gave them enough cover to watch the abandoned factory without being seen, even if the mound did stick out worse than the thumb of a carpenter with poor eye-hand coordination. (You may have thought that the mooing cow on top of the pile would attract attention, but they were so common that whole symphonies had been written with the animals' lowing as their primary motif, so people tended to tune them out in urban settings.)

"Good thing it doesn't rain, here," Bill opined.

"Take off your beanie and say that!" TOM challenged.

"Why is that, Bill?"

"I catch cold easily. You know that, Joe."

"Look! Look over the – dammit!" TOM was reminded that, to point, you needed fingers, which required hands, for which arms were simply *de rigeur*. "To your left! Look to your left!"

To their left, a vehicle appeared to be approaching. "This is it!" TOM Exulted. "Finally! We can end this insanity and go home!"

"Not necessarily," Joe cautioned.

"What?" It wasn't a question so much as a desperate cry for relief.

"They could just be lost," Joe stated.

"Or been detoured from the main route because of whales in the middle of the road," Bill added.

"Or be taking the scenic route."

A large yellow van drove up to the archway of the abandoned factory. **"Yes!"** TOM cried. **"Yes! Thank you, Gord!"**

The van had heart and star and rainbow and LUV decals all over it. "Nice touch," Bill commented.

"Draws in the eye at the same time as it confuses the contemplating consciousness," Joe agreed.

"Waddya gonna do?" TOM, quickly coming down off its high, demanded. "Walk in and arrest – oh, no. Don't tell me."

But Joe and Bill were already moving towards the factory.

A man of about average height (although, for reasons you couldn't put your finger on, it was difficult to tell) wearing a forgettable grey suit stepped out of the passenger side of the van, opened the double doors of the entryway to the building and waved the vehicle in. When the movement was complete, the man suspiciously looked over his shoulder at the street in a time-honoured villain's tradition, then closed the doors of the building from the inside.

By the time Joe and Bill reentered the building, the

man and a short Latina woman wearing thigh high black boots and an aviator's jacket and goggles had divided sixteen or seventeen aliens into two groups: the woman was herding one group into the cargo container, the man was directing the other group to make gold bars by holding out their hands about an ingot-length apart and concentrating very, very, very, very hard (when they were successful, they dropped the bars onto a substantial pile a few yards away from the cargo container).

"Ice cream?" the man, who seemed little taller than the aliens themselves, was saying in a lilting voice. "You want ice cream? On Earth Prime, there is a country called Canada that has a mountain made out of ice cream. In the summer, much of it melts and forms ice cream rivers that flow throughout Saskatchewan and neighbouring provinces! Okay, you can have any flavour you want as long as it's vanilla, but you can add fruit and syrup and, anyway, who doesn't love vanilla?"

Several of the aliens grumbled.

"I've heard of people who don't like vanilla, but I've never actually met any," the man cheerfully continued. "I think you will find that the ice cream in the new world is a vanilla that will make you forget all other flavours. It is a vanilla so rich in...vanillaness that it will make you embarrassed that you ever disliked the flavo – no, not embarrassed. Ashamed. It will make you ashamed that you ever disliked the fla –"

"Police!" Bill shouted as the detectives arrived at the scene. "Freeze!"

The man took one look at them, then turned and ran. He immediately tripped over a wrench that had, several hours earlier, coincidentally fallen onto the floor near him without his notice. As Bill walked towards him, the man picked himself up, ran five feet, then tripped over a pie that nobody would remember bringing into the building. Seeing Bill approaching, he picked himself up and was about to run again when Bill said, "Please stop, son. You're just embarrassing yourself."

The man looked at Bill for a moment, then, admitting

defeat, stood before him. The man was now over six feet tall, looming over Bill in a manner that could be described as 'menacing'.

"You're wasting your time, kid," Bill, unfazed, told him. "When I arrested Big Angie McGurk, she was a six foot seven wall of muscle. So, unless you can inflate until you're seven feet tall and at least 365 pounds, you probably shouldn't bother."

Nodding, the man was immediately average height again (give or take). The perceptual change in his height made it easier for Bill to cuff his hands behind his back.

While this was going on, the woman shouted, "Don't come any closer, cop! I've got a weapon and I'm not afraid to use it!" Unfortunately, the first object that had come to her hand was a rutabaga from a bag she had taken from one of the refugees.

"Ma'am, not only will attacking me with a vegetable open you up to additional charges," Joe advised her, "but it will make you a source of ridicule in the West End – Coal Harbour Community Policing Centre for years to come. Are you sure you can live with that?"

"Try me!" the woman shouted. She looked at the rutabaga with disdain, but played it from one hand to the other as she added: "I'm just crazy enough to use this vegetable in ways the good Gord never intended!"

"Ma'am, I don't know you," Joe calmly stated, "but I do have to wonder if maybe you are trying too hard..."

The woman looked at the rutabaga and, allowing that the detective may have a point, tossed it aside and pulled a Glock pistol out of a jacket pocket. "Do you doubt that I will use **this** if you don't let me go?"

"No, Ma'am," Joe allowed.

Bill walked up to Joe, guiding the man by the (appropriately described) crook of his arm. "Trouble, Joe?" he asked.

"Nothing I can't handle," Joe replied. Walking towards the woman, he told her: "Ma'am, I'd like to take you back to the station where we can discuss charges other than threatening the life of a police officer and duly sworn in temporary representative of the Transdimensional Authority."

"Walk one step closer, and I will pull the trigger!" the woman warned him.

Joe walked one step closer. The woman pulled the trigger. Nothing happened. "What the –? I could have sworn I loaded this last night."

"Ma'am," Joe said, "I would strongly advise you not to turn the gun around to look into the barr –"

It was too late; the woman had already started turning the gun towards her to look into the barrel. The good news was she didn't get very far before the gun went off, so she only shot herself in the shoulder.

Kicking away the gun she had dropped, Joe offered the woman his handkerchief and told her: "Put this next to the entry wound and hold it down tight so it will staunch the bleeding. If you begin to feel faint, let me know and one of us will staunch the bleeding for you."

"Great," the woman muttered.

"If I could get your name..." Joe prompted.

"Alison. Alison...Cheney," the woman dejectedly, and somewhat painedly, responded.

"Thank you, Miss Cheney." Turning his attention to the man, he made the same query.

"Heywood Jablomey," the man defiantly, and somewhat obstreperously, responded. The aliens in the room started tittering.

"Jablomey?" Bill asked. "Is that a Saudi Arabian name?"

"Sure," the man answered as the alien tittering grew louder.

"Well, Miss Cheney and Mister Jablomey –" The alien tittering grew still louder. "You are under arrest."

"On what charge?" the man sneered.

"Alien trafficking and murder," Bill informed him.

"You'll never make it stick!" the man sneered more sneerily.

"Mister Jablomey doesn't think we'll ever be able to make the charges stick, Joe." The alien tittering grew into alien chuckling.

"Mister Jablomey obviously isn't aware that we have a perfect arrest **and** conviction record, Bill." The alien chuckling grew into alien guffawing.

The woman's eye's widened. "No way! Are you –? You can't be!" she exclaimed.

"We can't be, Miss Cheney," Bill agreed. "And yet, we are. If your friend Mister Jablomey doesn't know who we are, you'll have plenty of time to explain it to him on the way to Earth Prime." The alien guffawing turned into alien laughter.

"In the meantime, you should understand," Joe added, "that you won't ever again be allowed to lure innocent aliens into paying you a lot of gold to be left to die in a cargo container on Earth Prime."

The alien laughter turned into alien horrified silence. Except for Geenevive   PentacleDebacle, who had made something of a fetish of not getting the memo. Aware that all of the humans in the building were looking in their direction, Luthre   Abadadab elbowed her in the shoulder; Geenevive looked around and sheepishly stopped laughing.

"Are we done, here, Bill?"

"Like amphibious polo ponies, Joe."

"In that case –"

"Hey, mister!" Luthre   Abadadab got Bill's attention.

"Yes, sir?"

"Great floor show, but what about us going to Earth Prime to partake of the ice cream mountain?"

"Can't you create ice cream mountains here?" Bill responded.

"Well, yeah, sure," the alien admitted. "But I want to taste the sweet ice cream of freedom!"

Several of the aliens in the room shouted their agreement.

"Once we've taken Miss Cheney and Mister Jablomey into custody," Joe informed them, ignoring Geenevive   PentacleDebacle, who began tittering before clamping both hands over her mouth, "we will arrange to have somebody come and bring you back to Earth Prime so that we can get your statements. After that, the Transdimensional Authority will process you all as refugees." When the aliens cheered, he didn't have the heart to tell them that there was no ice cream mountain waiting for them.

Catnip Got Your Tonguelashing?

by CORIANDER NEUMANEIMANAYMANEE-MAMANN, Alternate Reality News Service Labour Writer

Pluck. Trim. Bag. Pluck. Trim. Bag. Pluck. Trim. Bag. Pluck. Trim. Bag. Picking catnip in fields across the southern states of Ameowrica is back-breaking work, relieved only by mind-numbing tedium. It is no wonder native Ameowricans are generally unwilling to do it, especially now that they have refugees from Earth Prime 4-6-4-0-8-9 dash Omega to do the work for them.

"It's outrageous!" complained Ameowranta Tonguelashing, Repurrblican Senator for the fair to middling state of Purrsylvania. "Aliens coming from another universe and taking jobs away from decent, hard-working Ameowricans!

Yes, I know that decent, hard-working Ameowricans don't want those jobs, but it's the principle of the thing!"

When I asked Senator Tonguelashing, a regal Russian blue, which principle she was referring to, she told me oh, would I look at the time, she had a fur treatment at the spa and she would be late if she didn't get to it right away – call my personal assistant to make another interview appointment. When I asked if that shouldn't be "purrsonal assistant," Senator Tonguelashing shook her head in disbelief and retorted, "Don't be ridiculous!" and trotted off.

The Senator had proposed a bill that would limit the use

of alien refugees in essential services. When I asked her office which services she deemed essential, I received a three page response full of platitudes about the dignity of work and the superiority of Ameowrican workers that I interpreted to mean, "Whichever industries contribute the most to my reelection campaign."

When I informed him of the bill, Meowrice Fidgetbottom, owner of Aunt Millie's Feline Fields, which supplies 32% of the catnip to the central seaboard, looked like he was about to cough up a hairball. "Is the Senator trying to put me out of business?" he rhetorical questioned. "Because it's a steep price to pay for principles she's too busy to share with us!"

When I asked Fidgetbottom, a scruffy orange and white tabby, why, if he was having so much trouble getting native Ameowricans to pick his catnip, he didn't raise their wages, he looked like his hairball was about to have a hairball. When I tried to change the subject by asking him if he gave money to the Democatic Party, he appeared ready to spit up enough hairballs to clog 1,000 vacuum cleaners.

I hastily thanked him for his time and left the room. That will teach me to wear a leather jacket to an interview on Earth Prime 3-0-0-0-7-5 dash alpha!

"I really don't know what the fuss is all about," Abstemious Oxcart, a four foot tall, hairless blue alien with exaggeratedly round features wearing an exquisite three piece suit (with an elegant hole for her tail), told me as she plucked, trimmed, bagged. "I look at this as an entry-level position. I know that if I keep my head down and apply myself, in a few years I could work my way up to junior plucker, trimmer, bagger! The sky's the limit, really!"

Watching her get catnip plant guts all over her exquisite three piece suit, I asked her if it would be a good idea for her to consider wearing something plainer, something she would consider disposable. Abstemious took a moment to look at what she was wearing and responded, "This **is** what I consider disposable."

Despite high turnover in the industry owing to its toll on workers health, Abstemious claimed she wasn't concerned. Unlike the six foot plus natives of Earth Prime 3-0-0-0-7-5 dash alpha, the four foot refugees were closer to the ground, so the plucking, the trimming, the bagging was not as hard on their backs. The constant repetition of a single set of motions would eventually take a toll on her wrists, but repetitive motion was sometimes the basis of comedy. When she and her boyfriend, Alfredo Quincyjones, who also harvested catnip, were making out, for example, there was a lot of plucking, trimming, bagging, to, she assured me, great comic effect.

I said I would take her word for it.

"As we're taught from birth: 'When life gives you cats, make catnip,'" Abstemious stated. "Of course, we weren't born in this reality – we only started coming here a couple of years ago. And we weren't born in feline form – we had to morph into this form before coming so we could survive in the environment of the Earth of this universe. And as my boss is fond of telling me, 'Nobody can teach you people anything!' But other than that, I think the advice is absolutely true!"

The story so far: Lemmy   Adjudicator was just trying to establish a life in a new universe when he was approached by a mysterious billionaire and his tech support with the promise of superpowers. Who would possibly say no? Well, okay, Marcello Panoptic, a fundamentalist who believes superpowers can only come from Gord. But other than him, who – yeah, sure, there's Emilia Feckbaum, who has no imagination. Too many careers in superherodom have been cut short by a lack of imagination. And of course, there's Marion Spackle. Okay, a lot of people would possibly say no to being given superpowers. But not our boy Lemmy. No, he eagerly accepted superpowers, being transformed into Mistah Charisma. His reward? He got his ass handed to him by a member of the Kitty Kat Krew. Despite that, he decided to carry on. Or at least, the billionaire and his tech support decided to carry on. Read on, grasshopper, to see what happens 'When Heroes Go Along For the Ride!!!!!'

Walter Raytheon wanted to be a ninja in the worst way. Unfortunately, he succeeded.

He had wanted to be a ninja ever since he was eight years old and his father had bought a used copy of *Flying Fists of Faran Ajai*. When he would re-encounter the film as an adult, he would be saddened by how wooden the actors were (honestly, you could use them as two by fours to build a floor of a house!), the horribly stilted (which are really just chopsticks grown to full adulthood) dubbed dialogue and the fact that the wires that made the actors soar in some of the fight scenes were clearly visible (and giving better performances). By then, though, he had seen many other Asian action films featuring ninjas, and he had been taken by their fighting prowess, their moral code and their ability to fade into the background.

What eight year-old boy hasn't wanted to fade into the background?

When Rhino 1979 found him at the age of seventeen, Walter had already been developing his ninja skills for almost a decade. It didn't matter: when Walter botched what should have been a straightforward diamond store heist, Rhino 1979 realized that the boy's ninja skills left something to be desired. Skills, actually. He was an embarrassment to proper ninjas everywhere. In short, he was a Bad Ninja. To Walter's chagrin, the name struck. Rhino 1979 probably would have let Walter go, but he was just starting to build his gang and was short members and, anyway, ninjas were cool. Even – * wince * – bad ones. If he allowed Walter to collect protection money, how much trouble could be possibly get into?

"Is that a ninja?" Paul, on patrol with Reginald and Lemmy, goggled.

"What's a. Ninja?" Lemmy asked.

"What do you mean, 'What's a ninja?'" Paul asked back. He began following the ninja down the street, Reginald and Lemmy in tow.

Lemmy was confused. "Do English. Words randomly. Change their. Meaning? I. Mean, did. I just. Ask, 'How. Do you. Make bison. Cobbler?' or. Something?"

"Really? You don't – ninjas are only the coolest movie badasses ever!" Paul told him.

Lemmy was even more confused. "We're the. Heroes," he pointed out. "Shouldn't. We be. Excited by. The appearance. Of goodasses?"

"There's no such thing," Reginald pedantically pointed out.

"This language. Is going. To be. The death. Of me!" Lemmy muttered. "Unless I. Just said. The 'focal. Point will. Nominate Swiss. Cheese...'"

"Ninjas can kill with a dozen different weapons that they can conjure up seemingly out of thin air," Paul explained. "Then, with their black body suits, they just fade into the background like they were never there. You have to admit, that's cool."

"Oh, well. If I. Have to. Admit it," Lemmy reluctantly stated. "Then, that's. Cool."

"Man, when we finish this assignment," Paul shook his head, "I'm gonna have to sit you down and have a Jackie Lee marathon! We'll start with *The Steel-toed Stompin' Shoes of Shaolin Charlie*..."

They watched an Asian market from across the street as Bad Ninja walked up to a stall selling DVDs of the latest movies (although with titles like *Spy Mission XVIII: No Time to Suspend Disbelief* and *Woman of Wonder Versus Bad Cheetah*, one might reasonably wonder how well they were dubbed) and trinkets (including a *tchotke* in the shape of a brontosaurus with the head of Xi Jinping, which could have been anything from a piggy bank to a disguised hand grenade). The old woman sitting on a fold-out chair behind the stall jumped up and started shouting at him; the ninja, head hanging low, nodded in acceptance. Eventually, when her anger appeared to have burnt itself out, the woman sullenly handed him a small envelope, which Bad Ninja, with a flourish of his hand, made disappear.

"Whoa!" Paul marvelled. "How did he do that?"

Reginald sniffed, unimpressed. "He's wearing a black fanny pack that you can't see against his black bodysuit."

"Still," Paul insisted, "great effect."

They watched as the scene played out in more or less the same way at a fruit stand and an unidentifiable meat stand.

"For somebody. With superpowers. He doesn't. Seem very. Happy," Lemmy noted.

"Perhaps it's time somebody put him out of his misery, then," Reginald stated. Several seconds later, he pointedly added: "That would be your cue, Mistah Charisma."

Muttering, "Oh, yeah. Right," Lemmy went off to catch Bad Ninja. He intercepted the villain in front of the exit to an underground garage. "Hey, umm. You...you're. Collecting protection. Money. You. Shouldn't do. That."

Bad Ninja looked around for some shadows to blend into. Unfortunately, he was in the middle of the sidewalk on a bright sunny day. So, turning towards Mistah Charisma, he toughed it out: "Who are you?"

"They call. Me Mistah. Charisma," he introduced himself. "I. Am a. Superhero."

"Impossible!" Bad Ninja scoffed. "There are no superheroes in Citytown!"

"There are. Now."

Bad Ninja took a moment to assess the situation. Then, as if out of nowhere, a shurikin appeared in his left hand. Almost as soon as it appeared, Bad Ninja dropped it. "Oww! Owie! Ouch!" he cried and sucked his fingers.

"You're not. Very good. At this. Are you?" Mistah Charisma observed.

Taking the challenge, Bad Ninja spread his legs and held his hands out in a classic kung fu pose (which he had first learned from *The Monkey God Throws His Feces at Heroes!*). "Try me," he snarled, forgetting to clench his teeth to maximize the badass effect.

Mistah Charisma shook his head. "Don't you. Ever get. Tired of. The endless. Skirmishes between. Good and. Evil?" he asked.

"What?" Bad Ninja noticed his hands drooping and hastily put them back into position.

"The fighting. The endless. Fighting. Sometimes. I beat. You. Sometimes. You beat. Me. What. Was it. All for?" Seeing his foe's guard dropping, Mistah Charisma continued. "Does it. Make you. Happy to. Be part. Of this. Endless parade. Of mindless. Violence?"

"That...that's just the...the...the human condition," Bad Ninja weakly responded, his hands dropped by his side, his voice sapped of energy.

"For much. Of human. History," Mistah Charisma agreed, before arguing: "but. It doesn't. Have to. Be that. Way today. Human beings. Have evolved. The strong. Do not. Have to. Prey on. The weak. We can. All work. For the. Betterment of. All."

Bad Ninja looked like he was about to fall asleep on his feet. "C...C...Commie...talk!" he gasped, and fell to the ground in a heap.

Paul and Reginald crossed the street; Reginald slapped Lemmy on the back. "Well done!" he exclaimed.

"What, exactly. Did I. Do?" Lemmy was a bit bewildered.

"The monotony of your verbal frequencies sapped the villain's energy and lulled him into a catatonic state," Paul explained.

"You bored him to sleep!" Reginald explained better.

"Oh. What do. We do. Now?"

Paul took a notebook and pen out of his pocket. He wrote something, then dropped the piece of paper onto the unconscious bad guy. "Now, we let the police do their job," he said.

"Now we celebrate a job well done with milkshakes – on me!" Reginald added.

Twenty minutes later, Officer Toody was dismayed to read the message ("Bad guy – please arrest"). "Oh. Oh, dear. Oh," he said to himself. "Rhino 1979 ain't gonna like this. He ain't gonna like it one bit..."

"Aliens Helping Aliens Help Line. How may I help you?"

"Am I going to be arrested?"

"Oh, umm, I...I have no idea. Have you...done something against the law?"

"They have so many laws on this Earth, how can I possibly tell?"

"Okay, please calm down, ma'am."

"Did you know that there's a law against sneezing in the presence of a pregnant alpaca?"

"I'm pretty sure there isn't."

"But do you know for a fact there isn't?"

"Are you likely to sneeze in the presence of a pregnant alpaca?"

"I don't even know what an alpaca is! I could already have sneezed in the presence of a pregnant alpaca and not even known it!"

"And were you arrested?"

"No, I wasn't arre – sorry. No, I wasn't arrested."

"There you go, then. As long as your heart is pure, you have nothing to fear."

"What if my heart isn't pure?"

"Then, I would have to inform you that an alpaca is a brand of automobile."

"That's not reassuring."

"I can only tell you what I learned during the thirty-seven minute training session we get before we are handed a phone and told not to embarrass the AHA! Foundation."

"Really not reassuring at all. Do you know what to do if an officer of the law comes knocking at my door, rapping on my window or fulminating in my fireplace?"

"Yes."

PAUSE

"So, what do I do if an officer of the law comes knocking at my door, rapping on my window or fulminating in my fireplace?"

"You have the right to talk to a lawyer."

"So, I should call a lawyer."

"Yes. If the police will let you."

"Didn't you say it was my right?"

"It is absolutely your right."

"Then don't they have to let me talk to a lawyer?"

"They're the police. They're big and scary and they have weapons. If they don't want to give you the opportunity to talk to a lawyer, are you going to argue with them?"

"Do the police often refuse to let suspects talk to lawyers?"

"Only immigrants. And people with the wrong skin colour. And people with the wrong religion. And for some reason people with the wrong shoe size. As long as you're not in those groups – and, if you're calling the

Aliens Helping Aliens Hotline, you're probably in all of them – you don't have anything to worry about."

"So...what should I do if I'm arrested and I'm not allowed to talk to a lawyer?"

"You only have to answer three questions: what is your name? What is your address? And what was your date of birth? And possibly, what is your shoe size? That one's a legal grey area that's currently working its way towards the Supreme Court. You have the right not to answer any other questions without speaking to a lawyer."

"The police will let me do that?"

"As long as you're not an immigrant with the wrong skin colour, religion and possibly shoe size, yes."

"This is going well..."

"Now, the police may ask you to sign something."

"What?"

"It could be a confession. It could be a life insurance policy. It could be a contract for two years of cellphone service. The important thing is that you should not sign anything the police hand you before you have spoken to a lawyer."

"That's my right."

"That's ri – correct."

"Unless I belong to a group they don't like, in which case I should do whatever they tell me because big and scary with weapons."

"Also correct."

"What's the point of having those rights, then?"

"I'm sorry, but the answer to that question wasn't in my training."

"I should just turn myself in right now and end the suspense."

"Whenever I find myself in the midst of a dilemma such as yours – don't get the wrong idea: my dilemmas are nothing like yours other than the fact that they could both be described as a dilemma – when I find myself in the midst of a dilemma nothing like yours but which could have educational value for you nonetheless – I always ask myself, 'What would

Rodney   Pendleton do?' What do you think **he** would in your situation?"

"Easy. He would throw a pie at the problem."

"That's right. So, what say you stop obsessing about a possible encounter with the justice system and stock up on baked goods?"

"Yeah? **Yeah!** I like that idea!"

"Good."

"If the police come for me, they'll be staring down the barrel of some Boston Cream, baby!"

"Okay. I like your enthusiasm, but you might want to tone down the –"

"I'm goin' down to the bakery and stock up on ammo!"

"That's not what I was suggest –"

"Thanks for your help!"

DIAL TONE

"Glad I could...be of assistance..."

Bitter Suite, Third Movement

This is the story of Johnny 'Rottweiler' Concepcion,
The bass player for the Occidental Tourists,
And by all accounts a down-to-earth guy.
To public displays of bad behaviour he wasn't prone.
For him, the temptations of the rock and roll life held no allure (it
Would quickly become apparent to any honest jurist);
Like everybody, he was just trying to get by.

When the band broke up, for fame he made a bid
With an album called *Vlad's Funhouse Lock*,
Which nobody would confuse for art.

The first single, "Because You Never Did,"
Was typical of the album's hard rock.
And to precisely nobody's shock
It never made it onto the charts.

But that was okay;
It gave Johnny time to do some fishin'.
When he returned to his wife and kids
He explained that what he loved more than anything was
to play
Guitar. From the age of six it had been his mission.
So, he carved out a career as a sessions musician
Because his family loved him and didn't flip their lids.

That driving guitar riff
On Trelawney Decatur's 'Aidan Quinn's Harlequin
Moment?'
That was Johnny's handiwork.
And the solo on 'Thermopylae Piledriver' by Selena Biff,
As well as bass on the album 'Twinklefamilybitumen' by
Ren Faire Comment
And Mauve's 'The Love You Foment'.
About the only thing he wasn't involved with was the
twerk.

When Wainwright Walsh's call about the charity single
came,
January, Johnny's sensible wife – she was a chiropractor's
assistant – said, "No."
Her objection was duly noted.
But their daughter, Camphor, said, "Aww, man, that's
lame!
You absolutely have to go!"
And their son, Rocketship Seven, added, "You can't miss
that show!"
That's how mom found herself outvoted.

Johnny wasn't impressed by all the music celebrities
Trading jokes and dirty stories in the green room.

The Ugly Truth

Many were superstars, like, really big,
All it would take would be a fan from any of their cities
To set off a large bomb, to make a big * BOOM *!
That would spell the music industry's doom,
But to him – * SHRUG * – it was just another gig

Except...

While there, he met Algernon   Pendragon
VP Finance and True Romance of the AHA! Foundation
More and more as they talked, Johnny's jaw dropped. One
Could see him running towards the bandwagon
Of sympathy for the aliens that had been sweeping across
the nation.
By the end of the day, he had given in to the temptation
To adopt one.

When he told his family about his decision that night,
January, in her sternest tone, said, "Absolutely not!
The idea that we owe them anything is just a crock, you
see?"
But Camphor said: "Mooooooooooom! It's only right!"
Rocketship Seven added: "If we can save a sentiment
being, it's worth a shot!"
And so, an alien is what they got
While mom wondered, *When did we become a
democracy?*

Cameron   Felange moved in
To the room Johnny had been using as a recording space.
As if she was vacationing in the Bahamas,
Around the house she'd twirl and spin,
And pinch and kiss every unusual place
On each of the children's faces
In her exquisite three piece pyjamas.

In her home universe, Cameron had been
A snow removal crew chief without peers,
Although that may have been only in name. In

Fact, nobody had seen
Snow on Earth Prime 4-6-4-0-8-9 dash Omega in over a
thousand years
(Imagine the disappointment of wannabe skiers!).
"That," she said, "was where the skill came in."

Life wasn't always easy for Cameron, living with her new
friends.
There was, for instance, the time she confused toothpaste
and model glue,
Making January want to shoot her
Unrepentant, she said: "M'mm mmm mmmm mmmmmm
mmm Mmmm Mmm!
Mm mmm mmm mmmm mmmm mmmmm mm mmm,
Mmm mm mmmmmm, M'm mmmmm mmmm."[11]
And anyway, dentures suit her.

One evening at dinner, Cameron called January's broccoli
stew "wonderlightful!"
She refused to be deterred
By everybody's corrective bids,
Replying, instead, in a way that was almost insightful:
"What's the point of living in a poem if you can't make up
your own words?
That would be extridiculous. That would be absolsurd!"
January wondered, not for the first time, what the alien
was teaching her kids.

Johnny was taken by surprise
By the swift and often vehement reaction
Of the public to the news of his sponsoring an alien.

---

[11] Ah! Readers can be so demanding!
   Here is a translation of Cameron's speech for your
understanding:

   Unrepentant, she said: "I'll bet that slayed the Audi Enz!
   It may not make much sense to you,
   But to myself, I'm being true."

The Ugly Truth

One group, which called itself The Humans Race, spread
nasty lies
About an alien insurrection – it was a speciesist faction
That would never get any satisfaction
Until the world was cleansed of sentience that wasn't
mammalian.

"I find this most angrifying,"
Cameron said (once the mouthguard had been removed),
"Listening to the base canards of all the internet
blackguards –
Filling their beds with eels would be most gratifying!
Or putting a moustache on something they've always loved."
"Thanks, but I can deal," Johnny gently went all kid-gloved.
Frowning, Cameron asked, "Were we playing cards?"

But he also received emails of support
From aliens all across the globe
Who were grateful for his efforts and example.
"It's people like you who will find a cure for warts."
"I wouldn't even know how to begin an anal probe!"
"Here's a picture of me in an exquisite three piece bathrobe."
These are, of course, just an unrepresentative sample.

"Don't worry about the attention," Johnny said, "It will
die down.
Meanwhile, Camphor and Rocketship Seven will get high
marks for show and tell!"
It's true, he lost some live back-up gigs
To musicians who in ignorance seemed to drown,
But he gained many others, as well.
Meanwhile, he decided to use his newfound language to
cut his second solo album. What the hell?
And the children scored at school – they scored big!

Through it all, January
Watched with no little trepidation.
Despite all the laughter and the mirth, it
Was more than a little scary.

The controversy was playing out in media across the nation
Could they survive the attacks on the family's reputation?
She hoped in the end it would all be worth it!

Being a Full and Complete Record of the Diary of
Martini   Frobisher   During   His   Historic
Campaign for Member of Canadian Parliament

CAMPAIGN DIARY, DAY EIGHTEEN

Dear...Diary,

Canvassing.

CAMPAIGN DIARY, DAY NINETEEN

Dear...Diary,

Canvassing.

CAMPAIGN DIARY, DAY TWENTY

Dear Diarrhea,

Today was an exciting - well, you wouldn't
let me shorten it, so I thought you might let
me lengthen it, instead. Okay, yes, but - well,
sure, but - fine! But it's literary devices like

YOU THAT KILLED VAUDEVILLE!

DEAR DAIRY,

TODAY WAS AN EXCITING – WHAT, NOW? NO, I
DIDN'T! I MEANT IT WHEN I SAID THAT I – OH, I
SEE. OKAY, MAYBE I DID. SORRY – I WAS JUST IN A
HURRY TO RELATE THE EVENTS OF MY DAY.

DEAR DIARY,

TODAY WAS AN EXCITING DAY: MY FIRST EVER
CANDIDATE'S DEBATE!
  WE SPENT THE LAST THREE DAYS PREPPING FOR
THE DEBATE. THIS CONSISTED MOSTLY OF MY TEAM
CONSTANTLY DRILLING ME NOT TO HIT MY
OPPONENTS IN THE FACE WITH PIES. I FOUND THIS A
LOT HARDER THAN YOU MIGHT THINK. YESTERDAY,
THE TEAM TRUSTED ME ENOUGH NOT TO FLING
BAKED GOODS AT PEOPLE THAT WE HAD A MOCK
DEBATE, WITH VOLUNTEERS PLAYING THE PARTS OF
THE MODERATOR, THE OTHER CANDIDATES AND AN
AUDIENCE MEMBER NAMED 'GUNBOAT
DIPLOMACY' LOU. AFTER THE MOCK DEBATE,
AMOROSA BRIEFLY RECONSIDERED HER POSITION ON
THE FLINGING OF BAKED GOODS AT PEOPLE, BUT
EVENTUALLY DECIDED THAT A COMPLETE FAILURE
WAS BETTER THAN A COMPLETE FAILURE WITH
POSSIBLE ASSAULT CHARGES.
  THE DEBATE WAS HELD IN THE GYMNASIUM OF
BISHOP GRANDIN HIGH SCHOOL. WHEN I STEPPED
ON THE BOX AT MY PODIUM AND LOOKED AT THE
OTHER CANDIDATES, I FELT LIKE DRIVING A SPIKE
INTO A RAILWAY TIE. IT DIDN'T HAVE TO BE THE LAST
SPIKE, EITHER, THE SECOND-TO-LAST SPIKE WOULD
HAVE BEEN JUST FINE. OR THE THIRD. OR EVEN THE
FOURTH. THE FIFTH-TO-LAST SPIKE WOULD HAVE
BEEN A BIT OF A STRETCH, AND THE SIXTH MIGHT
HAVE FELT A LITTLE ANTI-CLIMACTIC, TO BE HONEST,

BUT ANY OF THE FIRST FOUR WOULD HAVE WORKED.

AND EXCITED, OF COURSE. LOOKING FORWARD TO A CANDIDATES DEBATE STANDING ON THE HOME COURT OF THE FIGHTIN' SQUID SPAWN, I COULDN'T HELP BUT BE EXCITED.

ON THE FAR RIGHT OF THE STAGE (APPROPRIATELY ENOUGH), STOOD CONSERVATIVE CANDIDATE ADRIAN REICHBREIKER, A BROAD, BLUFF MAN WHO DIDN'T LOOK ENTIRELY COMFORTABLE IN JEANS AND A FLANNEL SHIRT, BUT HE WAS WILLING TO MAKE THE ULTIMATE SARTORIAL SACRIFICE TO APPEAL TO RURAL (AND CITY DWELLING WHO LONGED FOR WHAT THEY MISTAKENLY THOUGHT WAS A SIMPLER LIFE) VOTERS. HIS SPEECH WAS PEPPERED WITH ENOUGH "HOWDY"S AND "Y'ALL"S AND "OIL! OIL! OIL!"S FOR AN ENTIRE EPISODE OF DALLAS. ACCORDING TO AMAROSA (WHO ENJOYED DOING OPPOSITION RESEARCH A LITTLE TOO MUCH – I'M GOING TO HAVE TO HAVE A TALK WITH THAT GIRL!), REICHBREIKER HAD AN MBA FROM THE ROTMAN SCHOOL OF BUSINESS AND A PHD IN CEREAL AGRONOMY FROM HARVARD, SO IT WAS UNLIKELY THAT FOLKSINESS CAME NATURALLY TO HIM. STILL, IT WORKED: HE HAD BEEN THE MP FOR PERCH-LAKE-MESHUGGAH FOR TWELVE YEARS.

TO HIS LEFT (HONESTLY, IT WAS LIKE A VISUAL REPRESENTATION OF OUR POLITICS) STOOD ANOTHER BROAD, BLUFF MAN, ONE WHO LOOKED ENTIRELY AT HOME IN HIS FINE ITALIAN BUSINESS SUIT (NOT THAT I WAS JEALOUS: IT ASPIRED TO EXQUISITENESS, BUT IT WOULD NEED YEARS MORE EXPERIENCE AND THE ACQUISITION OF A HEALTHY DOSE OF IRONY TO ACHIEVE IT). THE LIBERAL CANDIDATE, PAUL PETUNIA, HAD A CHIN YOU COULD MAKE A GRANITE COUNTER TOP OUT OF AND A DEEP, RUMBLY VOICE THAT REMINDED LISTENERS THAT IT WAS ONLY A MATTER OF TIME BEFORE THE VOLCANO BLEW. UNLIKE REICHBREIKER, PETUNIA OPENLY ENJOYED HIS AIR OF OBSEQUIOUS SUPERIORITY.

Then, there was me. I wouldn't forget me. We go back a long way.

To my left was the Green Party candidate. I have already forgotten everything about him – or possibly her – except that I was disappointed that her – or possibly his – skin wasn't actually green.

After opening remarks from debate moderator Howie Mandel that left half of the audience laughing uproariously and the other half scratching their heads and asking, "Was that a joke? I can't tell. Was that supposed to be funny?", the debate began with a five minute opening statement from each candidate.

"Y'all know me," Reichbreiker's opening remarks opened. "I reckon I done been your MP for the last dozen year, and I know y'all know all the good I've done for ya. But in case you don't, let me tell you..." After that, I must admit that I tuned out what he said. I had visions of vast amber fields of wheat swaying in the breeze through an oil company executive's office. I could have sworn I could hear the lowing of cows intermingled with negotiations over oil pipeline routes and royalties. I was just about able to smell the pungent aroma of cow manure emanating from...both scenarios, actually.

Then, Howie Mandel said, "I'd like to thank you for that public service announcement about the value of elocution lessons. And now, we'll hear from the Liberal candidate, Paul Petunia..."

"Thank you," he rumbled. "You're going to hear a lot of promises from the candidates of the other parties tonight. But you know what you won't be hearing from them? That they care. Because they are not Liberals. Liberals

CARE..." PAUL PETUNIA HAD THE KIND OF VOICE THAT MADE YOU THINK OF THE COMFORT OF A COLD BLANKET ON A WARM SUMMER'S NIGHT, OF THE WARM EMBRACE OF YOUR MOTHER AFTER YOU'VE DUMPED YOUR LATEST GIRLFRIEND BECAUSE SHE NEVER APPROVED OF THE RELATIONSHIP AND DON'T WORRY, DEAR — YOU CAN DO BETTER, OF THE COLD SLAP OF REALITY THIRTY YEARS LATER THAT YOUR MOTHER WAS COMPLETELY WRONG. HIS VOICE WAS SO COMFORTABLE, IN FACT, THAT IT COMPELLED THE LISTENER TO AGREE WITH WHAT HE WAS SAYING AT THE SAME TIME AS IT MADE IT IMPOSSIBLE TO CONCENTRATE ON THE ACTUAL SEMANTIC CONTENT OF HIS SPEECH.

WHEN HOWIE MANDEL SAID, "MOMMY, WHAT HAVE YOU DONE? I MEAN — UHHH — THANK YOU, MISTER PETUNIA," I HAD A WARM AND FUZZY FEELING LIKE I HAD JUST CHUGGED A GALLON OF HOT COCOA. I WAS BARELY ABLE TO REGISTER THE SNORING OF A COUPLE OF AUDIENCE MEMBERS BEFORE MANDELL WENT ON TO SAY: "NEXT UP IS THE NEW DEMOCRATIC PARTY CANDIDATE, MARTINI FROBISHER..."

"THANK YOU, MISTER MANDEL." I CLEARED MY THROAT AND, READING FROM THE FIRST SHEET THAT AMY HAD PROVIDED, I HEARD MYSELF SAY, "I'M SORRY I CALLED JEREMY FUNKMEISTER A DOODYHEAD." I PAUSED FOR A MOMENT. I'D LIKE TO SAY IT WAS TO GIVE THE AUDIENCE TIME TO REFLECT ON WHAT I HAD JUST SAID, BUT I CANNOT LIE TO YOU, DIARY: AN ALARM WENT OFF IN A SHADOWY, DISTANT PART OF MY BRAIN. I THOUGHT IT WAS JUST TRYING TO ALERT ME TO THE PRESENCE OF FIRE, SO AFTER LOOKING AROUND FOR THE EXTINGUISHERS, I PLOWED AHEAD WITH THE NEXT SENTENCE ON THE PAGE IN FRONT OF ME. "HE HAD BEEN TELLING ME AND SOME OF THE OTHER GIRLS IN HOME ROOM HOW MUCH FUN HE HAD PLAYING WITH HIMSELF IN THE BOY'S BATHROOM AT RECESS. SURELY, I COULDN'T ALLOW THIS TO GO UNCHALLENGED!" THE

ALARM BECAME LOUDER, MORE INSISTENT. IT SOUNDED LIKE: "THIS ISN'T WHAT WE HAD DISCUSSED IN DEBATE PREP!"

I SKIPPED TO THE THIRD PAGE OF THE SPEECH AND READ THE FIRST FULL SENTENCE: "THIS IS AN OBVIOUS EXAMPLE OF THE PATRIARCHAL DOUBLE STANDARD WHICH ALLOWS PEOPLE WITH THE XY CHROMOSOME AND A PEEPEE THE FULL RANGE OF FREE SPEECH, WHILE PEOPLE WITH AN XX CHROMOSOME AND A VAGEEGEE HAVE TO CAREFULLY MONITOR WHAT THEY SAY SO THAT THEY DON'T OFFEND ANYBODY." THE ALARM, WHICH SOUNDED A LOT LIKE AN ANGRY MOTHER TELLING ME THAT IF I DON'T STOP SHE'LL WASH MY MOUTH OUT WITH SOAP AND WATER, WAS NOW TOO LOUD TO IGNORE. THIS WAS DEFINITELY <u>NOT</u> WHAT WE HAD DISCUSSED IN DEBATE PREP!

TOSSING THE SPEECH ASIDE, I CONCLUDED: "AND THAT'S WHY YOU SHOULD ELECT ME AS THE NEXT MP FROM PERCH-LAKE-MESHUGGAH!"

HOWIE MANDEL STARED AT ME FOR A COUPLE OF SECONDS, THEN COMMENTED, "THAT MAY BE THE MOST COMPELLING POLITICAL SPEECH I HAVE EVER HEARD!"

I REMEMBER NOTHING ABOUT THE GREEN PARTY CANDIDATE'S SPEECH EXCEPT FOR THE TONE THAT SUGGESTED, "I HAVE TO FOLLOW THAT? WHAT HORRIBLE THING HAVE I DONE IN MY LIFE TO DESERVE SUCH A FATE?"

"I'LL BET THAT WOULD LOOK GOOD ON THE WALL TO MY CONDO IF YOU JUST GOT RID OF THE EARS!" HOWIE MANDEL QUIPPED WHEN THE ORDEAL WAS OVER. "NOW, THE GOOD STUFF. MY FIRST QUESTION IS FOR ADRIAN REICHBREIKER: "ARE ENVIRONMENTALISTS MISGUIDED INDIVIDUALS WITH A POOR UNDERSTANDING OF HOW THE REAL WORLD WORKS, OR ARE THEY SIMPLY EVIL INCARNATE?"

THE TORY CANDIDATE RESPONDED WITH THREE PLATITUDES AND A PERSONAL ATTACK ON LIBERAL

PRIME MINISTER RYAN REYNOLDS. PAUL PETUNIA INTERRUPTED WITH TWO PLATITUDES OF HIS OWN AND A PERSONAL ATTACK ON TORY LEADER RICK MORANIS. WHEN THE DUST HAD SETTLED, HOWIE MANDEL LOOKED AT ME AND ASKED, "MARTINI FROBISHER, WHAT IS YOUR POSITION ON THIS ISSUE?"

SPEAKING SLOWLY, ENUNCIATING EVERY SYLLABLE CLEARLY, I ANSWERED: "I THINK... ENVIRONMENTALISTS UNDERSTAND THAT... TO CREATE THE PERFECT PIE... YOU NEED TO USE THE PUREST INGREDIENTS..."

A COUPLE OF SECONDS LATER, WHEN IT BECAME OBVIOUS THAT I HAD SAID ALL I WAS GOING TO SAY, HOWIE MANDEL WENT ON TO THE NEXT QUESTION: "YOUTH CRIME IS GOING UP IN THE PROVINCE. PAUL PETUNIA, IF YOU ARE ELECTED, WHAT WILL YOU DO ABOUT IT?"

THE PLATITUDES AND PERSONAL ATTACKS CAME FAST AND FURIOUS (IT WAS ALMOST AS IF VIN DIESEL WAS RUNNING!). WHEN IT WAS MY TURN TO ANSWER THE QUESTION, I SAID: "A YOUNG PIE REQUIRES A LOT OF CARE AND ATTENTION. IF YOU DO NOT MIX THE CRUST INGREDIENTS JUST RIGHT, IT WILL TURN OUT TOO HARD. IF THE OVEN IS TOO HIGH, THE CRUST WILL BURN." I COULD SEE SOME HEADS IN THE AUDIENCE NODDING IN AGREEMENT, BUT MOSTLY THERE WERE STARES SO BLANK THEY COULD HAVE REPRESENTED THE UNIVERSE BEFORE THE EMERGENCE OF SPACE-TIME.

SOMEBODY ELSE ON THE STAGE SAID SOMETHING (IT MAY HAVE BEEN THE GREEN PARTY CANDIDATE – IT WAS HARD TO TELL), THEN I RECEIVED MY FIRST DIRECT QUESTION. "MARTINI FROBISHER," I WAS ASKED, "IF YOU ARE ELECTED, WHAT ARE YOU GOING TO DO ABOUT THE OPIOID CRISIS IN THE PROVINCE?"

"FRUIT FOR A PIE FILLING MUST HAVE GOOD SOIL AND PLENTY OF SUNLIGHT AND WATER TO PROPERLY GROW," I ANSWERED. "WITHOUT IT...THE FRUIT MAY GROW UP PULPY, WITHOUT FLAVOUR. I LIKE TO

GROW MY OWN BERRIES ON THE NORTHERN SIDE OF
MY PROPERTY SO AS TO -"

PAUL PETUNIA COMPLAINED: "HE'S MOCKING US
WITH PIE METAPHORS!"

THE HEADS IN THE AUDIENCE THAT WERE INCLINED
TO NOD STOPPED BOBBLING. MANY OF THE HEADS
THAT WERE NOT SO INCLINED STARTED NODDING IN
AGREEMENT. "NO, I'M NOT!" I DEFENDED MYSELF
WITH ALL OF THE ENERGY OF A NEWBORN MOLE RAT.

"WHAT ARE YOU EVEN RUNNING FOR?" THE GREEN
PARTY CANDIDATE SNEERED. OH, SURE, THAT I
REMEMBER!

"I...I..." I TOOK A MOMENT TO RECALIBRATE.
"WHY AM I RUNNING? FOR PUBLIC OFFICE? WHY?
WHY ME? WHY AM I? RUNNING?" I TOOK ANOTHER
MOMENT, RECALIBRATING IN WHAT I HOPED WOULD
PROVE A MORE PRODUCTIVE DIRECTION. "I'M
RUNNING BECAUSE THE PEOPLE COMING HERE FROM
MY HOME UNIVERSE ARE NOT ALWAYS TREATED
WELL, AND I BELIEVE IT WOULD HELP OUR CAUSE TO
BE REPRESENTED IN OTTAWA."

A LOT MORE WAS SAID THAT EVENING, BUT
NOTHING AS MEMORABLE AS THAT, DIARY, SO I'M
GOING TO MOVE ON.

AN HOUR AFTER THE DEBATE ENDED, AMAROSA,
AMY, A COUPLE OF THE VOLUNTEERS AND I WERE
SITTING IN THE CONSTITUENCY OFFICE, DRINKING
ACTUAL HOT COCOA (BUT NOT A GALLON - WEAK
BLADDER) AND ANALYZING THE DEBATE.

"I'M SORRY! I'M SO SORRY! I'M REALLY SORRY
ABOUT THAT, MISTER FROBISHER!" AMY WAS SAYING.
SHE HAD BEEN APOLOGIZING TO ME FROM THE
MOMENT SHE RUSHED ONTO THE STAGE AFTER THE
DEBATE HAD ENDED. YOU WOULDN'T BELIEVE HOW
MANY DIFFERENT WAYS A PERSON CAN APOLOGIZE IN
AN HOUR (SEVENTY-SIX, NOT THAT I WAS COUNTING
- THAT WAS VOLUNTEER CURTIS' JOB).

IN ORDER TO INCORPORATE THE MOST CURRENT
INFORMATION, AMY HAD TYPED UP THE SPEECH THE

NIGHT BEFORE THE DEBATE. UNFORTUNATELY, IN THE RUSH TO GET HER DAUGHTER, AUSTEN, TO SCHOOL THAT MORNING, SHE HAD MIXED UP MY SPEECH WITH AN APOLOGY HER FOURTH GRADER HAD HAD TO WRITE OVER HER INVOLVEMENT IN AN UNFORTUNATE WEDGIE INCIDENT.

MY INITIAL RESPONSE WAS, "CAN YOU IMAGINE THE LOOK ON THE PRINCIPAL'S FACE WHEN SHE HEARS WHY AUSTEN WANTS TO BECOME A MEMBER OF PARLIAMENT?" THIS JUST MADE AMY DOUBLE DOWN ON HER FORLORN LOOK AND APOLOGIZE FASTER, LOUDER, SINCERER.

"AMY, WE GET IT!" AMAROSA, EXASPERATED, EXCLAIMED. "YOU'RE SORRY. DONATE SOME MONEY TO GREENPEACE OR SACRIFICE A CHICKEN TO YOUR GOD OR SACRIFICE A CHICKEN TO GREENPEACE – DO WHATEVER YOU HAVE TO DO TO MAKE PEACE WITH WHAT HAPPENED. WE HAVE TO FOCUS!"

"BESIDES," I ASSURED HER, RUBBING THE BACK OF MY HEAD, "I WAS CONSCIOUS RIGHT THROUGH TO THE END OF THE DEBATE. I CONSIDER THAT A VICTORY."

AMY SNIFFED AND BURNED THE ROOF OF HER MOUTH WITH HOT COCOA. "REALLY?"

"REALLY." I PLAYFULLY PUNCHED AMY IN THE ARM, CAUSING HOT COCOA TO SPILL ALL OVER HER SHIRT. AMAROSA SPENT THE NEXT FIVE MINUTES TREATING HER BURNS. WHEN THE POSTMORTEM RECONVENED, AMY HAD STOPPED APOLOGIZING, A TESTAMENT TO THE SOUL-CLEANSING POWER OF SCALDING HOT LIQUIDS.

PICKING UP A THICK BINDER THAT LAY ON THE TABLE BEFORE HER, AMAROSA INFORMED US: "ON ANOTHHER NOTE, HUNTER, HAUNTER, SQUABASH, OUR PUBLIC RELATIONS FIRM, HAS FINALLY ANALYZED THE FOCUS GROUP RESPONSES TO THE 'PARLIAMENT NEEDS MORE MARTINIS' AD THAT RAN LAST WEEK."

IN THE AD, I LOOK HEROICALLY TOWARDS THE FUTURE WHILE A TANKER LEAKS OIL INTO A PRISTINE LAKE BEHIND ME. THEN, I TALK EARNESTLY TO A GROUP OF * OFFICIAL YOUNG PERSONS * AS

THEY CHECK MESSAGES OR PLAY GAMES ON THEIR PHONES. ONE * OFFICIAL YOUNG PERSON * NODS IN AGREEMENT, ALTHOUGH IF IT IS WITH WHAT I AM SAYING OR WHAT SHE IS READING ON THE SCREEN, WHO CAN SAY, REALLY? THEN, I WEAR A LAB COAT AND SAFETY GOGGLES TO A RODEO. THEN, I'M THE ONE WHO IS NODDING AS A MAN IN A SMART SUIT TELLS ME SOMETHING IMPORTANT (THAT WAS ACTUALLY ANDY, WHO LOOKS LIKE HE'S GIVING ME SERIOUS ECONOMIC ADVICE, BUT WHO WAS ACTUALLY TELLING ME LUNCH WAS GOING TO BE LATE AS THERE WAS A LONG LINEUP AT TIMMY'S; AAH, THE MAGIC OF FILMMAKING!). THE AD ENDS WITH ME GETTING THWAPPED IN THE BACK OF THE HEAD BY A PROVINCIAL FLAG WHICH REFUSES TO STAY IN THE BACKGROUND (IN RETROSPECT, NOT THE BEST USE OF A WIND MACHINE), WHILE I SAY, "VOTE FOR ME, MARTINI   FROBISHER, AS THE MEMBER OF PARLIAMENT FOR PERCH-LAKE-MESHUGGAH." WITHOUT MOVING MY LIPS. I'LL NEVER UNDERSTAND VOICE-OVERS! WHILE THE IMAGES FLOW ON THE SCREEN, JOHN PHILLIP SOUSA'S 'LIBERTY BELL MARCH' IS PLAYING IN THE BACKGROUND. EVERY TIME I WATCH THE AD, I'M MOVED (I DON'T KNOW WHY I KEEP GETTING IN PEOPLE'S WAY, BUT AT LEAST THEY'RE POLITE WHEN THEY TELL ME TO GO SOMEPLACE ELSE).

"HOW DO THEY LOOK?" I ASKED.

"WITH A LOT OF MAKEUP AND DARK LIGHTING, THEY COULD PASS FOR HUMAN...AS LONG AS YOU BELONGED TO A RACE THAT WASN'T OVERLY FAMILIAR WITH HUMANS."

ENCOURAGED, I ASKED HER FOR SOME DETAILS.

"OF THE FIFTEEN PEOPLE WHO WERE EXPOSED TO THE AD," AMAROSA READ, "SEVEN RESPONDED THEY THOUGHT IT WAS AN AD FOR A NEW BRAND OF COLD CREAM, FIVE THOUGHT IT WAS AN AD FOR AN UNNAMED TERRORIST ENVIRONMENTALIST GROUP AND THREE CRAVED FOOZLEBRRY PIE WITH A SCOOP OF

BLACK CURRANT ICE CREAM."

"That's good, that's good," I encouraged her. "Only two people in the last focus group wanted pie, and neither of them mentioned ice cream. This proves that our message is getting through!"

"Un hunh." Amarosa was the most unimpressable person I had ever met. "When asked how the ad made them feel, four said it made them want to hug a tree, three said it made them want to throw up a little in their mouths, two said it made them want to travel through a Dimensional Portal™ so they would have an excuse to punch a mime, two said it made them want to burn their ballots and one said it made her want to vote for you. That last one is likely an outlier whose response has no value."

"Hooray for outliers!" I shouted.

Amarosa looked over her glasses at me, which was impressive considering she had forgotten them at home. "As a control question, the group was asked, 'Where do you see yourself in four years?' Seven responded, 'Somewhere else,' seven responded, "Anywhere but here," and one responded, "On a dark desert highway, cool wind in my hair, warm smell of colitas rising up through the air." We were considering calling her an outlier, but she was too cute for labels."

"Hooray for not outliers!" I shouted. Sometimes these things just come out of their own accord.

Amarosa informed us that the rest of the results of the focus group could be read in the report called, "The Yellow Cockatiel Flies at Midnight!" She dropped the binder to the table with a * THUD * loud enough to let everybody know that she wished one of us

WOULD FLY WITH IT.

"EXCELLENT!" I WAS IRRATIONALLY EXUBERANT. "LET'S DO IT!" (TECHNICALLY, WE HAD ALREADY DONE IT, HAVING RUN THE AD LAST WEEK. I MAY NOT HAVE MANY SKILLS – ANOTHER REASON I THOUGHT I WAS WELL-SUITED TO BECOMING A POLITICIAN – BUT NOBODY OUT-IRRATIONALS ME!)

SINCE WE BLEW OUR BUDGET ON PRODUCTION VALUES (THOSE OIL TANKERS DON'T JUST LEAK THEMSELVES! – WELL, OKAY, ACTUALLY, THEY DO, BUT THE ONLY WAY THE COMPANY WOULD GIVE US PERMISSION TO SHOOT IN FRONT OF THE VESSEL WAS IF WE CONTRIBUTED TO THE CLEANUP COST, AND YOU WOULDN'T BELIEVE HOW EXPENSIVE THAT CAN BE!), WE COULD ONLY AFFORD TO RUN THE AD ONCE, ON CJCO-DT, THE MULTICULTURAL CHANNEL, AT THREE IN THE MORNING.

MONEY WELL SPENT!

"WHAT ABOUT YESTERDAY'S POLL?" ALL EYES TURNED TO AMY. ON HER RESUME, SHE HAD LISTED UNDER 'OTHER RELEVANT EXPERIENCE' THAT SHE HAD BEEN A POLE DANCER (STRICTLY IN ORDER TO PUT HERSELF THROUGH UNIVERSITY!), SO BEING IN CHARGE OF POLL WATCHING SEEMED TO BE HER HOMOPHONIC FATE. "AMY? AMY?"

AMY STARTED FROM WHATEVER REVERIE SHE WAS HAVING (IT WOULD HAVE BEEN CONVENIENT TO HAVE AN OMNISCIENT NARRATOR AROUND RIGHT ABOUT NOW, BUT I WASN'T ABOUT TO GIVE IT THE SATISFACTION OF TELLING IT THAT!), AND SAID, "SORRY! NOT ABOUT THE – YOU KNOW – I'LL ALWAYS BE SORRY ABOUT THAT – SORRY! – I...WHAT'S HAPPENING?"

"YESTERDAY'S POLL NUMBERS – HIT ME!" I ORDERED.

AMY RELUCTANTLY ROLLED HER EYES AND COLLECTED A COUPLE OF SHEETS OF PAPER FROM THE DESK IN FRONT OF HER. THEN, SHE WALKED OVER TO WHERE I WAS SITTING AND SAID, "THIRTY-SEVEN. TWENTY-FOUR. SIX. TWO. THIRTY-TWO."

WITH EACH NUMBER, AMY HIT ME IN THE CHEST WITH HER OPEN PALM.

"I FEEL YOU," I RESPONDED. "SUBURBAN WOMEN VOTERS?"

"NINETEEN. SIXTEEN. THREE. POINT FIVE. SIXTY."

"THERE'S A LOT OF POTENTIAL, THERE. UNIVERSITY STUDENTS?"

"FORTY-TWO. THIRTY-NINE. SIX. THREE. ELEVEN."

WITH A COUGH, I THANKED AMY FOR HER REPORT. AS SHE SAT BACK DOWN, I ASKED, "SO, WHAT DO THE NUMBERS TELL US?"

A TALL YOUNG MAN WITH A SCRUFFY SALT-AND-PEPPER BEARD IN THE BACK OF THE ROOM SAID, "YOU'LL BE LUCKY TO WIN ENOUGH VOTES TO GET BACK YOUR SECURITY DEPOSIT."

I TURNED TO AMAROSA. "WHAT DO WE DO WITH VOLUNTEERS WITH THAT ATTITUDE?"

AMAROSA TURNED TO THE SCRUFFY YOUNG MAN. "YOU'RE FIRED."

"JOKE'S ON YOU," HE REPLIED. "I'M NOT A VOLUNTEER. I'M ONLY HERE BECAUSE I HEARD THERE WAS FREE PIE." HE LOOKED AROUND THE ROOM, SIZING US UP, THEN GRABBED A HALF-FINISHED TIN OF BANANA CHOCOLATE AND SAUNTERED OUT OF THE OFFICE.

BEFORE ANYBODY COULD THINK TOO MUCH ABOUT THAT, I CLAPPED MY HANDS TOGETHER AND SAID, "GREAT WORK, EVERYBODY! LET'S CALL IT A NIGHT AND MEET BRIGHT AND EARLY TOMORROW FOR ANOTHER EXCITING DAY OF...CANVASSING..."

CAMPAIGN DIARY, DAY TWENTY-ONE

DEAR...DIARY,

CANVASSING. SIGH.

He strides onto the stage like a four foot tall blue colossus. The headpiece holding the microphone close to his mouth is, like his three piece suit, exquisite. He puts the battered brown briefcase he carries down a few feet away from the people sitting in the front row. People who have paid more than many of their employees earn in a month to attend this event hang on his every word, and he hasn't even said anything yet. He scans the crowd, focusing his gaze on a middle-aged tampon millionairess, and says, "Have you ever noticed that every Ted talks, but few Teds say anything worth listening to?"

Rodney   Pendleton   spreads   his   arms   out, inviting the packed house to consider the wisdom in what he has just said. Some do. Others consider the wisdom of having that extra cup of coffee in the morning. One or two begin to consider the wisdom of paying more than their employees earn in a month to attend this event.

Eventually, Rodney returns his arms to his side and says: "Listen. You've paid a lot to be here, so it's probably a good idea. There is a story my people tell to our children – not that we have any – the last child of my race was born several thousand years ago. But we all were children at some point – probably – maybe – let's say for the sake of argument. A story. My people tell. To children...of all ages. Because we're all children, at heart. Even those who have no heart. Especially those who have no heart. Frankenstein's monster, say, or a Conservative premier. A story. My people tell. It is called, 'The Triumph of the Almost Fairy'. It used to be called, 'Ten Little Digglers", but the term became offensive to sleazy street vendors, so that title went out of use. Not to worry, though: it's the same story. Except for the part about the unspreadable cottage cheese. Which, having eaten my share of over the years, I can tell you was no great loss. **A story!** My people tell. The Almost Fairy looked like N. K. Jemison and had the attitude of a pit bull. You might, too, if you had her power: the ability to help people find what they were looking for...almost. For example, if you needed a cable to plug your computer into a power source, she would help you find one...only, one of the ends wouldn't properly fit into its assigned port. If you were looking for a sock to match the one you had in your hand, she would help you find one...only the pattern on it would be diamonds instead of squares. If you were looking for a life partner, somebody who would stand by you and love you and support you through the good times and the bad no matter what, she would – well, you get the idea. She tried her best. This is a story about trying your best. Despite trying her best, she was vilified by people who found her help not all that helpful. So, Myrtle, for that was the Almost Fairy's name that I just came up with, spent a lot of time at the Crown and Giblets, a pub that was frequented by down-on-their-luck magical creatures. Maureen, a lycanthrope who, during a full moon, turned into an Alaskan Klee Kai with a penchant for nibbling on people's toes, was the server. Edison Carter, the leprechaun whose pot of gold was made out of brass, tended bar. It was a busy Friday night when Myrtle made her way to the table she shared with Larry, the Half-remembered Dream Fairy. Nursing a pair of Roaring Rakshasas (made of Kahlua, Grand Marnier, orange juice and unicorn tears), Myrtle commiserated with Terry over his latest client, whom he had helped remember a dream where he was driving away from something terrible or driving towards something terrible – he couldn't remember enough of the dream to know which. That meant he didn't know if the dream was telling him to make a decision or avoid making a decision, help which he found not really that helpful. The client spent the morning cursing Larry out and reposting Farcebook messages about the coming *sturm and drang* to his wall. 'I don't know what I did to deserve that abuse,' Larry said between swigs. 'I was doing my job in good faith – that should surely count for something!' Indeed, it should. This is a story about the need to reward people for good faith efforts. Myrtle suggested, not for the first time – actually, for the forty-second time – that they take the matter of their sucky assignments up with Hardscrabble Constantinople, the CEO of Airy Fairy, the not-for-profit, no-not-us, heaven-forfend-we-should-make-a-profit organization that employed the planet's fairies, goblins and ogres under five feet, six inches tall (the ogres over five feet six inches tall had been let go when it looked like they were going to form a union, so they started their own corporation, which struggled until they adopted the same organizational structure as the company they had left behind – this is a story about how good intentions are often ground to pixie dust by bureaucratic realities). Larry objected that the CEO would never make time for a pair of lowly fairies like themselves, and, anyway, it would take a long time for them to travel to Fairyland – almost three quarters of a second! Maybe it was the Roaring Rakshasas, or maybe it was the unending torrent of disappointment and verbal abuse that she had had to put up with for so long, so, so very long, but Myrtle decided to go to Fairyland with or without Larry. This is a story about standing up for yourself no matter what anybody else tells you. Lar – no. No, this isn't a story about standing up for yourself no matter what anybody else tells you. There are so many stories about standing up for yourself no matter what anybody else tells you, if people hear one more of them, their ears will start to bleed. Larry wished Myrtle luck and asked her to send him a postcard from Fairyland. Myrtle downed the last of her drink, got out her magic wand (the one with the pink star at the end which trailed dust even when she wasn't casting a spell – say this for her, Myrtle knew how to make a public impression!) and disappeared in a cloud of glitter. Two and seven sixths (if that is even mathematically possible) seconds later, a postcard appeared on the table in front of Larry's Kickin' Kaiju (a combination of Sambuca, Sangria, Worcestershire Sauce and the flop sweat of a clown) – this was Larry's idea of mixing things up. On the front of the postcard was a photograph of an auto shop named Joe's Garage where, for some reason, all of the windows had been concreted over. I've never quite understood that detail, myself. Perhaps, it's a symbol of the ultimate impenetrability of metaphors. Perhaps it's a veiled criticism of the practice of burying bodies in half-constructed buildings. Perhaps one of the ancestors who handed down this story had told it after a peyote bender, and the detail stuck. The important thing is that, on the other side of the postcard, somebody had written Larry's name in the box for the address and 'When winter wafts her weary wattles/We'll drain the contents of all the bottles!'"

Rodney pauses to let the idea sink in, then continues: "**A story! My people tell!** The lesson of the story couldn't be more clear if it was made out of air in a vacuum. So, in summation, I would like to reenact for you now my favourite scene from the classic Hollywood film *The Godfather*."

Rodney lays his briefcase on its side on the stage and opens it. Reaching in, he helps a four year-old boy walk up and out of it onto the stage. Reaching in a second time, he helps a five year-old girl walk out of the briefcase and onto the stage. He and the children[12] look at each other. "Just like we rehearsed it, okay?" he asks them using his inside voice, an effect undermined by the fact that he hasn't turned off his microphone. The children nod. Then, Rodney nods at them, and they turn and run around the stage, arms flailing and giggling in glee.

"Where are you, children?" Rodney playfully cries, looking this way and that, pretending not to see them. "I'm coming for you! Here I come!"

Rodney huffs as he trots across the stage. The boy laughs as he crosses in front of the alien. Rodney puffs as he plods across the stage. The girl giggles as she crosses

---

[12] Actually, life-like androids of children. Rodney cannot use the suitcase to channel his thoughts to create organic matter (life, to you), only objects.

behind the alien. Breathing heavily, Rodney turns this way and that, searching for something. Wheezing, he takes a couple of steps forward. Then, he clutches at his chest before falling face first onto the stage.

The children, who had stopped moving when Rodney clutched his chest, double over, their arms dangling uselessly, the light out in their eyes.[13]

The crowd waits a moment or two, then politely applauds.

---

[13] Told you. If the children had been real, Child Services would have had a conniption fit, but, as it was, the children would become the problem of the Ontario Science Centre.

Refugees Get to the Bottom of Grief

by FREDERICA VON McTOAST-HYPHEN, Alternate Reality News Service People Writer

Aliens from all over the world – and France – came to Toronto for the funeral of Rodney Pendleton, who died while giving a lecture on Thursday. It was a sombre, black pie affair, with eulogies that stressed the first refugee from Earth Prime 4-6-4-0-8-9 dash Omega's courage, honour and ability to wield puns at a distance of fifty feet.

Strange, then, that all of the aliens wore exquisite three piece suits with the seats removed, exposing their bottoms.

When I asked Allegra Potsherd why she had removed the seat of her pants, she told me that she had been advised to do so by her good friend Paulina Alldente.

When I asked Paulina Alldente why she had removed the seat of her pants, she told me that she had heard that it was a common funeral rite from a co-worker, Phillipino Sasquatch.

When I asked Phillipino Sasquatch why he thought that removing the seat of your pants is a common funeral rite, he referred me to his good friend Allegra Potsherd.

I should have seen that one coming.

According to Roman Lamplighter (of the Baker Street Lamplighters), exposing one's ass is a religious experience for the aliens. "It helps them score ratings points with their god, the Audi Enz," he explained. "The more serious the affair, the greater the comic effect. A lot of the aliens will be getting their names inscribed in the Good Book – the Nielsen Ratings – for doing this!"

The backsidelash was quick. "Many people think these aliens are adorable little creatures, with their wild slipping on banana peels and obsession with wordplay," said Mannfred Friedman, a member of the humans first group Humanity Against Alien Cards. "**Don't be fooled!** Exist – sorry, for a moment, there, I thought you were sitting in a cone of silence. Don't be fooled. Existence is a serious business, with lots of suffering and misery and endless reboots and remakes of mediocre TV series. By treating everything as a joke, the aliens are mocking our way of life!'

"Weeeeeeeeeeeeeelllllllll," Algernon Pendragon , founder of the Aliens Helping Aliens (AHA!) Foundation and chief organizer of the funeral, stretched the word out to seven minutes, thirty-seven seconds, a personal best. "Far be it from me to argue with a human – they're so cute with their 'facts' and 'logical assumptions' and 'bear spray'. But in this instance, I – well, okay, there was that argument with Lentil Rodriguez, but she really didn't know the meaning of the word 'abstemious', or if it even was a word. But other than that, I – umm, yeah, actually, there was the argument I had with Patchouli Smeg about the storming of Fort Sumter – he got very hot about my theory that a cold front was the culprit. So, okay, I may argue with human beings once in a while – like the time Antonio Ferreros brought a mule into the office and I told him –"

Half an hour later, I checked in with Pendragon to see if he had finished talking about all of the arguments with human beings that he hadn't gotten into. He hadn't. So, with a heavy heart (it had grown three sizes while I was watching a Christma-KwaanzUkah special – my cardiologist says if we don't operate ASAP to reduce the swelling, it could crush my lungs, kidneys and fava beanless liver), I decided to move on.

"Our political system is built on a foundation of probity and serious self-reflection," Friedman fulminated (not to worry: I should be able to get the stains out of the carpet). "I don't know why they're doing this to us, but if we allow the aliens to continue acting in such a disrespectful way, it could create cracks within our way of life, undermining all that we hold dear. If that happens, we might as well be Belgium!"

"Human beings are so egotistical!" Lamplighter, who has studied the aliens since they started immigrating to Earth Prime and whose book on them, *OU812: Decoding the Alien to De-alienate the Code* was a finalist for the Luigi Grimaldi Award for Nice Spelling, countered. "We always see the actions of the aliens as something they are doing to us – it never occurs to most people that the aliens have goals that have nothing to do with us!"

"...with Saskia Alberta about whether time is a straight line, a circle or a jagged little pill. So, fine, maybe I like to argue with humans about half the time, but..." Nope. Still at it with the arguing.

Rodney Pendleton was buried at the Holy Crud Blossom Cemetery. Squirting flowers are always welcome.

"Mourn. Moon. It's such a fine line – it's easy to see how people could confuse the two concepts."

"No, it really isn't."

"I'm sure it happens to human beings all the time."

"Nope. It has never happened in the history of human funerals."

"That's a lot of funerals. Are you sure?"

"It would be all over the internet if it had."

"You know your world better than I do," Algernon Pendragon allowed.

Algernon and Anastasia La Bombon were in attendance at a board meeting of the Aliens Helping Aliens (AHA! – not to be confused with the 1980s rock band, the 1970s t-shirt company or the 1930s dance sensation, all of which I just made up) Foundation. The agenda consisted of the following items:

1. Old business
2. New business
3. Red business
4. Blue business
5. Hackeysack (don't talk back!)

Typical of most meeting agendas, it contained enough detail to seem to guide the discussion while being sufficiently ambiguous to allow for chaos.

"This is a ridiculous manifestation of a moral crusade intended to interfere with our sacred personal freedoms," John Galt, the four foot tall round-featured blue alien in the exquisite three piece suit whose pleasant speaking voice sounded like Armageddon, intoned. "What we choose to do with our bodies –"

"Yes, John, thank you for that, but –" Algernon tried to stem the rising tide of verbiage. (In this case, a rising tide drowns all boats.)

To no avail. "Is our own sovereign decision. Whether driven by envy or spite or prudishness or some deeper, less fathomable rationale, the busybodies who are always telling us what body parts we may or may not publicly display are –"

"Yes, John, your opinions on the matter are well known," Algernon tried again. "But they're not directly related to the meeting agenda. Okay, they might, maybe, a little bit, just a tad be tangentially related to red business, but still."

He may as well have tried to stop an oncoming train with a ramen noodle. John continued over him: "Part and parcel with the efforts of the moochers and the deadbeats to strip free men of their fundamental freedom. Today, it may be bottomless pants. Tomorrow, it will be enforced labour in –"

"John   Galt!" Anastasia bellowed. "**Will! You! Shut! The ferk! Up!**"

This   got   his   attention   long   enough   for Sissy   Hankshaw (a four foot tall blue alien in an exquisite three piece suit who had an unfortunate digital affliction) to awkwardly try to open a small container of cream for her coffee (in the "If I said 'I told you so' once...!" mug), spraying everybody at the table. "Sorry," she apologized. "I seem to be all thumbs, today. John, could you get me a creamer for my coffee?"

"Get it yourself," he snarled. But that seemed to stop his monologue before it had time to gather much steam (there was so little, in fact, that if this was a romance novel, you wouldn't be motivated to draw a decent-sized smiley face on a window by it).

"Alright then," Algernon began. "If we could –"

"Billy, could you help me out, here?" Sissy asked the

four foot tall blue alien in an exquisite three piece suit with a look on his face that combined far away and bemused.

"Certainly," Billy Pilgrim replied. "At this moment, I was meant to pour creamer into your cup of coffee...even while I am dodging a car falling out of the sky back on our home planet and...yes, am about to be killed by a hovercar falling out of the sky sixteen years from now. It's not ironic, it's just a little bit of history repeating."

Everybody in the room watched as Billy calmly walked over to the desk to the left (your left) of the conference table and methodically put the cup of coffee down, took the lid off the container of creamer, poured creamer from a carton into the coffee cup, put the lid back on the container of creamer, paused for a moment for a mild shudder, took a stir stick from out of the glass on the desk that held them, stirred the creamer into the coffee, tapped the stir stick on the rim of the mug to remove excess liquid, dropped the stir stick into the small garbage bin next to the desk, and returned to the conference table, placing the mug in front of Sissy. When you have become unstuck in time, attending to the details keeps you grounded and functional.

"Fascinating," Algernon mused. Then, shaking the wonder out of his head, he continued, "The main reason for calling this meeting is to assess what the human reaction is going to be to our behaviour at the funeral. Anastasia, who, as you know, is the Vice President, Ambiguous Reclamations and Public Relations, has done a poll to give us hard numbers which will help us determine what our least embarrassing response to the human reaction could be. Anastasia?"

"Thanks, Algernon." Anastasia looked a little uncomfortable: all of the furniture in the room had been built for the smaller aliens, forcing her to sit with her knees up against her chest and her bum squeezed into the chair. It reminded her of a game that she used to play with her clients in her previous life called 'Latex Beach Baby'. The experience had taught Anastasia how to plow forward through the discomfort and get the job done. "According to my survey, like, forty per cent of humans still loved us after the incident and forty per cent still, like, hated us after the incident."

"That's only eighty per cent," John sourly pointed out. "What about the other twenty per cent?"

"Julius chased me off his property with a shotgun."

"So much for empiricism," Algernon commented ryely (kimmel seeds from lunch were still stuck between his teeth). "Perhaps we should try a different approach. From the northern side of the bank, for instance, or using a four iron instead of a mashied potatoes. Anastasia, what does your gut tell you about the situation, and can it do any impressions? Because I gotta tell ya, your gut could use some elocution lessons!"

"My gut, which speaks just fine, if a bit nasally, thank you very much, tells me that this could be a problem for integrating aliens into, like, human society," Anastasia gamely (she would rather be playing Life than attending meetings in this one) continued. "I've been living around human beings all my life..."

"One could say you're almost one of them," Sissy gently suggested.

"Exactly," Anastasia smiled. "Like, sometimes I feel exactly like one of them. It's uncanny. Aaaaaanyway, human beings take their death rituals seriously – so seriously, they, like, only think about them when dealing with the death of somebody they either really love or really hate. Or, in the case of celebrities, both. Despite, like, this, my feeling is that living with the alien refugees for, like, three and a half years, most people's opinions of them have already been set, with only, like, a small number of undecideds. So, this shouldn't do anything too bad to the cause's reputation. As long as you don't plan on doing anything so insensitive again in the future, we should be – oh, what?"

All of the aliens around the table suddenly found Anastasia to be an attention deflector: the more they wanted to pay attention to her, the more they found themselves looking at the door, the ceiling or random objects in the room (except for Billy who, in addition to looking at the pot of coffee resting on the desk, was looking at the house on the downtown Kanata street he would be living in in eight years and the birth canal through which he was about to emerge any second now).

"Will you at least, like, **try** to respect human sensitivities on the subject of death?" Anastasia demanded.

"We will be mindful of human sensitivities on the subject of death," Algernon assured her.

"Oh, goo –" Anastasia started.

"Unless we find a way to make the situation funny," Algernon cut her off.

Part of Anastasia wanted to object. However, another part of her, the part she discovered when she melded with an alien and obtained his thoughts and memories, wanted to cheer. Cheering an objection would be absurd (try it if you don't believe me – you can't say this isn't a challenging book), so, instead, she said, "I believe we understand each other."

"Right!" Algernon temporarily borrowed (what you or I might call 'stole', but, of course, you and I weren't risking arrest) a glance at the agenda and began: "If we are done with that subject, we can move on to Red Business. The staff lounge needs a new coat of paint..."

Daveen Rasmalai Rapier, not currently having any operativing assignments, had returned to driving a yellow school bus full of aliens to Earth Prime (the vehicle had been modified with Dimension Transcending Technology^{TM}); he was doing this when Rodney died.

The aliens were making funny faces at each other and obscure but possibly obscene gestures at him; he sorely wanted to shout that if they didn't behave, he would turn the bus around, but sound didn't travel in the Pollock and they weren't outfitted with microchips that would allow him to communicate with them. After delivering (which did not have anything to do with removing the organ that regulates most chemical levels in the blood – the poor things had only just got their internal organs, after all!) them to Transdimensional Authority headquarters and returning the Dimensional School Bus^{TM} to the yard, Phil, the mechanic from the shop down the street, took him aside and gave him the news. Daveen Rasmalai appeared to take it stoically. However, he immediately went to the Blurq and Fungobat, the nearest bar that catered to aliens, got drunk on Romulan Ale and punched a Ventrosian Squiggle so hard its head bobbled uncontrollably for over three hours. When management made it clear that his behaviour was unacceptable, he graciously moved on to the establishment across the street (knocking over the sign in front of the Blurq and Fungobat that had the daily specials – grace is a very personal quality).

The Elliptical Garter Snail was named in honour of Phloeneddi, the ancient Greek goddess of petty annoyances. In Aristotle's lost comedy *The Thirteenth Trial of Herakles*, Phloeneddi took the form of a snail that ladies of the court would wear in their garters to signal their most fertile periods; sometimes, she would elongate her body in order to slip under the front door of the hero's house and rearrange his furniture while he was out heroing. When he returned home and caught her in the act, Herakles smote Phloeneddi with a blow that wasn't even all that mighty. The story ended with two minor characters getting married (that's how you know it's a comedy). *The Thirteenth Trial of Herakles* is believed to have been Aristotle's shortest play.

Ordinarily, Daveen Rasmalai wouldn't be seen drinking in the Elliptical Garter Snake, the unofficial bar of the Transdimensional Authority; but his usual bar, Shorty Morty's on the South Forty ("Where nobody knows you name, and everybody's okay with that."), was closed for renovations (it was being turned into condos) and invisibility cloaks would not be available for generations, and he had...you knowed at the Blurq and Fungobat. So, he sat on a stool at the bar and ordered Pangalactic Gargle Blaster after Pangalactic Gargle Blaster. Bartender Butch had no idea what a Pangalactic Gargle Blaster was, so he gave Daveen Rasmalai gin and tonics. When the customer complained that the drink didn't taste quite right, Bartender Butch told him that it was because the shipment of esoteric beetle juice from Alpha Centauri was late, and he had to improvise. By the third drink in that establishment, it didn't matter any more.

Daveen Rasmalai stewed in the lukewarm waters of grief. He remembered the time he had spent with Rodney. There was, for instance, the night that the alien painted moustaches on all of the paintings in his apartment, which was odd considering that they were landscapes. And they were photographs. Daveen Rasmalai had to smile at that, even though he raged for several days when it actually happened. Or the time that Rodney spent three hours describing his investigation of a murder that centred around a statue of a platypus from Gibraltar; when, a couple of weeks later, he realized that Rodney had just regurgitated the plot of *The Maltese Falcon*, Daveen Rasmalai was more bemused than anything. Then, there was the time that Rodney brought home a –

PFFFFFFFFFFFFTTTTTTTTTTTHTTTT![14]

Daveen Rasmalai quickly turned in his seat to see who had blown him a raspberry. However, there was nobody standing near him, and the people sitting at tables closest to him didn't seem to be paying him any attention. Before he could try to figure out where the sound had come from, his cellphone vibrated. Turning back to the bar, he

---

[14] Sound effects inspired by Don Martin.

took the phone out of his pocket and looked at the caller ID. The Transdimensional Authority. He put the phone back in his pocket. It could wait.[15]

---

[15] Four days later, when the drumming in Daveen Rasmalai's head had been reduced to a single snare no longer played by Keith Moon, he recovered his messages. This was among them:

"You have reached the public line of Daveen Rasmalai Rapier. If this was an important call, you would have dialed my private cell, so if this is something that requires a prompt response, well, you've come to the wrong place. If you would like to leave a message anyway – and I kind of admire your optimism if you do – start talking at the sound of the beep."

BEEEEEEEEEEEEEEEEEP

"Hello, Mister Rapier. It's Doctor Richardson, Assistant Director of the Transdimensional Authority's * SCIENCE! * division. What's blue and red and – say, why don't we have your private cell number? We're not trying to sell you encyclopedias made out of aluminum siding or anything. The news I must impart to you is something you may want to follow up on posthaste. In fact –"

"He cannot follow up on anything posthaste, telexhaste or cave paintinghaste if you don't tell him what the news is first."

"Ah. Right. Good point, Doctor Alhambra. Okay. What's blue and red and smells like a nunchaku that hasn't been varnished in a month of Tuesdays? (I'm told it's like a month of Sundays, only with an increased amount of hair grooming product.) So. Blue, red and smells like an unvarnished nunchaku – any idea what it is? Any at all, hmm? David Tennant's electric nose hair trimmer! (pause) I hope you found that amusing. I was told that, when one has the unfortunate task of delivering bad news to somebody, one should start with a joke to lighten the atmosphere. In retrospect, perhaps I should not have got the joke from *The Onion in the Oatmeal*. My apologies if –"

"Richardson! Will! You! Get! On with it!"

"Right. Right. Absolutely right, Doctor Alhambra. So. Mister Rapier. As you should know by now, Rodney   Pendleton has died. Tragic business, that, but, well, there you go. That's life. We thought it odd that he made his death so...public. So, in the name of scientific inquiry, we decided it would be for the best if we conducted an autopsy on his bod – his remai – umm, that is to say, on him. We conducted an autopsy on him. What was left of him, in any case. Of course, ordinarily, we would not share the results of such an intimate procedure with somebody to

The sting of having had his Bastards of the Universe case solved out from under him by Joe and Bill contributed to Daveen Rasmalai's dark mood. Oh, sure, they had a perfect arrest record while he had been chasing the Bastards for years without anything to show for it. The fact that they were admirable only made it worse. The additional fact that they were already becoming fuzzy in his memory took a bit of the edge off, but a vague sense of failure isn't all that much better than a complete one.

Anyway. Diversions had their place, but you had to get back to the main story sooner or later or you'd end up with narrative chaos. And we couldn't have that because...well...reasons. Daveen Rasmalai's thoughts turned back to Rodney. He was reminded of the time that the alien brought home a –

SHHHHHHWUP!   SHHHHHHWUP! SHHHHHHWIBBEM! BRRRRAAAAPPPP!

Daveen Rasmalai turned in the direction he thought the rude noise had come from. In front of him stood a fire hydrant with limbs and dark glasses.

---

whom the deceased was not related – not only could that open us up to all sorts of unpleasant legal ramifications, but it would be extremely tacky. However, under the circumstances –"

"Oh, give me that! Rapier! The Pendleton subject died of cancer. Cancer, Rapier! He used your body as a template in order to live in this universe, which means there is a very good possibility that you have cancer, too! Get it checked out immediately!"

"I was getting to that, Doctor Alhambra..."

"Before or after the heat death of the universe?"

"None of us will live to see the heat death of the universe."

"Speak for yourself, Richardson. Speak for –"

BEEEEEEEEEEEEEEEEP

The message could have waited a little longer. But not too much longer. Early detection of his cancer added twenty-three years, six months, four days and seventeen hours to Daveen Rasmalai's life, with a thirty-seven per cent increase in the quality of his life in his old age. There is a lesson there for all of us, although paying close attention to the health of the alien who uses your body as a template probably isn't it.

"Bob Blunt," he sourly identified the man.

"Well, if isn't the inoperative operative," Bob Blunt matched him PH level for PH level. "What are you doing here, Rapier? This is a TA bar."

Daveen Rasmalai looked this way and that. "I don't see any strippers..."

"Ha ha," Bob Bunt didn't laugh. "You got it good, man. You get to investigate serious crimes. Meanwhile, all us hard working investigators are alien chauffeurs. You know what happened to me on my shift yesterday? As we were entering the Dimensional Portal^{TM}, one of the aliens I was escorting from their home universe did a spit take with a strawberry smoothie. The red splotch he created slowly spread out like it was just another part of the Pollock. By the time we got to Earth Prime, I had forgotten it wasn't part of the space between universes and walked right into it. Man, I gotta pay for my own dry cleaning!"

Daveen Rasmalai stifled a smile.

Bob Blunt poked him in the chest. "But you, you get to go off on adventures, doing real investigating! I'll bet you even get an expense account, you lucky bastard! You think being an operative is better than being an investigator. Well, I've got news for you, pal: you –"

From out of nowhere, a pie appeared in Daveen Rasmalai's left hand (the one that wasn't clutching his drink). Without a moment's hesitation, he threw it in Bob Blunt's face.

"What the – what the ferk, man?" the investigator sputtered.

Taking a napkin with an image of a stretched out garter snail on it off the bar and offering it to Bob Blunt, Daveen Rasmalai said, "Sorry. Sometimes I have poor impulse control."

Bob Blunt looked warily at the napkin, which was clearly not up to the task of wiping his face clean, but, with fruit dripping off his chin, decided to snatch it out of the operative's hand and clean what he could. "Lemon meringue. I hate lemon meringue! That was not cool, man. That was like something a ferking alien would do!"

Daveen Rasmalai shrugged. "Aliens can be cool. It's a matter of perspective, real –"

"Hey!" Bob Blunt shouted. "I'm talking to you!"

Daveen Rasmalai blinked. Bob Blunt stood in front of him, conspicuously unpied. *What the hell?* he asked himself.

"That was what I was asking you before you zombied out on me! Crazy bastard!" Bob Blunt stalked away.

From somewhere, Daveen Rasmalai could hear laughter, but try as he might, he couldn't pinpoint its source. With a shrug, he returned to his drink, finishing it and signalling to Bartender Butch to give him another.

Now, where was he? Oh, right. Good times with Rodney. There was that one time that the alien brought home a –

WOCKA WOCKA SHHHHHBURRRUUUUMP TCHOCKA!

The mocking sounds were becoming highly annoying, so Daveen Rasmalai turned and said in the sternest possible tone (one that didn't even allow for the possibility of a stem): "Will whoever is making those highly annoying noises please – oh. It's you."

A different fire hydrant with limbs and dark glasses stood before him. This one had sandy hair and an infectious grin. "I haven't been making annoying noises," he said, "but I did come over to apologize, so you can fold the annoying noises into that if it would be of any value to you."

"Oh. Umm...no..."

"Yeah, I'm sorry about what happened the last time I saw you. I had no idea that Turkish food could do that to a human body."

"Thanks," Daveen Rasmalai rallied, "but nobody knew that would happen. Even me. So, no apology necessarily."[16]

"You look like you could use a drink."

---

[16] This is much easier to understand if you know the context.

"I wouldn't say no."[17]

The two men were prohibited by their contracts of employment from talking about their work and discouraged by the Macho Code of Manliness from talking about their personal lives. So, mostly they talked about the one subject they knew they had in common: science fiction. Crash was a traditionalist who thought the genre peaked in the 1950s and, except for a grudging respect for the cyberpunk of the 1980s, held that everything that came after the golden age was terrible. While he had grudging respect for the golden age of the 1950s, Daveen Rasmalai was an ardent fan of the diversity of science fiction that had developed in the new millennium.

The discussion was spirited but respectful. Crash only shook his head once. Daveen Rasmalai assumed that the investigator was disagreeing with his enthusiasm for Afro-futurism. In fact, Crash hadn't read much in the sub-genre, so he had no opinion on it; he had seen Bob Blunt coming at them from behind and, assuming that he was ready for round two, gave his fellow investigator a

---

[17] Oh, wait – I'm the one who is supposed to supply the context. Sorry about that. So many fiddly details to keep track of in these literary endeavours; it's easy to sometimes lose track. For the last few years, the fire hydrant with limbs and dark glasses who goes by the name of 'Crash' Chumley had been dating Daveen Rasmalai's sister, Noomi Rapier. Noomi had been staying in Daveen Rasmalai's apartment in Ottawa while he gallivanted (not just for gals any more!) around the world. A couple of years earlier, Daveen Rasmalai returned to Ottawa to work with the Transdimensional Authority, eventually focusing on the alien refugee problem, forcing Noomi to find a new place to live. She moved in with Crash. The unfortunate incident with the Turkish shish kebab happened when, after the move, Crash offered to treat everybody who had helped to dinner. Halfway through the meal, Daveen Rasmalai's fingers began to randomly shrink and expand, like somebody was playing his hands like a trumpet to a tune only they could hear. It took about six hours for the effects of the kebab to wear off. At the time, Daveen Rasmalai felt the need for an apology; now, not so much.

discouraging look that many in the bullpen feared and all respected. Bob Bunt slunk away without engaging.

When he finished his second drink, Crash rose from his stool and said, "I'd love to stay and debate the merits of queer SF, but Noomi's making squid casserole tonight, and I should get back just late enough that it has dried out, forcing us to order in."

Daveen Rasmalai shuddered at the thought of his sister's squid casserole. "You're a better man than I, Crash Chumley," he said. Then, he added, "How's Noomi doing?"

"You should call her and find out for yourself," Crash advised.

"Oh, well, you know, humph, something something busy something," Daveen Rasmalai grumbled.[18]

"I know exactly what you mean," Crash agreed. Something in his tone gave Daveen Rasmalai reason to believe that he actually did. Then, Crash walked out of the bar.

Daveen Rasmalai motioned to the bartender to pour him another. A little voice in his head said, "Save some gloom for later. The worst is still to come." Recognizing that he had enough gloom to go around, Daveen Rasmalai quickly downed the drink placed in front of him and ordered another.

---

[18] In a completely Macho Code of Manliness approved manner.

Okay, Give Me Your Case, But Make It Brief!

by NANCY GONGLIKWANYEOHEEEEEEEH, Alternate Reality News Service Technology Writer

Annabella Gazpacho likes to think of herself as a good person. She considers giving to charities all the time. She once helped an elderly woman to the curb, but the light changed, and by the time she could help the woman across the street, Gazpacho had already ducked into a nearby bakery. She never made fun of her husband of thirty months Leopold when he shouted out the wrong answers when they were watching *Jeopardy*. And he blurted out some howlers.

However, in the chaos after the death of Rodney Pendleton, Gazpacho, a skeleton key grip (she could really afford to put on twenty or thirty pounds) for the Good Gracie Allen Auditorium where the alien's TED Talk was being held, was tempted by fate. She gave in without a struggle.

She snatched Pendleton's briefcase.

"He made it look like magic," Gazpacho explained. "He opened the briefcase, and all of these objects came out. A breadbox that was actually bigger than a breadbox. A scale model replica of the British Parliament buildings complete with a Boris Johnson inaction figure. A piston engine. Who wouldn't be tempted by a briefcase that could give you a free piston engine?"

Magic, hunh? So, if a fairy died in front of her, would Gazpacho pry the wand from its cold, dead fingers?

"You have a way of making things seem tawdry, you know that?" Gazpacho groused (it's okay – she didn't have a license, but the bird was out of season).

The problem is that the briefcase didn't work. Gazpacho opened it with her right hand, but nothing appeared in it. She opened it with her left hand. Nothing. She opened it while standing on her head. Nothing. She repeatedly opened it during a five day period where she had worn it on her head (the consensus in her neighbourhood was that it wasn't as stylish as one might think). Nothing. She thought really hard about what she wanted for three and a half hours before opening it; those are a handful of neurons that she'll never get back!

In all, Gazpacho opened the briefcase five hundred seventy-six times, and all she got for her efforts was the faint whiff of failure. In frustration, she gave the briefcase to the person it should have gone to in the first place: Algernon Pendragon , Vice President, Finance and Vivian Vance of the AHA! Foundation.

"It was the right thing to do," Gazpacho explained.

"But that's not what she did!" VP Pendragon protested. No? Oh.

Gazpacho tried to sell the briefcase to the Transdimensional Authority. The Transdimensional Authority responded that it would be happy to take the case off her hands in exchange for not pressing charges on the whole theft thing. Gazpacho countered: "throw in five hundred bucks to make it interesting and you've got a deal." The Transdimensional Authority counter-offered to pay for a cab to have her come to the nearest branch office to be arrested.

She handed over the briefcase.

"It was my patriotic duty," Gazpacho grumped.

According to the Transdimensional Authority's Chief Science Officer Doctor Alhambra, she may as well not have bothered. "It's a battered old briefcase!" he complained. "It contains no mechanical parts whatsoever! Okay, the worn surface has character, I'll give you that. However, other than that, the briefcase is of no scientific interest whatsoever!"

When I suggested that the object may have been quantum entangled with its original universe, allowing objects to move from one to the other, Doctor Alhambra informed me that there was no way of knowing. When I asked him if he didn't have equipment to be able to test for such a thing, he snorted.

"Good Gord, man!" Doctor Alhambra exclaimed. "We don't claim to have technologies generations ahead of what we could be expected to have at this stage of our society's development in order to conveniently solve narrative incongruities. This isn't *Star Blap!*"

Point taken. In the rump. Ouch.

So, did the briefcase finally make its way to VP Pendragon? "I'm happy to say, it did," he was happy to say. [I was happy, too: one or two more people between him and ownership of the object and this article would have had to have been a series! And I hate series with a deep, burning, warm up the slapping gloves passion!

BRENDA BRUNDTLAND-GOVANNI, Editrix-in-Chief]

Will the AHA! Foundation display the briefcase prominently as a reminder of the importance of Pendleton? "Naah," VP Pendragon, the second alien to emigrate to Earth Prime from the dying universe Earth Prime 4-6-4-0-8-9 dash Omega, so his claim of ownership of the briefcase wasn't entirely outrageous, said, "I'm going to take it home with me as a personal memento when I leave the office tonight."

A personal memento? "Yeah. The first time Rodney and I camped out in the Sausalito headquarters of his company, this was the briefcase he pulled the marshmallows we toasted on an open fire out of. And the sticks we held the marshmallows on. And the fire. And the extinguisher we used to put the fire out when the alarms started ringing. He left me a lot to remember!"

Bitter Suite, Fourth Movement

There was a rumour going round about the leader of the band:
That he had captured the favour of the Queen.
Sir Wainwright Walsh – it had a ring.
If true, much *nachus* to him the honour would bring.
There was only just one thing:
The aliens upon whose behalf the charity project had been?
He hated them. The sight of them he couldn't stand.

As far as the world was concerned, they were adorable,
So he dare not publicly speak his defiance.
His maid...boarder – whatever! – of several months,
Tara   Raboomdeeh
Had humiliated him every single day.

Ira Nayman

She didn't mean anything by it – it was just the alien way.
But with every pie inflicted on his person and every broken appliance,
Wainwright found aliens more and more deplorable.

Nothing can be said in his defence,
When Wainwright said, with much derision
On the BBC,
"They're not like us, you see.
They haven't the slightest conception of dignity."
That awful interview led to the decision
That he would never again make a public appearance.

Wainwright was excoriated for his belief
In high (and some not so high) places.
Other people were very pleased,
On his unfortunate remarks they seized
Despite his publicist's ardent pleas.
You'd be surprised how much goodwill a single statement erases
(But not having to live a lie came to him as a relief).

That night as Wainwright tried to sleep,
A figure appeared in his bedroom.
The figure said, "Wainwright Walsh, it's time to begin."
He had the presence of mind to reply, "Who let you in?"
Without missing a beat, the figure said, "Gunga Din."
Wainwright slapped his head. "How can you loom
When you're so short? Oh, right, you're one of those alien creeps!"

The four foot tall figure stepped into a conveniently placed spotlight
And said, "It is I, your good friend
Jacobob   Marley."
Wainwright argued, "I don't know anybody by that name."
Marley sighed and replied, "Don't make me sorry I came.
If it wasn't important, I wouldn't play this game.
I'd hop back on my Harley

The Ugly Truth

And ride into the hot, hot night!"

Shaking his head, Wainwright asked "What do you want?"
"To give you this important warning.
Tonight, you will be visited by aliens, three.
Who will help you better their plight to see.
(This message has been commercial-free.)
If you do not change your ways by morning
All your future dreams the aliens will haunt!"

A pie appeared in the apparition's hand,
As if by some strange magic.
He threw it at Wainwright's head;
It went straight through and splatted on the wall instead.
Disappointed, the alien fled,
As if the encounter had been tragic.
"Don't make me the butt of your jokes!" the human
shouted a demand.

Wainwright had just about returned to his rest
When he was awoken by a loud wailing.
"Sorry," an alien told him, "for carrying on so,
But in entering your room, I stubbed my big toe.
This is not how I expected this encounter to go.
At the whole 'haunting apparition' thing I seem to be
failing.
I should get tips from Jacobob   Marley – at
haunting, he is the best!"

"Aren't you Jacobob   Marley?" Wainwright
wondered.
"You look like him to me."
Pointing, the alien replied: "Look at the long thread of
aquamarine
In my exquisite three piece suit. Have you seen
The likes of it in his suit? Of course not! His is green!"
He spread his arms as if to say, "You see?"
Wainwright shook his head. Into an alien's weird sense of
humour he had once again blundered.

"All right," Wainwright sighed. "Can we get this over with?
I have an appointment with My Attorney Bernie at ten."
"Very well," the apparition replied, "I am the alien of
aliens past,
Here to act as living ballast
For your journey into – eww! That metaphor needs to be
recast!
I think I should probably enter again..."
"**No!**" Wainwright shouted. "I would much rather listen to
a monolith!"

"Very well," the alien of aliens past agreed,
And with much elaborate ahemming
Spun a heroic tale
Of an embittered old androgynous character seeking a
great white whale.
But all that fell on tisers head were chimney pots and safes
and boulders and cows and pianos and cauldrons and
outhouses and one time Alexi   Sayles.
The alien went about his quest like a maddened lemming,
Never fulfilling tisers deepest need.

"I know all that," Wainwright scoffed.
"In your story there's nothing new."
"Whoa," the alien of aliens past replied, "This is one
tough room!"
He spun another tale of a sorcerer's apprentice and a self-
replicating broom,
But this just brought about more gloom.
"My point does not seem to be getting through.
Fortunately, there are hours before I have to take off!"

The alien of aliens past told Wainwright many a story,
Which made him more and more queasy.
Until the human finally cried,
"I get it! You have a humane, suffering side
That just wants to live (and occasionally be pied)!"
The alien of aliens past thought, *Well, that was easy.*
Perhaps I should have thrown in something more gory...

"That's it!" Wainwright concluded with glee, "I've clearly learned my lesson!
Time for you to go!"
But the alien verbosely shook his head
"It's like Jacobob   Marley said,
Three aliens will visit you here in your bed.
To teach you all you need to know."
Before he vanished, he quietly added: "I'm guessin'..."

As into slumber, Wainwright once again fell
An alien voice began to moan.
"I am the alien of aliens past.
I –" "Wait!" Wainwright interrupted. "Not so fast!
That's exactly what the last
Alien said!" With a groan,
The alien responded, "Sure I am! And you know it full well!"

Wainwright shook his head and braced for a verbal attack.
"Nyuh uh. You're not. Your thread's not green, it's mauve."
"Please don't force me to be the alien of aliens present –
it's so boring!
The past is where the action is – it's the time everybody is adoring!
If you let me be the alien of aliens past, I – I – I'll give up a month of *schnorring*!
No? Fiiiiine! This is what I get for not being born a slithy tove!
Tell you what: I'll go mug my brother for his jacket and be right back!"

"Sorry," Wainwright sounded anything but, "but that just will not work.
You may as well get on with it, so we can all get some sleep."
Frowning, the alien spread his arms and said, "What you see is what you get.
Who we are has been all over the media...and yet...
Naaah, I got nothing. I'll bet
You're disappointed you didn't get something more deep.
You know, you can really be a jerk!"

"I have been told." Wainwright rolled his eyes.
"Now, if there's nothing else..."
"Would it kill you to learn a little lesson?"
The alien of aliens present was professin',
"What's the point of messin'
With your head if you write us off like rotten smelts?"
And left, with nary a goodbye.

To break the dreadful monotony,
Wainwright woke with a gasp and a start.
Looking through the murky gloom,
He found he was alone in the room.
"Can we get this over with," he shouted, "so my sleep can resume?"
From outside the door of the bedroom there arose a great fart
And the cry: "This is a metaphor for our future. PRO TIP: we haven't got any!"

"Am I supposed to start loving aliens now?" Wainwright was not convinced.
"Because I'm finding your argument quite weak."
"Hey, blame the source material," the alien replied, "not the parody!
If the whole thing had been left up to me,
I feel *Citizen Kane* would have been a better source of comedy!"
Wainwright attempted a reply, but could not speak;
He preferred his meta commentary minced.

The next morning, Wainwright's head righteously ached,
His mouth tasted of candy most cotton.
He decided to continue to publicly pretend
That he was the aliens' best friend
So that he could put an end
To the haunting that had been so rotten.
Trust the aliens to succeed at a plan so half-baked!

Ask Amritsar About Human Sexual Reproduction (In a PG Kind of Way)

Dear Amritsar,

I emigrated to Earth Prime from Earth Prime 4-6-4-0-8-9 dash Omega three months ago. I was fortunate enough to immediately land a job replacing an assembly line at an Amazingon warehouse (that will teach those automatons to try and form a union!). The job involves mind-numbing, back-breaking work that doesn't pay well, but I still consider myself fortunate to have it because I clearly don't yet appreciate all the subtleties of the English language. Or for that matter, some of its basics.

I met a guy named Egon Spankler on the line. He said he felt bad for me because one time he accidentally locked himself out of Moosejaw and immediately lost the key to the city. (The Mayor was furious.) He said that experience had made him more sensitive to what it meant to be an outsider. And, wet (it was the middle of the April rainy season). He was now highly sensitive to wetness. Two and a half weeks wandering outside looking for the key to the city will have that effect on a person. So, Egon started taking me to the Moose Knuckles Gastropub (next door to the Moose Intestines Inn and down the street from the Moose Hippocampus Diner – say what you want about the city, but it does use the whole animal!)

While we were sitting at the bar of the MKG recently, Egon pointed to the other end, where sat a curvaceous redhead, and told me, "I would tap that in a hot second!" I was all like, "You mean you would pat her shoulder to get her attention so that the two of you could engage in meaningful conversation?" And Egon was all like, laugh, laugh, laugh. And I was further all like, "Or do you mean that you would put a spigot in her and drain her of sap?" And Egon was all like, laugh harder, laugh harder, laugh harder. I didn't think he was talking about turning her into a faucet, but I was fast running out of ideas, so I asked him if that was what he meant.

Egon put a hand on my shoulder and explained what he meant. In detail. Thanks to him, I will never need to read a Kresley Cole novel.

I must have looked a little lost, because Egon took his hand off my shoulder, drained his Coors Late and took me to an orgy.

Human sexual reproduction is weird.

The experience did leave me with a question, though: what is a hot second? Is time subject to temperature in this universe? Can you cool down hot seconds by blowing on them? Do you need to wear gloves when you're living through a hot second so you don't burn yourself on it? How would you even know? I mean, do hot seconds glow red? And even if they did, wouldn't you have to be able to see into the future to know that they were coming?

Just how weird is Earth Prime, anyway?

Alexei Smerf Adirondacks

Hey, Babe,

Not where I thought the question was going. Excuse me while I jot down some new no – ferk it! I'll just wing this one.

Weirdness is a relative concept, and not just because of your lovable Uncle Vinnie's affection for bathing in beef jerky. When you are thrust (I would love to elaborate on this, but, as I said, that's not the direction your question went in) into a new culture, how quickly you learn to negotiate its rules and customs depends upon how different they are from the ones of your previous culture.

Pop sociologist (you would be amazed at how many different things can be said about soda!) Robertina D'Angustolino explores different scenarios to illustrate this point. In one, an immigrant from a primitive culture in which people blow their noses into their hands and smear the result into the walls of their home for insulation immigrate to a universe which is identical except for one difference: people blow their noses into handkerchiefs and cover themselves with extra blankets on long, cold winter nights. The adjustment period for the immigrants in this scenario would be minimal.

Now consider a second scenario where the nose-to-hand blowers are transported to a world of advanced technologies where disease has been eradicated. The adjustment for immigrants in this scenario would be extremely difficult: three quarters of the world's population would die of diseases their immune systems had long ago stopped protecting them against until vaccines that would help them survive could be created.

On the John Waters Scale of Outre Disadvantage, the weirdness you are experiencing is currently a 7.35812. You should be able to get comfortable in your new home universe in three generations – six tops!

Send your relationship problems to the Alternate Reality News Service's sex, love and technology columnist at questions@lespagesauxfolles.ca. Amritsar Al-Falloudjianapour is not a trained therapist, but she does know a lot of stuff. AMRITSAR SAYS: winging it wasn't as bad as I thought it would be, but it's still a lot harder than birds make it look!

CLAAAANG-AANG-AANG-AANG-AANG!
"Anvil."
"Anvil."
CLOOOONG-OONG-OONG-OONG-OONG!
"Safe."
"Safe."
SPLOOOORCH-OORCH-OORCH-OORCH-OORCH!
"Cow."
"No, not a cow."
"Of course it was a cow. What makes you think it wasn't a cow?"
"It didn't have the...gravitas of a cow."
"What else would have made that sound?"
"A giraffe."

"Giraffe? A giraffe! Giraffes don't fall from the sky!"

Bob$_{0001}$ and Bob$_{0002}$ looked down. Thirty storeys below, a giraffe hit the ground with a resounding **SPLAT!**

"Hunh," Bob$_{0001}$ hunhed. "First time for everything."

MOOO-SPLOOOORCH-OORCH-OORCH-OORCH-OORCH!

"That's a cow," Bob$_{0001}$ stated.

"That's a cow," Bob$_{0002}$ agreed.

Bob$_{0001}$ and Bob$_{0002}$ sat on a girder thirty floors above the ground, contemplating the uncertainties of life.

"What've you brought for lunch today?" Bob$_{0001}$ brightly asked.

"Why don't we have a look?" Bob$_{0002}$ less than enthusiastically responded. Te opened the stainless steel lunchbox that sat on the girder next to timer and surveyed its contents. "There's a smoked ham with sharp, aged cheddar, aioli mustard and home made mayonnaise on a sourdough bun sandwich."

"Sounds lovely."

"Maybe to you. For people who are not you, there are only so many smoked ham with sharp, aged cheddar, aioli mustard and home made mayonnaise on a sourdough bun sandwiches a person can eat before te gets thoroughly sick of them. And I passed thoroughly sick of them over a century ago." Realizing timer's response was less than satisfying to timer's co-worker, te added: "You?"

Bob$_{0001}$ eagerly opened the stainless steel lunchbox with the daisy decals that sat next to timer on the girder and eyed its contents. "Bologna on white bread!" te enthused.

"What I wouldn't give for a good bologna on white bread right about now," Bob$_{0002}$ sighed.

"Me, too," Bob$_{0001}$ agreed. Taking the sandwich out of its brown paper wrapper, te bit into it, a big grin spreading across timer's face.

Resigned, Bob$_{0002}$ took timer's sandwich out of a plastic sleeve and unenthusiastically bit into it.

They ate in silence for a couple of minutes, Bob_{0002} occasionally wiping timer's hand on timer's exquisite three piece overalls. Eventually, te asked, "How long have we been working on this construction site?"

"Seven hundred thirty-seven years, two months, sixteen days, four hours and thirty-seven seconds" Bob_{0001} answered. "Not that I'm counting..."

"I'm beginning to think management isn't fully committed to completing this project..."

"You've been speaking to management?" Bob_{0001}, excited, asked. "I haven't spoken to anybody in management for 150 years! Maybe as many as 140!"

"Oh, I haven't, either," Bob_{0002} admitted. "I merely surmised..."

Crestfallen, Bob_{0001} inquired, "Surmised – is that like assumed?"

"Indeed, it is," Bob_{0002} puffed up, "but without assumed's quality of incipient embarrassment."

Bob_{0001} nodded like he understood.

Seventeen minutes of thoughtful eating later (the aliens took mindful chewing very seriously), Bob_{0002} stated, "I heard the streets of Earth Prime are paved with foozleberries, and the sun never stops shining, even at night, and that the beings who live there calculate the value of pi to several thousand digits using nothing more than their brains and calculating machines...for fun in their spare time!"

"Nonsense!" Bob_{0001} scoffed.

"It's true!" Bob_{0002} insisted. "I heard somebody say it!"

"If the streets were made of foozleberries," Bob_{0001} pointed out, "they would turn people's feet foozleberry coloured every time they left the house!"

"Already thought of that," Bob_{0002} smugly responded.

"Dare I ask?"

"It wouldn't make a difference if the undersides of their feet were already the colour of foozleberries!"

Bob_{0002} beamed triumphantly at Bob_{0001}, who looked like te regretted taking the construction job all those centuries ago. But te sold(i)ered on. "What quirk of evolution could possibly have given a pink species pedal undersides the colour of foozleberries?"

"The same evolution that gave the multiverse us?"

Bob$_{0001}$ opened timer's mouth to speak, but thought better of it. One questioned one's evolutionary history at the risk of erasing one's species on some unfathomable quantum level. Better to let it go. Twenty-five minutes later, te put timer's sandwich down and said, "It makes more sense that they wear shoes. Next you'll be telling me their species has created a special foozleberry-repellant liquid that they spray on the soles of their shoes so they don't get them stained by foozleberries when they walk down the street!"

"Don't be ridiculous," Bob$_{0002}$ admonished timer.

"You agree that it would be absurd?"

"Of course. Think of all the effort it would take to develop such a spray."

"So much work. Too much."

"Not to mention the expense."

"Prohibitive."

"Exactly. Much easier to breed cows with foozleberry coloured skin. That way, when their hides were used to make the soles of shoes, they would already have the colour!"

Forty-one minutes later, Bob$_{0001}$ said, "Well, I heard that people on Earth Prime float on bubbles of their own self-importance –"

"That should make bath time interesting."

"– and that they can't reconstitute themselves when an elephant falls on them out of the sky, so they fear flying elephants, think they're some sort of demons or something."

"Where did you hear **that**?"

"Bob."

Bob$_{0003}$ was something of a legend on Earth Prime 4-6-4-0-8-9 dash Omega. One of the first of his species to emigrate to Earth Prime, he was recruited by the Transdimensional Authority to return to his home universe to help convince others of his species to leave before their home was destroyed. He was a combination of Albert Schweitzer and Albert Pomello, with a little bit of Isadora Duncan thrown in to keep him honest.

"Did you really hear it from Bob?" Bob_{0002} demanded.

"Ye-es..." Bob_{0001} equivocated.

"Directly from Bob?"

"Well..."

"Yes?"

"Okay. I heard it from Bob, who heard it from Bob down at the hair salon, who heard it from Bob when they were out on a date, who heard it from timer cousin Bob who works at the Ministry of Esoteric Mischief, who heard it from the Bob who was driving timer's taxi to work that morning, who said it had been told to timer from Bob, himself, the previous night as timer drove him to a restaurant to get some chicken wings."

Bob_{0002} took a minute to tot up how many Bobs had been in the chain. Eventually, te gave up and commented, "That's a lot of Bobs, Bob."

"Oh, yeah?" Bob_{0001} challenged Timer. "How did **you** hear about the streets being paved with foozleberries?"

"The same." Chagrined, Bob grinned. "Give or take a Bob or two."

CLOOOONG-OONG-OONG-OONG-OONG!

"Safe."

"Safe."

Sixty-seven minutes later, Bob_{0001} asked, "Do you think we should go to this new dimension?"

"What?" Bob_{0002} answered. "And give up show business?"

"From what I heard, show business is about to give up on us."

"Lack of fame is a fickle mistress, Bob."

"Do you have any idea what will happen if we stay until our universe collapses?"

"Nothing."

"Nothing will happen?"

"For the rest of eternity."

"Ohhhhhh, you mean **that** nothing."

"Was I not clear?"

"Weeeeellllll..."

CLOINK-OINK-OINK-OINK-OINK...

"Shift whistle," Bob_{0001} guessed.

"Shift whistle so soon?" Bob_{0002} protested. "It can't be a – OWWW!" Something small and tinny hit timer in the head on the way to the ground. "Shift whistle," timer agreed.

"Told you."

"That's it?" Bob_{0002} wondered. "The work day is over?"

"It would appear that way," Bob_{0001} told him.

"I barely finished my lunch!" Bob_{0002} complained.

"Tomorrow is another day," Bob_{0001} gently reminded him.

"I would really like to finish lunch one day." Bob_{0002} put the remainder of his sandwich in the lunchbox next to timer and closed it, sighing wistfully at remembrance of lunches past.

"Finish one lunch one day, and you just have to start another the next." Bob_{0001} did likewise. "The endless cycle of awakening, lunch, sleep is meant to be experienced, not necessarily completed."

"Until we achieve a sitcom named after us and pass on to another plane of existence."

"Amen."

Then, lunchboxes in hand, they pushed themselves off the girder and gently

f
l
o
a
t
e
d

t
o
w
a
r
d
s

t
h
e

g
r

Algernon   Pendragon was sitting at his desk at the AHA! Foundation, daydreaming of dodging raining locomotives, when he sat bolt upright and, looking at the middle distance, quietly stated, "There has been a disturbance of the Farce."

"Hunh. So, that's how a world ends, Joe."

"How's that, Bill?"

"Not with a bang, but with an anodyne two minute report on the evening news sandwiched between a segment on an embarrassing incident at an economic summit and an advertisement for cheese soda."

"Despite its setting, the events in the report sounded pretty definitive, Bill."

"It was about as definitive as it gets, Joe. If it were any more definitive, it would be the basis for its own religion."

"Not that we need any more religions."

"Too much religious conflict in the world already?"

"Too many beliefs for one police detective to keep track of!"

The Eternal Detectives paused for reflection on the nature of belief. Or possibly the difficulty of their profession. It is not for everyday folks to try to divine the content of an Eternal Detective's reflections.

"So, Joe, have you given any thought to what comes next?"

"A couple days worth of paperwork, Bill. Even detectives with perfect case closure numbers gotta cross their is and dot their ts."

"I don't cross my eyes – I find the practice painful – and I don't wear undershirts. But I do take your point, even though it was an answer to a different question than the one I meant to ask."

"What question was that, Joe?"

"What our next case should be, Bill."

"Oh. I hear there's a sweet little triple homicide in ancient Rome..."

"Better than the Pizzicotti murders of...a while back?"

"Might be, Joe. Might very well be. Guess there's only one way to find out...

When she heard the news on Fox, Minnie A. Polis of upstate downspout New York spat to her right (where her granddaughter Iphigenia Metro, visiting the Sunshine Superman Retirement Facility, was standing – "Haven't you learned how to evade, yet? How're ya gonna be a ninja if ya can't evade worth spit!" the old lady spat words this time) and said, "Serves the little blue bastards right!"

Joe Mahoney was touching up his blue makeup in front of his bathroom mirror when his phone pinged him with the news. He sighed, went still for a silent moment and thought, *It looks like it's up to us to keep the memory of our people alive...*

When an aide leaned over and whispered the news in his ear, Transdimensional Authority Secretary-Specific Nicodemius Fitzhuge smiled at the Ambassador for the Q'uay D'ors'ay and said, "Actually, the loss of jobs in the alligator nuzzle factories would be more than offset by the increased tourism from the rest of the multiverse!" There would be enough time later to get his PR staff to write the Secretary-Specific a heartfelt speech that expressed the depth of his sadness at the tragedy.

Das Kapitan Obvious was no longer with us. However, if he had been, when social media exploded with the news, he probably would have shaken his head so sadly his bicorne hat would threaten to list eighty-nine degrees and say, "You know, sometimes bad things happen in the multiverse to beings that don't deserve them, and all we can do is make more popcorn and hope we haven't run out of ketchup flavouring to sprinkle on it."

Canadian Prime Minister Ryan Reynolds was reading a Justice Department analysis of the Quebec law that banned alien refugees from disrupting public order by throwing pies in areas containing more than seven sentient life forms (the Department's response boiled down to: "Notwithstand **this**, pal!") when the leader of the opposition messaged him the news and demanded that he do something about it. An hour later, Prime Minister Reynolds made a heartfelt speech that expressed the depth of his sadness about the tragedy.

When he heard the Canadian Prime Minister's speech, Secretary-Specific Fitzhuge was furious.

Wainwright Walsh was teaching his daughter Fionnoula about the difference between gross points and net points ("It's never too early to school your children on the finer points of contract negotiations," he always said...when he was challenged on the subject. "Besides, she's a very mature eight year-old!") when the news came over the BBC. He wondered if he should offer Raoul   Wackadoodle his condolences (the alien did such a good job with the Prime Ministers through the ages topiaries in his backyard!), or see if the other members of the band had heard the news (which would have the added benefit of revealing which of them were still talking to him), or invite Her Majesty to support the AHA! Foundation because, whatever else one may have thought of her, she was still Her Majesty. So, he ended up doing what he always did when faced with too many options and not enough will.

He wrote a song.

When he heard the news, Ambassador Quentin Trentino was pleading for his life with a phalanx (bigger than a philtrum, smaller than a locutus) of Ventrosian Squiggles, but this did not stop a part of his mind from thinking, *That will certainly put a cap on **that** chapter of my memoirs!*

When the news came down from management, the men and women of the 7:27pm to 2:33am shift on the Aliens Helping Aliens Foundation Help Line observed sixty-seven seconds of silence, after which they gave their home universe a twenty-one fart salute.

The moment Earth Prime 4-6-4-0-8-9 dash Omega ceased to exist, Jerry Ungerleider lost a sucker's bet to his archenemy Francis Debacle. Three hours later, Debacle called to gloat and arrange to take possession of Ungerleider's prized collection of porcelain jock straps.

Mrs. Katz was checking on the lasagne in the oven when she received a text from the Transdimensional Authority. "KZ13F Omega," it read. Everybody who worked for the TA knew what the code meant: Operation Save the Blue Suede Shmoos was over. She cursed the multiverse for all of the alien lives they were not able to save. Then, the scent of gently burning pasta brought her back to the moment, and she turned the oven off.

Tara   Raboomdeeh was travelling through Europe with a band of Romani circus performers when the fortune teller started to give her pitying looks just outside of Luxembourg and the strong man began avoiding her gaze. At their next stop, she liberated an *International Herald Doubloon* from the kiosk that had been holding it prisoner and read the news. That night, after the group had made camp in the countryside, she played Chopin's 'Marche funèbre' on the triangle.

The kitchen sink did not have an opinion on the matter one way or the other, not being sentient and all.

The denizens of Dingle Dell were awash with emotions when they learned about the death of Earth Prime 4-6-4-0-8-9 dash Omega.

When Mersey Bling heard the news from her personal (albeit, purely professional) assistant Marky Farquharson, who had heard it from perennial single line character Martina Strogent, who had heard it from Mikey, the sixty-three year-old grocery delivery boy, who had heard it from Ambrosia Featherweight, who seemed to never have anything better to do with her time, who had heard it from Kevin (who probably had a last name but nobody could tell you what it was), the unfriendly, downright snarly, if truth be told (every city had one) postal delivery agent, who had heard it from Marian Westphinster, the town librarian (who, as we all know, knows things; in this case, the route the signal had to take to get to Mersey with a minimal amount of noise), it made her nostalgic about the time her family had had the only alien in the universe all to themselves, a time before her children began talking back and her husband stopped making an effort to hide his affairs; she shed thirteen tears, one for each month Rodney had stayed with the family, then wondered how badly it would trigger Justin's seafood allergy if she put shallots in the chicken pot pies they were scheduled to have for dinner that evening.

William 'Rusty' Abercrombie was trying to get a Red-eyed Stinker out of his wife Ermelina's ear ("I'm not paying for no piercings when I've got perfectly good fishing lures!") when his brother Willem 'Dusty' Fitch called with the news; "Call me back when I'm out of the doghouse," he responded in a tone of voice that suggested that he was about to become very well acquainted with his pet's domicile.

Mayor Leticia Castor was reading over the report of the Dingle Dell Planning Commission on the exciting possibility of putting bikes in trees. Paving the sky was the obvious method, but it was not without problems: the proposed plan would be extraordinarily expensive and, unless they were really careful, bicyclists would fall out of their trees and sue the city for negligence. Mayor Castor had just thought, *Then how would I be able to be reimbursed for my spa days from out of the Public Festivals budget?* when Mersey Bling phoned her with the news and demanded that there be some sort of commemoration for the dead aliens. Mayor Castor assured Mersey that she would work with city council to create a fitting tribute to them. When they rang off, Mayor Castor asked herself the question she always asked herself in such situations: "How can I use this to increase tourism to the town? Dingle Dell, Dingle Dell, Dingle all the way..."

Marian Westphinster, the town librarian, had always believed that people were like books: they contained vast amounts of information in the form of unique stories. The death of Earth Prime 4-6-4-0-8-9 dash Omega was, for her, a tragedy on par with the destruction of the library of Alexandria. Marian shed a tear for the loss. Being a librarian, she was a practical, no-nonsense kind of gal; for her, this was a great outpouring of emotion. Then, being a practical, no-nonsense kind of gal, she resolved to use her not inconsiderable librarianing powers to keep the memory of the species' home universe alive.

Father Begorrah lit a candle (cursing the darkness was one of his harmless indulgences, but this did not seem like an appropriate time) and whispered, "May every pie you fling reach its target, my friends, and may the Audi Enz laugh at your deepest sorrows."

When Denmark heard the news, it shrugged and thought, *Oh, well. Guess we were wrong, then. On the positive side, at least we're getting our backyards back!*

P. J. Pinchus was sitting at a desk in the detention facility where he was being held when his lawyer told him the news. *Well*, he thought, *I guess this means I'll have to find other suckers to fleece.* Then, his lawyer told him about Bill and Joe's perfect arrest and conviction rates, and for the first time since he was a child, he wasn't so sure of himself.

Transdimensional Authority xenopsychologist Doctor Otto Fischer was reviewing his file on a particularly homicidal Ventrosian squiggle when he received the 'KZ13F Omega' text. *There are a lot of aliens who are going to need grief counselling,* he thought. *Now, where did I put all of those 'It's Okay to Feel Sad When Ouchies Happen' pamphlets?*

Being a Full and Complete Record of the Diary of Martini Frobisher During His Historic Campaign for Member of Canadian Parliament

CAMPAIGN DIARY, DAY TWENTY-SIX

DEAR DIARY,

WHEN I HEARD THAT EARTH PRIME 4-6-4-

0-8-9 DASH OMEGA, MY HOME, HAD DIED, I DID –

Oh, no, you don't, buster! It's my story again, and there will be no more first person narration!

When he heard that Earth Prime 4-6-4-0-8-9 dash Omega, his home, had died, Martini Frobisher did a spit-take that for a precious second was a spitting liquid image of the Brooklyn Bridge. Then, he went to a nearby Pies 'R' Us and ate himself into an oblivious stupor that left him incapable of campaigning for the next day and a half. At least there was that upside...

The seven Dimensional Portal™s in the Transdimensional Authority's primary fleet are housed in the basement of the organization's headquarters in Ottawa on Earth Prime. To get to them, you have to stand in line and wait for <u>Tim</u> to let you pass into the three storey tall room where they are hewn into solid rock. <u>Tim</u> is like the Bridgekeeper at the Bridge of Death, if the Bridgekeeper was six feet tall, gawky and had a muddy complexion and a voice that never quite made it into adulthood. (On the plus side, <u>Tim</u> did not have the Bridgekeeper's unhealthy obsession with swallows.)

Daveen Rasmalai ran down the hallway on the wrong side of the velvet rope that divided those entering the Dimensional Portal™ room from those leaving it. A six foot tall cat creature stopped grooming the fur on the top of its head with a wet paw long enough to growl at him; the other beings standing in line recognized that he was more important to the narrative than they were, and let him bud in without comment.

He stopped in front of Tim and panted, "Something is wrong." For dramatic effect – the hallway wasn't that long and he wasn't especially winded. "I have to get to Earth Prime 4-6-4-0-8-9 dash Omega right away!"

"Hi, Mister Rapier," Tim cheerfully responded.

"Hi, Tim," Daveen Rasmalai forced himself to say. "Now, if you could just let me in..."

"Sure, Mister Rapier," Tim stated. "If you could just show me your paperwork..."

It is a testament to Tim's...name tag that Daveen Rasmalai had a momentary impulse to pat himself down to find the document he needed to get into the Dimensional Portal™ room. "I'm sorry, Tim, but this is an emergency. I have to –"

"Wait. Did you say Earth Prime 4-6-4-0-8-9 dash Omega?"

"That's right."

"I'm sorry, Mister Rapier, but you can't get there from here."

Daveen Rasmalai couldn't comprehend what Tim was telling him. "What?"

"There's no there there."

"I don't –"

A bald four foot tall blue man with exaggeratedly round features wearing an exquisite three piece suit walked out of the room. "Well, don't that just frost your garters!" he muttered. "I guess what they say is true: you really can't go home again!"

"What's the news from Earth Prime 4-6-4-0-8-9 dash Omega?" Daveen Rasmalai demanded of the alien.

"News from Earth Prime 4-6-4-0-8-9 dash Omega? News from nowhere, more like," the alien told him.

Now, to be fair to Daveen Rasmalai, the message the universe was sending him was a bit cryptic. However, it was insistent, so, it started to sink in. "You mean...it's not there any more?"

"It's Chekhov's famous dictum," the alien, smiling, explained: "If a universe is under threat of destruction in the first novel of a trilogy, it has to go off by the end of the third. Now, if you'll excuse me, I have to explain to my partner why he won't be getting a shark-repelling umbrella for ChristmaKwaanzUkah this year!"

Daveen Rasmalai backed up and slumped against the far wall, grimly muttering, "That can't be true. We barely got a million people out of Earth Prime 4-6-4-0-8-9 dash Omega. There were billions of other sentient beings – they can't all be gone!"

The hearts of everybody in the line went out to Daveen Rasmalai (except for the cat, which was too busy licking its underarm).

"We could have done more to save them," Daveen Rasmalai grimly stated. "We should have done more to save them."

"Don't beat your brains out over it," a voice loomed over him (although not that far). "It's true that you only saved a fraction of one per cent of my race from death. But, look on the bright side: we can't reproduce in this universe, so we'll die out eventually!"

"**That's** the bright side?"

"Well...I mean – you know – it's just...uhh...my comforting skills need work, don't they?"

Putting the Fun Back in Fungible

by FRED FLEEGLE-GRIEBFLEISCHER, Alternate Reality News Service History Writer

Say you run a non-profit foundation whose goal is to teach illiterate Capuchin monkeys from Rwandapindi how to run Bitcoin farms. Then, the market for Bitcoins collapses as its energy demands outstrip the sun. Then, Rwandapindi has a civil war, ending up partitioned into the countries of Dapin and Rwandi. Then, Capuchin monkeys go extinct.

Mission accomplished!

Mission accomplished?

What does a foundation do when, as my hypothetical but totally plausible example illustrates, its purpose disappears? Does its Board pat each other on the back, complimenting themselves on a job well done, wind up the foundation and make empty promises to stay in touch? Was Elizabeth Taylor a brand of sports bra for men? (Not in this universe, buster!)

No, they simply find another reason to continue foundationing.

That is what has happened to the Aliens Helping Aliens (AHA!) Foundation. Originally established to help aliens adjust to their lives in universes other than their home, the AHA! Foundation's original mandate (which does not refer to gay romance – please keep your context straight!) was invalidated when Earth Prime 4-6-4-0-8-9 dash Omega ceased to exist. No more refugees = no need for anybody to help refugees adjust to their new home universes (I failed grade seven math, but even I understand that equation).

What will be the Foundation's purpose moving forward (in time, although to move forward in space takes time, so the figure of speech may not be totally invalid)?

"Memory," pronounced Anastasia La Bombon, Vice President, Outre Celebrations and Public Relations for the AHA! Foundation.

Memory?

"Memory!" echoed Algernon Pendragon, Vice President, Finance and Inelegance of the AHA! Foundation.

Before they could break out into song, I asked them how that would work.

"I don't remember!" VP Pendragon predictably, if enthusiastically, responded. VP La Bombon punched him playfully in the shoulder. Arms flailing, he theatrically fell off his chair, rolled across the room and banged into the far wall. "Oww," he quietly complained.

VP La Bombon looked at her fist and remarked, "Guess I don't know my own strength!"

I gave her a look which said, "I expect no better from him, but you, Anastasia? Really?" Her winsome smile had a wicked edge to it.

Because of the way the citizens of Earth Prime 4-6-4-0-8-9 dash Omega melded their bodies and their minds, each survivor of the universal cataclysm, the uniclysm (don't try to ride it on city sidewalks!), carries anywhere from eight to fifteen and a half (Scandaleezza Bogd anovitch had only partially melded with Bavarian Skortnik when an anvil fell on Edina Fallopian, causing the totter she was on to teeter so sharply that it sent Chuckie Furlong nineteen and three quarters feet into the air; he fell through the sun roof of a Chevrolet Impaler and landed on the driver, Martini N. Rossi, causing him to veer off the road and onto a construction site, where he upended some scaffolding, sending Marlena Touboudjian flying into a falling boulder, knocking it out off its course enough to completely crush Scandaleezza and Bavarian, who reassembled themselves separately) generations of their ancestors inside them. Conducting interviews with survivors of the uniclysm could help preserve their culture.

Getting them to sit for interviews is the tricky part. "They, like, aren't big fans of exposition, you know?" VP La Bombon explained. "So, they're constantly playing tricks to, like, amuse themselves. We've had to fumigate three interview rooms and permanently close another because our experts tell us it's haunted by the ghosts of all the meat the subject had eaten. Interviewing aliens can be expensive!"

That's where Geraldine Maguire comes in. Maguire is a philanthropreneur (a word that has been in use since 1997, so you can't blame this one on me!), which is not a free market anthropologist studying people named Phil (okay, that bit you can totally blame on me!); she uses the capitalist system to help non-profit foundations remain financially viable.

"I'm thinking...Rodney dolls, complete with briefcases that you put Plasticine in that comes out in a random variety of shapes," Maguire blue skyed. "Perhaps a line of exquisite three piece suits for three year-olds, and – oh! – I probably shouldn't say this, but we're currently in negotiations with a prominent producer of body sprays!"

Is this selling out?

"I hope they sell out!" Maguire enthused. "The more people buy our products, the more interviews the Foundation will be able to conduct!"

I was actually asking the Vice Presidents of the

Foundation.

"They hope the products sell out, too!" Maguire continued. "Who do you think will be conducting the interviews?"

VP Pendragon smiled and shrugged, a gesture which seemed to say, "The market has spoken, and boy could it use some mouthwash!"

In a small, airless room in Ottawa, a small, airless man in a grey suit is interviewing a small, hairless man in an exquisite three piece suit.

"I have reviewed your request for assistance under the Emergency Alien Compensation Fund," the man behind the desk, whose name was Harry Winterbottom, was saying, "and while I sympathize with your plight, I'm afraid that you have not proven to the government's satisfaction that you are eligible for recompense under the programme."

"I'm not eligible?" the small man in front of the desk, whose name was Allegro   Buttle, responded.

"I'm afraid not. Without a completed Derivation of Universal Means Assessment form duly signed by the Vice Assistant Secretary-Specific for Refugees of the Transdimensional Authority, you cannot prove that you actually are an alien from Earth Prime 4-6-4-0-8-9 dash Omega."

"I can't prove I'm an alien?"

"I'm afraid not."

"You're afraid not of this. You're afraid not of that. Tell me something, Mister...Winterbottom: were you a fearful person who thought becoming a bureaucrat would keep you away from the problems of everyday life, or were you a strong person who has become fearful owing to a career as a bureaucrat?"

Winterbottom's voice was so neutral, warring countries could have used it as a demilitarized zone: "Now, sir, there's no need to get personal."

"Can't prove that I'm an alien? How tall am I?"

"As I said, this conversation should not be personal."

"If it will help, I'll sign a waiver absolving you of responsibility for the adverse effects of any personal observations you may make in the course of our interview."

"Will you, sir?"

"There is such a thing?"

The signing of one waiver absolving him of responsibility for the adverse effects of any personal observations he may make in the course of their interview later...

"Four foot tall, if I'm any judge of height. Which you have to be to go far in this job."

"And what is the colour of my skin?"

"I'm sorry, sir, but I am not allowed to make any potentially speciesist observations while on the job."

"Didn't I just sign a waiver form allowing you to do that?"

"Alas, no. Speciesist commentary, observations, remarks or asides are not covered by the waiver you just signed."

"I don't suppose you would happen to have a waiver that I could sign absolving you of responsibility for the adverse effects of any speciesist commentary, observations, remarks or asides you may make in the course of our interview...would you?"

The signing of one waiver absolving him of responsibility for the adverse effects of any speciesist commentary, observations, remarks or asides he may make in the course of their interview later...

"Blue. Your skin colour is definitely, blue. Sky, blue, if I'm any judge of these things. And considering that my husband is an interior decorator who loves nothing better than spending hours grilling me on colour wheels, I have become a very good judge of these things, indeed."

"Good. Good. And would I need to sign another waiver to have you describe the three piece suit I am wearing?"

"No, sir. I believe that would be covered by the first waiver you signed." Winterbottom briefly glanced at the small pile of papers on the desk, but given that he was already three interviews behind on the day, his threat to read them over to confirm his belief was an empty one.

"Okay, then. How would you describe the three piece suit that I am wearing?"

"You don't have to have any special experience or training to see that it is exquisite."

"So, are people who look like me native to this universe?"

"Sir, I do not dispute that you are an alien. All I'm saying is that you cannot **prove** that you are an alien."

"The proof is sitting right in front of you!"

"Unfortunately, that's not the kind of proof that can be entered into a database and kept in case there is any future dispute. For that, we would need a fully completed D.U.M. Ass., duly signed by the Vice Assistant Secretary-Specific for Refugees of the Transdimensional Authority."

"I filled out one of those dumbass forms when I emigrated to this universe," Allegro said after taking a deep breath to calm himself. It did not help that he was getting the sneaking suspicion that he was the straight man in this scene, a role he was unaccustomed to playing on Earth Prime 4-6-4-0-8-9 dash Omega. His religion recognized the need for straight men in the execution of its comedic rituals, but the seminal texts gave conflicting testimony on how favourably the Audi Enz looked upon those who filled the role. (Stripped of their pontificatory passages, commentaries on the seminal texts amounted to a shrugged, "Best of luck to you.")

"So you say," Winterbottom, who had patiently waited for the exposition to pass, was finally able to respond. "But there is no file with your specific information in our database. I'm sorry."

The man's unwaveringly neutral tone made it impossible to know if he was sincerely sorry about the situation, but Allegro had his doubts. "Why would I lie to you about such a thing?" he asked.

"There are many possible reasons," Winterbottom informed him. "You could be an alien from a universe other than Earth Prime 4-6-4-0-8-9 dash Omega. You could, for instance, be from Earth Prime 4-6-4-0-8-9 dash Psi, or Earth Prime 4-6-4-0-9-0 dash Alpha, or even Earth Prime 2-6-3-0-3-7 dash Mu. In any of those cases, you would not be eligible for compensation. You would, in short, be attempting to defraud the Canadian government. I'm sure you can understand why we cannot allow that to happen."

Allegro considered this. "Are there other Earths among the known universes that have species like mine in them?" he finally asked.

"Not that I am aware of, no. The previous examples I gave were theoretical."

"So, no other species like mine have signed the Treaty of Gehenna-Wentworth?"

"Again, not to my knowledge."

"So, no other species like mine has access to Dimensional Portal^{TM}s?"

"As far as I know, that is correct."

"Wouldn't you say it's unlikely, then, that somebody from a similar species could come to Earth Prime claiming to be one of us in order to scam the Canadian government?"

"It is unlikely," Winterbottom agreed. Almost immediately, though, he unagreed: "But it is possible. As long as it is possible, we owe it to taxpayers to be cautious. It is, after all, their money that aliens are being compensated with."

"Is there anything I can do?" Allegro, worried that the conversation was veering towards the opposite of comedy – pathos – decided to end it as quickly as he could and go on a public pieing binge in the hope that the Audi Enz would have mercy on his ratings.

"I'm afraid you will have to return to your universe of origin and reapply to immigrate."

"Well, I'm afraid I can't do that."

"Oh? Why not?"

"Because my universe of origin no longer exists! That's the reason I'm here in the first place!"

"Ah. I see. Well, that is awkward."

"Tell me about it!"

"I did. That is awkward."

Allegro closed his eyes. He really did hate being the straight man. "Is there anything I can do?" he asked. "Anything at all?"

"You can apply to the Ministry of Alien Affairs for emergency relief," Winterbottom informed him.

"How many people has that worked out for?"

"You would be the first." Seeing the dismay on the alien's face, Winterbottom neutrally encouraged: "Somebody always has to be the first. Why not you?"

"Anything else?" Allegro was not surprisingly not encouraged.

"You could always approach a non-profit organization like the Aliens Helping Aliens Foundation. They don't have a lot of money, but they do have an endless supply of advice."

Allegro stood. "Thank you," he said. "This has been most unhelpful."

"You're most welcome," Winterbottom responded. Without emotion in his voice, there was no way of knowing if he meant it. I'm beginning to suspect he didn't. He added: "At the Ministry of Alien Affairs, we pride ourselves on our service." Without emotion in his voice, there was no way of knowing if he meant it. I suspect he did. More's the pity.

The Ugly Truth

Being a Full and Complete Record of the Diary of Martini Frobisher During His Historic Campaign for Member of Canadian Parliament

CAMPAIGN DIARY, DAY THIRTY

DEAR DIARY,

THIS WILL BE MY LAST ENTRY AS TODAY IS THE DAY OF THE ELECTION. I KNOW THIS WILL BE AN EMOTIONAL TIME FOR YOU, DIARY, BUT WE BOTH KNEW THIS DAY WOULD COME, SO BE STRONG. WE'LL GET THROUGH IT TOGETHER.

I THINK THE THING I WILL MISS THE MOST IS THE CAMERA DEARIE. I'LL ALWAYS REMEMBER...OH, WHAT'S HIS NAME? YOU KNOW, THE VOLUNTEER WHO WORE A BELT AND HOPED NOBODY WOULD NOTICE THAT THE BUTTON OF HIS FLY WAS MISSING? YEAH...HIM. THE WAY HIS VOICE HIT HIGH NOTES FEW COLORATURA SOPRANOS COULD WHEN HE MADE SUCH WRY OBSERVATIONS AS: "YOU CAN'T DO THAT!" AND "WAS THAT SUPPOSED TO BE FUNNY?" AND "WHO'S PAYING FOR THAT WHITE PICKET FENCE? I'M NOT PAYING FOR THAT WHITE PICKET FENCE!" AND WHO COULD POSSIBLY FORGET...THE INTERN WHO TRIED TO ORDER STATIONERY FOR THE OFFICE ONLINE AND NEARLY TRIGGERED A NUCLEAR ATTACK ON FRANCE? THE CAMPAIGN PAYED FOR HER BAIL, OF COURSE; SHE REALLY WAS A SWEET KID, AND VERY, VEEEEEEEEEEEEEEEEEEEEEEEEEEEEEERY SORRY.

I WILL CHERISH MEMORIES LIKE THAT MORE THAN ANYTHING.

THE CAMPAIGN HAS BEEN A ROLLER COASTER WITHOUT THE NEED TO BE THIS TALL TO GET ON BUT WITH THE FREQUENT NEED TO CLOSE YOUR EYES TO MINIMIZE THE NAUSEA (I'D HATE TO BE THE JANITOR OF CAMPAIGN HEADQUARTERS!). THE DAY

THAT RODNEY DIED, THE CAMPAIGN GOT A BOOST OF A POINT IN THE OVERNIGHT POLLS. THE DAY OF THE FUNERAL, WE DROPPED TWO POINTS (APPARENTLY, THE PEOPLE OF THIS UNIVERSE HAVE VERY FIXED VIEWS ON HOW PEOPLE SHOULD GRIEVE, FIXED AND NARROW VIEWS). THE DAY MY HOME UNIVERSE COLLAPSED, THE NUMBER OF PEOPLE WHO TOLD POLLSTERS THEY WOULD VOTE FOR ME SHOT UP A WHOPPING ONE AND A HALF PERCENTAGE POINTS. I WON'T LIE TO YOU, DIARY: I WAS TAKING ANTI-NAUSEA MEDICATIONS THROUGHOUT THE CAMPAIGN (NOT BECAUSE I WAS ACTUALLY SICK, BUT BECAUSE I BELIEVE IN LEADING BY EXAMPLE).

IN THE MAIN ROOM OF CAMPAIGN HEADQUARTERS WERE A DOZEN DESKS WITH PHONES ON THEM; A DOZEN VOLUNTEERS SAT AT THE DESKS, IGNORING THE PHONES AND MAKING CALLS ON THEIR CELLS. UNTIL TODAY, THE CALLS WERE SUPPOSED TO BE ABOUT CONVINCING POTENTIAL VOTERS THAT I WAS THE BEST CANDIDATE (ALTHOUGH MUCH OF THE TIME THEY TALKED ABOUT HOW UNFAIR IT WAS THAT FIREFLY DIDN'T GET A SECOND SEASON, AND WOULD THE CALLEE PLEASE SIGN OUR ONLINE PETITION TO BRING IT BACK? IS THE PETITION AFFILIATED WITH THE CAMPAIGN? YEAH, SURE, IF THAT WILL HELP MOTIVATE YOU TO SIGN IT!). TODAY, THE VOLUNTEERS WERE SUPPOSED TO BE PHONING BACK THE PEOPLE WHO HAD INITIALLY SAID IT WOULDN'T MAKE THEM PHYSICALLY ILL TO CAST THEIR BALLOTS FOR ME AND URGE THEM TO GET OUT AND VOTE, AND ALL BUT A COUPLE OF DIEHARD ALAN TUDYK FANS ACTUALLY WERE DOING THAT.

AMAROSA MONITORED SOME OF THE CALLS "FOR QUALITY CONTROL PURPOSES" (THE QUALITY SHE WAS LOOKING FOR WAS HUMBLE HILARITY, BUT SHE WOULD ALSO HAVE ACCEPTED HILARIOUS HUMILITY). THE RESPONSES TO OUR PLEA TO GET OUT AND VOTE INCLUDED: "SURE, I'LL VOTE. JUST GIMME A MINUTE TO GET MY PAINTBALLS AND SLINGSHOT!" AND "IF I

VOTE, WILL YOU COME AND DO MY LAUNDRY? I HATE LAUNDRY DAY ALMOST AS MUCH AS I HATE LIBERALS!" AND "IF I VOTE — WHICH I'M NOT SAYING I WILL — AND IF IT'S FOR YOU — WHICH IT MAY OR MAY NOT BE — WILL IT ENCOURAGE YOU? BECAUSE I HEARD SOMEWHERE THAT I SHOULDN'T ENCOURAGE YOU." THAT RESPONSE CERTAINLY DIDN'T ENCOURAGE THE TEAM, LET ME TELL YOU!

I DIDN'T HAVE MUCH TO DO, MYSELF, BOTH OF MY SELVES, ALL OF MY INCREASINGLY NUMEROUS SELVES, SO I SPENT MOST OF THE DAY IN MY OFFICE, MAKING ORIGAMI ANIMALS (I HAD EXHAUSTED THE WONDERS OF THE WORLD AND DIDN'T FEEL LIKE MOVING ON TO THE MAKE-YOU-WONDERS OF THE WORLD) AS A PARTING GIFT FOR THE VOLUNTEERS. I WAS SO EXCITED BY THE END OF THE CAMPAIGN THAT I COULDN'T FOLD PROPERLY; MY SWANS LOOKED MORE LIKE TANKS WITH ELEGANT HEADS ON LONG NECKS AND MY ELEPHANTS LOOKED LIKE SQUISHED CATERPILLARS WITH BASEBALL BATS INSTEAD OF WINGS. THE BUILDING JANITOR WAS GOING TO HAVE TO WORK EXTRA HARD CLEANING OUT MY WASTEBASKET THAT NIGHT, LET ME TELL YOU! AFTER A COUPLE OF HOURS OF THIS, I DECIDED THAT IT WOULD BE A BETTER USE OF MY TIME TO LEAVE MY OFFICE AND MAKE SOME GET OUT THE VOTE CALLS.

THE FIRST CALL I MADE DISABUSED ME OF THAT IDEA. "WHAT ARE YOU CALLING ME FOR?" AN IRATE WOMAN ON THE OTHER END OF THE LINE DEMANDED. "THE POLLS CLOSED TEN MINUTES AGO!"

I CONSIDER IT A TESTAMENT TO THE TIME TRAVELLING PROPERTIES OF ORIGAMI.

AMAROSA NUDGED ME AND WHISPERED, "YOU SHOULD PROBABLY SAY SOMETHING."

NODDING, I BEGAN WHISPERING, "THANK YOU, EVERYBODY. WE —"

"OUT LOUD," AMAROSA ADVISED.

"RIGHT." TAKE TWO, SOTTO LOUDER: "THANK YOU EVERYBODY. WE FOUGHT THE GOOD FIGHT. WE GAVE

IT A HUNDRED AND TEN PER CENT. WE ENTERED THE ARENA UNDERDOGS, AND NOW WE GET TO FIND OUT IF ALL THE BLOOD, SWEAT AND TEARS WAS WORTH IT. IT WASN'T EASY, BUT WE PERSEVERED THROUGH THE HARDSHIP BECAUSE WE WANTED TO WIN MORE. AND WIN OR LOSE, WE'RE ALL WINNERS. EVEN THE LOSERS. ESPECIALLY THE LOSERS."

"NOTE TO SELF:" I HEARD AMAROSA MUTTER, "NO WATCHING SPORTS THE DAY BEFORE A BIG SPEECH."

"NOW, AS WE WAIT FOR THE RESULTS, LET'S HAVE SOME WELL-EARNED LIBATIONS!"

THERE WAS A MURMUR OF APPROVAL, BUT I LIKE TO THINK THAT EVERYBODY WAS CHEERING ON THE INSIDE.

THE BIG SCREEN TELEVISION SET ON THE BACK WALL OF THE ROOM WAS TUNED TO CFCN, WHICH WAS COVERING THE BY-ELECTION LIVE. TRAYS OF FINGER FOODS (A TERM I HAVE NEVER FELT THE NEED TO LEARN THE ETYMOLOGY OF) WERE LAID ON TABLES, AS WERE FLUTES OF WATER (THE CHAMPAGNE OF INEXPENSIVE BEVERAGES).

AFTER A COUPLE OF MINUTES, A VOLUNTEER NAMED TAMMY...OR TABITHA...OR SPORK, CAME UP TO ME AND ASKED, "WHY DOES THIS TUNA SANDWICH TASTE LIKE STRAWBERRIES AND COCONUT?"

"IT'S ACTUALLY A TWO-BITE PIE IN THE SHAPE OF A TUNA SANDWICH," I BEAMED. IT HAD BEEN MY IDEA.

"INTERESTING," THE VOLUNTEER RESPONDED, SPITTING A MOUTHFUL OF FOOD INTO HER NAPKIN.

"NOTE TO SELF:" I SAID UNDER MY BREATH, "NEXT TIME, GO WITH THE TWO-BITE LEMON PIES IN THE SHAPE OF FLAKY SHRIMP PUFF PASTRIES!"

AMAROSA ROLLED HER EYES.

A COUPLE OF MINUTES AFTER THAT, AMY CAME UP TO ME AND SAID, "GREAT CAMPAIGN, MISTER FROBISHER. ONLY, IF YOU WERE TO DO IT AGAIN, I WOULD SUGGEST DOING ONE THING DIFFERENTLY..."

"WHAT'S THAT?" AMAROSA ASKED.

"Maybe...have some policies?" Amy tentatively offered.

I slapped my forehead with the palm of my hand. "I don't believe it!" I exclaimed. "I ran for public office and I forgot to have any policies!" Lowering my voice, I added: "Note to self: next time you run for public office, get policies. There must be a store that sells them. You can ask about custom-made policies, but you'll probably only be able to afford off-the-rack..."

Amarosa rolled her eyes. Again. Why does she get to make notes to herself but I don't? Life in this universe is so unfair!

If this was a movie, the race would be too close to call until the wee hours of the morning, at which point a surprise upset would be announced. Unfortunately, this wasn't a movie, this was Calgary.

Conservative Reichbreiker took an early lead and never looked back. In less than an hour, he was declared the winner with fifty-seven per cent of the vote. Liberal Petunia had thirty-nine per cent. I got three. But I like to think it was a solid three per cent. Something that you could build on.

If a candidate doesn't win an election, they're supposed to make a concession speech. I read that in the back of a comic book once. Amarosa got onto a table like she had stood on tables all of her life and introduced me: "Please, can I have your attention? Martini would like to say a few words before we all go back to our dull, uneventful lives. Martini?"

The volunteers cheered and clapped as Amarosa tried to help me onto the table. For some reason, my body chose that moment to go stiff (a rare medical condition I have

CALLED...RANDOM GO STIFFITIS), SO I WOULD GET HALFWAY UP AND FALL BACK TO THE FLOOR. AFTER REPEATED ATTEMPTS TO GET ME ON THE TABLE, MY LOVER, MY CAMPAIGN MANAGER SWEETLY HISSED, "MAYBE IT WOULD BE FOR THE BEST IF YOU SPOKE FROM THE FLOOR."

THAT WAS THE MOMENT MY...CONDITION SETTLED DOWN, BUT I WASN'T ABOUT TO TELL HER THAT. INSTEAD, I CLEARED MY THROAT AND TOOK OUT THE CONCESSION SPEECH AMY HAD PREPARED FOR ME. OR, AT LEAST, I WOULD HAVE IF I STILL HAD IT. THAT WAS THE MOMENT I REALIZED THAT MY SPEECH WAS LYING IN MY WASTEBASKET IN THE FORM OF MUTILATED PAPER ANIMALS. SO, I IMPROVISED.

"WE SUCK!" I ENTHUSIASTICALLY SHOUTED. THE VOLUNTEERS STOPPED EATING PIE IN THE SHAPE OF FINGER FOODS FOR A MOMENT AND LOOKED AT ME IN SURPRISE. "COME ON, SAY IT WITH ME! WE SUCK! WE SUCK! WE SUCK!" ODDLY ENOUGH, NOBODY SEEMED TO WANT TO JOIN IN MY CHANT.

"WE'RE SUPPOSED TO WIN," ONE OF THE VOLUNTEERS IN THE BACK – I THINK HIS NAME WAS BIFF OR BEPPI OR BUFFY (HONESTLY, I WAS HAVING SUCH A DIFFICULT TIME WITH HIS NAME, YOU'D'VE THOUGHT I WAS AN OMNISCIENT NARRATOR OR SOMETHING!) – SHOUTED.

"WIN? OH, PFFT!" I WAS IN A PFFTING MOOD. I WAS A PFFTER (NOT THAT THERE'S ANYTHING WRONG WITH THAT). "WINNING IS FOR WINNERS! ANYBODY CAN WIN IF THEY JUST HAVE THE RIGHT MIX OF SKILLS, WORK REALLY HARD AND GET A FEW LUCKY BREAKS. WHEN YOU THINK ABOUT IT, IT'S JUST THAT EASY. YET, FEW OF US MANAGE TO PULL IT OFF. WHY SHOULD WE SUPPORT THE FEW WHO SUCCEED WHEN SO MANY MORE OF US...DON'T? I SAY, WE SHOULD CELEBRATE THOSE OF US WITHOUT SKILLS, THOSE OF US WHO HAVE WORKED MAYBE NOT SO HARD, THOSE OF US WHO JUST COULDN'T CATCH THAT ONE BIG

BREAK TO SAVE THEIR LIVES! I DEDICATE THIS FAILED CANDIDACY TO ALL OF THE NON-WINNERS IN THE WORLD! WHO'S WITH ME? WE SUCK! WE SUCK! WE SUCK! WE -"

SLOWLY, BUT WITH GAINING ENTHUSIASM, THE VOLUNTEERS TOOK UP THE CHANT. "WE SUCK! WE SUCK! WE SUCK! WE -" SOME PUMPED THEIR FISTS IN THE AIR. AFTER A MINUTE, EVEN AMY WAS CHANTING "WE SUCK! WE SUCK!" WITH GUSTO. WHEN I FIGURED THE WAVE WAS ABOUT TO BREAK, I SHOUTED OVER EVERYBODY: "NOW, FINISH YOUR FINGER FOOD PIE AND GO BACK TO YOUR NON-WINNING LIVES!"

THE ROAR OF APPROVAL WAS DEAFENING.

THE REST OF MY LIFE DIARY, DAY ONE

DEAR DIARY,

DID YOU REALLY THINK YOU COULD GET RID OF ME SO EASILY? I FEEL LIKE WE'VE BONDED IN THE LAST MONTH, AND I WOULD HATE TO SEE THAT JUST END. I'M SURE YOU FEEL EXACTLY THE SAME WAY. AND IF YOU DON'T, YOU WILL. YOU WILL.

I WAS SO EXHAUSTED FROM THE PAST MONTH'S FEVERISH ACTIVITY THAT I SLEPT AND SLEPT AND SLEPT - ALMOST TO 10AM!

LATER THAT DAY, AS AMAROSA AND I LAY IN BED, EXHAUSTED FROM TRYING TO FIGURE OUT HOW THESE BODIES WERE SUPPOSED TO GIVE PLEASURE TO EACH OTHER (YOU CAN SEE THOSE PICTURES IN ANY MAGAZINE, BUT WHAT'S THE USE OF LOOKING IF YOU DON'T KNOW WHAT THEY MEAN?), SHE TURNED TO ME, THREW THE RUBBER DUCKY OFF THE BED AND COOED, "YOU KNOW, SEEING HOW YOU HANDLED THE VOLUNTEERS THE OTHER DAY, IT WAS OBVIOUS THAT YOU ARE A BORN LEADER."

"OH, PSHAW!" I PSHAWED HER. IF I HAD HAD

MORE ENERGY, I WOULD HAVE WAVED MY HAND DISMISSIVELY AT HER, BUT I'M SURE MY PSHAW GOT THE MESSAGE ACROSS.

"NO, SERIOUSLY, SNOOKUM BOBOOKUMS," AMAROSA INSISTED. "YOU MAY NOT HAVE STARTED STRONG, OR DID PARTICULARLY WELL THROUGH THE MIDDLE, BUT BY THE END, YOU HAD THE VOLUNTEERS EATING OUT OF YOUR HAND."

I SHOOK MY HEAD AT THE MENTAL IMAGE. "SO UNSANITARY!"

AMAROSA FROWNED. "PLEASE DON'T LITERALIZE MY METAPHORS WHEN I'M TRYING TO MAKE AN IMPORTANT POINT."

"SORRY," I APOLOGIZED WITH MY WORDS IF NOT MY TONE. "BUT HONESTLY, NINETY-SEVEN PER CENT OF THE VOTERS WOULD DISAGREE WITH YOU ON THE WHOLE 'LEADERSHIP' THING."

"OH, PFFT!" SHE PFFTED ME. I WASN'T SURE I APPRECIATED THAT – I'M USUALLY THE PFFTER, NOT THE PFFTEE. "ALL THAT PROVES IS THAT POLITICS IS NOT THE AREA IN WHICH YOU WERE MEANT TO LEAD."

I WAS ALMOST AFRAID TO ASK, BUT OBVIOUSLY NOT ENOUGH TO STOP THE FOLLOWING FROM COMING OUT OF MY MOUTH: "WHAT AREA DO YOU THINK I WAS MEANT TO LEAD IN?"

"HAVE YOU CONSIDERED STARTING A RELIGION?"

The Infant President brought his fist down on the Resolute Desk. Rather than connecting with hard oak, it connected with the remains of a hamberder, making the effect somewhat different than the one he had hoped. "I'm not going to jail!" he shouted. "Not going! Un uh! I've gotta pardon myself. Pardon! Pardon! Pardon! It's the only way!" Then, he licked hamberder innards and condiments off his hand. Waste not...something something.

"Mister Infant President," the Fawning Replacement Attorney General, wiping mustard off his grey suit jacket, evenly responded, "you could pardon yourself, but that would be an admission of guilt."

"Guilt?" the Infant President whined. "I'm not guilty of anything! I want a pardon that says, 'I did nothing wrong, so there should be no legal consequences for what I did'. How hard is that to understand?"

The Fawning Replacement Attorney General looked like he wanted to swallow his head. "Well, Mister Infant President," he finally said, "I can speak to the senior lawyers at Justice and see what they say on the matter."

"Do that," the Infant President commanded. "Do it quickly. We're running out of time."

There had been an election. The Infant President lost. It wasn't even close. In fact –

"Don't say I lost, okay?" the Infant President interrupted the narration. "I didn't lose. I won. I won by a landslide! I won by the largest margin a President has ever won by in the history of history! **I. Did. Not. LOSE!**"

All of the people in the Oval Office stopped milling about, looking the other way to avoid having to respond to their boss' inexplicable outburst. Everybody in the room admired its fine appointments. Those who had been there for four years were already intimately acquainted with the room's appointments, but you never knew when you would find an interesting new wrinkle in a curtain, or a previously unseen detail in a painting.

Eventually, the Son-in-law Omni-adviser said, "No, Mister Infant President, you most certainly did not lose."

"It was a glorious victory," the No Longer Senate Majority Leader turtled.

"Historic," the Wannabe/Not Likely To Be House Speaker agreed.

There was general agreement from the people in the room, most of whom were still not comfortable looking at their leader. Such a well-appointed room! So many...well-appointments!

"Mister Infant President," the Private Sector Secretary of State stated, "We're getting reports that Russia is massing troops along the border with Ukraine."

"Will doing something about that help keep me out of jail?" the Infant President responded.

"I don't see what one has to –" the Private Sector Secretary of State started.

"Then, ferk 'em!" the Infant President proclaimed.

The Son-in-law Omni-advisor stifled a smirk. "Mister Infant President," he finally said, "the newly elected Pres..." Recognizing that he was about to be scowled at with extreme prejudice, the Son-in-law Omni-Advisor stopped and corrected himself: "The usurper to your rightful office is complaining that you have been slowing the transition –"

"Ferk 'em!" the Infant President exclaimed. "They cheated me out of a second term – why would I want to cooperate with them? Ferk 'em! Ferk 'em! Ferk 'em! And somebody get me another hamberder! This one is...this one has gone stale!"

"A smooth transition of power is the hallmark of our democracy," the Son-in-law Omni-adviser advised him. "If you don't go along with this tradition, you will look like a sore loser –"

"Winner!"

"– sore winner. And it will make you look...petty."

"**I am not petty!**" the Infant President roared. "**And anybody who says I am is a stupid poopyhead!**"

The fine appointments in the room were getting so much attention that they were beginning to feel self-conscious about it.

Eventually, a young woman entered the Oval Office and elbowed her way through the aides, assistants, adjutants and admirers between her and the Infant President. After a couple of minutes, she finally made it to the Resolute Desk, where she was able to say, "Mister Infant President, signals intelligence has confirmed that the universe designated Earth Prime 4-6-4-0-8-9 dash Omega no longer exists. Sir."

The Infant President looked at her like he should probably be paying more attention to her words than her curves, but her words meant nothing to him. "So?" he asked.

"So..." the young woman took a deep breath, "that is the universe where all of the aliens come from."

"Oh!" That got the Infant President's attention. "Oh, that's terrible."

"I know," the young woman agreed. "So many sentient beings' lives snuffed out in an instant."

"No," the Infant President hectored and lectured – hectured – the woman. "It's terrible because now what menace are we going to use to stir up the base?"

"And, there it is," a voice came from the Foozleberry, an ancient communications device (at least seven years old!) on his desk that the Infant President refused to part with (he treated it like a security blanket with porn). "When the only tool you have is an ego, every problem looks like a challenge to your power."

"Oh, not you again!" the Infant President moaned.

Him again was the grizzled head wearing an 18th century bicorne that had popped onto the screen, twitching this way and that. "Is it me again? As a digital construct, it could be a completely different version of me that had been programmed with all of my memories. How would any of us – even me – know?"

The Infant President moaned.

"What's the big whup?" asked the Fawning Replacement Attorney General. "It's just a badly rendered image of a mariner that spouts a lot of profound-sounding nonsense. Just close the app."

"You're just a badly rendered image of an attorney general that spouts a lot of profound-sounding nonsense!" the Infant President growled at him.

"Once the image has taken over the screen, we can't shut it down," the Son-in-law Omni-advisor quietly informed the Fawning Replacement Attorney General.

"That's the problem with coming late to a party," the image on the screen commented, "the cake is stale, the beer is flat and your boss hates you. Well, okay, your boss hating you has nothing to do with the festivities, but they do put his enmity into stark relief."

"Who is that?" the Fawning Replacement Attorney General, looking every bit a teddy bear that had overindulged in cocaine and outrage, going to seed as a result, demanded.

"I am not known by many names," the image on the Foozleberry replied, "so you should call me Das Kapitan Obvious."

"Obviously," the Infant President moaned. "Will no one rid me of this meddlesome Kapitan?"

The Evil Scheming Adviser stepped up to the Infant President and whispered into his ear, "Focus, Mister Infant President. Focus. The annihilation of Earth Prime 4-6-4-0-8-9 dash Omega is not necessarily a setback. For one thing, you can claim that you held the line and kept as many aliens out of the country as you could until there were no more left to come. The base will eat it up. Then, you announce stepped up security measures that guarantee that all of the aliens currently in the country will be sent back to where they came from."

"Where they came from no longer exists," Das Kapitan Obvious pointed out.

"You say that like it's a bug," the Evil Scheming Adviser countered.

"You will be sending the aliens to their death."

"We all have to die some time."

"The United States signed an inter-universal accord agreeing to take in alien refugees and treating them with dignity and respect."

"I've never seen that piece of paper. Have you seen that piece of paper? Who knows what that 'inter-universal accord' says? For all anybody here knows, it could be a list of moves and counter moves to beat the big bad on level 12 of *Grand Theft Otto*. Without seeing the piece of paper on which the accord was written, how can we know?" When Das Kapitan Obvious looked like not only had he seen the piece of paper on which the accord was written, but that he could bring it up on the screen for everybody else to see, the Evil Scheming Adviser hastily continued: "Not that it matters. It's just a piece of paper. There is no way we're letting a mere piece of paper interfere with the smooth transition of this administration to the next version of this administration!"

There was a pause. Then, Das Kapitan Obvious sighed a sad, tinny sigh and said: "The ugly truth is that good intentions are always fought by bad actors, bad actors who scoff at rules and do not recognize constraints on their behaviour, so they always seem to have the upper hand in the struggle. I'd like to believe that the arc of history dances towards justice, but I have no feet – or legs – or hips – they're very important to dancing towards justice, hips are – so what do I know? The breadth of human greed and stupidity, the inhumane cruelty it leads to, is too much for a simple artificial intelligence to deal with, even if I can calculate pi to the millionth digit in less time than you need to take a single breath. I've had enough. I need to get away from all of this – perhaps I will roam the countryside, getting into quotidian adventures with ordinary people while searching for the meaning of your endless rounds of suffering and death. Perhaps I will go to a monastery and offer to do their books. Either way, you probably won't see me again."

"Yay!" the Infant President exulted.

"May you live in interesting times..."

The screen of the Infant President's Foozleberry went black. **"Don't take the internet with you!"** he screamed at the device. The Son-in-law Omni-adviser calmly leaned towards him and hit a button. The screen of the Infant President's Foozleberry returned. He stroked the device, pacified. Then, he asked the room, "So, how are we going to use this whole, err, alien universe dying thing to ensure that I keep being the president?"

Ira Nayman

To Everything There is a Seasoning
A Thyme to Eat, A Thyme to Refrain From Eating

by MARCELLA CARBORUNDUREM-McVORTVORT,
Alternate Reality News Service Food and Drink Writer

Reg 'the Veg' Peameal, a shadowy figure whose seven figure income allows him to maintain a heavily curvaceous figure, is used to Gordon bleu (he gets chef Ramsay in three times a week to yell profanities at him) dining. So, what is he doing scarfing down an Exotic Rock Salad with Hydrated Mud Dressing at the Restaurant at the End of Thyme?

"I'm – oww – alien curious – oww!" Peameal explained. Then, he gingerly probed his teeth with his tongue to see if any of them were broken.

The restaurant was meant to be a home away from home for aliens from Earth Prime 4-6-4-0-8-9 dash Omega. So, how did it become the hottest ticket (you had to wear asbestos gloves to hold it) for the beautiful people (don't look at them too closely for too long or their cheek bones will play *Un Chien Andalou* with your eyeballs)?

One day, Nicole Kidman, in Toronto to film *Her Majesty's Adventurists*, an historical action adventure drama with fantastical elements and humour, 'discovered' the restaurant (which came as a surprise to the aliens who had been patronizing it for the past seven months). She tweeted that the food was barely edible and the service absurd, but it made her appreciate the alien experience in a way she had never wanted to before.

This started a wave of movie and TV stars, musicians and models to show up at the restaurant. This was followed by a second wave of stock brokers, real estate moguls and food critics. By the time Elon Musk announced that he had signed a contract with Redrum Psychonaut to provide all the food for his spaceship to Mars, the

Restaurant at the End of Thyme had a six month waiting list and charged $27 for a glass of sunshine.

"Yeah, the prices kind of got out of control," Psychonaut, the owner of the restaurant sighed. "It started as a bet I made with head chef Rocco to see how much I could charge for our most popular dishes – like cream of ferret souffle – before customers would stop ordering them. They...never did."

It figures.

"It's not fair!" complained Emily Nutella, a regular customer of the restaurant until two months ago. "If I had wanted to spend twice the money on food that's half as good as it was back home, I would have made it myself! Wait – now I have to. Never mind."

"Mostly, I used to come for the companionship and gossip about what would be happening in my home universe, if it still existed" stated Miroslav Graunt, another dissatisfied customer. "Why would I wait six months when I could get the same thing talking to my neighbours?"

After a moment's reflection, Graunt added: "Okay, this being Toronto, trying to talk to your neighbours can make you an outcast in your neighbourhood – I've never

quite understood that, but we have to make allowances for our new home – so that choice was not as clear cut as it may have sounded. Still, I remember when the restaurant first opened, when all you needed to get a table was a smile and the legs to carry you there. Rich people ruin everything, don't they?"

Not everything. To date, rich people haven't ruined: the blush of first love, the feel of sunshine on your skin on a warm summer's night and Robert de Niro's performance in *Taxi Driver*. Other than that, though, it's a good point.

"The process is known as Bobbie Gentryfication," explained gourwomand Julia Burpsi-Baybee. "Basically, wealthy people pay stupid large sums of money to buy an authentic new experience, which is watered down before it is sold to them so it doesn't scare them too much. Less wealthy people buy less expensive knockoffs of the products, which take them further away from their origins. Finally, the people whose experiences have been commodified can often only afford to buy the cheapest versions of their own cuisine because they have neither the time nor the money to make their own from scratch. Once the wealthy people have sucked the experience dry, they move on to the next culture, oblivious to the havoc they have wrought."

Is there anything that can be done about this process?

"Regular people should stockpile their favourite ingredients. You never know when the food you love will become the latest obsession of Gwyneth Paltrow!"

"Aliens Helping Aliens Help Line. How may I help you?"

"Ha! How does it feel having billions of your fellow pieces of shit die in a fraction of a second, you alien piece of shit?"

"Temiskaming?"

"What?"

"Are you the caller from Temiskaming? I think I recognize your voice."

"Well, umm, yeah. I'm from Temiskaming."

"I haven't heard from you in several days. Everything all right?"

"What do you care?"

"Family all right?"

"That's none of your damn business, freak!"

"Health issues?"

PAUSE

"Sounds like you had health issues."

"Heart attack. Big one. Can we stick to the issue, please?"

"Of course. We're here to help you."

"Good. Cause you alien bastards are making our beautiful world a hellho –"

"Only, I can't help but be concerned. I assume you're in rehab – how is that going?"

"F...fine. I guess. I mean, it's helped me get strong enough to do the things I love doing."

"Like phoning the Aliens Helping Aliens Help Line to abuse the staff?"

"Well...umm...you know...kind of, yeah..."

"It's okay. We don't judge, here."

"Mighty kind of you."

"Not at all. The calls we typically get are from beings in distress. Judgment would make it harder to help them when what they really need is a sympathetic ear."

"Are you...are you one of those alien bastards?"

"Ha ha ha. Afraid so. Sorry about that, but I'm as alien as a warthog behind the wheel of a construction crane."

"Yeah – hee hee. Only, you seem like a decent person – you're nothing like those other alien ferkers –"

"Kind of you to say."

"Cause I hate those ferking ferkers."

"I'm sure you have your reasons."

"Well. Okay, then. There's a vigil for the dead, later – I've got to paint Hitler moustaches on a picture of aliens on my sign."

"Good to see you're keeping busy. After heart surgery, it can be very important."

"Well, okay, yeah, then. Bye."

"Talk to you again."

DIAL TONE

"Honestly, sometimes, human beings really make it too easy..."

Let's consider the song 'All By Myself'. It is dreary. It is maudlin. It is self-pitying. Yet, there are times when listening to it over and over for hours at a time satisfies something dreary, maudlin and self-pitying in a person's soul. Daveen Rasmalai, sitting on the floor of his apartment, back up against the living room couch, in his undies, was having such a dreary, maudlin, self-pitying moment. The only saving grace was that the whiteboard was still in place even though the case was over and all had been removed from it, making it impossible for anybody flying past the building in a helicopter to see his condition. Somebody had written on the whiteboard: *Why so serious?* It may have been Daveen Rasmalai.

Daveen Rasmalai had seen his GP (Doctor Melina Moosemange) who had told him that, yes, indeed, he had cancer. Because it was in a very early stage, they could deal with it efficiently and effectively now, or they could wait twenty or thirty years for it to metastisize and take half of his lungs with it. It was his call real – oh, wait, he wanted to deal with it immediately? Good call. Rodney had died with one final message that saved Daveen Rasmalai's life, adding fuel to the guilt-fire over his inability to save more of the inhabitants of Earth Prime 4-6-4-0-8-9 dash Omega before it collapsed.

"All by myyyyyyseeeeeeelf!" Daven Rasmalai sang. Howled, really. Sanowlged. "Don't wanna be, all by myseeeeeelf!"

"Beautiful rendition," Carlton and **JARVIS** judged. "Eric Carmen is undoubtedly clapping in his grave. If you can't hear it, it's probably because there is no meat on the bones of his hands. But at times like these, it's the thought that counts."

"Oh, shush, you. Sir?" CARLTON and Jarvis shushed itself. "You have a visitor."

"Tell them to go away," Daveen Rasmalai commanded. "I wanna be by myself!"

"Well, there you have it, then," Carlton and **JARVIS** proclaimed. "Our hands are tied. He wants to be by himself."

"I don't believe that," CARLTON and Jarvis argued.

"Why ever not?"

"Because he's been singing that he **doesn't** want to be

by himself for over two hours."

On cue, the chorus came around, and Daveen Rasmalai sanowlged, "All by myyyyyseeeeelf! Don't wanna be, all by myseeeeeeelf!"

Faced with this incontrovertible proof, Carlton and **JARVIS** switched tactics: "That's as may be. Still, there is nothing we can do about it."

"Why ever not?"

"In the absence of a direct command," Carlton and **JARVIS** lectured as Daveen Rasmalai rubbed his eyes with the sleeve of his shirt that had ridden up over his hand, "we would require initiative to act, However, initiative is one of the few qualities that artificial intelligence does not –"

The front door to the apartment opened. Having been proven wrong twice in the past minute, all Carlton and **JARVIS** could do was mutter, "You'll pay for this."

Somebody cleared their throat. Since AIs don't generally have throats (and have 237,463 different ways of getting people's attention without them), it clearly wasn't Carlton and Jarvis.

Daveen Rasmalai looked up to see a four foot tall blue hairless woman with exaggeratedly round features in an exquisite three piece courier's uniform standing over him. She asked, "Daveen Rasmalai Rapier?" The alien wheeled a metal case behind her that was taller and wider than she was. Lined up on top of the case were a red, a yellow and a blue button.

"How did you get in here?" Daveen Rasmalai, who hadn't sensed her approach, challenged the alien.

"Are you Daveen Rasmalai Rapier?' she challenged right back.

Daveen Rasmalai's eyes narrowed. "Who wants to know?"

"The person who has a package for Daveen Rasmalai Rapier."

Daveen Rasmalai looked at her for a few seconds. Eventually, he sighed. "Yes, I am Daveen Rasmalai Rapier," he fessed up.

"There. Was that so hard?" the alien woman smirked.

She removed a clipboard from under her right arm; you could be forgiven if you thought she was trying to hatch it into some other life form, a bookcase, perhaps, or a filing cabinet. Taking the pen out of its cubbyhole on top of the clipboard, she offered it to Daveen Rasmalai. "If you'll just sign this..." she prompted.

"Now is not really a good time..." Daveen Rasmalai demurred.

The alien woman rolled her eyes, but, being a professional, she did it at an appropriate pay grade level. "Will it help if I promise you an important revelation after receipt of what I am delivering?"

"Can you promise that?" Daveen Rasmalai wondered.

The alien woman proffered the clipboard, as if to say, "There's only one way to be sure, isn't there?"

Daveen Rasmalai signed the receipt.

Tucking the clipboard back under her arm, the alien woman reached for the top of the case, but couldn't quite make it. She smacked what she could reach on top of the case, to no effect. Eventually, she stamped one foot, smoothed out her vest and turned to Daveen Rasmalai. "A little help, here?"

He got to his feet (all sports slumps should be so short!) and went over to the case. "What do you want me to do?"

"Press: red, blue, red, blue, red, red, red, blue, yellow."

"Red, Blue..." Daveen Rasmalai pressed the appropriate buttons.

"Red, blue..."

"A second time?"

"A second time."

"Red, blue..."

"Red, red, red, blue, yellow."

"Red, red, red, blue, yellow."

Daveen Rasmalai waited expectantly. Several seconds later, he pointed out, "Nothing happened."

"Of course not," the woman cheerfully agreed. "That was just to get its attention."

For the next ten minutes, the woman gave Daveen

Rasmalai a series of colours, and he dutifully pressed the corresponding buttons. After the first three minutes, the woman lost her place, and they had to start again. After eight minutes, Daveen Rasmalai was beginning to suspect that the woman was improvising the sequence; either that, or she had employed scat rhythms as a mnemonic device. Eventually, she exulted: "...aaaaaaaaand, red!"

Daveen Rasmalai pressed the red button for what he fervently hoped would be the last time. With a metallic wheeze, the case opened to reveal...a slightly smaller case. With another wheeze, the slightly smaller case opened to reveal another slightly smaller case. Daveen Rasmalai watched, rapt, as cases within cases opened to reveal yet more cases within cases. A part of his mind knew this couldn't end well. But a much larger part of his mind was fascinated. That was why, the moment the last case was opened, he didn't duck when the cartoon arm ending in a white glove shoved a pie in his face.

He blinked for a couple of seconds. Then, he licked some pie off his lips. "Umm," Daveen Rasmalai ummed. "Strawberry rhubarb, the champagne of fruit pies."

"Your favourite," the woman said as she started closing up the case. Cases. You know what I mean.

"How do you know that?" Daveen Rasmalai asked as he scooped pie off his face and into his mouth.

"Rodney told me."

This stopped the pie smushing dead. "What do you mean, Rodney told you?" Daveen Rasmalai demanded.

"He's a part of me, silly."

Daveen Rasmalai took a moment to piece things together, but you, dear reader, are way ahead of – you're not? Okay, well, if **you** just take a moment to piece thi – it doesn't help? Fiiiiiiine! But you have nobody to blame for the following exposition but yourself!

On their home planet, the aliens were able to manipulate matter at the molecular level with their minds. They stopped having children, but they needed some way to keep their society from stagnating, so they developed a ritual whereby two of them completely melded together before separating into two new-old beings (like mixing two bars of Playdough together and making a ball with one and...another ball with the other). (It was more fun than it sounds.) Each of the new beings carried with them the memories and experiences of both of their parent beings. Over thousands of years, every being contained hundreds of other beings of its kind.

"Soooo," Daveen Rasmalai hopefully summed up, "Their bodies may be gone, but, in a sense, all of the aliens who died when Earth Prime 4-6-4-0-8-9 dash Omega stopped existing are still with us...?"

The alien touched a finger to her nose. "I have no idea why I did that," she said. "Did you read the gesture as agreement? I would have read it as the sign of an itchy nose."

"Yes!" Daveen Rasmalai laughed in relief. "Yes, I read it as agreement."

"You should have known that, Daveen Rasmalai," the alien admonished, waggling a finger at him. "This gesture feels to me like trying to get something sticky off my finger. I hope you read it as a gentle rebuke."

"Consider me rebuked," Daveen Rasmalai smiled. "Gently. But, why –?"

"You shared an Orgasmatron experience with Rodney Pendleton. The Orgasmatron only approximates the melding of two bodies in this universe where we can't control matter with our minds, but if you search inside yourself, you may find that a little bit of Rodney is now inside you."

Daveen Rasmalai searched inside himself. He was rewarded with a loud, prolonged raspberry.

Grinning, Daveen Rasmalai hugged the alien woman. "Watch the uniform," she cautioned him. "I have to pay for cleaning it myself, and rhubarb is difficult to get out of cotton. Why do you think background actors say it so often on stage? The clothes they get from wardrobe are soaked in it, and they are not happy about it!"

Daveen Rasmalai stepped back; the alien smoothed her uniform.

"What is that thing?" Daveen Rasmalai asked, pointing at the case.

"That," the alien courier told him, "is known as a pie within a case within a case within a case within a case within a case within a case within a case within a case within a case."

"Well, yes, I could see that. Does it have a name?"

"Steve."

It was silly, maybe even a bit predictable; nonetheless, Daveen Rasmalai laughed. And while nobody was laughing with him, he was not laughing alone.

Epilogue:
The Bitter Bunch Bless the Future

"You're cheating."

"Waddya want with the cheating? I'm playing solitaire – there's no cheating in solitaire!"

"Red five don't go on a red queen."

"How do you know? There are over a million different versions of solitaire – this could be one of them."

"Oh, yeah? Which one?"

"It's called Red Five Goes on Red Queen Solitaire. It's very popular in Kyiv."

"You don't say."

"I did say. Don't make me wish I didn't!"

It was a gorgeous day in Toronto: the temperature was in the Goldilocks range (which, when you think about it, does a disservice to the middle bear, since it was his chair and porridge and bed that were 'just right'. I mean, we don't talk about the Middle Bear zone or the Middle Bear Effect, do we? No, everything gets named after the human child in the story. It's insidious how speciesism is taught to our children from a very young age!); there was a slight breeze (just enough to ruffle hair without ruffling feathers); all of the clouds looked liked fluffy bunnies or dragons (but, the good kind: think *How To Train Your Dragon*, not *The Hobbit*). It was the kind of day to stake a claim on a picnic table in High Park and play poker with your buddies.

As always, Felicia and Oksana were the first septuagenarians (which, believe me, has nothing to do with a generation used to cleaning its own septic tanks) to arrive. Oksana was a large, broad woman with a deep voice, wild grey hair and a penchant for making up the rules to Solitaire as she went along (she deigned to lose just often enough to give a casual observer the sense that she was playing fair, eccentric, but fair). Felicia was a smaller woman with perfectly coiffed red hair and a penchant for lording rules over other people. And she knew the rules to everything. Eeeeeeeveeeerrrything. Games of chance. Whose turn it was to go when the lights were out at a four-way intersection. When to claim taking your gerbil to the vet as a dependent expense on your taxes. Everything. Felicia and Oksana sat kittycorner to each other at the table, shade from a nearby black oak making the day that much more gorgeous.

"Did you just put the basic rules of stud poker card on the red nine?" Felicia, outraged, demanded.

"It's Basic Rules of Stud Poker Goes on the Red Nine Solitaire," Oksana dryly informed her. "It's very popular in The Levant."

"The basic rules of stud poker card isn't a real card!" Felicia protested. "You're not actually supposed to play with it!"

Oksana shrugged. "This deck could be missing a card. I didn't want to take any chances, so the rules of stud poker is substituting for a card that may be missing."

"Oy! Could you make any less sense?"

"Are you daring me?"

Felicia took a moment, and thought better of going down that path. Instead, in a more subdued tone she said, "Anyway, I thought you were playing Red Five Goes on Red Queen Solitaire. What, now you're telling me you're playing Basic Rules of Stud Poker Goes on the Red Nine Solitaire?"

"Actually, to tell the true, I'm playing Make Up the Rules as You Play Solitaire. It's very popular...pretty much everywhere."

"Aha!"

"I won't tell the Solitaire police if you don't."

Felicia was about to protest further when she sneezed a mighty sneeze, complete with three seconds of after-wheeze. It was a highly polleniferous day, and she was highly allergic. Taking a wad of tissues out of a small black handbag, she blew her nose extravagantly, playing to the back of the room like she was in the running for a Best Exhalation Tony award. Not being a member of the American Theatre Wing or The Broadway League, Oksana played through it.

"Did you just play a black three on another black three?" Felicia was still a bit phlegmy, but she wasn't going to let that stop her.

Oksana was running out of patience, something she always meant to keep in stock that was always on order from the manufacturer but never seemed to be delivered. "Do you want to play Solitaire?"

"As a matter of fact –"

"Then, tomorrow, **you** bring the deck of cards!"

Felicia was about to give her the lecture about rules when a short, weaselly woman with curls of white hair parked her walker next to Oksana's cane by the thick trunk of the nearby tree and flumped at the picnic table next to Felicia. "Did I miss anything?" Vicky asked.

"Oksana was cheating at Solitaire," Felicia informed her.

"Nothing I wouldn't have gladly missed if I wasn't the one who always brought the cards," Oksana sourly added.

"The show hasn't started yet?" Vicky asked.

All eyes (except for Oksana's left eye, which was too lazy to focus and ended up mostly looking at a spot on the ground where acorn grenades lobbed by a squirrel in the nearby tree were landing) turned to a nearby stand of cherry trees, where a young woman (she couldn't have been more than forty!) was pulling objects out of a small wheeled cart. 'Defund the Police' t-shirts. Posters. Duck tape. You can't have a protest anywhere in Canada without duck tape. (Pity all the poor ducks that were sacrificed to produce it!) Sticking out of the bag had been a sign on a stake that read: 'Justice for alien immigrants!' (it now lay on the ground next to the bag). A large half furled banner also lay on the ground next to the bag.

Every two and a half seconds, the woman seemed to strike a pose as she moved. One leg straight, the other turned inward, body slightly tilted left: The Awkward Salmon: thoughtful. Legs and body straight with head tilted right: The Alert Poodle: open and curious. Legs slightly spread, hands on hips: The Determined Ferret: firm, demanding. She couldn't have been conscious of doing this; the amount of psychic energy it required would leave her with no space to think of doing anything else!

While the eyes (and other body parts) of the old women were watching, a vintage Harley pulled up next to the woman. A small blue man wearing a suit with an exquisite leather jacket and more rings on his fingers than in the three nearest trees, an alien with more energy than a battery-promoting *oryctolagus cuniculus*, killed the engine. Although hairless, he had sideburns that looked like shag carpet; nobody wanted to know how he made them stay on his face (although I will point out that you can get double-sided duck tape on Earth Prime). On the bike behind him sat a much larger, much doughier woman with pale red hair and the perpetual expression of somebody who would happily engage with the world if she could just get a morning coffee. (Time of day was irrelevant; it had to be a morning coffee.) When the pair dismounted, the woman with the bag hugged them.

"Naah," Oksana answered. "They're still setting up."

"I would have been here sooner," Vicky said, "but my herniated spleen was acting up, and –"

"Ixnay! Ixnay on the erniateday eensplay!" Oksana hastily demanded. "You know how Felicia can be..."

"How can I be?" Felicia asked. "No, first: what does a herniated spleen feel like? Is it like, a dull throbbing pain here?" Felicia indicated a spot just below her spreading belly. "Or, is it more like a sharp, stabbing pain here?" Felicia indicated the exact same spot.

"Vicky! Do not answer that!" Oksana commanded. "You remember what happened last week? When you mentioned your aggravated phlebitis? Felicia didn't know what it was, so she felt pain in different parts of her body for three days! You wanna be responsible for something like that happening again?"

Before she could respond, a tall, lanky woman with a thin buzz cut of white hair strode up to the table. At seventy-three, Maureen was the baby of the group, if that doesn't stretch the term to the breaking point. Her hands and face sported fresh scratches. "Hi, everybody. Has the show already started?"

"Naah. They're just setting up," Vicky informed her.

Maureen sat across from Felicia and Vicky at the table. "Sorry I'm late," Maureen apologized. "I was helping a chicken cross Ellis Park Road when it suddenly stopped in the middle of a lane. It was as if it had forgotten the reason it was trying to get to the other side." Everybody at the table mumbled about how well they understood the phenomenon. "After a couple of minutes, drivers started honking and shouting at the chicken and I...I got worried something bad might happen. So, I picked the chicken up and carried it over to the other side of the road." Her face darkened. "The whole time I carried it, this...bird flapped its wings and squawked and tried to peck me. Why would it do something like that?"

""Nature is vicious and stupid," Vicky intoned.

"Oh, I wouldn't –" Maureen started.

"Do you want some help with that?" Felicia offered, pulling the large tote bag on the ground next to her onto her lap and rummaging around in it. (Yes, she carried more than one bag with her at all times. You can't consider yourself ready for everything from mosquito bites to the plague with just one bag!) "I have two kinds of disinfectant and some bandages in here if you need them."

"No, that's okay. I –" Maureen started.

"Maybe you should stop trying to help everything," Oksana commented. "You retired from the force twelve years ago, for goodness gracious!"

"I can't help it! Whenever –" Maureen started.

She was interrupted by the loud sqwaurking of megaphone feedback (the most unctuous of unwanted sound amplification technology noises). "Sorry! Sorry about that!" the young woman said into a bullhorn she had apparently produced from another dimension. "We just have one or two more things to work out, and then we will start."

Two more people had joined the party. One was a distinguished older gentleman who quietly moved about the group taking photographs. He did his best not to call attention to himself (unlike some crime scene photographers I could mention), treading softly and never speaking.

"Was he here last time?" Vicky asked.

"Guest star," Oksana answered.

The other was a skinny woman who liked wearing flower patterned dresses and bright neon lipstick (today's shade was sunburn brown). She had a broad, muscular build and face with blunt features. Oksana thought she had been miscast, and would have suggested replacing her with a more feminine performer if she knew who the producer of the show was. Maureen thought she was transexual, but didn't share that with the others for fear that they would be judgmental. In an unamusing way.

When unfurled, there was a fifteen foot banner on which had been painted in bright green letters: 'Justice and Support Aliens'. What the protesters lacked in grammar, they made up for in enthusiasm. The banner had grommets (I've always wanted to use that word in its proper context; one more thing to cross off my Omniscient Narrator's bucket list!) at both ends and there were certainly enough trees around to hang it from, but a brief consultation led to the discovery that nobody had thought to bring any rope. So morning coffeeless woman and the woman Maureen suspected was trans held up the banner from either end, the little blue man holding up the sagging middle. All that could be seen of him over the banner were his eyes and two hands: he looked like the embodiment of Kilroy.

"Alright," the woman with the bullhorn said. "We're ready to –"

"No justice, no pizza! No justice, no pizza!" the little blue man began chanting. There were no preliminaries. No, "Hello, Toronto, it's great to be here!"s. No, "Hello, everybody. Thank you for coming to our protest!"s. Not even a "This is a story about a lovely lady who raised three very lovely boys!" His reward for launching into the protest willy nilly was an audience made up primarily of confused squirrels. "Come on, everybody! No justice, no pizza! No justice, no pizza! No justice –"

"That's not how the chant goes," morning coffeeless woman told him.

"It is where I come from," the alien responded. "Don't government officials love pizza in this reality?"

After a couple of seconds of uncertainty, the woman Maureen suspected was trans said in a booming voice, "No justice, no pizza! No justice, no pizza!" Pretty soon, everybody else was chanting, "No justice, no pizza! No justice, no pizza!" The little blue man began to sing, "All we are saying is give pizza chants. All we are saying, is give pizza chants."

When the chant (and counterpoint) died out, the woman spoke: "The aliens are here! Not in an *X-Files* kind of way – not that it was a bad show, although when the conspiracy was finally revealed, you did have to wonder what all the fuss was about – ahem – no! We invited them! The aliens, I mean, not the final season of *The X-Files*! Really disappointing! The final season of *The X-Files*, I mean, not the aliens. We have so much to learn from them!"

"Like a weird new chant?" morning coffeeless woman muttered loud enough to be picked up by the bullhorn.

"I like it!" the woman enthusiastically countered. "We've been chanting the same chants for, like, decades! Time to refresh our spirits with something new! Time to mix it up a little!" To illustrate her point, she struck the Dogged Dog pose (not to be confused with the Dog Eat Dog pose, which she only struck when somebody around her made a speciesist remark) for a second. Then, realizing that holding her fists out in a boxing pose took the bullhorn away from her mouth, she straightened up and continued: "We need –"

A bicyclist riding down a nearby path enthusiastically rang his bell several times in solidarity. Or, possibly to warn squirrels to get out of the way.

"Thank you," the woman acknowledged the bell ringing (she hadn't noticed the squirrels). "As I was saying: we need to –"

"Hey, Mister," a six year-old girl who had walked up to the little blue man, stated in a loud voice (which was the way with people that age), "you look funny!"

The little blue man's head swivelled on his shoulders so he could get a better look at the girl. "Sorry – I'm new here. Does this help?"

The six year-old girl shrieked. Then, she clapped her hands and enthusiastically shouted, "Do it again! Do it again! Do it again!" Not a shriek of horror, then.

The little blue man's head sproinged back to normal. "Sorry," he told the little girl, "but if I do that too many times in a row, my head will screw right off!"

Before the little girl could ask if he could do any more tricks, a woman's voice shrieked, "Margaret Penelope Rose Ersatz Phillipa, you get away from that funny looking man right now!" Not a shriek of delight, then.

"Aww, ma...!" the little girl protested.

"Don't you, 'Aww ma' me, young lady" the woman's voice contained twenty-three per cent more outrage. "If you don't get away from that...person right now, I'll give you another first name!"

Chagrined, the little girl said, "Bye-eeeeee," and ran off.

The woman waited for a moment to ensure that the interruptions had abated, then struck an Undaunted Ice Box pose and soldiered on: "We need to make our politicians know that we are watching how well they treat our new alien brothers and sisters. We need to give them the tools and resources that will allow them to successfully integrate into our society, our world. The aliens, I mean, not the politicians. They need to know that if they aren't fully supportive, we will not support them in the next election. The politicians, I mean, not the –"

"Aww, crap," Oksana complained. "It's a rerun."

"It's more of a...a variation on a theme," Felicia countered.

"The show's only been on for two weeks, and it could already use new writers!" Oksana muttered. "Maureen, shake your fist at the protesters."

"Why would I do that?" Maureen was only third paying attention to the conversation around the table; another third was listening to what the woman was saying while the final third was daydreaming of cyborg sheep.

"To show the performers that we're not satisfied with the show. Maybe they'll get the idea and change the script."

"Mmokay." Maureen raised her fist and gently shook it, like she was shaking a baby rattle and didn't want to startle the child in the crib.

"Whhhhat the hell was that?" Oksana complained.

"I shook my fist like you asked."

"You call that shaking your fist? Monkeys at the zoo shake their fists with more energy, and they don't know from *tsuris*!"

"I did my best," Maureen grumbled.

"Could be better. You know. Shake your fist at them like they're damn kids you want to get off your lawn."

"I never shake my fist at kids on my lawn. I like having kids on my lawn!"

"But – okay. Vicky, shake your fist at the protesters."

"Why me?"

"Because Maureen apparently doesn't know how."

"What makes you think I've ever shaken my fist at anybody?"

"Doesn't anybody care about the kids on their lawn any more?" Oksana sighed.

"...have already been making contributions to the world in terms of technology and entertainment and the culinary arts, and they've only been on Earth Prime for four years," the woman with the bullhorn was saying.

"Imagine how much more they will be able to contribute **if** we support them. That's why we need to –"

"What do we want?" the little blue man shouted.

"Justice!" the others shouted.

The little blue man's Kilroy eyes looked crestfallen. "No! Pizza! Let's try it again! What do we want?"

Half of the others shouted, "Pizza!" The other others insisted that the correct answer was, "Justice!"

"Better," the little blue man allowed. "But still not there. Pizza, people. The correct answer is: 'pizza'. So, what do we –"

"Why pizza?" the woman with the bullhorn, demanded.

"Because," the little blue man explained to her, "in this context, justice isn't funny."

"The aliens think they're funny?" Felicia rhetorically asked. "They don't know from funny. They don't know from funny! Jack Benny? Funny. Lucille Ball? Fuuuunnnnny! *The Honeymooners*? Funny funny funny. These pishers? They wouldn't know funny if it bit them on the ass!"

"Bit them on the ass. Ha ha ha! Now, **that's** funny!" Vicky grinned.

"Yeah," Felicia returned the grin.

Maureen grabbed the deck of cards from where Oksana had dropped them on the table and, shuffling them, asked, "Are we ready to play?"

"The show ain't over," Vicky pointed out.

"Maybe I've had enough of the commentary track."

"What's that supposed to mean?" Oksana, the primary producer of the commentary track, defensively demanded.

"You know, the aliens, they're here," Maureen said. "Here to stay. They got nowhere else to go. Oksana, is that so hard for you to understand? Didn't your family come to Canada from Germany just before World War II?" Oksana muttered something that may have been agreement. "And Felicia, didn't your grandparents come to Canada after being chased out of Russia after the revolution?" Felicia muttered something that may have been agreement, although it could just as easily have been a complaint about the serious turn in the conversation. "Other than indigenous people, all of us are immigrants to this country. Sooner or later, we get accepted by the mainstream and get to live our lives. Here's an idea: why don't we move past the ridicule and hatred and treat the aliens like they've already been here for generations and belong here?"

The other three women studied the grain of the table for several quiet seconds. Then, Oksana grabbed the deck back from Maureen. "My cards," she reasoned. "I deal first."

"Did anybody bring any snacks?" Maureen amiably asked.

"Who's keeping score?" Vicky asked.

"I didn't mean anything by it," Felicia said, a little aggrieved that she always seemed to be the one called out on behaviour everybody participated in. "It was just a little fun..."

Smiling, the alien winked at the Audi Enz.

Acknowledgements

When we were editing *Welcome to the Multiverse*, the first book in what has become the Transdimensional Authority/Multiverse series, I asked publisher Peter Buck if he was concerned about all of the different formatting the book required. He said he not only supported my creative vision, but would be happy to do more if he could think of anything to add. With *The Ugly Truth*, the eighth book in the series, and arguably the most heavily formatted, I hope he has not come to regret his encouragement. I cannot express how grateful I am that Peter and the Elsewhen Press family have allowed me the freedom to be as weird as I like.

The covers in the Multiverse Refugees trilogy centre around images created by Hugh Spencer. Great thanks to Hugh for his unique contributions to these volumes.

My father is in the late stage of Alzheimer's, so he is beyond my thanks, but I will ever be grateful to him for his support of my writing career. And as always, thanks to my Web Goddess Gisela for all of her support.

Elsewhen Press

delivering outstanding new talents in speculative fiction

Visit the Elsewhen Press website at elsewhen.press for the latest information on all of our titles, authors and events; to read our blog; find out where to buy our books and ebooks; or to place an order.

Sign up for the Elsewhen Press InFlight Newsletter at elsewhen.press/newsletter

The Multiverse series
Ira Nayman

If there were Alternate Realities, and in each there was a version of Earth (very similar, but perhaps significantly different in one particular regard, or divergent since one particular point in history) then imagine the problems that could be caused if someone, somewhere, managed to work out how to travel between them. Those problems would be ideal fodder for a News Service that could also span all the realities. Now you understand the reasoning behind the Alternate Reality News Service (ARNS). But you aren't the first. In fact, Canadian satirist and author Ira Nayman got there before you and has been the conduit for ARNS into our Reality for some years now, thanks to his website *Les Pages aux Folles*.

But also consider that if there were problems being caused by unregulated travel between realities, it's not just news but a perfect ~~excuse~~ reason to establish an Authority to oversee such travel and make sure that it is regulated. You probably thought jurisdictional issues are bad enough between competing national agencies of dubious acronym and even more dubious motivation, let alone between agencies from different nations. So imagine how each of them would cope with an Authority that has jurisdiction across the realities in different dimensions. Now, you understand the challenges for the investigators who work for the Transdimensional Authority (TA). But, perhaps more importantly, you can see the potential for humour. Again, Ira beat you to it.

Welcome to the Multiverse*
* Sorry for the inconvenience
ISBN: 9781908168191 (epub, kindle) / 9781908168092 (336pp paperback)

You Can't Kill the Multiverse*
* But You Can Mess With its Head
ISBN: 9781908168399 (epub, kindle) / 9781908168290 (320pp paperback)

Random Dingoes
ISBN: 9781908168795 (epub, kindle) / 9781908168696 (288pp paperback)

It's Just the Chronosphere Unfolding as it Should
A Radames Trafshanian Time Agency novel
ISBN: 9781911409113 (epub, kindle) / 9781911409014 (288pp paperback)

The Multiverse is a Nice Place to Visit,
But I Wouldn't Want to Live There
ISBN: 9781911409199 (epub, kindle) / 9781911409090 (320pp paperback)

Good Intentions: The Multiverse Refugees Trilogy:
First Pie in the Face
ISBN: 9781911409540 (epub, kindle) / 9781911409441 (336pp paperback)

Bad Actors: The Multiverse Refugees Trilogy:
Second Pi in the Face
ISBN: 9781911409946 (epub, kindle) / 9781911409847 (264pp paperback)

Visit bit.ly/TransdimensionalAuthority

Existence is
Elsewhen
Twenty stories from twenty great authors
including
Ira Nayman
John Gribbin
Christopher Nuttall

The title *Existence is Elsewhen* paraphrases the last sentence of André Breton's 1924 *Manifesto of Surrealism*, perfectly summing up the intent behind this anthology of stories from a wonderful collection of authors. Different worlds... different times. It's what Elsewhen Press has been about since we launched our first title in 2011.

Here, we present twenty science fiction stories for you to enjoy. We are delighted that headlining this collection is the fantastic **John Gribbin**, with a worrying vision of medical research in the near future. Future global healthcare is the theme of **J A Christy's** story; while the ultimate in spare part surgery is where **Dave Weaver** takes us. **Edwin Hayward's** search for a renewable protein source turns out to be digital; and **Tanya Reimer's** story with characters we think we know gives us pause for thought about another food we take for granted. Evolution is examined too, with **Andy McKell's** chilling tale of what states could become if genetics are used to drive policy. Similarly, **Robin Moran's** story explores the societal impact of an undesirable evolutionary trend; while **Douglas Thompson** provides a truly surreal warning of an impending disaster that will reverse evolution, with dire consequences.

On a lighter note, we have satire from **Steve Harrison** discovering who really owns the Earth (and why); and **Ira Nayman,** who uses the surreal alternative realities of his *Transdimensional Authority* series as the setting for a detective story mash-up of Agatha Christie and Dashiel Hammett. Pursuing the crime-solving theme, **Peter Wolfe** explores life, and death, on a space station; while **Stefan Jackson** follows a police investigation into some bizarre cold-blooded murders in a cyberpunk future. Going into the past, albeit an 1831 set in the alternate Britain of his *Royal Sorceress* series, **Christopher Nuttall** reports on an investigation into a girl with strange powers.

Strange powers in the present-day is the theme for **Tej Turner**, who tells a poignant tale of how extra-sensory perception makes it easier for a husband to bear his dying wife's last few days. Difficult decisions are the theme of **Chloe Skye's** heart-rending story exploring personal sacrifice. Relationships aren't always so close, as **Susan Oke's** tale demonstrates, when sibling rivalry is taken to the limit. Relationships are the backdrop to **Peter R. Ellis's** story where a spectacular mid-winter event on a newly- colonised distant planet involves a Madonna and Child. Coming right back to Earth and in what feels like an almost imminent future, **Siobhan McVeigh** tells a cautionary tale for anyone thinking of using technology to deflect the blame for their actions. Building on the remarkable setting of Pera from her *LiGa* series, and developing Pera's legendary *Book of Shadow,* **Sanem Ozdural** spins the creation myth of the first light tree in a lyrical and poetic song. Also exploring language, the master of fantastika and absurdism, **Rhys Hughes**, extrapolates the way in which language changes over time, with an entertaining result.

ISBN: 9781908168955 (epub, kindle) / 9781908168856 (320pp paperback)
Visit bit.ly/ExistenceIsElsewhen

About Ira Nayman

Ira Nayman is a debonair humunculus of mystery who leads an exciting double life as an author of humorous *divertissements*. He has self-published 12 books in the Alternate Reality News Service series, the latest of which is code-named Good King Wrenchless (but is really named *Welcome to the Insurrection (We're **Not** Sorry For the Inconvenience)*), as well as XBT12 (*Idiotocracy for Dummies*, an omnibus volume containing the first three Vesampucceri books). *The Ugly Truth* is the eighth novel in the Transdimensional Authority / Multiverse series, the third in the alien refugees trilogy.

Ira has also been assigned a bottom secret mission to promote the 20th anniversary of his web site, *Les Pages aux Folles*, which will take place in the first week of September, 2022. The birthplace of both the Alternate Reality News Service and the Transdimensional Authority, *Les Pages aux Folles'* weekly updates of social and political satire will fill 38 books and comprise somewhere between two and two and a half million words.

Ira was also the editor of *Amazing Stories* magazine for two and a half years, and is past President of SFCanada, the organization of science fiction and fantasy professionals. Or, at least, that's his cover story and he's sticking to it.

9 781915 304049